It aint where you from. How you do anything, is how you do everything

PRAISE FOR ERIC JEROME DIC~~KEY~~

"Dickey's fans flock to his readings. . . . He's perfected an addictive fictional formula." *It's how and* —*The New York Times, when you throw the interception that counts*

"Dickey has the knack for creating characters who elicit both rage and sympathy." —*Entertainment Weekly*

Control what you can

Control: THE BUSINESS OF LOVERS

"[A] heartfelt erotic drama . . . The setting is artfully crafted, the characters' struggles are real and moving, and the sex those characters have is flaming hot." —*Publishers Weekly*

"Bestselling author of street-wise romance, Dickey's latest is a contemporary erotic tale of ambitions delayed." —*Booklist*

"In this sensual road trip across LA there are deep conversations, adult situations, and a sweet love story at every turn." —*Kirkus Reviews*

BEFORE WE WERE WICKED

"From wanton to wicked, the love-hate relationship between Dickey's characters burns with rapid-fire dialogue and plenty of steam." —*Kirkus Reviews*

"The love story Dickey tells . . . is potent. Readers will want to read *Bad Men and Wicked Women* again after being immersed in this edgy, emotional adventure." —*Booklist*

"A passion-filled prequel that puts a new spin on the familiar conflicts that have made him a household name." —*Essence*

"Nobody currently publishing today writes sex better than Eric Jerome Dickey." —*Electric Review*

BAD MEN AND WICKED WOMEN

"Quentin Tarantino's *Pulp Fiction* comes to mind as Swift and Ellis cruise through Los Angeles's wealthy neighborhoods debating issues of racism, inner-city poverty, and the lingering effects of slavery. . . . Suspense builds with an action-packed finale." —*Library Journal*

GENEVIEVE
NAACP IMAGE AWARD NOMINEE

"[A] sizzling, sexy, downright gritty love story." —*Library Journal*

"Explicit . . . red-hot . . . sex-drenched . . . [and] instantly engrossing."
—*Publishers Weekly*

DRIVE ME CRAZY

"Smart, gritty, and gripping . . . Another winner." —*Publishers Weekly*

NAUGHTY OR NICE

"A very funny and engrossing novel, , , Laugh-out-loud humor."
—*Booklist*

THE OTHER WOMAN
NAACP IMAGE AWARD NOMINEE

"A fast-paced tale." —*Essence*

THIEVES' PARADISE
NAACP IMAGE AWARD NOMINEE

"Passionate, sensual, rhythmic. If Eric's previous novels are food for the soul, *Thieves' Paradise* is the nectar and ambrosia of life."
—*The Chicago Defender*

"No one does it like Eric Jerome Dickey."
—The Black Expressions Book Club

BETWEEN LOVERS

"Provocative and complex." —*Ebony*

LIAR'S GAME
NAACP IMAGE AWARD NOMINEE

"Steamy romance, betrayal, and redemption. Dickey at his best."
—*USA Today*

BY ERIC JEROME DICKEY

The Business of Lovers

Before We Were Wicked
(Ken Swift)

Harlem
(eBook)

Bad Men and Wicked Women
(Ken Swift)

Finding Gideon
(Gideon Series)

The Blackbirds

Naughtier Than Nice

One Night

A Wanted Woman

Decadence

An Accidental Affair

Tempted by Trouble

Resurrecting Midnight
(Gideon Series)

Dying for Revenge
(Gideon Series)

Pleasure

Waking with Enemies
(Gideon Series)

Sleeping with Strangers
(Gideon Series)

Chasing Destiny

Genevieve

Drive Me Crazy

Naughty or Nice

The Other Woman

Thieves' Paradise

Between Lovers

Liar's Game

Cheaters

Milk in My Coffee

Friends and Lovers

Sister, Sister

ANTHOLOGIES

Voices from the Other Side: Dark Dreams II

Gumbo: A Celebration of African American Writing

Mothers & Sons

Got to Be Real

River Crossings: Voices of the Diaspora

Griots Beneath the Baobab: Tales from Los Angeles

Black Silk: A Collection of African American Erotica

ERIC JEROME DICKEY

THE BUSINESS OF LOVERS

DUTTON

DUTTON

An imprint of Penguin Random House LLC
penguinrandomhouse.com

Previously published as a Dutton hardcover edition in April 2020

First Dutton trade paperback printing: March 2021

LIBRARY OF CONGRESS CATALOGING-IN-PUBLICATION DATA

Names: Dickey, Eric Jerome, author.
Title: The business of lovers / Eric Jerome Dickey.
Description: New York: Dutton, 2020.
Identifiers: LCCN 2019013455| ISBN 9781524745202 (hardcover) |
ISBN 9781524745226 (ebook)
Classification: LCC PS3554.I319 B87 2020 | DDC 813/.54—dc23
LC record available at https://lccn.loc.gov/2019013455

Dutton trade paperback ISBN: 9781524745219

Printed in the United States of America
1   3   5   7   9   10   8   6   4   2

For Uncle Darell and Auntie Carol

Youth is a blunder; Manhood a struggle; Old Age a regret.

—Benjamin Disraeli

Broken crayons still color.

—Ihadcancer.com

No man's born ready for marriage; they have to be trained.

—Joan Crawford as Harriet Craig

THE
BUSINESS
OF LOVERS

CHAPTER 1

BRICK

THE TIMER ON my iPhone went off.

An hour had passed, but I didn't see Penny at the gate to the mansion. Feeling ill at ease, I called her cell. By the second ring, I'd opened the glove box to get my snub-nosed revolver. By the third ring, I was out of my car, heading down the driveway to that mansion, ready to kick down the front door, but then Penny answered. I took a breath but didn't turn back around. There was laughter and erotic moans in the background.

I said, "Code phrase."

"Your cockeyed momma eats Mexican food and farts the third verse of the national anthem."

I turned around, headed back toward my car. "You wrapping up in there?"

High heels clip-clopped across either wooden or tiled floors.

She said, "One second."

She put me on hold long enough for me to get back in my ride.

Penny returned to the line, caught her breath. "Clients want another hour."

"Who are they?"

"Hollywood heads from a big-time casting agency getting coked up and talking about actors and shit. They know who has swallowed to get a five-and-under and who took it up the ass to get a movie deal."

"Get paid first."

"There are three other dates-by-the-hour here."

"I didn't see them come in."

"They were here first. They're staying too."

We were in the prestigious Hancock Park neighborhood, a palm-tree-lined, melanin-deficient area off of Wilshire Boulevard. It was a luxurious bubble, the type of place where owners complained about immigration while a team of immigrants was cleaning their estates, babysitting, and cooking them five-course meals.

I said, "The next hour I wait will be at my overtime rate."

"You know I have to pay my car note, rent, and tuition for next semester."

"My rent ain't free and my student loans are not going to pay themselves. Time and a half or call an Uber."

"You're a jerk, Brick."

"You know what you are?"

"Fuck you."

Penny hung up.

I put my daddy's snub-nose back in the stash spot; then I kept my eyes out for the local George Zimmerman.

My phone buzzed. A text message came in from my ex. Feelings rose.

> Hi, I have a missed video call from you. Not sure if it's in error. Hope all is well on your end.

I checked my phone. I hadn't accidently sent her a call. Hadn't called her in six months.

FIFTY-SIX MINUTES LATER, a thick white girl jogged out of the estate, phone at her ear. She was a ginger rocking UCLA sweats, a very sexy size twelve. A Kia pulled up. She eased in and the car zoomed away.

The clock hit fifty-seven minutes and I reached for my gun, but Penny appeared near the palm-tree-framed gate, a shadow carrying a USC backpack. When I had dropped her off, she'd dressed like she was going to a dinner party at the White House. Now she rocked a gray pullover, skinny jeans, colorful socks, and *Doctor Who* high-tops. I assumed the elegant gear was in her backpack. I turned my timer off just as Penny paused mid-driveway. Two women caught up with her. A congregation of beauties. Minorities standing around in one of LA's preferred zip codes turned on a white man's bullhorn. I stepped out of the car and waved for Penny to hurry the fuck up. She headed toward the car. The other two girls sashayed right on her heels, dragging along duffel bags. One girl looked Latina and wore a UCLA sweat-shirt, black jeans, and ballet flats. She had dark eyebrows; her hair was Hitchcock blond.

She grinned. "Good evening."

Penny said, "Christiana, this is Brick."

With a nod, Christiana evaluated me, then yielded a dazzling smile that could lure a man to Jesus or to the gallows. My suit was light gray. The Latina's eyes told me she liked my contemporary style. I liked hers too.

Christiana laughed. "Penny, is this gorgeous man your boyfriend?"

Penny said, "We're neighbors. I hire him as a chauffeur-bodyguard when I work."

A girl carrying a Moschino bag came up next to her. She wore New Religion jeans, pink Uggs, and a pink Gap hoodie. She rocked Goth makeup and shades. Her hair was short and natural, dyed a dark red.

Penny said, "And this is my girl Mocha Latte."

Her expression was terse. Something had happened in there and she wasn't happy about it.

I didn't see any other rides pulling up, so I asked, "What's going on?"

Penny turned to me. "They're rolling with us."

"Ass, gas, or cash, and I don't accept the first two on that list. Same for EBT."

"Stop popping off and open the trunk so we can put our stuff in Miss Mini."

My ride was a red-white-blue UK-branded 2005 Mini Cooper, about 138,000 miles on the odometer. Paid for since 2009. Worth about four grand. Clean as a whistle; looked new. I wasn't a fan of UK politics, but riding around like a billboard for Brexit was less trouble than riding around in something Africa branded.

I stuffed the weighty duffel bags inside the trunk and regarded the women. They smelled freshly showered and sweet, like trouble.

Mocha Latte and Christiana took the back seat.

Mocha Latte couldn't get relaxed, made a face like she was living in agony. Already I didn't like her.

I asked, "What's wrong with her?"

Penny replied, "A little proctalgia."

"Occupational hazard."

"Every job is a pain in the ass."

CHAPTER 2

BRICK

WESTBOUND TRAFFIC ON Wilshire was horrible, which was par for the course, day or night.

Penny said, "Hope you don't mind my coworkers coming along."

"Kinda late to ask since you've already invited the brood of chicks, don't you think?"

"Don't call them chicks. That's disgusting."

"Not tall enough to be a tower of giraffes. Pride of lions, a pace of asses, a romp of otters."

"Don't insult my friends."

I asked, "How'd the band of coyotes get here from where they were before they came here?"

"Uber. And stop with the stupid grouping."

"Convocation of eagles. Charm of finches. Leash of greyhounds."

"Stop it."

"I'm going back to pace of asses. I like the sexy way that sounds. Pace of asses."

"Stop it. Last time."

"Even when women work in pairs, it's not wise. Bad shit happens."

"But it's safer. If I keep doing this, I need a work buddy. Need a partner."

I asked Christiana, "Where do you and your friend live?"

"We were roommates in Santa Monica. Now we are homeless together."

Penny said, "I told them they can crash at my place for a couple of days."

Christiana said, "We lost our apartment; got evicted two days ago. Landlord didn't like us. Asked me for my fuckin' immigration papers, and when I didn't show them, said he would call ICE."

Mocha Latte's phone rang. She answered with a frowning face but a fake-cheery voice. "Hello? Who is this? Oh, you. I remember. You liked to do that thing. Whassup? Well, yeah, it's been a while. Thought you had forgotten about me. When do you want to meet? Let me check my schedule. I'll have to move some things around, but I can be available for two hours. Two minimum. Pay through PayPal. PayPal. Yes. Once the payment clears, I will call. I will come to you. No, I don't work out of my home. Hotel or your place. No, I don't do bareback. No, you can't pay me enough for that. I don't care if you saw it on Brazzers. No watersports. Mild BDSM is cool. No slapping. Do what? Slavery reenactment? No, I don't get down like that. We straight, then? How much to do what? Well, double that number and let me think about it. But no promises. Okay. Yes. Love you too. What's your name again? Ethan Shine."

I peeped in the rearview mirror. She hung up, frowned out the window. I knew that irritated look. That silence. Penny wore that expression the first time she did this. She hated herself for what she was doing.

As I battled traffic I asked, "Roscoe's, T.G. Express, Tim's Kitchen, or Pann's?"

Penny beamed. "Roscoe's is calling my name. I love my Obama Special."

I asked Christiana, "How long have you been living here in California?"

"In Los Angeles, only a few months. I came from Miami."

"You've done this gig the whole time?"

"Before Miami, I was an attorney. I wore business suits and heels every day."

"An attorney? Really?"

"Yes. *De veras.* Once upon a time I was attorney. *An* attorney. Excuse my English."

"Your English is fine."

"I make mistakes. I forget words. That is why I say my English is horrible. I like to talk to people, so I can practice. Everyone's English is very different. Everyone uses different words, phrases."

Christiana laughed a little, then leaned to Mocha Latte and whispered in her ear.

Penny asked, "Okay, what was that all about?"

"I told Mocha Latte that the energy I feel tells me that you and Brick are lovers."

Penny rolled her eyes. "There is no energy between us, other than hostility."

"Am I wrong, or am I right?"

Penny said, "Once."

"Once?"

"Once."

I said, "Twice."

"Long time ago."

"Not that long ago. Five months ago, more or less."

Christiana asked, "Really?"

Penny said, "I was drunk. Emotions were all over the place. Needed a fix."

"You like him?"

Penny said, "I used him the way men use women."

I said, "I guess I was just doing a brokenhearted neighbor a ten-minute favor."

Penny kissed her teeth. "You couldn't keep it hard."

I said, "Why would I stay hard for a drunk woman blowing snot bubbles over a dude that bankrupted her and left her for some other chick that he married in Vegas a week later? You think that was a turn-on?"

"I was upset, dammit."

"When you stopped crying I had your ass on your sofa going, 'Ay ay ay.' Like Shakira. 'Ay ay ay.'"

"*Dios mío*." Christiana smiled. "That's the cute noise you make. You were moaning loudly and saying 'ay ay ay' a lot tonight. Especially when the fat bald man was behind you while you and Mocha Latte—"

"Shut up, Christiana," Penny snapped. "Never talk about work in front of Brick."

"You said that Brick was cool."

"What happens in Vegas stays in Vegas."

I said, "I was in Vegas."

"No, you were in Barstow."

Mocha Latte shifted again, made another pained sound.

Christiana said, "Penny, you and Brick may have been lovers twice—"

Penny cut her off. "For the last time, the only reason it happened was because I had broken up with Javon, that jerk. He spent all my money, dumped me, then married some thot the next week. Yeah, that left me fucked-up in the head. Drunk dialed Brick to talk and cry on his shoulder. I was so damn drunk. Wasted. Stressed. Depressed. Heartbroken. Lonely as hell. I trusted him not to try and sleep with me, and he violated that trust."

"You called me over."

"Not to smash."

"You answered the door naked."

"I had a towel on."

"Then you were as naked as Erykah Badu when she was looking for a window seat."

"I had just showered and didn't expect you to show up so damn fast."

"You told me to come right over."

"The way I remember it, you pushed me back onto the sofa, gave me head like Jill Scott on the mic, and—"

"Don't revise our history. She had a three-level-deep orgasm and begged for me to do it to her again."

Christiana asked, "Three-level orgasm? *Mierda*. What is that?"

"When a woman has an orgasm inside an orgasm inside an orgasm. I took her three levels deep. Made her feel so good it scared her to tears. Penny lay on the floor, crying, like she'd had an out-of-body experience."

"Orgasm inside orgasm inside orgasm." Christiana laughed harder. "You are so very funny, Brick."

Penny grumbled, "Nobody begged."

I mocked her, "Ay ay ay."

Penny combed her hair. "Every woman has *at least* one 'wish I didn't' affair. He's mine. Twice."

Christiana asked, "Did you not come like that? Was there a three-level orgasm?"

Before Penny could answer, sirens blared a block back. Lights from squad cars lit up the night. I pulled over to the right, kept my hands on the steering wheel at ten and two, implemented the Negro survival training passed down from generation to generation. They hadn't taught a black man how to make the LAPD treat him like a blond white woman from 90210, and since my skin looked very 90220, this was the best I could do.

After they passed and I started driving again, Christiana exhaled. "So, Brick, Penny mentioned that your girlfriend left you not long ago?"

Penny laughed. "She used him to have a place to live rent-free, and as soon as he wised up and brought up money matters, she dumped him for someone with a better hoopty and a bigger paycheck."

That offended me, touched an open wound, but I manned up and grinned through the pain.

Christiana went on. "What went wrong with your girlfriend, Brick?"

Mocha Latte snapped, "I wish all of you would shut the fuck up. Who gives a shit?"

Penny and Christiana looked at that slice of chocolate like she was possessed by the devil.

I PULLED DEEP into the run-down, L-shaped parking lot of Roscoe's on Pico.

As we crossed the lot, a good-looking woman appeared from the entrance of the eatery, laughing. I recognized her and frowned. She was tall like the Nilotic peoples, indigenous to the Nile Valley. A brown-skinned woman caught up with her. I recognized her too. She kissed the darker woman on the lips; then she took the darker woman's hand.

The Nilotic woman was dressed in a glamorous suit in the hue of oranges and reds, her hair touching the middle of her back, in one braid. The tall brown woman with her rocked an oversize Afro so large it made her look like a moving tree. She wore a hot yellow dress, tight over her breasts, her hips, her ass, and sweet Madden boots. Her name was Coretta. I had bought her those boots. That tight dress too. Maybe her underwear as well. The brown-skinned woman saw me and stopped laughing. The Nilotic woman followed suit. Smiles became frowns.

Coretta was my ex.

We made eye contact, and I couldn't help but make a face like I had an intense anal fissure and a cluster of hemorrhoids the size of a grapefruit. She did too. I regained my composure first. We walked by each other without a word, like we never meant anything to each other, like we'd never known each other in the biblical sense, like strangers.

Tried not to, but I looked back and my heart turned to stone.

Coretta eased into her woman's Maserati. The glamorous Nilotic woman kissed my brown-skinned ex, did that to show possession, and drove away. A bitch who broke hearts and took no names now had a bitch of her own. If I had noticed that Maserati when I came into the lot, I would have kept going, or I might've hit the accelerator and rammed that car, but she had parked deep in the back corner of the backward-upside-down-L-shaped lot, hidden between two Range Rovers. My world had stopped moving and now I had stopped walking.

The pace of asses stopped too, looked back at me to see a man disturbed.

Christiana asked, "What is wrong, Brick? That look on your face; did you see a ghost?"

Penny said, "The bad attitude in the yellow dress was his ex. The one who dumped him."

"Brick, that was the girl you were in love with?"

Penny went on, "The jet-black girl with her licked the clit and turned her out."

"Turned her out? What does that mean?"

"His hard dick wasn't as strong as a woman's soft tongue."

Seething, I said, "Shut up, Penny."

I hoped the pace of asses would move on, but Christiana took a breath, gave me a kind smile, and regarded me as if she were beholding my soul, her face filled with empathy and understanding. "We're complicated creatures. All of us are. Yet we are simple, almost predictable, at the same time. Our needs are not always the same as those of our lovers. That is the part of dealing with each other, with other humans, that we must understand. Many of us need different things, but we all need something specific, and that can change year to year, or moment to moment. Some will take what they need from you, ruin your heart, then go. Do not be offended when someone does not live up to *your* needs or *your* expectations. It is part of living, part of life."

Penny and Mocha Latte considered her, shifted like those words had touched their souls too.

Christiana took a deep breath. "I've been through every kind of heartache and misery imaginable. You have no idea what I've sacrificed and endured. I am just like Penny. Just like Mocha Latte. And, Brick, I am just like you."

Those sincere words jarred Penny, woke up some pain she felt within.

The mini-sermon had the same impact on Mocha Latte. Buried feelings had been called to the surface for the girls. Couldn't be laughed or joked away. Then Penny marched on toward the diner, Mocha Latte barely keeping up with her. I stared toward the spot where Coretta had been.

CHAPTER 3

BRICK

WITH A TENDER smile and an expression of pure concern, Christiana stayed behind with me.

I needed a minute to get the intrusion of cockroaches out of my brain and the feeling of flaming grapefruits in my ass to fade away.

She waited a few more seconds before she asked, "You're okay?"

Another five seconds passed before I responded, "I'm okay."

"I saw your heart. It was on your sleeve."

"You saw dandruff on my sleeve. Nothing Head and Shoulders can't wash away."

"I saw her heart too. Both of you were so startled. When was the last time you saw her?"

I felt uneasy but answered, "Six months ago, more or less."

"She held that woman's hand, but the way she looked at you, love and jealousy remain. Seeing you did something to her. I saw that in her eyes and body language. She saw you and no longer wanted to hold the woman's hand she was with, but that woman held her hand tighter. In fear. I know in my heart that she had love for you in hers."

"That's not what I saw."

She asked, "What does she do? Is she a model?"

"Dresses like one, but she's a speech pathologist."

"She is attractive, and I can tell you are kind. What happened?"

"Philosophies collided. Reality and fantasy had a big disagreement."

"What does that mean?"

The question made me uneasy. Made me feel like Christiana was studying me, accumulating information that somehow could be used later. Or maybe that was just one question too many. Maybe she was just profound and the kind of talks she wanted to have required self-reflection, honesty, and emotional labor.

I said, "There was a song that went, 'Nothin' from nothin' leaves nothin'.' Man sang it long before I was born. It feels like a woman's anthem. Women tell men, 'You gotta have somethin' if you want to be with me,' but she didn't want me to know how much she made, how much she had saved, yet she wanted a wedding ring?"

I caught myself before my issues dragged me away like a team of wild horses.

Christiana asked, "So, you were almost married, Brick?"

"We were in the preplanning stages. We looked at rings but were never engaged."

She asked, "What kind of girlfriend was she?"

"Now that I can see clearly? A user."

"Then be glad you are free. It is hard to let beautiful things go, but at times we must."

I asked, "So what do I do?"

"You go on. You live with sleepless nights until one night you surprise yourself and sleep soundly. You allow the recovery process to happen. You may feel like you are the only one awake at night, like you are the only one in the world feeling what you feel, but you are not alone. There are more than many."

We took slow steps toward Roscoe's. A couple of bros were out front passing out pro–African American literature. The militants noticed Christiana and had to hold their family jewels to keep their balance.

Roscoe's was crowded. Lots of chatter, but not every table was taken. I passed by the cashier, near where they had President Obama's picture on the wall, servers whizzing by carrying plates filled with chicken, waffles, red beans and rice, grits, mac and cheese, and collard greens. After we were seated and had ordered, Penny and Mocha Latte went to the ladies' room together. Christiana sat next to me.

"Brick, you're only a chauffeur and not in the other special parts of the business?"

"What special parts?"

"There are amazing women, rich women who just don't have time to date, or don't feel like doing the work, but want to find a good-looking, fit lover they can spend quality time with. I have made contacts along the way."

"So, you have a client list that consists of male miscreants and wayward women."

"LA is the perfect place for this profession. Women come to LA on business, are here for only a night, maybe only for an afternoon, and love to have the boyfriend experience. They are women of power and means."

She pulled out her phone, showed me pictures of women. Schoolteachers. Housewives. Politicians.

Christiana said, "A restless woman is a very unfaithful woman. So is an unhappy woman."

"I've never met a woman who wasn't restless or unhappy."

"And I've never met a man who was so happy he wasn't restless."

I noticed a pack of guys, rappers, stop Penny and Mocha Latte on their way back from the bathroom, trying to holla. One was halfway famous, and all the way interested. The rest were that joker's henchmen. Probably on his payroll, being paid in leftover tennis shoes plus all the chicken and waffles they could eat. Penny and Mocha Latte put on smiles and sat down with the rapper and his crew. I could hear erections growing as they exhaled.

I asked Christiana, "How was it the first time? Who was your first customer?"

"He was a minister. He was fifty years old, very kind. I cried after."

"A real minister?"

"It was in a church, saw Jesus looking down on me as he did things to me."

"In a church?"

"I was foolish to have gone into that church by myself. I needed money and took risks. I am more careful now. I prefer that Mocha Latte and I work together. That way, we can watch out for each other."

I nodded. "If you need a driver, I can work for you, same rate as I charge Penny."

"There are people who will buy a parking space for a million dollars or pay two hundred thousand for a bottle of champagne. They will pay seven thousand for a night. I need to find those clients, and I could earn five hundred thousand in one year."

"That's about seventy-two nights."

"I'm worth it."

"I would love to take a selfie with a seven-grand-a-night pussy."

"I would love to feel an orgasm inside of an orgasm inside of an orgasm."

"And I would love to see a unicorn."

"I am a very smart woman, but I am also very self-aware, and I know that before time runs out, or there is an accident or illness, this fleeting beauty is to be used to my advantage. I have been through seven kinds of hell. I deserve heaven. I deserve to be rich in adventure, health, and knowledge. I deserve love and family. I dream big and I work hard. I remain humble, and I try to help other people become successful."

I told her, "You're gorgeous. I'm sure a rich man would wife you in a heartbeat."

"If I don't have my own money, I'll just be a whore wearing a diamond."

The conversation ended when Mocha Latte and Penny came back. The rappers looked at me, sizing me up. Saw that I wasn't a joke. They broke first, giving me a head nod. I did the same. Respect.

The food came. We ate, people watched, and talked about nothing memorable.

Christiana finished her meal, sipped tea, and asked Penny, "You work often?"

"Not often. I'm in college so everything is scheduled around classes and studying."

Christiana asked, "What is not often for you?"

"Once a month. Maybe twice. But my money is funny now, so I'll have to work more."

"If it is okay to ask and not be offensive, how did you start doing this, Penny?"

Christiana had a way about her, a disarming tone. Penny was usually closed off, but she opened up. She told Christiana that she had fallen in love, moved in with the man of her dreams, before she found out about his other girlfriend. Dude ran up her charge cards, wrecked her car, then walked away and left her fifteen grand in the hole. Money was needed to survive. Not long after, she ended up doing quickies for quick bucks.

Penny said, "The first time I did it, rent was due and I hadn't eaten for three days. Thought, do that a few minutes, eat like a queen, get my Whole Foods on, and not have to worry about that for the rest of the month. Once wasn't so bad. Done in twenty minutes. Nobody knew. So, I put an ad online at Ebony Escorts. Still needed money, you know? A Jewish girl at USC did the same, turned me on to other parts of the business, showed me other websites, showed me where to go after the fast cash. Smart girl. Cunning. She's going to be an attorney. Will probably end up on the Supreme Court. Anyway, I was only going to do it a couple more times, and that was, by my estimation, at least four months ago."

Christiana nodded as she listened. "You haven't done this that long."

"Yeah. Four months. Closer to three. Did it five times, five dates. Still not comfortable with it, but not as uncomfortable."

"You looked very nervous when you came into the house tonight."

"I was. This scares me. Was shaky until I met you and Mocha Latte. Then I felt safer."

"What's your goal?"

"Pay my debts and stack enough chips to get through six months of living; then I'm done."

"How much longer do you think you'll do this?"

Penny's phone rang. She looked at the number, made a face, answered. "What took you so long to call me? Uh-huh. Bro, you don't sit on my number for a year, then call me and talk about taking me out in the next hour. Six months is a year. Keep it real. Yeah, I know I sound different than I did six months ago. Lot has changed in my life. Not your business. You see the time? Don't call at this hour trying to disguise a booty call as a dinner invitation. I don't do booty calls for cheesecake. If you can't call ahead of time and invite me to church, or Bible study, then just lose this number. I'm blocking you on social too. God bless you and, boy, bye."

Mocha Latte chuckled, gave Penny a smooth high five.

As they talked and finished their meals, Christiana and I got in line to pay.

I asked, "What is it like?"

"What is what like, Brick?"

"To go to a room and not know who's waiting to . . . to make love to you?"

"There is no love waiting. Only a stranger who desires to be intimate with another stranger. Someone who wants to control you or needs you to control them."

"How does it feel knowing you're going to have sex with someone you've never met?"

"Imagine, you open a door, see a smiling woman, and know that in a matter of minutes she will invite you to touch her, to please her, that she will invite you inside her body in some way. A woman you just met."

"You're good at making what you do sound very erotic, intriguing, and profitable."

"We are psychiatrists that raise orgasms to soothe the souls of prevaricators and the restless."

"Now you're in the medical field."

"We are therapists too. Orgasms are healing. Cure illnesses. They take away pain. Calm your mind and body. Orgasms get rid of tension. You and Penny did that for each other two times. That was kind."

"Won't be a third act of benevolence; no caravan of orgasms. Not with Penny."

"Just be sure that you are as sure as she is sure. Even if the woman is not yours, once you have been intimate, with that connection, some will become jealous of certain things."

"We're friends."

"Friends who have been lovers will never truly be friends again."

The rest of the pace of asses joined us as we left.

I said, "Where next? Comedy Club in Long Beach? My brother is on tonight."

Penny said, "I don't want to see André's little comedy act again."

Christiana said, "Dancing. I want to go dancing."

Penny began to move. "I know where to go. Inglewood. My spot in Inglewood."

CHAPTER 4

DWAYNE

THE LOBBY OF the comedy club was café style. Checkerboard floors, wooden ceiling fans, pictures of every comedian from Charlie Chaplin to Richard Pryor covering the walls. There was access to the bar and itty-bitty kitchen, so I got a whiff of everything from Bacardi to Budweiser, from refried beans to greasy burgers.

My younger brother André and I were outside the top comedy club in downtown Long Beach, taking in the cool ocean air under the palm trees. I'd just landed at LAX two hours ago and surprised him at his show. I had on black joggers and a white T-shirt underneath a Jedi hoodie. André had on slim jeans and a WAKANDA FOREVER T-shirt. He sat on his yellow BMW motorcycle, helmet at his side, while we watched the crowd file into the club.

My younger brother asked, "When you get back?"

"Plane landed two hours ago."

"Glad you're back home. For how long?"

"Not sure. I have to deal with Frenchie. Court. Family court."

"Again? You're down there so much, they should be sending you a paycheck on the first and fifteenth."

"And I haven't seen my son in three months. We talk all the time, but I need some face time."

"Been that long? I don't see how you stay on the road with those shows year after year."

"It's theater. We live on the road. New city every week. Some folks have been on the road thirty years." I motioned at the time. "Showtime, Baby Brother. Get me a seat in the back. Don't want to upstage you."

"You wish."

"Get me a drink too. A greyhound."

"You talked to Brick?"

"Not yet. He coming down?"

"Said he might."

I wanted to tell him about the disturbing text messages I'd gotten from my son, texts that had my anxiety through the roof, but it wasn't the type of thing you dropped on an entertainer before he stepped onstage.

I'd let him finish working, then go by his crib, bring up my concerns. I was worried about my son, Fela, and his well-being.

André had to do three one-hour sets that night: he was headlining the seven, nine, and eleven shows. First show was always the hardest because people weren't drunk enough. Second show, they were just right. By the third show, people could be too intoxicated. Intoxication always woke up a hoard of hecklers.

AT THE LAST show, André stood onstage, laughter coming down hard, talking about his years of unprovoked run-ins with the cops, same experience damn near every black in America seemed to have had at some point. He did a new bit about when he was getting fucked with by the cops in Beverly Hills a few days ago.

"I was not speeding. No missing front plate. No broken taillight. Wearing my seat belt. Hadn't broken any laws. I don't look like OJ or Rodney King. Basically, I was in a very nice car, as nice as those driven by the white people being allowed to go from point A to point B unprovoked, enjoying my motherfucking Sunday, driving while black. I didn't have a white woman at my side, which, for this story, is very important to note, because that means there was absolutely no reason for anybody of any race to fuck with me on my Sunday, black women or white men. But I'm a black man in America. Who needs a reason? Shall I proceed?"

People in the crowd shouted, *"Yes, proceed."*

He let the laughter die down a bit.

"So, I was in Beverly Hills, in a drop top . . . going *under* the speed limit . . . minding my own fucking business . . . and that has somehow disturbed the police, the way that chilling in Starbucks now is like sitting at a lunch counter at Woolworth's during the civil rights era. So. Was minding my motherfucking business."

A heckler in the front row yelled out, *"Get to the punch line."*

He had disrupted the two acts that came on before André too.

André walked to the edge of the stage, looked down on him, smiled. "Oh, I will, white boy."

"White boy?"

"Yeah, I called you a boy. Did I get the gender right? I don't want to assume."

"Racist."

"Did you call me racist? Well, you have to remember that no black people work at the Department of Racism. That's all white people, *Chuck.* Doesn't he look like a Chuck? Now, you could've called me a bigot and I might have agreed, or a nigga and I would have agreed, then beat your ass, not in a violent manner, but in a very intellectual and educational sort of way that ended with a punch line and maybe a standing ovation."

His snark brought out waves of laughter.

"Call me a racist? Nah. Bigot? Yes."

Laughs kept coming.

"Racist? Never. But you also have to remember that if I am a bigot, the Department of Bigotry is secretly funded by the Department of Racism. They set the rules; we just follow their lead. The Department of Racism, where most of the employees are white men. I'm joking. They're all white men. That's where it all started and that is who is still in control. Yeah, I might be a bigot, but that's only because I'm in a country of racists. It's a defense mechanism. You get rid of the head office and all of this shit might go the fuck away."

Huge applause and laughter. He was Dave Chappelle, Chris Rock, and Richard Pryor 2.0.

Chuck yelled, "Asshole."

"Former asshole, Chuck. Former. Let me explain this to you. Chuck, did you know the first body part developed in an embryo is the anus? The asshole comes first. My point? We all start off as assholes, but the rest of us have developed into decent human beings, Chuck."

Hilarity ensued.

"I'm the clap-back king, *Chuck*. You're probably the king of bringing the clap back. White people. Infecting America since 1492."

People died in the aisles; women had to run to pee.

"You get what you get, Chuck. You're barking orders, basically said, 'Nigga, hurry up.' Like you're my comedy overseer."

He paused as the heckler whispered something to his date.

André asked, "What was that? You can say it to your woman, so say it to me."

Then my brother took it down to a whisper. "This is between us. You don't like that I called you boy? Neither did my people when your momma and daddy did it, yet little white boys called our black grandmothers by their first names. This is for them, Chuck."

Applause and laughter showed who was in charge. This was André's house. The heckler's girlfriend was laughing so hard it was twice as contagious as the measles. Her laughter was fuel; André pointed at her, and everyone had a show just watching the pretty girl struggle to stop laughing.

André asked her, "Okay, I'm not that goddamn funny. Wish I was. What's the joke, Tammy?"

She wiped her eyes. "You. Keep. Calling. Him. *Chuck*."

"And?"

"His. Name. Is. *Chuck*."

The room erupted in explosive laughter, except Chuck the Heckler. He needed an enema.

André addressed the heckler's date. "Don't tell me your name is Tammy."

"No." She could barely talk for laughing. "My name is Becky."

"Becky?"

"Yes. Becky, not Rebecca. My name is actually Becky."

"Like Becky . . . with the good hair?"

"Yes. It's orange and yellow this week, but it's good."

"Beyoncé's after your ass, girl. Don't drink any lemonade."

The room fell out laughing again. People rolled in the aisles.

"Where did you find Chuck? DealDash-dot-com? Or does he work at the Department of Racism?"

She laughed. "He works for the government."

"So, yeah. At the Department of Racism."

André died laughing and the room loved it. Chuck was pissed the fuck off.

With a kind voice and a genial smile, André said, "Chuck. If you're thinking about kicking my ass, I'll let you know that will be a one-way trip. No need to pack, because you won't be coming back. Always bet on black."

André was crude, rude, likable, intellectual, very funny, and in your face at the same time.

"Anyway, I was driving and *minding my own motherfucking business*, just like I was doing a second ago when I started this joke, and next thing I know, Johnny Law was up in my window, looking all tense, gun at his side. I thought his IBS was acting up and he needed me to drive him to the emergency room . . ."

André got back to his routine, his segue as smooth as butter.

When he finished, he dropped the mic, threw up two fingers, then left to a standing ovation.

Chuck the Heckler stormed out of the room and left his date smiling at the stage, clapping hard for André, until finally she disappeared, shadowed her date into oblivion. She had laughed harder than anyone else in the room.

Watching my baby brother own the room, feeling how the crowd loved him, I was jealous. Proud, but still jealous. That used to be my life. His star was getting brighter and I was trying to stop mine from dimming.

CHAPTER 5

DWAYNE

"André. Becky is watching you."

"She's out here?"

I said, "By the front door."

He turned around and saw Chuck the Heckler's front-row date. She was staring out toward Pine Avenue and the convention center. Her butt had a nice hook. Shoes looked like Ferragamo. Her legs looked smooth. She had a single-button jacket on, so I couldn't tell if she was firm or soft around the middle. She shifted from one high heel to the other. Something about the way she moved her thighs warmed me up, sent a tingle up my spine.

André said, "She ain't looking at me. She must be waiting on Chuck to pull up in his heckler-mobile."

"She's using the window and checking you out in the reflection."

"When did she come out?"

THE BUSINESS OF LOVERS 27

"When you were talking to that producer about being in some movie at Lionsgate."

"Think she's waiting on Chuck to pull his car around? Women in sexy shoes don't like to walk far."

"Never know until you ask." His words stayed with me, but his eyes were on her.

André said, "So, you're back in town to do that court thing again?"

"Now that you bring it up, you owe me two grand. I need that cash to pay my attorney."

"Since when do I owe you two grand?"

"A year."

"For what?"

"I loaned you two grand. I don't know what you did with it."

"Did you?"

"Nigga, please."

Becky shifted, moved her thighs in a way that gave a man wild thoughts. Her reflection smiled. André shifted like he felt that tingle, like her electricity had enveloped him; then he slid his chair back.

I asked, "Where you going?"

"To holla at Becky before Chuck gets back and starts saying that I'm a racist."

André moved in her direction. She didn't turn around. André stood next to her and looked out the window.

André asked, "Where's Chuck?"

"He left."

"Was he your ride?"

"No. Thank God."

"How'd you end up with Chuck?"

"Guy I was seeing, we broke up, so I was online and swiped right."

"Why you and the guy you were seeing break up?"

"Getting caught makes a motherfucker have to decide."

"He decided?"

"I decided."

"You smell nice."

"You're handsome. Very."

André grinned. "Enjoy the show?"

"You come at them hard."

"When you call a black man selling loosies a criminal, yet you have Manafort, you get what you get."

She said, "I've never laughed so hard in my life. But when you smiled at me, when you looked me in my eyes . . . you're so handsome I guess I zoned out and went to another plane. *Chuck* noticed. Said I was flirting."

"Were you?"

"I was."

"*Chuck* coming back?"

"Fuck *Chuck*. Fuck my ex and fuck *Chuck*. He embarrassed me by heckling you. *Chuck* was mad because I wouldn't walk out and leave like he wanted to, then mad because I had a great time without him."

"My name is André."

"I know your name."

"I know yours. Becky."

"I lied."

"Egads."

"Joëlle is my real name. Becky was the name I told Chuck. My Internet name."

"Surprised you stuck around so long."

"A lot of people were talking to you after the show, so I googled you. Had never heard of you. Impressive résumé. I decided to hang around. I was wondering if or when you were going to notice and say something to me."

"I thought you were waiting on Chuck."

She nodded once. "You're very funny. That's all I wanted to say. I'm going to leave."

"Can I go with you?"

"I'm not that kind of girl. I just wanted to thank you for being the best part of my night."

"I've been looking at you, and you've been looking at me. You know what that means?"

"What?"

"We've been looking at each other."

Her face switched to the enamored stare she had on when he was onstage.

Her hips shifted again.

She put her hand on the door, pushed it part of the way open. "Nice meeting you."

"You're really going to leave without me?"

She took a step, turned her eyes back to André, asked, "You shoot pool?"

"Yeah."

"I'll be in the parking lot. Dark green Nissan."

"I'll follow you. I'll be on the yellow BMW motorcycle."

"That's yours?"

"Yeah."

She was impressed. "Bet you ride women around the way Prince did Apollonia."

"Bet you'd look good on the back of it going down the Pacific Coast Highway with me."

"I've never been on a motorcycle."

"I could be your first."

André came back over to me.

I said, "We running in the morning?"

"See you at seven."

"Brick running?"

"He hasn't been running lately."

"Was going to crash at your pad."

"Snap, bro. You got somewhere else you can go? Just in case."

I was stressed about money, about life, worried about Fela, and didn't want another nasty confrontation with his mother, sort of needed my brother emotionally, but I nodded. "I'll book a room."

CHAPTER 6

BRICK

I CHAUFFEURED THE pace of asses to Inglewood, then parked on Market Street. They changed in the car and sashayed into Savoy Entertainment Center in dresses barely long enough to cover a man's number one obsession. Those showstoppers had made money and wanted to drink and dance because the eagle was flying high, and drink and dance we did. I love to dance. Dancing increases happiness. Drinking numbs problems and fears. The pace of asses hit the floor together, attacked the beat, and were in the middle of thirty other people, tripping the light fantastic like yesterday didn't matter, today was a done deal, and there was no tomorrow. My phone vibrated. A Florida area code. My older brother. A little worried that he was calling so late, I stepped off to the side and answered.

Dwayne said, "I'm back in LA. I'm in Long Beach with André."

"Cool. Was going to call you to check in tomorrow."

"You have all my documents from CSS?"

"Yeah, I have your child support notices stacked up. Your other mail is there too."

My older brother claimed my address as his residence to keep his fifteen-year court case in California and guided by the rules here. The pussy you fuck gets you fucked in the end. If he used his address in Florida, he'd have to pay for a lot of other shit, and he'd be broker than he was now.

I asked, "You okay? I hear that sound in your voice again."

"Stress. This shit is killing me. Different city every week, and the show was falling apart. Everyone was getting fired, from musical director to choreographer. Even the lead was replaced. They let me go too. I spoke my mind and asked them to, so I could be eligible for unemployment. Fuck 'em. Pay was so low that when I worked it out, between all the rehearsals and performances and this and that, I was making ten bucks an hour."

"Nothing back in New York on Broadway?"

"Nothing right now. I'm back. My agent will get me some auditions while I'm here. I'm working on something else too. But first I have to get a court date to see about getting child support lowered again."

"How long will that take?"

"Will take a minute. Couple months at the earliest."

Christiana saw me, beckoned me to the dance floor seductively.

I said, "Dwayne, let me call you back."

He ranted, "She said she couldn't get pregnant. Polycystic ovaries. She lied. Soon as she missed her period, she called a top-shelf attorney to figure out how to file for child support right away."

"Dwayne."

"'Gold digger digging all the gold out the child star's mine.' My attorney said that. The first time we went to court she demanded sixty grand a month and wanted it to be increased each year by fifteen percent. She got laughed out of the room. The judge rolled his eyes at her and her attorney. She got *four thousand* a month and left family court outraged, crying like she was the one being robbed. Forty-eight thousand a year, tax-free, and she was mad because she didn't score enough money to buy the west wing up at Hearst Castle."

"Y'all been fighting a long time."

"Sixteen years."

I had to yell over the music. "Dwayne, checkmate. I'm at a club. Dancing. Gotta go."

"You have company tonight?"

"Not sure. I'm with Penny right now, getting my dance on."

"Penny?"

"My neighbor. The USC girl."

"Brick, I need a favor. Hate to ask, but I need you to check something out for me."

Music kicked up louder and I could barely make out what he was saying.

"Brick, check on my son because he told me that the lights and water were cut—"

"Do what?"

"My son sent a lot of text messages, freaking out, said his mother hasn't paid the—"

It was a struggle to hear Dwayne over a Yemi Alade mix playing. "You have to pay for what?"

Naija music bumped like a 7.0 earthquake and I couldn't hear Dwayne.

Christiana pranced her way over, took the phone from my hand, and hung up. "Dance with me, Brick."

She led me back to the party. I showed her some moves to go with the Afrobeats. Her expression told me she was surprised I had skills. Even did that Ethiopian chest-pump thing, the dance called the *eskista*, for kicks. Salsa came on and she did some Latin moves hotter than the sun. We boogied for thirty, maybe forty-five minutes nonstop, and all the while, Mocha Latte and Penny were burning up the floor next to us. Penny was in the zone, dancing like she wanted to chase the sins she had committed in the name of capitalism from the center of her soul.

TWO HOURS LATER, we sat in Penny's living room, sipping wine. Her place was always disorganized, every room in a state of confusion. Books on black history and art were stacked unevenly on her two overpacked Ikea bookcases. Still, even though it was disorganized, it was clean.

Penny was on the sofa, blanket up to her chin, eyes closed. Mocha Latte was cuddled up behind her.

I shook Penny, told her to go get in her bed; then I stretched and grabbed my coat.

Penny yawned. "Let me pay you for tonight."

I waved her away. "I'll get it tomorrow. You've got your hands full."

She shrugged with her inebriation. "Sorry about the things I said about, you know."

"Needed to hear those things."

"You saw your ex tonight."

"Next subject."

Penny pulled her lips in. "How are your parents?"

"They're good."

"Your brothers?"

"Dwayne's back in town. André is being André."

She nodded, awkward, out of things to say. "I'd better clean my face and shower again."

She rose from the sofa, stretched, yawned, and headed down the short hallway, her short dress caught in the crack of her ass.

Christiana called my name. "Are you going to bed?"

"Not right away. I have trouble sleeping. Runs in the family."

"Penny might shower a long time. May I shower over there?"

"Sure."

She took towels and toiletries from her duffel.

She told Penny that she was going to my place to take a bath and would be back in a few minutes. We pulled the door up behind us. I picked her up and carried her across the walkway. Twenty steps to my front door. My place was nothing special. Classic sofa. Love seat. Coffee table. Five-year-old flat-screen. Chess set.

I turned on the ceiling fans in the living room and kitchen, let the cool desert air circulate.

She saw the chess set in the living room. "Do you play well?"

"I hold my own against those who have lesser talent."

"That's good to know."

"Why?"

"It's a skill set to be considered." She went to the kitchen. "What other hobbies?"

"Jazz. Snow skiing. Protesting injustice that started in the New World back in 1501."

"I see a very nice karaoke machine in the corner over by your very nice sofa."

"I like to have drinks, call people over, fire it up, and act a fool now and then."

"You swim?"

"Shallow end of the pool. If you find me floating in the deep end, it was murder."

"Skydive?"

"If the airplane was about to crash. But every airplane crash is involuntary skydiving."

She drifted into my kitchen. "*Dios mío.* You have so much wine."

"Only the good stuff."

She read some of the labels. Gentle Jack Morgan. Haan. Casamigos. Michael Mondavi Red Blend. Château Lynch-Bages Pauillac.

She asked, "Expensive?"

"Not all. I have wine ranging from eight dollars a bottle to about seven hundred a bottle."

"This is your job?"

"A side hustle. Do it for fun. Make a few tax-free dollars. And because I like wine. If nobody buys it, then I get to drink it."

"Where do you work?"

"At a widget factory. On leave for a while."

"You are a professional."

"Yeah. I'm an executive, more or less."

"I can tell. You are articulate. And how you carry yourself."

"Yeah. White-collar with blue-collar tendencies. Grew up blue-collar. Hard habit to break."

She didn't ask for details. "Well, may I have a glass of the wine that costs eight dollars?"

I put on music. Opened a bottle that sold at two hundred. We shared a glass of wine without sharing a word. Soon, my tipsy guest danced her way to the shower, used up all the hot water, then came back out, sexy in mikado-colored satin. She was a regular girl. Pretty, but regular, stripped down to the bare minimum.

She said, "Brick, your phone is buzzing."

I picked it up, saw about twenty CALL ME text messages from Dwayne.

He wanted to know if I had company. He was trying to crash on my sofa.

Couldn't deal with him. His anxiety was a bit much at times.

I went and stood in the shower, under cold water. A smack of emotions assaulted me. Coretta was a stranger to me. It was a good thing I saw her. I needed to see them holding hands, laughing like newlyweds. Could've been worse. Could've been revealed after a wedding, after two kids, and this grief I held on to now would be nothing compared to the pain, heartache, and financial destruction that would have cost. You could be with someone a year or twenty years and realize you didn't know them. People rarely rose to the level of being beyond intimate strangers.

WHEN I CAME out of the shower, Christiana was already in my bed.

I asked, "You want the television on?"

"No. But we can talk some more until we sleep."

"Sure."

"You have a lot of pills on your dresser. Maybe twelve bottles of this and that."

"Vitamins."

"'Vitamins' with complicated names given by prescription. I recognize one. It is for nausea."

I eased into bed next to her. She scooted over, cuddled up against me. I was on my left side. I wrapped my right arm around her, let it rest under her breasts. It felt good to touch a woman. Damn good. The curve of her body was against the firmness of mine. Heat disarmed me. Aroused me. She smelled like heaven. She smelled like love.

She asked, "What's on your mind?"

"This job you and Penny and Mocha Latte do, you know men who do this?"

She turned and faced me, smiling. "Of course."

"What kind of men do women like to rent?"

"European women love black men. But not to marry, only to have experienced at least once. I have heard women talk. It makes her feel naughty. You are their fantasy. Their forbidden fruit. Some want an adventure."

"What about black women?"

"Most desire exotic men. Some love seeing their skin against a differing skin color in bed. A man's accent, be it Spanish or French or Moroccan, makes a clitoris dance. Some feel like they are doing something taboo. I am only guessing, only saying it the way it appears to my eyes and ears. For some, it is how they battle depression."

"You know every type."

"Sometimes we simply provide love to the unloved or the misunderstood. Imagine no one touches you, no one kisses you, no one wants you in a sexual way. It can be very, very depressing to feel rejected by the rest of the world. So, people like that, they come to people like us to feel what feels like love."

All she said, I could imagine. It was my life. I responded, "But you don't love them."

"We make them feel loved. And not always with sex. Many don't want to have sex."

"What do you do with them?"

"Hold them. Talk. Go to dinner. Go hiking. Go skiing. Pay attention. Some only want to look at me."

"Why pay to look at you if they can touch you?"

"Some men are not capable. The emoji no longer functions. They pay to give me oral."

"Never heard it called an emoji."

"Not all emojis work."

"That's a win-win situation, I'd guess."

"Or some call it bamboo."

"And the league of wayward women would want to pay me so they can be bamboozled."

"Some clients want it rough; some want sex sensual. I find out as much about them as I can before I meet with them. Some men want sex and they want it the moment you enter the room. No conversation. No drinks. Women are different. They usually want to book far in advance and meet you, see how you get along, see if they like you face-to-face before inviting you into the bedroom. They might want to meet for drinks to feel more relaxed."

"You never know what to expect."

"Everyone is different. Some orgasm and are done with you, want you to leave right away. Some will feel guilty, ashamed of what they have done, and cry like babies." She hummed. "Are you intrigued?"

"You're busy at night."

"Our busiest times are early in the morning. That is when rich men in business suits are supposed to be on their way to work. Or during lunchtime. They have us meet them for a quickie. Evenings, married men go home to their wives and children and pretend to be perfect husbands and fathers and grandfathers. Women, too."

I digested, shifted, then asked, "You said you were an attorney?"

"I was. The best at my firm."

"Why do this dangerous work, why risk going to jail, if you were an attorney?"

"I was a lawyer back home, but I wasn't able to be one here in the States."

"Where are you from, Christiana?"

"Cuba."

"Caribbean girl."

"Born in Old Havana."

"Hard life?"

"Day and night. Poverty for breakfast, bribery for lunch, corruption for dinner."

"Ah."

She yawned. "So Penny never talks to you about what she does?"

"The most Penny will say is that she is an escort. She is paid for her company, and then whatever happens, happens. She says she has never been paid for sex. That's the lie she sticks to."

Christiana hummed. "Call it what it is. I have no shame. I sell a man his own orgasm."

"Sounds messy."

"Can be. With my Nigerian client, I should wear goggles, Saran Wrap, and a bib."

I asked, "Do you like doing what you do?"

"I do not always want to go to work and I do not like every customer."

"How much time do you actually spend having sex?"

"Lots of foreplay, but I try to be done with that part in no more than ten minutes."

"Really?"

"You look surprised. I know how to give fake sex, to make a drunk or high man think he's inside of me, but he is between my thighs. I can hide my face with my hair and use my hands and they think they are in my mouth."

I put on a Maxwell Smart voice. "The old cock-between-the-thighs trick."

"Most of the time, I try to make them finish before they get to put it inside of me."

I asked, "Then what?"

"I say to him that I enjoyed my date with him and if he wants me to stay longer, that can be arranged with a cash donation, PayPal, Apple Pay, or verified gift card. But I prefer cash. US dollars or British pounds. Never take Caribbean money, same for African money. It's worth nothing; no one will change it for American money."

"You have it all sorted out."

"I like you, Brick." She laughed. "We will get along very well."

"Really. Why?"

"You don't judge us. You talk to me like I am a human being."

"No, I don't judge. People are people. We're all trying to get paid or get laid."

She chuckled. "You make women feel safe."

"Most of your customers are married men?"

"Yes, many are married. Women too. Some women want a sewing circle."

"Sewing circle?"

"Code for women desiring lovers of the same sex. Many women want to be with women."

"Bisexual?"

"Some. Others are lesbians and some just like to be with women. It is different than being with a man. Some only do it once."

I asked, "Ever have any serious problems with a client?"

"I was at a bar in South Beach with a man, and his wife walked in and slapped me in the face. She was Dominican. She had followed him there, thought I was the girl he was having an affair with. He had paid in advance, PayPal, and we never even made it out of the bar. So, I just laugh and call that the one-thousand-dollar slap."

I said, "You're funny."

"So are you. I like you. You are nice."

"Nicer than some, meaner than others."

"I'm surprised Penny isn't your girlfriend."

"We're just friends."

"Two times. She will never forget she made love with you two times."

I shook my head. "She will forget a lot of things and a lot of people. She will marry, have kids, move to a nice home, and days like this, people like me, people like you . . . she will forget us all. What say you?"

"She will not forget. Not all the way. We pretend to forget the things we can't help but remember."

"I'm sure you've made love twice with someone you had nothing in common with."

Her playfulness waned. "Yes, my ex-husband."

"You were married?"

"Until he had sex with my younger sister."

"Sorry to hear that."

"Like you said, we had nothing in common. I realized my dream was based on many lies, but we were legally married, man and wife, and we stayed married for another year after he and my sister were exposed."

"Why stay married after that?"

"We are Catholic. God gave me that man to be my husband. We

didn't want to divorce, no matter what. That unhappiness tested my faith, made me question my religion. It was the longest year of my life, a century of what the doctor called melancholia. I had so much sadness. After he slept with my sister the first time, after I found out, I slept with him again. Took a while, but I did. Out of obligation. I was still his wife. And he was still my husband. Did it to show my sister that I was better than her, that I was good at being a wife, that he loved me more than he did her, and it was her fault he slept with her. I blamed her for the way she dressed, for how she danced and flirted, blamed everything but my husband's dick. It was a foolish, emotional thing. It was . . . the phrase . . . the phrase . . . yes . . . it was a *territorial* fuck. It was the fuck of ownership, to prove I was the queen of my house, not making love for forgiveness. I could not forgive. It was not the same. Hated myself for being with him again. After that, never again. I wish I could take that night back. He became my regret fuck. The lover I despised. And I do not regret what I did to my sister."

"What did you do to your sister?"

"I collected my tears in a coffee cup and splashed it in her face."

"You cried that hard?"

"Well, I said they were tears."

"What was in the cup?"

"Tears from my vagina."

"Guess you were pissed off."

She wiped her eyes. "She deserved it."

"You've had quite a journey."

Christiana said, "I hated my husband even before he slept with her. He told me I worked too much, but I was an attorney and he did nothing but drink cervezas and party, spent what I earned before I had earned it. Then I had to work even more to pay for his debt. Now he's divorced from me and married to my little sister. He married her, and my stepchild became my niece on the same day we were granted our annulment by the Catholic Church. So now, in the eyes of God, I have officially never been his true wife. Only had sex with him. He married her, and everyone thinks that something was wrong with me and I was not a woman, not a real woman. And they pity me because I was unable to give him a child. Or they think I was not a capable wife in bed. They blamed me for his affair. They blamed the victim for being victimized. They live with my parents, the same place he lived with me when we were married. No way I could stay in that house. No way could I watch them be husband and wife, sleeping in the bedroom next to mine. I would wake up and he would smell like her; then he would slap my ass and smile. It was too much."

"He married her, and then tried to make love to you?"

"There was no love between us. He would have raped me, and I would have been blamed."

"I stand corrected."

"At night, I slept with a knife at my side."

"You were around selfish and coldhearted people."

"He brought out the worst in me. I needed to get away to remove that darkness from my heart. I needed to start over. I told no one I was leaving. Not my mother. Not my father. Only told God. I didn't expect God to make it easy for me, not when God had never made life nor love easy for no one I have ever met."

"How did you end up here in America?"

"I walked out one day, pretended I was going to work, left everything I owned, and prepared for a journey that I might not live to see to the other end. I took all of my savings and paid to come over with more than fifty other people from the islands on an overloaded boat. Our journey was treacherous. We found our way into a storm. I almost drowned twice but I refused to die. I refused."

She shook. Heartache and pain were palpable.

"I was dying and clung to men who tried to get sex from me. Men touched me and said they would protect me if I slept with them once we were in America, and I refused those men, would pray for a dolphin to be sent by God to rescue me. I struggled. Before I bargained with them, I would rather drown first, and in the end, those opportunistic men drowned. The coast guard tried to force the boat away from the land. Everyone screamed. Panicked. I was terrified. I told myself that God is always in control, from Jesus's birth to his death and resurrection, and I knew that if this were not the will of God, I would not survive."

She stopped talking, rocked harder, and I whispered, "What happened?"

"I jumped into the ocean."

"You jumped from the boat?"

Her voice shuddered. "I jumped from the speeding boat into the Atlantic Ocean."

"How far out?"

Her foot bounced. "They said we were two miles away."

"That's a long way in dark waters."

"It felt like two thousand miles. Ninety miles from Cuba, two miles from Florida. The water looked like black ink. Cold, black ink. I swam toward America in the dark. Others were caught in the water, were sent back to Cuba. I touched sand before the police could catch me. I crawled on my knees, looked up, crossed myself, and prayed. I was in a new world. I could breathe the air, see the sky in America. Refugees from Haiti and the Dominican Republic were on the same boat, but they were sent back to their homelands. I had my papers. Had my passport. I was free from Cuba. They could catch me, but they couldn't send me back to everything I wanted to escape. *Never.* America has a special law for Cuban refugees but not for the Haitians and not for the Dominican Republicans. Only for Cuba."

She was back in time.

I said, "You were lucky."

"I was lucky. I was homeless, penniless."

"How did you get by?"

"Cleaned toilets. Washed sheets. Worked in sweatshops."

"You're a survivor."

"I was working in a sweatshop, dealing with racism. Hungry, eating once a day if I could. An attorney in Cuba. *Nothing* in America. My education counted for nothing. For years I cooked and cleaned for the rich and lazy. I watched other young girls like me, very young girls, lease themselves to horrible men. I said that I'd never do that."

Her voice had hardened, then softened, as she followed the rugged path down memory lane.

She turned her back to my front, cuddled up against me again.

"Brick?"

"Yes?"

"Thinking of my past makes me very stressed." She moved against me in a nice rhythm, hummed. "I am very stressed now and I need therapy to relax. I need to orgasm to be able to sleep at all tonight."

I moved against her, felt her heat. I was stressed and restless too.

She hummed. "Penny is not your girlfriend; am I correct?"

"Nah. Penny is not my girlfriend. Ain't no benefits over there waiting on me."

Christiana went to the bathroom, came back rubbing her palms with lotion. She took my rising emoji in her hands. Stroked me and licked my nipples. She made me rise, made me strong.

"See, Brick. I do this, smile this way, flirt like this, and a man will do or pay whatever I ask."

"I ain't got seven thousand dollars."

Christiana smiled. "This unwinds me."

"Does it?"

"Tonight, it relaxes and arouses me."

She had talked to me the way she would have a client. This was unexpected, but it would not be rejected. It had been too long since Coretta. Too long since Penny. My energy had moved, was in one part of my body. Nerves were fire. Her rhythm was smooth, a gentle kneading, hands working like she was mastering a musical instrument.

It was getting good, too good, had me moaning; then there was a fast, hard knock at my door.

The doorbell rang over and over.

Startled out of the moment, Christiana whispered, "Someone is angry. Very angry. Is that your ex?"

CHAPTER 7

BRICK

I ASKED CHRISTIANA, "Why the hell would it be my ex at my door at this hour?"

"Because love for you lives in her heart."

"Love don't live here anymore. Don't live there either. It's probably my brother."

I groaned, panted, pulled on my jeans and a T-shirt, pushed my stiff emoji up vertical against my belly, and limped to the front door. It was Penny. I let my neighbor in. Mocha Latte was with her, dressed in Nike tights and a T.

Penny tried to blink the alcohol out of her system. "Your power is still on?"

"Yeah."

"Mine went off. I got up to go use the bathroom; lights didn't come on. MacBook won't come on. Phone not charging. I'm screwed. Didn't pay the stupid bill."

"What you need?"

"I need to put my food in your fridge so it won't spoil."

The pace of asses followed me to Penny's place. I grabbed what she told me to grab and soon we were stumbling back into my spot. I put Penny's food in my fridge. Everybody else had phones, laptops, and chargers and were more concerned with plugging them in and getting my Wi-Fi password than with the food. Once the fridge was loaded, we all crawled into my bed, got comfortable underneath my ceiling fan. Christiana and Penny chatted while Mocha Latte clung to a pillow and drifted off to sleep. Penny tried to stay awake, tried to keep talking, but thank the gods, she failed. The sandman won. Christiana was bouncing her foot, like it was a signal, staring at me. When Penny was breathing softly and Mocha Latte was doing the same, we eased out of the bed. We stood where we could see Penny and Mocha Latte. I turned Christiana around, took her in the doorframe. We moved from there and got on the carpet in the living room. She got on top of me and made me want to scream. She held on to me. Her orgasm had her. I clamped my hand over her mouth, muffling the beauty of her sounds. She gave it to me good and I came so hard it hurt not to be able to shout it out of my body. We stayed like that a moment, letting it die down. We eased up off the carpet and peeped into the bedroom. Penny had shifted in the bed. So had Mocha Latte. No one heard us tiptoe to the bathroom to wash up. No one moved when we eased back into the crowded bed.

We stared at each for what seemed like an eternity.

She asked, "How soon can you make your emoji ready to go again?"

"Why?"

"I need to know what kind of emoji you have."

Again, I asked, "Why?"

She eased from the bed and called for me by bending her finger. I took slow steps and I followed her into the kitchen. I put my hands on her waist, lifted her up to the counter, eased her down gently.

She bit my ear, whispered, "This is not comfortable. Why do men love to put women in so many uncomfortable positions? On hard surfaces like this, on our knees, in the bathtub, on rugs, it does not feel good. Men are comfortable, and women are left with aching backs, sore knees, and rug burns."

I took her to my sofa, then sat down with her straddling me. "Better?"

"Much. Now I can focus on you and not wish I had on two pairs of kneepads."

We started again, our movements short, intense, hot.

Soon her hand covered my mouth while my hand covered hers. She sucked my fingers while I licked hers. She moved like she was famished, starved. I felt the sun rise, then swell, and want to explode inside of my body. She put that much fire in the heart of my soul. She made me see the god who made the gods who parented the god I worship. While we panted, we turned our heads and saw that Mocha Latte was in the living room, two feet away, standing near us in silence. Christiana stopped moving. I held her, eyes wide, my mouth opened in surprise.

Christiana whispered, "Mocha Latte?"

Mocha Latte sat down on the sofa next to us and looked around without blinking, then stood and walked around the living room. She headed toward the front door, walked into the wall, then backed up and stopped.

Christiana eased away from me and went to her. She touched her friend's face.

Mocha Latte jerked and blinked a few times. "What just happened?"

Christiana said, "You're sleepwalking again."

"I'm sleepwalking."

"Where are you?"

"Paradise Island. At the Atlantis Hotel. With my ex. The attorney. The day he asked me to marry him."

"Stay in the Bahamas with him. Stay with your dream."

Christiana took care of Mocha Latte, put her back in bed while I sat on the sofa recovering. Soon Christiana came and stood near me, rocking side to side. She nervously ran her hands over her hair.

I asked, "How bad is Mocha Latte's sleepwalking?"

"Once she drove a hundred miles wearing her panties and a bra."

"I hope she wears sexy panties."

"She wears merino wool panties. They cost forty dollars a pair."

"Wool panties?"

"Wool doesn't embrace moisture; they dry swiftly and don't hold on to odor."

"That part."

"You asked."

I nodded. "She won't remember?"

Without giving me a definite answer, Christiana reached for me. I followed her. She showered, was done in two minutes. I washed up again, yanked on gray UC Irvine joggers and a red T-shirt. Christiana wiggled into a fresh pair of wool panties herself. We moved Penny and Mocha Latte and got back on the bed. Underneath a slow-moving ceiling fan, the warmth from four people amalgamated as the coolness of the desert air circulated in the bedroom.

Christiana whispered, "You are a good lover."

"Better than some; worse than others."

"Better than most. Again, a talent not to be wasted waiting to find the love of your life. Orgasms are therapeutic. You can keep a healthy prostate and earn some quick money at the same time. Women between the ages of thirty-five and fifty-five. All are mature, rich, and would reward you for being in their presence."

"I'll put that so-called talent on my résumé and post it on LinkedIn, see how that works out."

"You have a skill that can be exploited to better your life."

She eased from the bed, went to her things, came back, and put three one-hundred-dollar bills in my hand.

The Cuban said, "So we are clear on what happened here tonight."

"Can I now pay you for the same thing you paid me for?"

"My prices are much higher. I can afford you, but you can't afford me."

"I can't afford any woman who pays forty dollars for her panties."

We stared at each other a while, inhaling, exhaling, pondering in silence.

I asked, "What?"

She spoke softly. "Let me present you to a client."

"Nope."

"Just one."

"Why would I?"

"To see what it's like to walk in a room and meet a beautiful stranger. Because nothing from nothing leaves nothing. Because the girl your ex was with has something and you want something too."

"You played me. Handled me like Olivia Pope. I won't forget this."

She winked. "No one ever forgets their first customer."

"Or their last."

She whispered, "Why the strange expression?"

"That round of how's your father was nothing to you."

"It was an interview. It was a test."

"I don't think I've ever had sex and it meant . . . What did we just do?"

"It was business, and at this point in my life business is everything to me."

"Good night."

She grinned. "You did not warn me."

"What you mean?"

"You come like a blue whale. I did not have goggles, Saran Wrap, and a bib."

We laughed.

She asked, "How long has it been since someone other than you touched your emoji?"

"Months. Not since Penny."

"Your emoji works. You're very handsome. Why no one since Penny?"

Mocha Latte mumbled, "Jesus, Christiana, shut the fuck up. People trying to sleep."

A stream of buffalo-size curse words followed; then she went right back to dreamland.

Christiana asked, "Can you take me shopping tomorrow?"

"Sure."

"And then I need to go downtown. I will pay you to be my driver and protector."

"Sure."

She whispered, "I saw bright colors, constellations, planets with a dozen moons, mathematical equations, solar systems, then more oceans. I saw deserts, lands that had never been touched by man."

I said, "That was only the start of level two. We should have continued."

Mocha Latte mumbled again, "Jesus Christ at a skating rink on Easter. People trying to sleep."

Christiana and I chuckled again.

At the same moment, we both whispered, "Good night."

I saw Christiana as a little girl who had grown into a woman who happened to have been an attorney in a foreign land, not as what she did on this pit stop between her successes. Same as I saw Penny as a USC student figuring out how to rule the world. I didn't see people as occupations, as cogs in the wheel. Christiana was soft on the outside, focused and hard within. I took no offense at what she had done and didn't expect more. She was a human being. Once upon a time, Maya Angelou worked as a prostitute. The poet of all poets, the Grammy-winning, calypso-dancing streetcar conductor in San Francisco. The friend to Malcolm X, the woman who had been a teen mother, the legend who delivered a powerful poem at the presidential inauguration for the first black president, had once been a female pimp. I read in a book that even Malcolm X had been in the same momentary quick-money occupation. For survival. Judge not in the moment, not while we are works in progress, but hold all verdicts until the end.

The pace of asses was on their own journey.

This was where our journey intersected, for now, not where we joined forever.

We were all adrift, being pulled by separate currents.

Sleep found me.

I dreamt I was at City of Hope cancer center in a chair, being fed poison to kill what wanted to kill me. From the window, I saw a Maserati taking my unfaithful past away from my unsure future. The Maserati began smoking; then it burst into flames. I woke sharply. I smelled smoke. The smoke wasn't in my dream. My apartment was on fire.

CHAPTER 8

DWAYNE

ANDRÉ AND I ran between nine and ten miles.

Neither one of us had slept much last night. André finished strong, then jogged in place, waiting on me. My body was damp from the top of my head down through my Thorlo socks. At the start of the run, when we were doing junk miles, I had told André about the musical I was just in, almost one hundred and forty in the touring cast. Told him how stressful it was, how I had to be on at almost every moment. Someone was always taking a personal day, so it was a different cast every night. I'd gone from a white show to a black show to a black show to a white show to a black show over the last year. Had seen large cities and small towns and had never been able to unpack my bags. Overworked and underpaid. It left me agitated, and I needed to run that demon called anxiety away every day.

Workout done, I took my Beats earbuds out of my ears, said, "Mind if I shower up at your crib?"

He did the same with his Beats. "Make it quick. Don't use up all of my goddamn hot water. I have to shower too. You get in a shower and start singing and use up all the hot water every damn time."

I showed him my traffic fingers. "I saw Brick last night, but he didn't see me."

"How did that happen?"

"I was going to stop by his crib, to check in, and when I pulled up, he was coming out of Penny's apartment and had some hot little number riding him piggyback. He took her into his crib. I drove off."

"What time was that?"

"About two in the morning."

"Booty-call hours."

"And he was carrying booty."

"Why were you out in the streets so late swinging by his crib?"

"Had shit on my mind. Was out driving around after your show, to clear my head. You'd gone to shoot pool with Little Miss Becky."

"It's dangerous riding around outside of Leimert Park. Been shootings and murders. We had a triple homicide on the back side of the post office on Crenshaw. A lot of the fools around here came from Eastside. This area is their version of moving up, and they have brought that gang mentality with them."

"Well, I was going to hang with Brick, kick it there, but he had a woman riding his back."

"He told me he had to drive his neighbor Penny somewhere."

"Wasn't Penny. Small woman. Fair skin. Had long hair."

"You can't say fair skin. That makes it sound like black women have unfair skin."

"Point taken. Light-skinned. Any idea who that one is?"

"No idea. I know he broke up with Coretta; Coretta is dark-skinned, tall, and wears a big Afro."

"Who is Coretta?"

"You've been gone too long, bro. Girl he was shacking up with. Broke his heart. He was superhot on her. Was talking marriage."

"What happened?"

"That's all I know. He won't tell me too much because he knows when he tells me more, it somehow magically ends up in the relationships part of my act."

I laughed as I wrestled with my thoughts. "One more thing. I need to use your laptop and printer. I wrote a script. Need to make three copies. Want you to read it for feedback."

"Read it? Printed, like a book? I'm a millennial, nigga. Your Myspace ass better send me a PDF."

"I'm trying to meet Brick for breakfast tomorrow. You should come if you're around and awake that early."

"Gladstones?"

"Around the corner at the new café by Eso Won bookstore. Black-owned."

"I might tag along. I'll set an alert. We should have Nephew with us. Manpower. I can't remember the last time the four of us were in the same spot, at the same time, breaking bread and chopping it up."

My son's dire texts were on my mind. "You heard from my son?"

"Haven't heard from Nephew in a few weeks."

"Frenchie?"

"Haven't heard from his mean-ass mom either. She fell off the radar."

"Fela said their power got cut off."

"With all the money you're paying?"

"He said they didn't have food."

He repeated, "With all the money you're paying?"

"I've been texting him and now he's ghosting me. Frenchie is ghosting me too."

"You're worried."

"I need to know what's going on. I called Inglewood and had the police go by there."

"Whoa. You called the cops?"

"Few days ago when I was on the road. Fela sent these texts, said shit was bad over there, and Frenchie didn't return my calls or answer my texts. The cops said everything was fine, so I don't know what's going on."

"Fuck, man."

"Had me so stressed that I didn't handle things well at work."

"You text him this morning?"

"Three times. Nothing. Texted Frenchie three times too."

I grabbed the carry-on from my rental while he stretched. When we climbed the concrete stairs and André opened his apartment door, I faced a black-framed Martin Luther King picture, a raven sofa, and a love seat. It was dusty because he'd had a few road shows last week. There were photographs on the walls from all over the country and world. André was also a photographer, had camera equipment scattered all over the place. He did head shots and made YouTube videos too. Everyone had to get a PR firm and self-promote to stay relevant.

From the front door, I saw why he hadn't gotten but about two hours' sleep last night.

Joëlle walked in from the kitchen. She was thick, solid, shapely. Sexier than sexy and she knew it. She gave me a blank expression, then gave André a big smile, the grin of first-time lovers, a smile that lived somewhere in between pleasure and unsure. A smile that had hoped he'd come back home alone. He returned the smile and the happy expression on her face got bigger. She had on one of his shirts, his boxer shorts, and no bra. Nipples were hard. Her colorful hair was pinned up at the top of her head, and her makeup was off; pimples on her skin showed.

André kicked his Nikes off at the door and said, "You woke up."

"I didn't know if I should stay or go since we had, ahem, you know."

"Were you gonna leave me a way to get in contact with you?"

She shrugged. "You know the deal."

"Then I'm glad you stayed."

"Really?"

"I'm working later, but maybe we can hang out or chill."

"We can chill. I'm going to need some sleep."

"Me too."

"That's why I didn't leave. I made it to the door but was too tired to drive out to my father's."

"So, you have parents."

"Daddy lives out in Riverside."

"Where's your mom?"

"Barstow area."

After a moment of silence I said, "Good morning."

She looked at me like I'd just appeared, but said nothing.

André said, "This is my brother. Dwayne, Joëlle. Joëlle, Dwayne. I was with him last night, remember?"

"I didn't notice him. I was focused on you. All evening."

"I have another brother who lives two blocks over."

"Why you live so close?"

"Because we're brothers."

"Why don't you guys live together?"

André laughed. "Because we're brothers."

"This brother staying for breakfast?"

André considered me. His date's rock-hard nipples watched me too. The doorbell rang, like a shock. The chimes were old-fashioned and loud. Joëlle jumped, gazed at André, shifted her stance a bit, face tensed with fear.

He laughed a little, said, "Relax, it's probably our other brother. His name is Brick."

She yawned and moved toward the bedroom, a slow-moving cat wagging its tail. As soon as she opened the bedroom door, a phone chimed. It was the cellular inside her purse. She went to her phone, then closed the door.

There was a twentysomething in a short skirt and Gap hoodie at the front door. Someone André saw horizontally from time to time.

He sent her away, told her he was busy with me, family issues, and would call her later.

She kissed him like she loved him, told me good-bye, and left, a fast-moving cat wagging its tail.

Like it was when he was onstage, his improvising was impeccable and his timing was perfect.

Then the nameless girl was gone down the stairs, disappointed she didn't get to stay for breakfast.

We looked out the venetian blinds and saw Nameless get into her Celica and leave.

I took my bag and headed into the bathroom and took a shower with much on my mind. When I was done and dressed, I went to the kitchen in time to catch my brother seated on the counter, getting a blow job.

I went into the bedroom used as an office, grabbed the three copies of my ninety-page script from the printer, and headed back toward the living room. This time André was between Joëlle's legs, on his knees, returning the favor and enjoying her flavor. She heard me, opened her eyes, looking like she was in an opium-induced trance.

I said, "André."

"Yeah, bro?"

"I need to borrow some money."

"Nigga. Man. Fuck. Whatever. Wallet by the door."

I went to his wallet, found a stash of green begging me to take it for a ride.

I said, "Taking four hundred."

He moaned.

I said, "I'll deduct this from the two grand you owe me."

"I don't owe you."

"Bullshit. I gave you two thousand in cash. I need my money back."

He moaned again.

"Better yet, I'm taking five hundred. One hundred will be late fees."

"I have to pay my rent."

"Nigga. What rent? You own the goddamn building."

"Mortgage. Still have a mortgage. Tenants be paying late and shit."

"I'm taking six hundred."

He moaned in protest but refused to allow me to be the marplot to his sexcapade.

"You owe me fifteen more Benjamins. Fifteen hundred. André, I need it when you can get it."

Something flew and hit me upside the head. Popped me good. It was a wooden spoon, and André wasn't the one who threw it. Joëlle frowned at me, both middle fingers aimed in my direction.

I nodded, then left the strangers getting acquainted without saying another word.

IT WAS HOT as hell outside. Tasted soot in the air. Ash had dusted cars overnight. Hills were on fire an hour away. California was having a devastating wildfire season because climate change had given the city years of drought. I had a couple of hours to kill before meeting with my accountant. I drove around awhile, counting the snowy-faced predators who had invaded the Nubian area, to make the morning go by. I didn't want to burn up too much four-bucks-a-gallon gas, so I headed to the mall. I parked halfway between Debbie Allen's dance studio and the restaurant that specialized in crab legs, let my seat back, and put my window halfway down. I had some escitalopram and tra-zodone with me and debated taking a couple of pills to ease my stress, but passed on it. I could sleep eight hours on that shit; it would be too hard to wake up. Just needed a nap. I slept hard and sweated a bit. I'd been living in this rental car since my plane landed, so I guess it was my mobile home. Had a problem with my credit card so my Airbnb fell through and couldn't impose myself on my brothers, who were busy entertaining their female guests. For now, I'd tough it out. I felt like I was a failure, and my failures were my failures. I'd deal with them on my own.

I woke up an hour later looking like I'd been through the desert on a horse with no name, and right away, I grabbed my phone and sent my son another text. No text back. Baby momma drama had me by the balls.

I sent Frenchie a text. I want to see Fela. This is my tenth time asking.

No reply.

I sent Fela another text. I'm in town, Son. Let's hook up. Ask your mom when.

No reply.

I sent Frenchie a message, all caps, screaming, If you're going to ghost me, fine. IDGAF. But grow some balls and at least let my son tell me he doesn't want to talk to me anymore himself, if that is what the fuck is going on. I came back to see him. Let him message me. I don't need to hear from you ever fucking again. But don't come between me and Fela. Have the decency to reply so I won't spend the foreseeable future thinking that there is something wrong between me and my son, and you won't come across as a bitter, cowardly, immature twat.

Twat wasn't the four-letter word I had written at first, but I backspaced and changed it.

Bubbles danced for ten minutes, but in the end, she had lost it, typed a long, nasty message; then she backspaced, deleted it all, gave me no reply. Anything typed can be used in court, but so could her nonresponses.

I had gotten to her. She heard me. I exhaled hard, wiped away a tear, and smiled.

AN HOUR LATER, I was in View Park, sitting on the back porch of my accountant's minimansion on her wicker rattan patio furniture, her backyard framed by hedges, palms, and evergreen trees. She had left a spread of fruit, chips, and hummus, and I ate that finger food like it was a gourmet meal. I waited on her to come back outside so we could have a meeting, go over my investments, debts, budget, child support, everything financial. While she went to argue with her teenager, I sat in her comfort and looked around, happy for her and her brilliant husband, smiling at all I saw, envious at the same time; so envious I started talking to myself, grumbled, "Yeah. My life was sweet, pure honey, for a while. Thought I was the next Denzel, maybe even better. I believed the hype, until Idris fuckin' Elba showed up. I thought I'd be a star, living in View Park in a five-thousand-square-foot house that had six bedrooms and six baths, with an Olympic pool in the back, like my accountant, Geneviève Forbes. Thought I'd be married to someone on Halle Berry's level, someone who would have made us a power couple in Hollywood, and I would be three kids deep with her, and Fela would be living here with us, all of us existing under my roof as the perfect Hollywood family. That was the plan. The dream. Instead, television shows came and went. I got that one chance white Hollywood gives black men and flopped. Broadway got me, and I got ahead of myself. I became arrogant. Then it became hard."

I knew this meeting was only going to tell me I needed to make more money or spend less money. The first was hard to do and the second wasn't an option. Mortgage, IRS payments, and child support were fixed numbers, not flexible. I might be able to refinance the house in Florida, and with my income, going to court to reduce child support was the only other choice. Adulting was not fun. I wished I was seventeen again, living with my parents. For each dollar I made I barely saw fifty cents, and that money was only in my accounts long enough to pay my bills. But I knew my reality. The burdens I had, I had placed upon myself. I didn't run away from any and I owned them all. Child support and failure to pay their taxes were the two things that broke many men and left them ready to jump, and even though it was hard to keep up, I wasn't behind on either. I was a few days, maybe a week behind on my obligation to Frenchie, on what Fela deserved, but I couldn't pay her before my check arrived from the people I worked for. Catch-22. Didn't want to have to sell my only property in

Florida, because it was finally rebounding from the loss I took back in '08. I was fine struggling, but knowing my son was hungry and stressed too, knowing that Frenchie had somehow squandered every dime meant for child support, that hit me hard. I had it in the back of my mind that my middle brother, Brick, had a gun. He had the gun that he'd borrowed from Nigga Daddy. I could get that heater. Banks were all over. If not for my fear of being recognized as soon as I'd handed the teller a note, it would have been a done deal. I might've succumbed to dark thoughts, to the movie in my mind, one where I got away with armed robbery, written a note and made another bad decision. I'd do anything for my son, but I wouldn't do something that would bring him irrevocable shame. As I sat in the lap of Geneviève Forbes's luxury, in the middle of her better choices, I reminded myself that wherever I was, whoever I was, I was not what has happened to me. I was what and who I choose to become. I just wanted to be a dad worthy of having a son named Fela. That was my mission statement.

CHAPTER 9

BRICK

A STRANGER HAD tossed my kitchen and invaded my home.

She was dressed in ripped jean shorts and a T-shirt that had seen better years. She stood at the counter in front of the blender. What I smelled were pancakes and bacon being cooked in my tiny kitchen. She had burned one pancake. Fruits had been cut up. The chef had her fancy purse in front of her, white earbuds in, music jamming on her phone, as she counted a stack of bills, at least two grand in cash. I wondered if she had made that last night in two hours. At two grand a night, she could earn enough to buy a small island by next February. Her laptop was on the kitchen table, opened to a dating site, one exclusively for the highly educated. My guess was she was up working, hunting for new customers, ones who had the IQ of a Mensa. I eased into the kitchen, saw her new face. The makeup was gone. Mocha

Latte looked different, was a brand-new person, this one with softer edges, and better edges.

She saw me, then jumped and put the wad of money in her fancy purse, set it aside.

She removed her earbuds and said, "Good morning, Brock."

"Brick."

"Good morning, Brick."

"Egad. She talks."

"In English. Nouns and verbs that agree, until they don't."

"Feeling better?"

She closed her laptop. "Woke up dehydrated like a big dog."

"You had a bit to drink last night."

"Mixed pain pills and booze." She nodded. "I need to eat. Or I will be an evil black woman."

"What was wrong last night?"

"I sold another chunk of my soul to the devil last night."

"What happened?"

"Skip it. Hungry?"

"You threw down like you're trying to outdo Sunny Anderson and the Galloping Gourmet."

"Earning my keep. Cooking helps me relax. Woke up feeling anxious. Got carried away."

"I can eat with you, if you want company, at my old wooden table bought from Goodwill."

"You're a thrifter?"

"Been called worse."

"I love thrifting."

"We have something in common."

She checked out my T-shirt and put on a sudden grin. "Oh my God. I'm stealing that."

I had pulled on one of my T-shirts without looking at the message. My wrinkled red T-shirt announced: MAJORED IN COMPUTER ENGINEERING. TO SAVE TIME, LET'S JUST ASSUME I'M ALWAYS RIGHT.

She laughed a curious laugh. "You're a nerd?"

"Between the hours of nine and five."

"What's your specialty?"

"Was a programmer."

"Was?"

"Now I'm a project manager. Manage a team of about twelve. I'm out on leave at the moment."

She asked, "You have your master's degree?"

"And the student loan bill to prove it."

"Impressive. That puts you in a different category."

"Yeah, still paying the bill for that accumulation of knowledge. How did you know?"

"Saw your diplomas on the wall in the hallway. I took a tour of the castle. Hope you don't mind."

"*Mi casa, su casa.*"

"Who are those guys with you in the other pictures?"

"My brothers."

She hesitated, then looked at me with sincere eyes. "Your spot hiring?"

"The widget factory I work at is laying off, if anything. They'd love to move operations to Mexico."

"Closet nerd. You might be cool after all."

"Likewise."

She motioned at my counter. "You have a lot of wine."

"More than some, less than others. Feel free to have a drink."

"Too early in the morning."

"Always five o'clock somewhere."

"I see prices on a few bottles. You sell it?"

"I only sell wine to people who suffer from oenophobia. As a hobby."

"Nice chessboard too."

"You play?"

"Nah. Never learned." She shook her head. "Interesting apartment. You don't own a lot of stuff."

"I'm a minimalist, more or less. I limit myself to owning no more than three hundred things."

"That's a cry for therapy, same as it is for hoarders."

"I buy only what I will wear or use. Except for the wine. I buy and sell those on the side, make a small profit."

"You're weird."

"Have you seen you at midnight dancing to Afrobeats at the Savoy?"

She laughed softly. "You have a Schnadig sofa. Those cost three grand a pop. It's awesome."

"Got it for forty bucks at the Goodwill."

"Forty for a three-thousand-dollar sofa? Get the fuck out."

"They had no idea."

She laughed a pretty laugh. "Blueberry pancakes work for you?"

"Waffles for dinner, flapjacks for breakfast. God bless America."

"My pancakes are better than the waffles at Roscoe's."

"They smell delicious."

"I can throw down in the kitchen. Used to want to become a chef."

I went to the counter, to my bills. I could tell she'd been nosey and looked at my investments with Oppenheimer, and mail from Kaiser and City of Hope. My older brother's child support bills were mixed with my documents.

She opened her computer again. Mocha Latte had a Samsung Galaxy View, the Android tablet with an eighteen-inch screen, and the swag to make it look like a laptop.

I asked, "How many gigabytes on that?"

"Sixty-four with Exynos 7580 and two gigabytes of RAM. Not easy to carry, but I like it."

I yawned. "Didn't mean to interrupt you while you were working."

"This website isn't for customers. It's personal. A dating site."

"Didn't mean to pry."

"Maybe you could give me your opinion. A man's perspective on some shit."

Mocha Latte showed me her page on the singles website. Her pictures were wholesome, professional, smiling, effervescent. There were images of her hiking, dancing ballet, and rollerblading.

I read her quote. "'I'm *looking for love*. Real love. Ridiculous, inconvenient, consuming, can't-live-without-each-other love.' Sounds to the point."

She said, "That's a quote from *Sex and the City*. When Carrie was in Paris."

I shrugged; that show meant nothing to me. "That quote is pretty direct."

"Is it too much? Sound too thirsty? Desperate?"

"Out the gate, it could be jumping the shark."

"I would use a quote from Marquis de Sade, but I don't want to seem pretentious."

"Do a biblical quote."

"Quote the Bible? I'll never get a response. Not from anyone sane."

"Put up a sexy picture and a passage."

"What passage?"

"Try the passage 'I am a wall, and my breasts like towers.' That's from Song of Solomon."

"That would wake up the perverts who want me to squeeze the juice from their pomegranates."

"You want a boyfriend."

She nodded. "*Boyfriend* sounds so high school. I want a *partner*. Would be nice to date someone who ain't dating everybody else. Or fucking everybody else. Would be nice to hold hands. To fall in love."

"You have a hard time meeting guys?"

"I meet guys. But I want one outside of work. I wouldn't date a guy who knows what I do. I don't date clients. I wouldn't date a man I knew would sneak away and pay for sex. At some point, he'd throw what I do now back in my face, even when I'm not doing it anymore. I want someone to engage me as a human being worthy of respect and consideration. I don't want to be judged by my weakest moments and my darkest hours. I want a man who will celebrate me and not just want to see his dick between my lovely tits. I want someone to have my back. You know how it goes. A man knows what I do, and all he sees is a woman in the world's oldest profession."

"Gigolos get lonely too."

"I just want someone to go to the movies with. We can check out a matinée. And we can take it from there."

"Then post that. 'Someone to go to movies with. A matinée. We'll take it from there.'"

"Think that would work?"

"Unless you expect him to pay and buy a large popcorn."

"I eat a small popcorn."

"I stand corrected."

"I'll buy my own popcorn and buy his popcorn, if he eats a small one too."

"Why not buy a large and share?"

"I don't like people touching my popcorn."

"Would you spring for Raisinets?"

"I could do that."

"And a large bottle of water?"

"Don't push it."

"Double standards."

"A bottle of water at the movies costs more than two gallons of gas."

"That's the problem with the black woman."

"He'd best be willing to roll with a frugal sista who will fill her bag up with goodies from Walgreens and be ready to drink a two-for-a-dollar soda. Only an idiot pays five dollars for a bottle of water you can get at the grocery store for twenty cents, if you buy in bulk, and I buy in bulk."

"That's the Mocha Latte I met last night. Welcome back."

We made plates and sat at my small kitchen table. She was chatty.

An irritating morning person. Mocha Latte said nothing about seeing me and Christiana on the sofa last night, as one colloquy led to another.

I asked, "What's the worst thing you've ever done?"

"That's an odd question to ask someone over delicious blueberry pancakes."

"I'm an odd guy, especially when I'm eating delicious blueberry pancakes."

She shrugged. "I was engaged to two guys at the same time."

"How did that work out?"

"One guy had met my family. The educated one. I love smart men. Want to have smart babies. The other one hadn't, and never would meet my family. He had a little too much thug in his blood. A street warrior. I want strong babies. My family would have crucified me upside down and burned the cross if they knew about him."

"Tell me more."

"One of my baes grew up in the streets. Eastside dude. I liked his common sense. You can't get that from a textbook. He was the one I really wanted to marry. The bad boy fed the beast in me, but the logical part of me rejected him. I didn't see a good future. He was always broke, didn't have a degree, would never be rich enough to travel the world like I want to do to get this wanderlust out of my system. I knew we'd never have much, would never be much better off than we were at the start because we'd spend the whole marriage in a box living off my salary, if I had a salary. But I was happy when I was with him, and he was amazing in bed. He was a fantasy. He could go and go and go. He was twenty-nine and I knew that when he made it to fifty, he'd still be screwing like he was half his age. But I knew my family would have had a fit if they had ever seen me with him. He let his pants sag, had tats on his neck. But he had sixteen-inch arms and a dick to match. Yeah, I wanted the bad boy who had no real potential."

"You must have fantasies about being a single mom and conjugal visits every Thursday."

"I have never seen a prison, nor do I know where one is, and will never go to one. Like my daddy says, 'If a nigga goes to jail, do not call me for bail. Enjoy your cell and pray your way out of that hell.'"

"Good to know you know where to draw the line. South of solidarity."

"The nice Westside lawyer was the résumé-perfect guy. Nice house. No kids. *But* he wanted kids. *Kids.* All he talked about was us having six kids. That scared me. Six kids? Who has six kids these days? That would be me being knocked up and wobbling on swollen feet for fifty-four months of my life."

"Eastside dude. Rapper or drug dealer?"

"Neither. But he had to hustle to get what he had. I want a leader, not a breeder."

"Breeder?"

"Those guys breed you and leave you in the Single Mom Sorority, then go off to drag more women across the burning sands to initiate them into the same sorority, just to keep you from being lonely."

"At least they're considerate."

"Eastside turned me out. I had a rude-boy awakening. Lots of sex makes a woman feel happy all the time, even if the relationship isn't the best. Helped with my migraines too. I get migraines bad. Sex always helps. Like medicine. Things would get bad for a minute, but sex would wipe that all away. We did it everywhere but the bed. It was good for him too. Reduced his chance of getting prostate cancer later on in life. Men who come at least twenty-one times a month have a better chance of not getting prostate cancer."

"You're not only adventurous, but thoughtful and selfless."

"I looked out for my man. Actually, I looked out for both of them."

"The other guy, the Westside lawyer, he wasn't a good lover?"

"Traditional. You know, same positions, no toys. Kinda quiet in bed. He made love. It was emotionally good. I needed that too. He treated me like I was his Meghan Markle. Opened car doors. Bought me flowers. Candy. Husband material. He was responsible. Had a great credit score. Cops would pull him over and not harass him."

"You found him safe and boring."

"My family saw prestige; my relatives saw dollar signs; and everybody kept pressuring me about the damn wedding, but I was considering going to Vegas to marry the roughneck. Almost did once. We headed to Vegas. Before we got to Victorville, his hoopty overheated and broke down, thank God. He was glad too. He wanted a big wedding. Wanted a backyard wedding at his momma's house in Moreno Valley. Wanted his family, everyone from Compton to Chicago, to be there. The lawyer's family wanted a big wedding too. Only they wanted it to happen in Beverly Hills. Would have been filled with professional people. His momma liked me. And I didn't want to disappoint our families. I was stressed. Had migraines every day. Head hurt so bad I thought I was having a stroke. Skin broke out. Had a rash. I literally was trying to figure out how I could pull off two weddings and have two husbands. The only way it could work would have been for me to tell both of them the truth, become both of their wives, and come up with a deal. But that shit wasn't gonna happen. I think I liked it better knowing that they didn't know. That was the part that stimulated me. I got to be two people. We all have this thing called duality, you know? I rocked the hell out of mine."

"Do you have regrets?"

"Enough to fill an Olympic-size pool. I know I sound confusing. I know I do. But I guess you have to be inside of me for it to make sense. I want to be liberated, and I want to be in a relationship. I want stability, but when I had the option to marry a man who had a career and everything together, I kept dealing with a guy who would give me nothing but good dick and hard times. And now that I've lost my job, now that I'm hustling like this, I crave stability. I want my old life back. I took it all for granted before my life went downhill. I'll admit that. When I was engaged to both men, I was living in the moment more than really thinking about the future. Then the future found me. Yeah. I had the best of both worlds because one man had money and status, and the other man was making me sweat. Do I have regrets? Fuck, yeah. Every fuckin' day I live and breathe regrets."

I nodded. "Everyone has regrets about something."

"I made a bad turn. Life went south. Someone else is living my life and I'm living a lie."

"How old are you?"

She grinned. "I'm twenty-three online. Sometimes twenty-one. Clients like young girls. But on my dating page, I'm twenty-nine. I use my real age. No lying about my age if I'm going to end up dating."

"You look twenty-one."

"I keep it tight."

"Kegels?"

"You got jokes. Early in the morning, you got jokes straight from the corny farm."

"There's a farm?"

She asked, "How old are you?"

"I've been alive over one billion seconds."

"You count every second?"

I nodded. "Sure do. And I try to make every second count."

"One billion seconds." She chuckled. "Do the math on that one for me."

"I'm thirty-one, give or take a few hundred thousand seconds."

"You look younger. No more than thirty."

I swallowed a forkful of pancakes, washed it down, then asked, "Where are you from?"

"I was born in Malakoff, Texas; lived there until I was eight, then grew up in Bakersfield."

"You don't sound like Texas and don't smell like Bakersfield."

"Yeah, I was a farm girl in Texas and was a bougie middle-class black girl in Bakersfield. Both of my parents are professionals. I went to private schools, went to church every Sunday, Bible study on

Wednesdays, sang in the choir, but I've always had a rough side that only the bad boy knew about."

"College?"

"The UCLA Henry Samueli School of Engineering and Applied Science. Took differential calculus, integral calculus, multivariable calculus, linear algebra, physics, mechanics, electricity and magnetism, material chemistry course, and computer programming. That doesn't include the writing requirement and the university's humanities and social science distribution requirement."

"Get out."

"Long way from driving a tractor, but I still love driving a tractor when I'm back in Malakoff."

"You're a genius."

"Thirty-six courses in four years. While I was working, engaged to two men, and juggling two lives."

"All that, and you like bad boys."

"Bad boys, but not criminals. I don't date men who have records."

"Why not?"

"I don't have a record player."

"Corny."

"But true."

"What did you do between driving a tractor and now?"

"I was an electrical engineer. I led a team of six people."

"No shit?"

"It bored me. I think I enjoyed college and research and learning and being under pressure for projects better than I did living and working in the real world. College was exciting. Greek shows, keg parties, football games."

"You invested all that time in college and didn't like the gig?"

"All we did was go to meetings and talk about the work we should have been in the lab doing."

"You were fired?"

"About two thousand were made redundant. People with master's and PhDs were sent home like our degrees were worth less than a GED. I noticed how blacks and browns were let go but white men were safe."

"How did that make you feel?"

"Being a black woman with a degree, a woman who had followed the white man's blueprint for achieving the American dream, without a job and not hirable because I was *over*educated, that was some disappointing shit. Was on unemployment until that ran out, then went two more years without getting a bite. Burned through my 401(k) paying a mortgage on a town house on the ocean I'd eventually lose. Yeah. Shit was a humbling wakeup call. I learned that black Harvard graduates have the same shot at a callback as white state college grads. White people are assumed to be smart. Black people are assumed to be dumb, even with an advanced degree. You feel me? And being a black woman, that puts us last on the list, no matter how well educated we are. I think I fucking gave up for a while."

"How'd you end up taking this exit off the freeway?"

"I was sleeping in my car. Was too proud to go back to Bakersfield or Malakoff. Going back would mean I had failed. One bad decision led to another and the missed-meal cramps kicked in, so I took a chance and did like Penny said she did, went after that quick-money thing. By the hour, it can pay more than having a PhD. Work smart for a week, then go on vacation for two months. You say you'll do it once, or twice. No job was coming my way, still had bills, still had to eat. We live in a capitalistic society. Without money, you're no one; you're invisible."

I nodded. "And once upon a time you had two men ready to get you to jump the broom."

She laughed. "Once upon a time, this black girl from Malakoff had *two* bad-ass engagement rings, from two men born in California. Had to wear one based on who I would see that day. Once I mixed the rings up. The lawyer noticed. I told him I was getting the one

he bought me cleaned and had borrowed one from one of my sorority sisters to wear in the meantime, so men would always know I was
engaged."

"You were a hot mess."

"It was wrong, but never really felt wrong, not as wrong as it should
have felt. No one man can give a woman all she needs. I had fun and
intellectual stimulation. I had love. I had great sex. Miss it sometimes.
I'm at an age where I shouldn't play around. If I'm going to have kids,
I need to start over and get serious with somebody. With the right
somebody. With someone who can support my dreams and won't be
turned off by my nightmares. My life seemed so much better then. I
was still an engineer. Now I'm someone else. Where I am now, I never
saw this occupation as an option, let alone as becoming a part of my
reality. A temporary part. Shit. I am tired of being broke. I need a
break. I need to be carried. But I want to be crazy about him too. I
want the love to be red-hot fire."

"You want to have kids."

"Yeah." She paused. "Having a baby and not being married wouldn't
fit into my image. No matter what I've done, being pregnant and not
married is . . . I just can't go that route. Others can, and good for them.
I can't. My mother is all about image. I was raised that way. Money,
image, and associations. I'm a sorority girl to boot."

"Anyone else know that you had a double life?"

"My former best friend knows everything. She tried to do an inter-
vention."

"She dropped a dime?"

"Not sure. She knows my business. And I know her business as
well. She needs Jesus and ten interventions. I picked up her cell phone
by accident. She had all kinds of dick pics in her phone."

"Really?"

"And you, Brick? My blueberry-pancake-loving friend, what's the
worst thing you've done?"

"Guess I'd have to go back to when I was fourteen."

"What happened? Did you rob a bank or kill somebody? I told you my life; now tell—"

She stopped talking when we heard someone leave the bedroom.

CHAPTER 10

BRICK

PENNY DRAGGED HERSELF into the kitchen. "Y'all are louder than a Pentecostal church in here."

I said, "And good morning to you, grumpy person who lives somewhere else."

Mocha Latte hugged Penny, then made Miss Cantankerous a plate of flapjacks.

Mocha Latte said, "You were all over Brick last night."

"Was I? When?"

"You were wrapped around him like a snake."

"You're joking, right?"

"What in the world were you dreaming about?"

"Idris."

"I'm jelly. Stop cheating with my boyfriend."

"That British accent."

"*Grrrrrrl.*"

I said, "Y'all know I'm sitting right here, right?"

Christiana showed up a couple of minutes later. "*Buen día.* Good morning, everyone."

She stood in the doorframe, yawned, stretched, then touched her toes. Penny turned on music. Mocha Latte sang, danced, and made me and the pace of asses smoothies. My apartment was suddenly party central.

Christiana sang, "*Soooo?* Mocha Latte, should I book us for tonight?"

"I can't do two nights in a row. I can't be that girl right now."

"Talk to me. What is wrong this time?"

"I throw up when I'm done. Last night I let a little dick man I'd never met take me to Greektown."

"He paid you a lot to be your first."

"What a fool believes."

"He paid top dollar to live out his own fantasy. They are all the same. Need you to be a virgin in some way. They want to know how you have not been violated or humiliated, then beg to pay to do that."

"Sick and twisted."

"Most of them are. That is why we must protect each other."

"The things they said while they were with us, the way they talked down to us. The uncouthness gets to me. I mean, I know I have a black pussy, but do you have to call it a damn black pussy over and over?"

Mocha Latte stormed toward the living room. The front door opened fast and closed hard.

Penny asked, "Does she always have a meltdown?"

Christiana motioned for us to let her be. "She gets like this after she works."

"I can't work with her if she's going to flip out every time she has a job."

"Some people can be intimate with strangers and it means too much, while another woman can sleep with her sister's husband, knowing that will destroy her sister and their familial bond, and see no wrong in what she has done. Some can have sex with close friends and it means nothing. Everyone's soul is damaged differently."

"Will she be okay?"

"Sometimes we get too comfortable with our demons and ask them to pull up a chair, when we should be pulling it away before they get a chance to sit down. Never let your demons get too comfortable in your life."

"Is that what she has done?"

"That is what she refuses to do. But it feels like what I have done."

Again, her words did something to Penny. Penny searched inside herself for her own demons. I did the same. Silence befriended us. Music played as we ate and did more smoothie shots. Christiana washed the dishes.

Twenty minutes later Mocha Latte came back. "Let's see what we can find for tonight."

Penny asked, "You okay?"

"What was I thinking?" Mocha Latte shook her head. "Blew it. Should've married the lawyer."

Christiana said, "Mocha Latte, I will start making calls soon."

"I turned down two calls this morning."

"What is wrong? Talk to me."

"Am I any good at this shit?"

Penny said, "Mocha Latte is a damn Bruna Surfistinha and asks if she is any good."

"*Sí*, she is very good. The men wanted her more than they did either of us."

I asked, "Who is Bruna Surfistinha?"

The shrewdness of women groaned, and it rang out like three middle fingers in my direction.

Christiana asked, "What do you want, Mocha Latte? I do not want you so unhappy."

Mocha Latte paused. "I want to be a wife. A mother. Don't y'all ever feel lonely?"

Penny spoke, and I heard her brokenness. "We will get past this part of our lives."

Christiana grinned, but I saw pain from Cuba. "We will all be richer than we were at the start."

Mocha Latte pulled a collection of bridal magazines out of her bag. The others gathered around her and softened up, had looks that said that they all hoped to be able to wear a wedding dress, either again, or for the first time, one day. To find true love, feel like the Duchess of Sussex, and leave these days, these secrets, behind them.

Driven by my own curiosity, I googled Bruna Surfistinha.

Mocha Latte took a call, then came back to me. She kissed my cheek.

I asked, "What was that for?"

"Felt good to be able to talk and be honest with someone."

"Blueberry pancakes are like truth serum."

She waved as she walked out the door. "And we have to finish our discussion."

I gave Christiana my spare key. Told her she and Mocha Latte could float between Penny's crib and mine. Penny left. Christiana sat next to me on the sofa. I was watching Bruna Surfistinha do the do on my phone.

Christiana said, "I can have you booked as soon as next Friday night."

"You are relentless."

"Imagine a beautiful woman waiting for you."

"Thanks for the offer to get paid to get laid, but I will pass on the cash-for-ass."

She smiled and nodded. "Well, at least you earned three hundred last night."

CHAPTER 11

BRICK

GOING EAST ON Slauson, I transitioned from the black zone to the area where Mexican and Central American street vendors ruled the streets. Two miles from where I lived was a different kingdom, one where the citizens hustled day and night and favored Spanish-speaking groups like Los Bybys, Los Llayras, and Jorge Meza.

It had been a year. I was going to see him.

His popular car wash was on the east side of Los Angeles. As soon as I pulled my UK-branded Mini Cooper into the lot, the Latino staff all started singing "Stairway to Heaven." I parked and flipped them all off as I smiled, then went toward the Creole man who was fifty-eight, but dressed in joggers and the latest Air Jordans like he was sixteen. An exotic dark-skinned Latina woman half his height and a fourth his age was clinging to his arm like a bracelet.

The Creole man was my father, Dwayne Sr. The name of his car wash was in Spanish, Tres Dwaynes.

Dwayne Sr. lived, for an old man, an adolescent life. That flaw was in my older brother's DNA too.

My father asked, "You here for a discount car wash?"

"Just stopping by, Mr. Duquesne. Was on the way to work out and stopped by."

"Haven't seen you in almost a year."

"Car wasn't dirty."

"Lying ass. Heard you take your ugly car to the Mexicans down Vernon at Bryan's Car Wash."

"They're cheaper than what you charge me."

We went back into his office. The girl on his arm followed, then made both of us a cup of coffee.

He said, "I ain't got no money."

"Have I ever asked you for any money?"

"Would set a bad precedent."

"Dwayne is in town. The oldest is back."

"Nigga Son is back. Acting or child support?"

"Both."

"Tell Nigga Son I ain't got no money. His bills are his bills. You make 'em, you pay 'em. You make the baby, you pay the lady. That's what the court says and that's what a man has to do for at least eighteen years."

"Thought maybe we should all try and break bread."

"For what?"

"So, I guess I shouldn't try and get us all together like a family. You ain't getting any younger."

"He sent you?"

"This is my idea. Haven't talked to him about it. I didn't know he was coming back until yesterday."

"Nigga Son knows how to find me. Same house, same business,

same phone numbers I've had since before he was born. Nigga Son ever wants to talk to me again, fine. He doesn't, that's fine too."

"Don't be that way."

"I was struggling and asked Nigga Son to invest in my business back then. He was too good to help me out."

"You asked him for half a million."

"He could afford it. I see his face on television every day on reruns of that stupid show. If he hadn't been down on Venice Beach with me that day, he never would have been discovered by those Jews. I had to give permission for him to do anything, had to sign off on him being on that dumb show. What did I get out the deal?"

"Twenty percent."

"I got fifteen. Fifteen is nothing. Then he fired me and got him a white boy as a manager."

I let that go.

He asked, "How is your momma's other rug rat, that other brother of yours . . . Arsenio?"

"André. He's okay."

He was still bitter that my mother had divorced him, remarried, and had a baby by another man.

That resentment was in his voice when he asked, "How's your momma?"

"Mom went down to Texas for the last Seminole Nation Days and hasn't come back since. Stepdad says living in LA is for the rich or for fools and it's a lot cheaper to live down there. They get more for their money. Haven't talked to her in a minute, but André talks to her all the time. She goes to his shows when he's performing in Texas."

He made a face like he remembered something. "What Nigga Son baby momma look like?"

The rugged transition in conversation wasn't unusual for him. When he asked you a question, he was never listening when you answered, had already gone on to other topics in his mind.

I told him, "You met her."

"All white girls look alike to me. White men too, for that matter. What Freaky look like?"

"Frenchie."

"I was at Venice and I thought I saw her. I spoke to her, but she acted like she didn't know me. If it wasn't her, then an orange-haired girl who looked like her was down there on the sidewalk singing for money."

"You think Meryl Streep looks like Taylor Swift."

"All white women look like Muppets to me. Especially when their hair is wet."

"I'm sure you look like Kermit the *Dog* to them."

"Then I was at a restaurant eating dinner, and there was a nice-booty, redheaded, singing waitress that looked like her. I spoke to her, called her Freaky, but that white girl acted like she didn't know me too."

The phone rang, and the elder Dwayne picked up.

"Why the fuck you keep calling my place of business? I told you no, and there is no ambiguity in the word *no*. You're a woman, and when you tell a man no, but he keeps *asking*, *asking*, *asking*, how does that make you feel? Well, that's how I feel, like you're not listening to me, like you don't respect me. Men have feelings too. I have another call. I don't give a fuck if we are related. Tell your momma too. Don't call back unless you want a discount car wash."

Business first. New pussy second. Old pussy third. Family brought up the rear.

When he took another call, his clingy girlfriend refilled my coffee, doing her best to befriend me. While my old man was in the middle of his call, I told the girl that I was making like Elvis and leaving the building.

Maybe I'd stop by and try again in a year. Maybe not. Doing this off and on was the definition of insanity. Still, he was my father. So I stopped by to say hi every once in a while, even though he couldn't care less. He was never happy to see me. I think he saw me and saw money that could have been spent on other things. Same for my older brother. I looked at that colorful business sign as I left: TRES DWAYNES. None of his sons had ever worked here, and not one had ever wanted to. Across the street was Tres Dwaynes Barbecue and Sandwich Shop. On the third corner was Tres Dwaynes Barbershop and Sports Bar. The parking lots were full of cars fighting to get in. On this side it was stacked with customers getting cars detailed at a C-note a pop. The barbershop was packed and the line for the barbecue joint was out the front door. That was his money. That old man who loved to wear a young man's clothing would spend his wealth on trendy sweat suits, tennis shoes, and a collection of loose women before he offered any of his struggling children a dime. He wasn't a man who was going to work hard so his children could live soft.

When a man had sons, and none wanted to be like him, that was sad. I had to stop looking back. I had to move forward. When you stopped chasing the wrong things, you gave the right things a chance to catch you.

I HIT HOLLYWOOD, parked in the neighborhood on Franklin, then hiked Runyon Canyon. I took the hard trail, was in the sun for two hours. I felt healthy again. I used to hike the trails with Coretta. But I also hiked with girls I dated before Coretta. I hiked, and while I was in the hills, I tried to recover as much of the old me as I could.

WHEN I GOT back to the crib, Christiana was dressed in yoga pants, ready to run her errands. I took her to the ninety-nine-cent stores in the area. She stocked up on tampons, sanitary pads, ChapStick, face wipes, body wipes, sunscreen, small books for children, deodorant, and razors. We had three carts filled with bras, panties, condoms, and feminine hygiene products. After she had spent about five hundred dollars, she organized the items into care packages and had me drive her to the heart of downtown LA. We stopped on a crawl overrun by a community of homeless living curbside in tents. Some had inflatable beds. She passed out products to the women, some not yet in their teens. She needed me with her. A man could rob her, then sell it all on the streets.

She told me, "Desperate people can be very thankful, or they can become very violent."

The women were appreciative, grateful, glad someone cared, and gave hugs and shed tears. When something was free, it attracted a crowd, and attract a crowd we did. Two hours later, Christiana was done.

We fought traffic down the 110 to MLK and headed back toward my apartment in Gentrification Central.

Christiana said, "This is how I redeem myself. I commit sins so others will not have to. I help others."

"You're this wonderful, compassionate attorney, and your husband went to your sister?"

"She looks more European, so to many, especially to the Cuban men, she is prettier."

I absorbed her hurt, said, "If only people were forced to wear their personalities on the outside."

"Then we could see who they are. It would save us a lot of time. Bad marriages."

"Yeah. And heartache."

AFTER WE ALL had dinner, I took the pace of asses to a spoken-word performance at World Stage. When that wrapped up, we took in the jazz two doors down. After the jazz ended, we joined the last moments of a free weekly salsa class at the business next to that. Dwayne texted me, asked if I was home. I told him I was out dancing; said I was T'Challa on a date with Ororo and we were dancing up a storm, and I would holla at him and André in the morning. When that sidewalk party was over, we headed back to the Savoy. The pace of asses drank and danced until lights came on at one thirty. Once we got back home, everyone showered, and again, we all ended up in my bed, all up on one another like a litter of kittens. I woke up not too long after. Sat up when I felt a cold draft. I jumped to my feet and crept to the living room. My front door was wide open. I ran outside, then had to sprint barefoot until I caught up with her. Mocha Latte was in her cerulean pajamas sleepwalking, scratching her ass and staggering down the street like a drunk. Christiana ran and caught up with me. We guided Mocha Latte toward my apartment. Penny came out behind us, jogging. I picked Mocha Latte up, carried her back to my place. Christiana put her friend back in the bed. I made sure my door was locked, then moved the classic sofa down enough to block the door from opening again.

CHAPTER 12

BRICK

THE NEXT MORNING, I showered and left the pace of asses sleeping in my bed. I hit Degnan and hiked a block south, took a slow walk into the cool of the morning and went back into the heart of Leimert Park. Had to meet my brother at Hot and Cool Cafe at seven, right when traffic in the area was becoming hysterical.

Dwayne was on the old piano situated in front of a red sofa. Always in search of the spotlight. He was dressed in ripped skinny jeans, a THIS IS AMERICA hoodie, and a big dark green fedora.

I joined him on the keys, and we jammed most of "Bohemian Rhapsody," then chatted at the piano.

He said, "You look like a black man who's doing good in a white man's world."

"You've lost some weight."

"Down twenty pounds. Been running between eight and twelve miles a day."

A dozen hipsters passed by outside. A collective of trouble. People with melanin-blessed skin passed by too.

He said, "I see a lot of snow on the ground in areas that ain't had snow since the sixties."

"Gentrification is an airborne virus. No vaccine for this shit."

"I just see whiteness. A room of white rattlesnakes, and you're trying to befriend the ones who promise not to bite you. Even a good rattlesnake benefits from the evil done by bad rattlesnakes, and rattlesnakes don't bite each other, or if they do, they don't die from the poison. Rattlesnakes give you the right to vote, then make it impossible for you to vote, or impossible for your vote to count, treating the entire black culture like convicted felons."

"How's Frenchie?"

"Go to hell."

"Rattlesnake bit you good, then went back to the other rattlesnakes."

He started playing and singing "Stairway to Heaven" by the O'Jays.

I said, "Oh, it's like that?"

He laughed.

Dwayne's stomach growled. "Brick. Hungry?"

"Always hungry."

"My treat."

On the way to the counter, we passed pictures of Obama, MLK Jr., Mandela, and Malcolm X laughing, smiling. Dwayne paused at a display with the colorful Leimert Park swag that the coffeehouse was selling.

He asked one of the owners, "How much for the hoodies?"

The tall brother with the hue of an unsullied African king said, "Sixty-five."

"Give me a large." My brother turned to me. "These are hot. Want one? My treat."

"I'm good."

Dwayne was thirty-seven. When he was a kid, he was discovered walking along Venice Beach, then thrown on a Disney-type show for five seasons. Overnight, he became Middle America's African American teen heartthrob. But all kids grow up. He hit Gold's Gym, buffed up like Erik Killmonger. By the time he was twenty-five, he'd added some facial hair, created a new look, and landed a part on a gritty adult series, a typical cable cop show that stole plotlines from the news, only it was set in the 4.4 square miles that made up Jefferson, Texas. It had a mostly melanin-free cast, and Dwayne played the part of a first-generation Afro-Mexican in Texas serving the law and snatching down Confederate flags alongside Brad Pitt, Billy Bob Thornton, and Pamela Anderson types. It tanked after two seasons, and he went to theater, to Broadway, and had been touring in musicals ever since.

I ordered a large chai latte. He ordered a large bowl of the three-bean soup, a blueberry muffin, avocado toast with hummus and honey, and a large coffee with honey. I don't think he'd eaten in a while.

Dwayne got my attention when three women came in. Afro puffs. Bantu knots. Braids in Mohawk.

I said, "A collection of queens."

"A snack of thick girls."

"Queens. I see queens."

His American Express charge card was declined. So was his Visa. And his debit card.

By then, the collection of queens was behind us talking, debating the politics of colorism. All under twenty-five. The first one held a book, *Objectivism: The Philosophy of Ayn Rand*. The second carried *Think and Grow Rich: A Black Choice*. While the queens were in their conversation, I paid for it all, hoodie included. Dwayne didn't thank me. This was why he hadn't ordered anything before I got here. He'd played me, like many times before. We stepped to the side, walked by the bright orange walls, the Afrocentric art, and took to the stairs, went up a level and spied down on the café from the openings in the giant loft above.

A sister in a motorized wheelchair approached the café. She'd have a hard time getting inside since the double doors weren't automatic. I spotted her, then hurried down to the glass doors. She was dark and lovely, had a cute little dog at her side. Her eyes were light brown and hypnotic. She wore a sexy summertime yellow T-shirt, one that was pretty tight, and had the Spanish phrase YO TAMBIÉN! across her breasts. A black purse and an intricate wooden box were in her lap.

She took a breath. "Thanks, my brother."

Her mane was wavy, full of life and power, parted down the center. Her lips were like a soft heart, painted an alluring dark hue. She drove herself over to the area on the other side of the room, big smile, eager to set up what turned out to be a Marinakis handmade Egyptian metal chess set in a wooden box. Her smile lit up the room. Her body was sexy and that stirred me without warning. Everything about her was mesmerizing. Made me wish I had worn something better than joggers and a Nina Simone T-shirt. If I'd known I'd meet her, I would've worn my best suit and shined my shoes. I stared at her too long and her dog barked twice. I barked back. Her dog growled. I growled.

She spoke like a mother would to a child. "Strawberry, hush."

She looked happy. My guess was whoever she was waiting on was the one putting that smile on her face.

I went back and waited with Dwayne; we chatted until the food and hot drinks were ready; then we grabbed the last open table, next to the girl. I reached in my man bag, took out all of his bills and notices from CSS.

I asked, "How much have you paid to support Nephew since this journey began?"

"Factoring everything plus child support? Over a million so far. At least."

I whistled. "Most people don't make that much in a lifetime."

"She had me in court as soon as the umbilical cord was cut. I was touring with an off-Broadway number, and she came at me hard. She said I wasn't around to see my son. Fela was just a few months old. I was there for the birth, like I had promised. I made sure she had everything she needed. She told them I had committed to doing a six-month road tour; called me irresponsible for being a working thespian, for doing the same job I was doing when we met, and the kind courts gave her full custody, did that and demanded more money. I couldn't quit the show and pay four grand a month in child support and be able to eat at the same time, and she wouldn't settle for a dime less."

I said, "Checkmate."

"She didn't even let me name my own son."

"I know. But he was named after Fela Kuti and has a cool name."

"To top that off, she gave my son *her* family name. Schlesinger. How could she deny me the right to name my own firstborn son?"

"Because you didn't marry her."

"I had to make sure the kid was mine and not her ex-husband's. She was still sleeping with her husband just like I was still sleeping with my girlfriend. He came to a few shows and she ignored me."

"Check. Mate."

Dwayne headed to the bathroom. While he was gone, his phone rang. A 1-800 number. I answered.

It was good old American Express calling about an overdue bill.

I said, "I'm just the janitor. No one is in the office. It's a bank holiday. Call back day after tomorrow."

I hung up on Mr. Bill Collector, and the phone rang again. It was an automated message.

"This message is to inform you that the IRS is filing a lien—"

I killed that robotic message just as a four-door Porsche was being parked at a meter out front.

When Dwayne came back, I didn't mention the calls, but asked, "You okay?"

He reached into his bag. "Read this script. Tell me what you think."

He ate two squares of avocado toast, downed most of his bean soup, ate two more squares of avocado toast, and polished off half of his muffin. His phone rang again. He looked at the number. He rejected the call, cursed, then grabbed his coffee and went back to the piano to give me time to read. Shit was heavy on his mind.

A guy eased out of the Porsche that had parked outside. He was about six foot four, a well-built Trevor Noah with dreadlocks down his back. He took in the urban area, then put some time on the meter and came inside. He had a strong smile, high energy. Slim jeans. Avengers T-shirt. Suede loafers. Beaded bracelets. Silver cross.

The women in the room shifted, perked up, fixed their posture. The girl in the wheelchair saw him, became excited, waved, and glowed, but he looked confused, lost his smile as he took slow steps toward her.

He said, "You're Allison?"

"Yes. I'm Dr. Allison Émilie Chappelle. You're Paul?"

Mouth opened in disbelief he said, "You . . . you're . . ."

"Early? Or is that look of surprise because I changed my hair from my profile picture?"

Three seconds of contemplation passed, three seconds of being about to say something, then changing his mind, before he eased his wooden chair out, sat down as the dog barked its intruder alert.

Sounding put off, he said, "You brought a chessboard?"

"You said you played."

"With expensive chess pieces that look like warriors."

"That way it feels like you're playing country against country."

He said, "You have a dog."

"Did the barking give it away?"

"In a black café? Black people don't do dogs in cafés."

She laughed. "I was going to bring my pet peacock, but I didn't want to show off."

He wasn't amused.

She said, "Strawberry goes wherever I go, most of the time. Emotional support."

Voices carried in the café, so I heard their conversation as Dwayne supplied a soft soundtrack.

She asked, "So, Paul, what was the last book you read?"

"Book?"

"Conversation starter for our first date. I brought some basic questions for us to break the ice."

"Let me think about that." He leaned away from her. "You go first."

"Last novel I completed was *One Hundred Years of Solitude*. Before that, I devoured *1Q84*. I have *Things Fall Apart*, *Children of Blood and Bone*, and *Binti* on my nightstand. You? What are you reading?"

"I don't really read books. Not for recreation. Reading gives me a headache."

"I'm a writer. As a hobby. Well, I try to write like Neil Gaiman. I love sci-fi and fantasy stuff. Comics too. But I have my PhD and I've been published in a few obscure magazines and journals."

"Your profile said you ran track?"

"I did. Used to dream of being in the Olympics."

"Your profile said you . . . you're twenty-six?"

"Twenty-five. It says I'm twenty-five. You look about ten years older than it says on your profile, but that's okay. If not books, then what was the last movie you saw?"

"It's not a movie, but *Luke Cage* on Netflix. You?"

She said, "*Bienvenue à Marly-Gomont*. A French film."

"I don't like to read movies."

"Okay. Well, ever watch *Game of Thrones*?"

"It's all white people in England or something."

She corrected him, "In a fictional realm known as Westeros and Essos."

He shrugged, unaffected. "Lots of killing and sex between a brother and a sister, right?"

"It's epic and all you can fathom is murder and incest?"

"Like I said"—he shrugged—"just a bunch of white people, you know?"

"What shows do you like?"

"*Power*. Shows like that."

"Okay. You only watch the single-narrative stories filled with the drug dealer, prisoner, criminal, and racist tropes we're trying to escape. It has an audience. But at the same time, from a much broader POV, in my opinion, I'd have to agree that every ghetto or hood tale reflects blatant oppression and pockets of dystopia in a prosperous country. If that entire genre was attacked from that perspective, if it showed the connection between white poverty and black oppression, if it truly revealed everyone's enemy, in my opinion, the subgenre would be elevated immensely."

"What would you consider Luke Cage? He's a superhero. That's basically black sci-fi."

"Luke Cage. Superhero who started off not as a billionaire . . . *drumroll* . . . but . . . wait for it . . . *incarcerated*. Sweet Christmas. His version of Harlem is appreciated but isn't exactly the next Wakanda."

He tapped his fingers, paused, searched for what to say next. "Music. I like music."

"Okay. I see what channel you're on. Adjusting my dial. Jazz? Afrobeats?"

"Rap. Hip-hop."

She laughed. "Oh, a fan of the n-word, are we? I won't even address the misogyny."

"We've reclaimed the n-word, flipped it, made it ours, and now it's powerful."

"Black people trying to own a slander created by white people, wouldn't that be appropriation? Black people *reclaiming* the n-word makes as much sense as women *reclaiming* the word *cunt*."

I watched her search for common ground. It was like watching oil and water separate.

It was like watching the last days I spent with Coretta. Nothing in common, yet still grasping.

She put on a big smile to hide the simmering disappointment. "We can stop talking and play chess."

I watched them. She started the game by moving her pawns to the center. She had strategy. A novice would make random moves from the start, hoping luck or bad moves on the other side of the board worked in their favor.

He lost the first game in six moves. They played again. In five moves, she slaughtered him. Her smirk made it seem vindictive. The way he had looked at her when he entered the coffee shop had set her off. In conversation or chess, it was pointless challenging her, and that was her muh-fuckin' point.

Dwayne called out from the piano, "You reading my script or not?"

I started reading, but my heart was more interested in the magnificence of Dr. Allison Émilie Chappelle.

She asked her date, "What's wrong? You keep looking at me like you just realized we're living in a fractal-holographic matrix and that space and time are woven together in a seamless continuum, permeating the universe. That or you just found out an asteroid is about to strike the earth and we're all going to die."

Seconds passed before he responded. "I didn't know you were crippled."

It became quiet at her table. She sat there, not blinking, jaw tight, breathing hard.

Then, as if confused, she repeated, "Crippled?"

"You're in a wheelchair."

"I thought this was a Tesla masquerading as an Uber for one."

"Am I being punked?"

Another wave of uncomfortable silence passed between them as Dwayne sang an old Al Green cover about being tired of being alone. Paul's cruel energy painted the walls, would linger like the measles.

Her happiness was gone.

In a darker, offended tone she said, "The best part of me still works."

"You can still have sex? I mean, can you feel anything? I've never . . . with a cripple."

"My brain. My brain is the most important part of me, always will be, and it goes unnoticed."

"We met on SmashAndGo. People don't meet on that app to . . . date and get to know each other."

"You're intellectually inadequate, smell like cigarettes, dress like a high school kid, and have a pre–middle school mentality, and you see me as the one crippled?"

"*You're in a wheelchair.*"

"*Knights move in an L.* You moved yours like a pawn. *You know nothing about chess.*"

Her anger was strong. The dog become a defense dog, growled like it was a grumble of pugs.

She calmed her dog, then told her date, "Swipe left. Go. You're dismissed."

His wooden chair screeched across the concrete floor when he stood. He strolled out of the coffeehouse, eased into his Porsche, and drove away. She sat there, barely blinking. Soon she went back to playing with her dog.

Dwayne called out, "Brick, bro, are you reading the script or not?"

I went back to his pages. Had to go back to the beginning and try to focus.

The lady in an Uber for one's phone rang. She answered, listened, then replied, "*Otra vez, Sobrina. ¿Cómo que? Claro.* No, let's do this in Spanish or French. You decide. Okay, Spanish. *Siga. Uh-huh. ¿Y dónde se almacena la información cuántica del universo? ¿Y cómo podríamos extraerla . . . y traducirla . . . y comprenderla? Claro. Escúchame, Sobrina. Hay muchos detalles, Sobrina, que desconocemos acerca de la relación intenso entre el espacio-tiempo, la materia y la información, Sobrina, sobre cosas cuántica.*"

Over and over she impressed me. The way she inhaled and exhaled excited me. She was thunder and lightning in a bottle. I wanted to pack up and go to her. As she chatted, she gathered her thirty-two chess pieces, collected her pawns, rooks, knights, bishops, and kings, and lastly the queens. Then, with tender loving care, one by one, put them all away, as if she was, piece by piece, locking away parts of her heart.

CHAPTER 13

DWAYNE

WHILE I PLAYED and slayed the piano and watched Brick read over my labor of love, I remembered the breakup with Frenchie over sixteen years ago. I was living back east then. New Jersey. An hour out of the Big Apple. That fall day was burned in my mind. The sun was setting as the last of the golden-brown leaves fell from the trees.

I stood in the third-floor apartment window, in a daze, my life falling apart. Soon I heard the shower turn off. Frenchie stepped into the hall wrapped in a huge blue towel. She looked like a woman of French or Spanish blood, depending on how she colored her hair. That day it was blond on the sides and red on top. She had come to see me for resolution, and we'd ended up making love. Soon as we were done, she started crying, then showered.

Frenchie said, "I don't believe in abortions."

"I don't want you to have one."

"Glad we're clear. This is really happening."

The woman who carried my child dried off, eased into her loose Levi's, then bumped past me to get to the bedroom. She fumbled the tumbled sheets until she found her red bra. She folded it, slid it into her back pocket. She pulled on her RENT T-shirt, then slid into her RENT sweatshirt and pulled both sleeves up to the elbow.

She said, "After the baby is born, if we're not married, I'm filing with the courts."

"You're putting me in court?"

"To keep things clean and fair. I don't want you to be surprised when you're served."

"Thanks for the heads-up. When should I expect that love letter?"

"As soon as the baby is born, if nothing between us has changed."

"If we're not married."

"Don't take it as a threat. Just doing what I have to do to protect my baby."

"You tried to file already."

"I thought I could file while I was pregnant. This is my first time."

"Baby has to be born first."

"Are we getting married?"

"You're already married."

"With your baby in my belly."

She was married when I met her, and I had a girlfriend, but that didn't stop us from traveling with the show and living like husband and wife. She stood in the mirror combing her hair and fought back the tears. She walked to me with her head low. I reached to wipe the tears from her eyes. She intercepted my hand.

"*Chicago*. You get to move on to another production and be Billy Flynn."

"Role of a lifetime, Frenchie. It can put me back on the A-list."

"You'll be on the road a year. At least. People have been on the road for twenty years with some productions. You could be one of those people. Touring is in your blood."

"Don't worry. I'll be there when my child is born."

"Dwayne, I've had to cancel all of my work. Not a lot of parts for a pregnant woman."

"Voice-over work? Can you move into that arena for now?"

"I'm here for Broadway and films. If I don't stick to that, next thing I know I'll be a singing waitress."

"Studio singing?"

"I burned that bridge a long time ago. No one cares about a one-hit wonder."

"You had a hit record. That's more than most."

"No one remembers me."

She took my hand and held it. I felt her flesh, captured the softness. She said, "I don't want to be pregnant and not married."

"You are pregnant and married."

"Not funny."

We walked down the long corridor, to the elevator, across the parking lot to her rental car.

We stood outside of her car. The sunlight was almost gone.

"I love you, Frenchie."

"Onstage. When you were in character. Now I see the real you. The great pretender."

"I love you offstage."

"I love you more. Always have. I don't see the barriers you see. People called me a *wigger*. I ignored it, but you couldn't. In this age, I was called a nigger lover by a theatergoer when they realized we were lovers in real life. The word got out. Guess it's different for us off the road in the real world. On the road, we lived in a microcosm. We were safe from the rest of the world. This is hard. This is wrong. But I love you. I was your biggest fan, Dwayne Duquesne, had a crush on you when you were a child star, loved you before I met you. Loved you more when I met you. Too much. But I guess it's not enough, not when a baby is involved, not in the kind of world we live in."

Tears flowed from her.

"Maybe, sometime in the future, after the baby is born, if you're not too busy being a superstar, maybe we can get together and get a cappuccino and talk about it, try to understand how we got here."

"Frenchie, you're going to be a star too."

"Pregnancy impacts a woman's career, not a man's. There is no color line on misogyny."

I didn't know what to say. There was no way to undo what had been done. People had been hurt.

She said, "Now that you're free of me, will you be going back to your girlfriend?"

"I told her about us. It wasn't easy to do. But I told her, so she left me."

"She's why you won't marry me."

"This has all but destroyed her, Frenchie."

"Now you care about her."

"Don't do that."

"She'll be back."

"She won't. She's knows you're pregnant. It got ugly. She's taking a cruise-ship show now. Will be working it for the next year, to get over me, to deal with this the only way she knows how."

"Wish I could do the same. My happy place is onstage. That stage has been taken away."

"Frenchie."

"She wants to get away from you. Same as it is with my husband with me. He hates me now."

"Frenchie. We made a mess of things. I didn't want to cause you to get a divorce."

"I'll get nothing. My marriage had a prenup. I cheated. I'm pregnant by another man, and you'll be gone in more ways than one, so I have to go through this, through divorce and pregnancy and childbirth, alone."

"Frenchie. I have to work. The show. I have to pay for a baby now. I have to work my ass off."

"*Chicago.*"

"You should understand this lifestyle more than anyone. It's a hard lifestyle and you know that."

She shook her head and gave me the final hug, the last kiss.

"I'll call you from the road. Will call you from rehearsal."

"We used to talk every day. Now, when I need you every day, I get this. I get what you gave your girlfriend when you were cheating on her; I get what I gave my husband when I was being unfaithful to him."

A moment rested, and what she wanted to tell me bubbled to the surface.

She said, "Full disclosure, my attorney will need to know how to get in contact with you."

"You will always know where I am. I'll always take your calls."

"Fellow thespian; use a condom while you're out there in Groupie City. Use one every time. Don't end up like Bobby Brown and have baby mommas at every cardinal stop."

"I don't want you to leave angry."

"I'm angry, but I guess I have to move on. We're not getting married; I see that now. It's fine. I'll survive. I have to focus on the new star of the show. I have to be prepared for opening night. And every night after."

When our affair had started, from that first kiss, we had made love almost every night; that had kept us feeling high. This was a one-eighty. Lots of thespians on tour were daytime friends and became nighttime lovers. Our story was nothing new in the land of Broadway stories with Hollywood dreams, and neither was the hard outcome.

I watched her drive away like we were at the end of that classic film. I expected to see movie credits creep by in front of my eyes, all while I heard Al Green in my head, singing, asking how to mend a broken heart.

Two days before Frenchie had come, my now ex-girlfriend, another Broadway actress, was in my leased condo going off on me and collecting her things. My ex was beautiful, tall, willowy, and as dark as *Eigengrau*, the color a man saw when he opened his eyes in a pitch-black room. That was what everyone called her: Eigengrau.

When I was forced to admit my infidelity, as Frenchie had been forced to admit hers, Eigengrau was upset with a fire that rivaled hell. She had shouted, "You just had to sleep with that bitch, didn't you? I knew something was up. Bet you fucked her city after city. I came to your whack show, met the whack cast, and you and that whack bitch pretended nothing was between you. The whack bitch smiled in my goddamn face and sucked your dick when I left. You got the whack ho pregnant. A whack-ass white-ass slut. All y'all whack niggas just alike. Soon as you make some cabbage, you become fucking whack-ass Miss-Ann-chasing motherfuckers *porque yo sé que tenía el alma* of a whack-ass *blanca*. Motherfucking whack-ass sellout. I hope she takes all your goddamn money, your whack ass."

Eigengrau pointed two fingers at me like snakes and cursed me to poverty, and the Dominican queen did it in in a way that shook me to my soul. I'd been in love with one woman, then fell deeper in love with another. Then lost both. There was nothing that could justify my irresponsibility. Frenchie was married and pregnant by me. Eigengrau loved me and was devastated, now living with the knowledge that someone else had had something that should have been hers and only hers. I was sure that Frenchie's husband felt no better and was having sleepless nights.

Frenchie had come for closure, to close this wound before the new one burst open. I had needed resolution, and it became emotional, and we ended up in bed, used intimacy to salve our emotional pain. She had left distressed, crying like her life had fallen apart. Our lives were converted by the life growing in her belly. We were to have our affair, our fling; then she was to go back to her husband, and my girlfriend would have never been the wiser. But we fell in love, got careless. I was in so much fuckin' pain. Felt like I was being pulled in a dozen directions.

After New Jersey, I went back to California and told my brothers that I had a baby on the way by a girl I was in the show with, and not my Dominican girlfriend. I took them to Gladstones to break the news. They were happy for me. Then I drove down Slauson and went to the car wash, went to Tres Dwaynes to tell my daddy the same, that I had a baby on the way and he'd become a grandfather within a few months, Lord willing.

He sat at his cluttered desk wearing an Adidas tracksuit. A young Brazilian girl came in, made him a cup of coffee, didn't offer me one, then kissed him on his cheek and left us to have our conversation.

He sipped his brew. "Nigga went and got a white girl pregnant."

"Look, I just wanted to let you know."

"What happened to the singing-and-acting pretty black girl with the ugly name?"

"Eigengrau."

"Gesundheit."

It hurt my heart to say it, but I manned up, nodded. "We had to break up because of this."

"That's the one you should've knocked up. You fucked up across the board."

"You're one to talk."

"Don't come in my office and start no shit."

"Wanted you to know you'd finally be a grandfather."

"Was that on my wish list?"

"Should be."

"Won't be my bill to pay."

"I know."

"Have to set precedence. Have to let you know that there is a line you can't cross."

"I'm not here to ask for money."

"You in a trick bag. What you gonna do?"

"She wants to get married. I love her, and I think I should marry her as soon as the baby comes."

"Where she from?"

"Vermont. East Montpelier."

"Oh, that snow bunny real white. Only thing scarier than down-south white is up-north white."

"No whiter than other white folks."

"She rich?"

"That's not the point. We're going to have a baby. We should get married for the kid."

"Don't do that. You're gonna lose enough paying child support for eighteen years. You gonna feel that mistake at the first of every month. Like I felt it. Nigga like you famous, so you can't run and hide and make money under the table. She got you, and she got you good. Don't marry her, not unless she rich. Trust me. Marriage don't benefit a man. You'll end up paying child support and alimony and in ten years lose everything you worked for."

"She's not like that."

He laughed. "You gonna learn. You done lost your control. You should've kept your pecker in a condom and invested with me. I'm about to get those two properties across the street and expand my business, gonna open another set of businesses. You'll be in the poorhouse. You'll be down here begging for a job before you know it."

I'd been stressed and turned to him for advice, maybe had tried to bond, needed him because even though I was a grown man, I was afraid, and I was a son who needed his father, but he smirked and took joy in my misery.

Tears ran from my eyes.

I said, "God gave me a nigga for a daddy. The nigga of all niggas. Momma didn't deserve you."

"Fuck you. Get the fuck out of my goddamn office."

"Nigga Daddy."

"You'll need me before I need you."

"I don't fucking need you. Never have."

That was the last time I saw him.

I hated all he had said, but it stuck with me, fucked me. His words were a seed planted in my brain.

I never should have gone to see Nigga Daddy. I should've just bought a wedding ring and run to Frenchie.

The next time I saw Frenchie was in court. She was a different woman, a mother who'd come to do battle.

After New Jersey she refused my calls, never replied to an e-mail or a text message. But she made sure I was there when Fela was born, to sign the birth certificate.

She was no longer the girl I'd been in love with. I didn't know her anymore.

The nasty things she said about me, the lies in the court papers, cut into my heart. She made me out to be some kind of a monster. I don't know how much of it came from her lawyer. A woman could say anything in court papers, and it didn't have to be the truth. Men could assassinate a woman's character in black and white, but I didn't say anything, told my three-hundred-dollars-an-hour attorney to not respond to anything Frenchie had said. She made me sound untrustworthy, manipulative, worthless. She left out the fact that she was married when we met, only said I'd promised her marriage, then abandoned her while she was pregnant, and now she wanted to recoup every dime she had spent on health care during that nine-month period. Her husband had divorced her before the baby came, and that was a strategic move, done in a hurry because if he was married to her when the baby came, he could be legally responsible for my son. He was embarrassed enough being a cuckold and refused to end up a white man with a white wife and a black child he'd be forced to pay for. That was left out too. Frenchie had said career-damaging things out of spite, and it all became part of the public record. Frenchie thought I was richer than I was, and I thought the same about her. She had grown up in Vermont in a big house and skied every winter. White people were poor too, but she wasn't one. She claimed zero income and zero savings. I knew that was bullshit. She had stopped working and had hidden her money, whatever she'd saved. She claimed any residuals from her one hit were insignificant by then. My attorney told me I'd have to pay an accountant to do forensics to prove she was lying, but I let it go, let her lie stand and kept it moving. There was no way I could do the same. All of my numbers were on the table, furnished by tax papers. I left there feeling like Emmanuel Eboué, the man who lost everything to his first wife, including his three kids, his mansion, his automobiles, and their first house in North London, when he was ordered by a UK court to surrender ownership of everything he had worked for. It wasn't as bad, back then, when the order was handed down; it just felt that way. I'd wanted to kick over a car. Like Nigga Daddy had predicted, the new Frenchie would be in my pockets deeper than lint for the next eighteen years. I'd left court with so much animosity the world had become a shade of red. It was what it was. It became a paycheck relationship.

Money changes things and people, and not always for the best, but I got an amazing son out of the deal. My million-dollar kid. I would've paid ten times that if I'd had it.

I had been blessed with a son I loved more than anything. A son I worried about night and day.

CHAPTER 14

BRICK

I HANDED DWAYNE back the ninety-page script. The table where the woman in the Tesla masquerading as an Uber for one had been had a set of new Nubians having a meeting there. Every chair in Hot and Cool was taken.

"Well, Brick?" Dwayne asked, finishing the last of the avocado toast. "How does that read to you?"

"Most films are community theater. This is Stanislavski level. The ambiguous ending is brilliant but will be wasted on an audience used to being spoon-fed every aspect of a story line."

"Oh ye who hates like the best of the hating haters, line up the backhanded compliments."

"Change it to white characters, Dwayne. Give Hollywood what Hollywood wants. Hollywood will force something this good to be just another forgettable urban movie. And a movie with a white lead gets a bigger budget."

"Brick, I'm not changing my script to accommodate racism."

"Create some green, pay some bills, then come back with that cash in hand so you can be your own producer and stop begging people to finance your shit. *Then* you can focus on the black aesthetic."

"I could get this made for under four million. Could probably do it with two."

"Then do it. Round up the usual suspects and have them finance it."

"Can't do shit on that level yet, not until I have control of my money. I have a script but need capital. Don't want to end up a passenger on my own project. I wrote this screenplay as a vehicle for my big comeback."

We headed outside, moved into the sunshine and desert air.

When he took a breath, I asked, "Seen Nephew?"

"Frenchie has me blocked out. Can't see my own son until court."

"Until then, what you going to be up to?"

"Going to pitch this *Stanislavski*-level screenplay and see if I can get some auditions."

I tapped the manuscript. "How long you worked on this screenplay?"

"Two years."

"It shows. Great job." I took a sip of my chai latte. "So, what else is going on?"

He said, "Plane ticket left me a little short on cash."

I opened my wallet, slid him two hundred bucks. Another loan that would never be repaid.

He asked, "Can you loan me some frequent-flier miles? In case I get an audition in New York."

I nodded, decided this date had gotten too expensive, then said, "I have to go meet somebody."

"I reported her. I had to call the police to do a wellness check on Frenchie."

"Wait, Dwayne, reported her for what?"

He pulled his lips in like he always did when something was going on in his life and it was hard to say the issue out loud. "My son texted me and said there was no water in the house. No gas. No electricity. No food."

"You shitting me?"

He took a breath, then showed me a thread of messages from my nephew. He wasn't lying.

He said, "It was a hard choice, but since I didn't have eyes on the situation, I called it in."

"You're paying your note?"

"My accountant pays her before I get a dime to buy myself a sandwich."

"Where is the money going? Frenchie on something?"

He huffed. "Brick, I need you to come by there with me. Just knock on the door for me. I'll stay in the car."

"You called the cops. You're persona non grata with Frenchie."

"*I was touring with the fucking play.* I had no choice. I needed eyes on the situation. If my son was with me, and he had sent her the same messages, said he hadn't eaten in two or three days, said he couldn't flush a toilet and had to shit at the local library, she would have had eight squad cars at my door and three helicopters over my spot."

I sighed. "You're right. I would have done the same."

Dwayne said, "Look, we need to check on my son."

"Why didn't you say something before now?"

"Brick. Nigga Daddy taught us that black men handled their own problems. He put that ideology in my head like it was his own religion. Hard to undo all of the brainwashing, even as an adult, even when I know better."

"I know."

"Hard to ask for help. For certain kinds of help."

"I know."

"When I do, when I have to, it makes me feel like a failure. Was trying to see how I could fix this. I can't."

I understood. "You can't go by there. It could get ugly and compromise your standing in court. Text me Frenchie's address and I'll check it out if I can. No promises, though. Uncles become hashtags too."

He sighed like ten thousand pounds had been lifted from his soul.

I said, "Change that script to white people and pay some bills."

"Not selling out."

I motioned outside at one of the few black middle-class areas from sea to shining sea, motioned at an area that was shifting, one real estate transaction at a time. "You see half the businesses are closed in the area?"

"I noticed."

"The train is coming down Crenshaw. Area is changing. Gentrification is coming. White flight has flipped and now it's the second wave of the European American arrival; they are buying up everything."

My big brother smiled. "Problem around here is our people are leasing. All of these black businesses have white landlords. We have to sell out or get out when the rent gets too high. When you own your shit, your real estate or your intellectual property, you don't have to sell out, not when you have something of value. *You have to own something.* That's the rule for the winners. I own my work. I own this script. If nothing else, this Stanislavski shit is mine. Court can't take it away. I don't have to fight for visitation. No one's name is on this labor of love but mine. You have to own something to be somebody in this city, Brick. You have to *own.* Bro, I don't even feel like I own the kid I made. But this, I own this. I might lose in family court, but I can win at this. Not selling out. Not this time."

We made eye contact and I saw a man struggling with his sense of self-worth, in need of validation. Maybe the script was more important because it was the only thing in his life that he felt like he could control.

I let two seconds pass, then softly said, "Checkmate."

He nodded. "Might stop by your place later."

"Got two girls staying at my spot."

"What, you're an Airbnb now?"

"They lost their place, need a spot to crash for a few."

"I was going to crash over there."

"Shit, my place is packed."

"I have an audition in a couple hours. Geico commercial. Will check in to see if you've been by Frenchie's."

He went back into the café, back to his table. A half block later I felt bad, went back, was going to tell him let's go do a drive-by. I looked in the window. He'd been recognized. Women grinned at famous people a certain way. Sisters rocking Afro puffs, Bantu knots, and braids in Mohawk realized who Dwayne was and suddenly had perky breasts and wide smiles. Dwayne had a new audience, went to them, positive smile. Spotlight was on him.

A moment later, they were all seated around the piano, and Dwayne was performing ballads for them. I headed toward home, looking down and reading the names in the sidewalk as I strolled. African American stars, singers, politicians, writers, and poets had been given their own version of Hollywood's Walk of Fame. Restless, I looked south toward Vernon, searched east and west. I hoped to see the good-looking woman who happened to chill in an Uber for one. Dr. Allison Émilie Chappelle. With each step, I listened for a barking dog. Heard nothing.

CHAPTER 15

DWAYNE

AFTER MY AUDITION, I needed to eat up some more day until I figured out where I could sleep tonight, so I followed the scent and trail of the displaced, went to Venice Beach. I was tired, but at least I could pace around in better air. The area was so crowded it was like Times Square by the sea. Took forty minutes to find a free spot. I parked near the roundabout by the post office and headed toward the main drag. To add insult to injury, I heard someone playing Frenchie's old pop song, "Everybody Knows." The tail end of the song played in the distance. Then her angelic voice was gone, lost in pandemonium, overpowered by all the other noises coming from every cardinal direction. Venice was a madhouse. Happily contaminated and a haven for alazons. Henna, weed shops, smoke shops, incense in the air, street comedians, palm readings, religion pushers, religion haters, atheists, pro-black-literature pushers, anti-white-literature pushers,

Buddhists, hemp products, gluten-free Twinkies, dancers, singers, chainsaw jugglers, weight lifters, tattoo shops, T-shirt vendors, people pushing tickets to watch TV shows or movie screenings, psychics, and people carrying Amazon-size snakes—everything considered good and bad could be found along the one-mile strip.

I sent Frenchie a text. I want to see my son.

No reply.

I texted her again. One word. One that came from the heart. Please.

Still no reply.

Two girls, one dyed blond and the other a natural brunette, bumped by people like they owned the world and everyone else's lease was up. They were barely over four foot ten inches tall, resemblance so strong they could be twin sisters, both wearing delicate iridescent T-shirts so thin they revealed the outlines of their gym-perfected bikini bodies. I didn't get out of their way. The blonde bumped into me, then gave me eye contact with no grin as we went in opposite directions in the foot traffic. The rude blonde looked back at me again, then said something harsh to the brunette.

That was how hashtags were made. I picked up the pace, disappeared in the crowd.

My attention was arrested again when I heard "Everybody Knows" playing a hundred yards away.

I fought my way upstream, then passed by the dyed blonde and the natural brunette again, the four-foot-ten-inches-tall women who could pass for twin sisters. This time they both looked at me, stared hard.

I grabbed a hot dog and smoothie, sat in the bleachers on the court where they filmed *White Men Can't Jump*, watched a full-courter in progress. Nine brothers and one white guy. Same ratio as the NBA.

While I watched the game, my phone buzzed.

It was a message from Frenchie. Please refrain from sending me text messages. Please have your attorney communicate with mine or directly with the courts regarding all custody matters.

I called her every name I could think of. A million dollars, and this bullshit.

I texted her, How's Fela? Just let me know how my son is doing.

No reply. Then those bubbles that said she was typing. Then a message, screaming at me in all caps.

DON'T FUCKING TEXT ME ANYMORE. YOU HAVE NO FUCKING REASON TO TEXT ME. EVER. PAY YOUR GODDAMN CHILD SUPPORT ON TIME AND KEEP IT MOVING. ONE MORE TEXT AND I WILL FILE AN ORDER OF PROTECTION.

As I fought the urge to send the nastiest text ever written, I saw the rude girls who had bumped into me a moment ago. The rude blonde and the ruder brunette. Again they bumped through the stream of pedestrians. I thought they were passing by, heading toward the part with the hard-bodied weight lifters, but they saw me and came toward me, hurried like they were coming to tell me off for bumping into them. The rude blonde gave me hard eye contact again.

The ruder brunette asked, "Like, aren't you . . . Dwayne? I mean, *the* Dwayne of all the Dwaynes."

"Yeah, I am."

The blonde set free a ginormous smile. "Oh my God. Like, I knew that was you."

The brunette became overexcited. "Like, oh my God. I'm a big fan. I am your number one fan."

The blonde came closer. "Like, I'm a huge fan too. There is no huger fan than I am."

Frenchie's voice, the woman who once loved me more than anyone ever created and now hated me more than anyone on this planet, her voice was in the distance, corrupting the air while I made two new friends. The blonde and brunette were both ambiguous so far as race. We talked about my old show, laughed about this and that, walked together and stood on the dirty brown sand at the ocean. After I'd felt like shit for days on end, they gave me adulation and genuine smiles. Was amazing how it was easier to get that from strangers than from the people you loved. It made me feel good.

CHAPTER 16

BRICK

WHEN I MADE it back home, I grabbed wine to be sold, then sent a text to Christiana. She sashayed out to my car wearing a golden dress and nude patent leather heels, hair whipped. She was as elegant as Grace Kelly.

I gave her two thumbs up. "Your client is going to fall in love over lunch."

"He is a movie star. He falls in love with no one, no matter how beautiful."

"He will see you and realize you're the woman of his dreams."

"Do you fall in love, Brick?"

"I do fall in love. Wife. Kids. Grandkids. A dog. A cat. I imagine those things. Okay, no cat."

"You don't seem the type. But to me, right now, knowing what I know, no man seems like the type."

I took her to the Beverly Hills Hotel to entertain one man of many living in a pity of husbands.

She said, "Just drop me off. He will bring me back to Penny's apartment in a limousine. He likes to make love in the limousine while we are being driven around Los Angeles, Hollywood, and Malibu. Or we cruise down Pacific Coast Highway, tinted windows hiding his marital sins committed at sixty miles per hour."

"Must be nice."

"It is. It is very nice. And when you are ready, I can arrange the same for you."

As she walked inside, every rich man looked her way in awe as she passed by. For a moment I fantasized about being paid to be a part of someone else's reality. I wondered what that would be like, to be in a stretch limo, being chauffeured, sipping champagne and eating peeled grapes while I had a good time with an A-list movie star.

AFTER I DROPPED off the wine, I doubled back to my apartment long enough to pick up Penny, then drove south to Inglewood. I was going to check on Dwayne's problems. His problems were our family problems. I had called André, wanted him to roll with me, but my call went to his messages, and I didn't leave one. The middle brother had to play the role of the big brother while the younger brother was out doing whatever younger brothers did.

When we crept up to the planned community of Pine Court, the college student had my music bumping the latest by the Internet. The colony of houses was in a sector where single-family homes sold for between seven and eight hundred thousand. Houses that sold for less than a hundred grand back in '79 sold for more than four hundred grand in '13 and now cost almost eight hundred grand. A real estate agent could pull twenty grand off one sale. I knew that much because when someone gave you their address and you dropped the info in Google, the Internet regurgitated all of their business.

Penny paused from texting someone regarding a date long enough to look up, take in the hidden area, and say, "Had no idea this neighborhood was built behind Faithful Central. Thought it was all industrial back here."

"They have a real nice tract of homes. Gets very little traffic after the businesses close."

I parked in front of Frenchie's crib. A postal carrier passed by about the same time we got out of Miss Mini. I pulled my suit coat back on. I had changed and was dressed like a hip professional, the way I wished I had dressed this morning at the coffee shop. Penny was dressed in worn-out USC swag. Hair pulled back. Eyeglasses. People would still call po-po on a black man in a suit, but in this town, no one would call the police on a nerdy girl from USC, not unless they were hardcore UCLA fans. I regarded the rest of the cul-de-sac, steeled myself to deal with a woman who had no love for my oldest brother; then we marched across a patch of grass to get on a narrow walkway that led to the front door. The lawn needed a lot of love. It looked like it hadn't been kissed by a lawn mower in at least a month. Grass was high enough to make me think no one lived here. Penny went to the front door while I stayed a step behind. The windows were open, but the blinds were closed. Penny pushed the doorbell twice, back to back.

Penny asked, "Did the doorbell ring?"

"Dwayne said the power might be off over here."

"In a house this nice?"

I knocked a dozen times. Somebody moved around inside. One row of the plantation shutters moved a bit.

I called out, "Frenchie? You home?"

"My mom's not home. Who is it?"

"It's your favorite uncle, the one you never call, not even on his birthday."

"Uncle André?"

"Fela, you are breaking a black man's broken heart. Try again."

"Uncle Brick?"

He peeped out the plantation shutters next to the door. "Who's that lady? Is that social services?"

"You don't have to be scared, Nephew. Open the door. Just checking on you and Frenchie."

"Mom told me not to open the door for anybody. Especially my daddy or the police."

"Open. The. Door. Nephew. I'm not coming in. Let me see you. Then I'm gone."

The locks came undone. The door opened.

Nephew was sixteen and six feet tall. He was a slim, dimpled, mixed-race boy with a light-brown Mohawk that needed to be shaped and edged. Nephew was the handsome boy all the girls would chase, black, white, or Mexican. He had on worn red joggers and a wrinkled yellow T-shirt. He looked as scared as he looked hungry.

I asked, "What's up, player? What you doing at home?"

"No school today."

I waited a beat, then got to the point, asked, "Your power and water off?"

He hesitated, afraid to say. "Been that way a couple of months. Maybe three."

His eyes watered. He was humiliated. I was shocked, and my expression gave me away.

Penny looked beyond him inside the home. She clearly didn't like the mess she saw.

I softened my disposition, and in a concerned tone I asked, "What's going on, Nephew?"

"Dad sent the police over here to check on me." He shrugged. "Police said everything was okay. I had hoped they would tell Mom I had to go live with my dad awhile, but they just looked around and left."

"I mean, why are the lights and water off? Did something happen over here?"

"Mom says she ain't got no money." Nephew almost looked excited. "Dad back in town?"

"He's really worried about you. That's why I stopped by."

"Are they going to court again? I heard Mom on the phone arguing with her lawyer about a court date."

I bit my tongue and nodded. "Where is your mom?"

"I don't know." He shifted. "She left early this morning."

"She working?"

"You have to ask her."

It hurt, but I stated the obvious. "You look hungry."

"I am. A little bit."

I took a breath. "Last time you ate?"

Nephew hesitated; then tears of shame fell from his eyes. "Three days ago."

"What you eat?"

"Just some snacks from the dollar store."

Nephew looked like a young man who had no idea where his next meal would come from. His lips were pale and looked dry. I mentioned food, and in a Pavlovian response, his stomach perked up and growled.

"Your mom working?"

"You already asked me that. You have to ask her."

"So, she's living off your money."

Penny said, "Brick."

I reeled it back in. I was getting upset, had to dial it back.

Nephew said, "Dad showed me how much he's paid. He wanted me to know that he's never missed a payment. Makes me feel bad. I feel bad for him and my momma. I'm the reason she's not famous and I'm the reason he has to spend so much money. I feel like this is my fault for being born."

"It's not your fault. Never think this is your fault."

"I just want to graduate, move as far away as I can, and not look back."

The frustrated teenager said that and we all stood in Vatican silence.

I asked, "How're the grades looking?"

"I got a C in English, a B in social studies; the rest are strong As."

I said, "Talk to the English teacher and ask what you have to do to bring your grade up to a B."

"Already did that. Working on a short story as extra credit. It can get me up to a B."

I asked, "You still shooting b-ball?"

"Naw. Tendinitis won't let me jump. Just exercising my mind to make sure I'll be able get into college somewhere. I have to learn to do for myself and depend on myself and take care of myself."

He'd calmed down a bit.

I asked, "Nephew, can you ride to the store with me?"

"I can't leave the house."

"Won't take but twenty minutes."

"Nope. Not leaving."

"Not even to get food?"

"She'll be mad. I have to live with her. You don't. It's hard enough as it is."

"Don't you have friends you can kick it with?"

"People tease you when you don't have food or money. I can't ask people to feed me and not get talked about. So, I just don't do anything but go to school and come back home and do my homework."

CHAPTER 17

BRICK

I WENT TO the Mexican grocery on La Brea near Florence and bought five bags of food and a case of bottled water. Penny picked what to buy, most of it nonperishable, and nothing that had to be cooked. When we returned, Nephew smelled the roasted chicken in the bag and his eyes screamed that he was ready to eat. I didn't go past the front door, just handed him the bags and water and told him to find out how much it would be to get their power and water turned back on, told him to have Frenchie message me as soon as she could, since he didn't have a phone. She'd taken it from him as punishment.

I asked, "You have some WAM?"

"What's WAM?"

"Walking-around money."

"No WAM. Your nephew is WAB. Walking around broke."

I handed him a twenty. He took it and looked at that paper like it was gold bullion.

We hugged, kissed cheeks. I loved Fela like he was my own son. He's the son I'd love to have.

On the way out, I snooped in their mailbox. The postman had just dropped off Frenchie's past-due bills. I committed a federal crime and took them. I sent Dwayne a text, told him I had seen Nephew and had dropped off food.

When we got in the car and started driving away, Penny was crying. She shook her head nonstop. "That's the life I don't want. I'll do anything to not have that life."

"That was too much for you."

"Who wants to have kids only to have them suffer?"

"Dwayne is the one keeping them afloat. Has since Nephew was born."

"That's what I'm afraid of. Depending on some man to send a check on time. A nigga doesn't feel like sending a check that month, or stops sending a check because he has a new car note, or has moved on to some new pussy and he'd rather finance some new ass than pay for his own child. Nah to being a single mom. We made a baby together, we stay together. Get me pregnant, and where you go, I'm the fuck going. Where you live, I'm the fuck living. Married or not. And you can get married, but know I'll be living with you and that bitch, and me and the baby will be in the same bed sleeping between both of you. If we have a baby, then we're family. If people made a baby and stayed together . . . lived under one roof . . . combined incomes . . . everybody could do better . . . instead of everybody pulling everybody down . . . paying lawyers . . . making them rich . . . half of your money over here, half over there . . ."

I said, "And losing everything you've worked hard to get along the way."

"Your nephew looked so weak. He'd probably had some water, and that fooled his stomach for a minute, but the need to eat is real and the throbbing will come back twice as hard. You try to sleep it away and sometimes it lets you. You catnap to conserve energy, but you wake up in unbearable agony, and once you do, you will not be able to sleep again. Not for a long while. Time seems to move in super slow motion. Your head aches. Your brain tells you to find a way to eat. Steal. Kill. Sell pussy. Eat, then deal with the consequences on a full stomach."

When she ended her rant, I said, "I had no idea it had been that bad for you."

"I came from nothing."

"I know. We're black in America. We all did."

"You've been middle class for at least a generation, not me. We were Section 8 and government cheese."

"Okay. I stand corrected."

"It's not fair. Two things you can't find in Los Angeles; bookstores and justice."

"That part."

"The inside of Frenchie's house looked like it's been on the decline for a while."

"Yeah. I could tell the maid ran away with the gardener a long time ago."

"I hate men who can't *at least* take care of their financial responsibilities."

"I hate a woman who can't keep a clean house."

"Men walk away and force women to become superwomen."

"Checkmate."

"Eat a dick. Checkmate that, Brick. Your rude ass. Dwayne is all over the world and his son is here, starving to death. If everybody was under one roof . . . If Dwayne could work it out with Frenchie . . ."

"That would help Nephew, but Dwayne and Frenchie would kill each other. I hate double funerals."

She said, "Couldn't you take Nephew with you? Let him kick it at your apartment?"

"Yeah, and the cops would be at my door in an hour and I'd get locked up for kidnapping."

"Frenchie like that?"

"She'd blame my brother, have him locked up too." I sighed. "My brother had the cops go over there to make sure his son was okay. Cops saw what we saw and said it was okay by them."

"Not having water and not having power is okay? My bad. I guess it is for black people."

"A black kid."

"If she has a black kid, in my book, she's officially black people now."

"At least Negro adjacent."

Penny hesitated. "What are you going to do about it, Brick?"

"Penny. Dwayne and Frenchie have to work that out. They're due in family court soon."

"I needed to see that. I was studying, wasn't going to stop and go with you when you called and asked, but God spoke to me. God knew I needed to see that with my own eyes to keep me motivated."

"You okay over there? You're a simmering volcano trying not to erupt."

She wiped her eyes, her smile as ugly as a frown. "I'm fine. Just paying a fat bill my ex left behind with nobody to hug at night. Just out here on my own. Hard coming from the family I come from. You don't know who you can trust or who will be your friend tomorrow. So, yeah, Brick, I'm okay over here. Everything is hunky-dory."

"What's going on, Penny?"

She twisted her mouth. "My ex called me this morning."

"Recidivism in progress?"

"Said he misses me. Said the other girl was a mistake. Cried and said marrying her was a mistake."

I softened my tone. "How you feel about that?"

"I don't know. Right now, he's flying around my head like a bunch of bats."

"Cauldron of bats."

She made a face of hurt and anger. "I see things a lot clearer now that he's gone. I was looking for a soul mate and he just needed a place to live. All he needed was a place to stay and a warm orifice to deposit an orgasm in a few times a week. He's gone and each month I'm getting bills to remind me how I fucked up by falling in love."

"He owes you enough money to fix the water problem in Flint."

"He owes me a lot of money. Jesus, I'm glad we don't have a kid. I can take the L and walk away. I can delete his photos from the cloud, block him on Twitter and Facebook, and pretend I never met him. I can remove his name from my vocabulary and make him cease to exist in my world. He can become the boyfriend I dated that no one I meet and date moving forward will ever know about."

I said, "I never would have thought you two would break up, not like that."

She retorted, "You and Coretta. I thought you two were the happiest couple on earth."

"Yeah. Everybody is happy until they aren't. Some pretend to be happy for a while."

"I didn't pretend. I was happy. Then all of a sudden I wasn't."

"Nothing happens suddenly. You pretended. You posted happy pictures on social media."

"Yeah. I guess I did. Mailed out Christmas cards. Posted a picture when we were on vacation last year in Cabo, smiling, but the rest of the time we were arguing. We did shit to look happy to the rest of the world. I kept our problems off social media . . . until we broke up. Then I had a moment and blasted his ass out."

"I never would have known. But there had to be signs. There were signs with Coretta."

"I feel like it's my fault, like I did something wrong. He cheated, left me for that bitch he married, and that made me feel so insecure. Still makes me feel like I'm not woman enough. It really fucked with my head, Brick."

"You came to me."

"I called you over. My neighbor. My friend. I needed to be comforted. I needed to be fucked by someone who wasn't him. I needed to suck a dick that wasn't his. I needed to let you fuck my pussy, let you fuck my ass, and do whatever it took. I needed to be a woman to a man and not feel insecure. That's why I answered the door naked."

"You had a towel on."

"I didn't want you to come over and we sit around talking. I didn't want any games, needed you to look at me and know what it was all about. I needed you. I needed to prove to him that I was more woman than the bitch he left me for. Yeah, he cheated and messed me up in the head. I needed you to look at me and find me desirable."

"I did."

She said, "And now he calls and says he misses me."

"Do you miss him?"

"A lot of men have made me come, and some have fucked my brains out, like you did, but not one single man has ever made me come hard enough to end up being a goddamn fool, except him. I let him ruin my fuckin' life."

"You miss him."

Penny took a breath and used the heels of her hands to move a mountain of tears. "My period must be coming, because I'm feeling superemotional and hypersensitive to everything right now."

I asked, "Need anything?"

"Wine and popcorn. All I need is wine and popcorn and reruns of *Scandal*."

Penny turned on the radio, found a song from the album Urban Flora, and cranked it up.

Our relationship, this friendship, had always been awkward, uneven, and undefinable.

Once upon a time, Penny had a client who didn't pay her. She came home that night and told me she was an escort. She had been scared to tell me, but she was more scared of the guy who had shorted her, and she needed that money to cover her rent and food. She was desperate for help. I took my daddy's snub-nose and we went and got what she was due, plus a tip for her inconvenience. I'm not sure if she asked me to or if I had volunteered, but I started driving her after that. Men didn't hesitate to rob women but conceded to other men.

Especially if he carried his daddy's snub-nose and cared about the woman in question.

WHEN I PARALLEL parked Miss Mini in front of my two-level building, Mocha Latte was running down Stocker, coming hard from the west, drenched in sweat. Penny went to her place and I waited on Mocha Latte. She was a block back; came to me walking, breathing hard, hands on her hips. She had on runner's gear, shorts that hugged her butt, and a sports bra, so she was more than half-naked, the best parts under dark spandex. The sweat on her skin made her shine like she was the richest chocolate. She said she had just run to the beach and back.

I said, "Beach is ten miles away. Round trip would be twenty."

She stretched. "Don't forget. I need you around seven. I'll be done by nine."

"Sweat is making your skin shine. Your skin is beautiful. You look like black silk."

She looked at me like my words had stunned her. "Thanks. I think."

"Stunning like Aïssa Maïga. Calves to kill for. Solid thighs. Stomach flat. Ass popping. You are a marathon-running Nubian queen who looks like her church is a gym and you worship three times a day. Saw you running. Impressive as fuck. Your body is perfect, and your skin is amazing. I don't think I've seen a prettier woman."

She stood speechless for a moment, watched me ramble, then said, "Wow. And who is Aïssa Maïga?"

"French actress. Born in Dakar. Malian father, Senegalese mother. She's so gorgeous it's a shame. You're magically delicious. Just like her. Maybe even more so because you're superfit. Marathon Mama."

She looked at me like she didn't know what to make of my honesty. "Again, wow. And thanks."

My phone buzzed with a number I didn't recognize. It was Frenchie. She said hello like we had issues.

As I waved good-bye to Mocha Latte and headed to my crib, I asked Frenchie, "What's going on?"

"Just wanted to thank you for the blessing."

"Why didn't you call somebody, Frenchie?"

"I'm calling to say thanks, not to start an argument."

"We're family."

"You have my number. All of you have my number."

"No matter what's up between you and Dwayne, you and Nephew can reach out to me."

"Don't make me wish I didn't call to thank you, Brick."

"No need to thank me. Dwayne gave me the money to buy the food."

Her animosity was so strong I felt her giving me the side-eye through the phone. "He's back?"

"He's back."

"I'll tell my attorney the absentee father who refers to this full-time mother as a gold digger is back."

"If things are rough and you want to let Nephew come and stay with me a few days, I can—"

Frenchie kissed her teeth and ended the call.

CHAPTER 18

DWAYNE

BRICK DIDN'T ANSWER when I called to check in, neither did playboy André, so I put my phone away and got back into bed and continued the conversation we were having about show business and being part of a touring show.

As we lounged in the nude on a Murphy bed, I told the racially ambiguous brunette, "It's not like you think. Very few five-star moments. Overall, it's racist as hell. If I'm with a black cast or a white cast, I'm treated differently."

She traced her finger along my skin, wiggled her ass, asked, "Like, how so?"

"A black cast gets the shitty rooms by the loud-ass ice machines or has to hike what feels like a route longer than the Trans Canada Trail to get to their rooms. Especially in the South. They still hate blacks in the South. They try to be slick and create a colored section away from everybody else in the hotel."

"They treat white casts that much better? Like, people still do that?"

"I've been with both, same hotels, and it's like night and day. They see a black cast and they're all attitude behind the desk. You see it in their eyes, in their fake smiles, how they loathe your troupe for coming to their hotel. *The Color Purple* won't get the same service and consideration as the cast of *Waitress*."

"But you're famous."

"They see black first. Always see black skin first. If a black troupe shows up, they just see black people they don't want to deal with. Just like they see white skin first and treat them all like stars."

"You had a television show. I liked the other show you were in too, the cop one. It was canceled so fast."

"Some places, if you're black you're never the right kind of famous to them. Ask Oprah."

"So, between the black productions and the white productions, does one pay more than the other?"

"Depends on your role. But all things being equal, white tours, generally speaking, pay more."

"I had no idea."

"But you can feel alienated. I'm a black man."

"Duh."

"Not being around other black people can get lonely."

"I can see that. Never thought about white plays paying more money than black plays."

"Whites pay more to see theater."

"Why?"

"Whites have a different level of disposable income. It costs twelve hundred dollars to see *Hamilton*. Costs five hundred to see *The Book of Mormon*. That's rent money. Whites grow up on theater and black folks grow up on gospel plays, and half the time they're watching a bootleg version of that second-rate production."

"Dwayne."

"Yeah?"

"Can I take a selfie while we, you know? Like, I really want a selfie with us."

"No photos while we're intimate. I have a kid."

"It'll be just for me. How about just my face? Won't nobody but me know it's you."

"Nah, I have a kid. We can step outside and take all the selfies you want, but not with me with my shirt off or in your bed naked. It would make you a Kardashian and I'd get the Ray J treatment."

She straddled me. I sucked her nipples. She raised up and put me in right away, took as much of me as she could stand. She moaned almost every vowel. She took it up and down, went in circles.

I smiled at her, then asked, "What are you?"

"My father is British Chinese and Cherokee American, and my mother is Black Jamaican and Irish."

"Your friend?"

"I think her mom is Puerto Rican, Scottish, German, and Jewish. I know her dad is from Sri Lanka."

"Yeah?"

"You?"

"Black with some Mexican in our blood. Mom is black and Mexican."

"So you're like the singer Miguel."

"More or less."

The door opened; the brunette's blond girlfriend was back, holding a bag of beer, wine, and snacks. Blondie undressed, then sat and watched, a finger twirling her hair as she bit her bottom lip. She waited for her turn. When hers came, I was behind her, had her facedown. The brunette smiled, sipped beer, and danced until it was her go again. I positioned myself, held Blondie's hips, went in deep, came out to the tip, then went in as deep as she would let me go. I did that over and over, slapping her narrow butt. Brunette opened a beer, gave me a swallow.

"We're in America having a sex party with a celebrity."

"I know, right?"

Brunette licked her lips, anxious for another turn.

I asked Brunette, "This your one-bedroom number on the beach?"

"Heck no. Like, this is our Airbnb. We've been here two days and leave for London tomorrow."

"Where you from?"

"Vancouver. She's from Quebec. We met and became BFFs at University of Toronto."

"Okay if I stay the night? I've missed my check-in time at the Beverly Hills Hotel."

"We would be offended if you didn't. But we're going to party awhile. We want to catch an Uber and hit a couple of bars before they close. We can get our selfies while we party like rock stars with a big-time celebrity."

"I lost my wallet and charge cards, think I was pickpocketed, so you'll have to pay."

"No problem. I'm using my dad's charge card anyway. It will be my honor."

The brunette came over, kissed me, joined in the fun. The price of fame.

The brunette moaned, then pouted, "He won't let me take a selfie like this."

Blondie said, "Too bad. It would break the Internet. And break up your relationship. Be smart."

"I just . . . want to . . . see . . . what . . . what . . . what I look like."

"Do I make faces like that?"

"If he let you . . . take a selfie . . . you would know."

They worked me, took my lion king roar down to a soft meow. I left both of them purring like cats.

We slept an hour, then hit a local bar, had drinks, danced, came back, had another session. Strangers fucked like it was fucking National Fucking Day. The brunette let us know she was coming, as the blonde touched her again. The brunette was demolished by orgasm, fell away from me. The blonde laughed, took her place. The brunette eased out of the bed, dancing. She moved in slow motion, went to do a line of cocaine, then sipped beer. The blonde gave me a sloppy blow job until the brunette insisted she could take care of that part. She was my number one fan. Said she would be honored. The way she used her mouth, she was the goddamn devil. It was a good orgasm, one that was voluptuous and substantial, a much-needed one that rivaled the Hoover Dam bursting. This was therapy, the kind that wouldn't cost me two hundred bucks an hour. This killed anxiety, kept me from popping a pill that would turn me into a zombie.

I needed a place to hide until the sun came up, a place that didn't have four tires and a seat that reclined. My charge cards were maxed out, and I didn't want to blow the little skrilla I had. I'd followed the groupies, done this so I could get off my feet, get a hot shower, and rest a few hours, horizontal, in a bed, even if that bed was crowded.

I did what I had to do to make sure I had money left when I got to see Fela.

CHAPTER 19

BRICK

MOCHA LATTE LEFT Penny's crib and came out to my car looking like a movie star. She had on a va-va-va-voom black backless midi-dress, a curve-loving stretchy number that hugged her figure. The rounded neckline exposed her back down to where her butt started to bubble, and there was a kick pleat at the back.

She eased on her big glasses, asked, "This too much?"

"Sensual, sexy, and sophisticated."

"This dress makes me feel pretty."

"You make that expensive dress feel the same way."

"Goodwill. Seven dollars. No, wait. Purple tag. Three dollars."

"Damn."

"Your gray suit. Those shoes will give a woman a shoegasm. Spectator shoes. Like in *The Great Gatsby*."

"Our daddy made us take pride in our appearance at all times."

"Your clothes are expensive. Nothing cheap."

"Every man or woman has a habit they have to keep under control."

"I see why you have a ten-thousand-dollar debt to the IRS. Four thousand in credit card bills. Most of that four grand was spent on wine. You buy wine the way a woman buys shoes and lingerie."

I said, "You went through my mail. Cooking. Snooping. Do you think you're my wife?"

"You owe Kaiser over one hundred thousand."

"Not cheap to stay alive in the USA."

"You sick or something?"

"Been better, been worse."

"Yes or no."

"I'm fine."

"Still being vague. Yes or no."

"Nothing to worry about."

"Move to Canada. Use their health-care system. Save that money."

I said, "Marry a girl who loves to eat poutine, Montreal smoked-meat sandwiches, and Nanaimo bars."

"Hockey-loving Canadian girls across the border love two things: Tim Hortons and black men."

"You date white men?"

"I was engaged to one." She eased into a nervous grin. "My dichotomy runs deep."

"A white man."

"A man who happened to be white."

"Still white in my book. Not judging what you prefer, just saying."

"My grandmother told me to marry a white man and improve the race. She is Portuguese, dark-skinned, and she believes in the philosophy behind the famous painting called *The Redemption of Cain*. You marry white, create a mulatto; they marry white, and now your family tree is officially white. That's her brainwashing, a way of being accepted, safe in a hostile world. You marry white until all the lynching vanishes from your family tree."

"For protection. To keep other white people from fucking with you and your kids."

"She used to say, 'Marry white, create a better life.' No, wait. It was a rhyme. Wait. Yeah. It was, 'Be a white man's wife, have a better life.' Same difference, I guess."

"At the risk of being stereotypical, I assume the white fiancé was the attorney?"

She nodded. "We were a striking couple."

"You'd make any man look good."

"We got so much attention. Too much at times."

"What about the Eastside guy?"

"We were Hood Prince Harry and Chocolate Meghan Markle." She smiled. "Nobody noticed me with him, not in a big way. I was invisible, just half of a good-looking black couple, unless we were in white spaces; then it felt dangerous being with him, or dangerous to be too black, like we could become hashtags based on our looks."

"Which scenario did you prefer?"

"No one wants to feel invisible. But no one wants to be stared at like an animal in a zoo."

"I understand your granny's philosophy, one based on fear, but I don't agree."

"You date white girls?"

"Never have."

"Why not?"

"Because God made black girls."

"Not once?"

"We need to see healthy and meaningful relationships between black people."

"It's evolving. Bit by bit. I read on Twitter that only two percent of white British people date interracially, compared to almost thirty percent for black British people."

"Your point?"

"It's that way over there and will be that way over here soon. I'm ahead of the tsunami."

"Renaissance woman in a three-dollar dress."

"You know it."

I looked behind us as we got into Miss Mini. Penny was in her living room window, watching us. Hair pulled back in a ponytail, dressed in leggings and a T-shirt that showed her belly, collegiate book in hand, in study mode.

Mocha Latte knew about my monthly debts like she was my brand-new woman. Coretta had known about my debt, but she had kept her own bills hidden. Hers had been diverted to a post office box over in the Ladera Center. She changed the passwords on her phone and social media at least twice a month. She kept all of her truths hidden like they were more valuable than the KFC recipe. Mine were always on the table. I was like that in a relationship, when I was a fool in love. If I loved you, all that I owned also belonged to you. No limits. She knew how much I made at my white-collar gig, how much I owed my creditors. She didn't know about Kaiser and City of Hope, but that didn't happen on her watch, so I had no guilt. It was like Coretta walked out and cancer walked in. She didn't know I'd been ill, had stopped working, had done treatment, had endured weeks of poison while my mom and stepdad were in Texas, while Dwayne was away on tour and André had so many comedy shows from coast to coast he was never in town either. Taking my issues to Dwayne Sr. would've been like spitting in the wind. I decided to deal with it until I needed help. I'd caught it in the early stages. I was scared. Numb. And at the same time, I didn't want anybody to worry. It was selfish of me. I knew that. Part of me had wanted to call Coretta, tell her, maybe get that ex-lover's sympathy, or enough "I still love you" empathy for her to want to take that journey with me. Now I was better. I'd done it alone.

Coretta hadn't been around long enough for me to trust her with that issue.

Maybe it was because of the way I'd found out about Coretta and Maserati Mama.

One Saturday morning, a week after Coretta had left me, while I thought that maybe she'd cool down and come back to me, I was in a barbershop on Crenshaw and Forty-Third, and a tall, dark-skinned woman sweet-walked in and sat next to me. It was Maserati Mama. I didn't know who she was then. But the Nilotic woman got in my face and laughed a nasty laugh, and when I asked the gorgeous creature what was so funny, she told me we had something in common, more like someone in common. She said Coretta was living with her in Fox Hills. She told me Coretta was her woman and wanted it to be clear that Coretta had left me, was happy now, and told me to stay out of their way. Maserati Mama said it in a room filled with black men, was in my face like she'd kick my ass if necessary, then got up, did a smooth Naomi Campbell walk to her ride, slapped on shades, and drove away. Not for that, I might've called Coretta.

We'd only been broken up seven days, but it already felt like a year in the desert with no sign of rain.

CHAPTER 20

BRICK

CENTURY BOULEVARD. LAX'S hotel row.

I parked in the pay lot, then accompanied Mocha Latte to the festive and crowded lobby. Her date hadn't arrived yet. First the plane was late; then Mocha Latte received a message, saying it was stuck on the tarmac.

It was going to take at least thirty more minutes to hear back, so we went to the bar.

I told Mocha Latte, "This is how it works when you're with me. I will give you a code phrase. It will be the first thing you say when I call your phone, or the first thing you say when you call mine. After that, I will know that things are okay and we can talk. If you say anything different, it means things are bad and I will come kick down the door. I am here to protect you. What you do is your business, but I am here to make sure you are safe."

She was nervous. Kept bouncing her leg while she sipped wine. Across the bar, I saw a good-looking woman, an Amazon of a certain age, looking at us. Our eyes met. She was a woman who looked powerful, important.

Mocha Latte pulled my attention from the woman. "Worst thing you've ever done?"

"I slept with my high school history teacher."

A surprised smile took over her face. "No lie? How old were you?"

I saw my teacher in my mind, and just like that I was back in time. She was under me, looking up at me, smiling as I stroked, her hands caressing the sides of my face. While I came, she smiled the way a proud mother did.

I answered Mocha Latte, "Fourteen."

"How old was she?"

"In her twenties. About ten years older."

"Was thinking she was in her fifties or sixties."

"Gross. If I was hitting granny panties, it would be gross."

"Ageist. There are some sexy older women out there. But twenty-four is still wrong."

"Pedophiles come in all genders."

"What was her pedigree?"

"She had a master's from Stanford."

Mocha Latte's cellular rang. She answered, then told whoever called, "No, I don't accept Bitcoins."

I chuckled. "Coochie for cryptocurrency? Is that a thing?"

"I'm not TurboTax and this ain't free free free."

She ended the call, rolled her eyes, checked her messages, went back to her drink, then back to me. "Anyway. You were fourteen. Damn, bro. Get caught getting your education? How long did that affair go on?"

"Nope. Went on for two years, until she got married and moved away."

"Until she got married or until she moved away?"

"Until she moved to Texas. She saw me after she was married."

"A pedophile and an adulteress wrapped in one."

"She married on a Sunday, and the next Sunday she took me to a motel."

"What did she say about her husband?"

"We didn't even talk about her being married."

"Sounds like she had a double life too. That duality thing is a father-fucker."

"One day she asked me to meet her in Compton. At a restaurant called Coco's. Rode my bike an hour to get there. Saw her for ten minutes. We had sex in her ride. She kissed me good-bye. She was crying. She drove away. She was just . . . gone. There was no confirmed good-bye."

"What was it like being with girls your age after that?"

"Disappointing. Physically and emotionally disappointing."

"You're good at keeping secrets."

"It's only a secret if one person knows. Therefore, technically, I own no secrets. I have some information that is, as far as I know, only shared by two, but even that is not guaranteed."

The refined woman across the bar was on her phone, her face intense, like a CEO giving orders. She looked monied, definitely high-class, and very confident. I stared; she did the same. Then I sipped my drink.

Mocha Latte said, "The teacher, Penny, your ex. You have had a rough go with women."

"As rough a go as some women have with men, only because they pick the wrong ones."

"That story fascinates me. You were sprung at fourteen, then heart-broken at sixteen."

"Young, dumb, and full of come. Now older, with two-thirds of the same irrepressible traits."

"Use protection with your pedophilic teacher?"

"Never did."

"She didn't bring any?"

"Nope."

"She was your first orgasm?"

"The first time, it was like she had taken control of my soul. I thought she had broken my penis and killed me. Twenty minutes later I wanted her to kill me again. I thought she was a witch and had worked black magic."

"She took you three levels?"

"She did. I did the same with her. She taught me how to make love to a woman."

"Whatever with that bull. Can't no fatherfucker do no three-level-orgasm shit like that."

"Seemed like we would go for hours until I was drained."

"Bareback."

"That bothers you?"

"Just surprised. You could've been a dad by the time you were fifteen."

"Me and my older brother would have had kids the same age."

"Wow, Brick. Wow. I didn't have sex until I was a junior in college."

"So that's the long answer to your question."

She smiled, shook her head with her thoughts, chuckled, and moved her faux-Afro from her face.

I asked, "What?"

"This is odd, but nice. Talking. Laughing. Being honest. No holds barred. Getting to know each other. Drinks. Dressed up at a bar. Sitting this close. Sort of feels like a date. Or the way I want one to feel."

"Yeah. Drinks. Music. Good company. Sort of does feel exciting . . . like a date."

She said, "You have BDE."

"What's that?"

She winked. "It's a good thing. You have BDE and don't even know you have BDE."

I looked around the room at all the women and wondered how

many were here for the same reason as Mocha Latte. Knowing Penny and this pace of asses made me see the world in a different way.

I said, "The cougars are on the prowl. That table over there is MILF City."

She asked, "You know the tale of two wolves?"

"That wolf you feed becomes stronger."

"We're watching them struggle with the two wolves inside. They have husbands. Wives. Boyfriends. Girlfriends. Children. And they are here, at a bar, dressed up, struggling, surrendering, feeding a wolf."

I asked, "Why are they here, still searching, still hungry, never satisfied?"

"Life is too much for them, and not enough at the same time. They probably have love, or lovers, but they're hungry for a better love. In the meantime, they deal with the wolves inside begging to be fed."

"So it goes."

As if she had read my mind, she said, "At least six, maybe eight, people in here are working."

"You can tell?"

"That white guy talking to the brother with the locks? The brother is working. The white guy is his client. Subtle body language. I've seen the brother around here before. The redheaded girl having dinner with the man old enough to be her grandfather is working too. The two Filipina-looking girls at the bar are looking for work."

"This is your world."

"I'm an engineer. This is their world. This is just a layover for me, not the destination."

"I stand corrected." Then I checked the time again. "You said you know this client?"

"Doctor from Yale. Born in Detroit. Passes through here once a month or so."

I asked, "How long you want to wait for your paycheck to show up?"

"Twenty more minutes. We can chill and watch people struggle with the seven deadly sins."

"If you get stood up, we can get dinner at Katana in Hollywood, eat sushi, maybe go dance."

She brightened up. "That would be nice."

"I like the way you dance."

"Yeah? You were watching me at Savoy?"

"Hard not to look at you. The way you move. You almost shut it down."

She faced me head-on. "Is that right? Why were you looking at me?"

"Beauty is an aphrodisiac of which you are not in short supply. I see an abundance. You're intelligent and gorgeous, and you make the best pancakes. I'm just being honest and speaking my mind."

"Don't play with me like that. Don't say things like that to me. It does stuff to me."

"Don't make me blueberry flapjacks. Don't be smart. Don't make me laugh. Don't make me sit here and wish I had met you instead of Coretta. Don't smile at me the way you smile at me. It does stuff to me."

"Stop playing, Brick."

"You're the perfect woman."

"Nobody wants me."

"Bullshit. A man will get with you and not know how to let go."

"Look at Angelina Jolie. Brad Pitt grew tired of fucking her. Ain't no hope for me."

Again, there was a moment between us. Eye contact. Imagining.

She raised her drink to mine. "Here's to the people who know the real me but still stick around."

Jazz played as our fingers almost touched.

She said, "I saw the medicines lined up on your dresser. Ondansetron. Sildenafil. Terbinafine. Prednisone. Hydroxyzine. Prochlorperazine. Gabapentin. You know I had to google all that shit."

"The sildenafil was for Coretta."

"I'll bet it was."

"It was. What I have left is what we didn't use."

"She was working you that hard?"

"We were pretty hot for a while."

"Who is the pill for now?"

"Nobody. I don't need it. We just used it for kicks. Was like being on steroids."

"On the serious tip, you're okay? Those other meds add up to cancer."

"I'm fine. Never been better. I was one of the lucky ones. Got in early before it took root."

"You sure?"

"Had some peripheral neuropathy, but it's gone now. Doctor said being young and fit helped."

"Did you try using ice gloves?"

"Oh yeah. Bought a pair of NatraCure cold therapy socks on Amazon."

"Those are still experimental."

"Doctor said they were for people on a different chemo, but I used them anyway."

"Too many black men don't go to the doctor, and when they do, it's too late."

"Girl I met in chemo, Ericka Stockwell, she told me the same thing."

"Oh, got an empathy hookup? I hear cancer patients do that."

"Met her in passing on her last day, actually. After your final treatment is done, you get to ring the bell. She was with her fiancé, or husband, didn't ask. It's an emotional moment. She cried. Her man cried. I cried. Cried again when I got to ring that bell for myself. Felt like the world applauded for me that day. I got my freedom back."

"Who was there with you when you got to ring that bell of freedom?"

"Nobody. I was by myself."

She touched my hand, looked sad. Just like that, I was closer to her than I'd ever been to Coretta.

She said, "You know I was engaged to two men at once. I told you all of my business. So, tell me about your past girlfriends, before the one we saw at Roscoe's, and after your freaky teacher."

I told her about Stephanie Nwabuzor, from Savannah, whose parents were Nigerian and wanted her to marry a fellow Nigerian. That was four years ago. Miko Crawford from Little Rock, three years ago. Ann-Marie Moreau, a black French girl from Houston, was right before Coretta.

I said, "When I met Coretta, I thought she was the end-all, be-all."

Mocha Latte asked, "Who was best in bed?"

"It wasn't a contest."

"It's always a contest. Who?"

"Each brought her own sexual proclivities and skill set and was perfect in her own way."

"Who was the smart one? Mr. Master's Degree, I can tell you like shrewd girls. You have to see how keen a girl is, what her personality is like, and then you decide if she's beautiful to you."

"Maybe. All had advanced degrees."

Mocha Latte put on a devilish smile. "Brick, tell me the most embarrassing thing you've ever done."

"Oh God. We going there? Are we really going there?"

"I see it in your face. The memory. Tell me."

"When I was nine, I had to pick a song at random, a church song, and do a solo."

"Okay."

"I picked a song I heard my momma singing at home all the time."

"What song?"

"'Stairway to Heaven' by the O'Jays."

"Get out."

"Had the word *heaven* in the title. Momma's favorite song. Learned every word, taught myself to play it on the piano. I sat in front of the congregation of three hundred, played the piano, and sang my heart out."

"That song is straight up about sex and having an orgasm."

"I thought the O'Jays were praising Jesus and talking about going to see God."

"You sat in church on a Sunday and sang a song about busting a nut?"

"I was nine. I had no idea what a 'road to ecstasy' was. And I don't think half the women in church knew either. I thought it was about people trying to get into heaven, going up one step at a time. I tore it up when I got to the part about heaven being right here on earth, was expecting them to open the doors of the church and take new members. I sang my heart out. Sang every word. When I was done, the church was quiet, and my mom was mortified."

"What happened when you finished singing about sex on a Sunday in the house of the Lord?"

"Preacher asked me why I picked that song. I said it was my momma's favorite church song."

"What did your momma do?"

"She spanked my ass, we changed churches, and I was never allowed to sing again."

"Yeah, that shit was embarrassing. I can't top that."

"No, tell me the dirtiest thing you've ever done."

"One client paid me to watch him suck himself off. Autofellatio. He was huge."

"Wow."

"A mouth is a mouth, quite simply. Even if it's your own."

"What else?"

"There was another client who practiced eproctophilia."

"I have no idea what that is."

"Eproctophilia is the sexual fetish of farts."

"That's a thing? Someone paid you top dollar to . . . to do what exactly?"

"So, Mr. Poot Lover would feed me cans of beans, then put his face in my booty and I'd . . . *dammit*."

Mocha Latte's phone buzzed and startled her. She looked at the text message, lost some of her teasing smile. She wore the look of a woman who was suddenly disappointed about something.

I asked, "What happened? Client's not coming?"

Mocha Latte waved toward the entrance to the bar. "The opposite. My client is here."

Curious, a little jealous, I wanted to see the scoundrel who was going to feed one of his wolves tonight. I saw men of every nationality entering the bar, powerful men in suits; then I saw the customer wave at Mocha Latte.

CHAPTER 21

BRICK

COMING TOWARD US, smiling, was a curvaceous lady. She was a freckle-faced woman, each freckle a snowflake. She had the type of well-to-do beauty that was hard to see and not become transfixed.

I told Mocha Latte, "I'll go and come back when you call."

"Chill out here. I'll be done with her in thirty minutes, no more than an hour."

The client wore a beautiful, multicolored, high-fashion hijab. She rocked skinny jeans and a loose, faded, long-sleeved jean shirt that covered her arms to her wrists. When she was closer, I saw she had eyes the color of sand. At least five nine in low heels. I'd guess she was in her mid-twenties, early thirties at the most.

The client asked Mocha Latte, "How's my favorite marathon runner?"

"You made it. I was getting worried."

"Did I interrupt your conversation?"

She had a nice voice, professional, sounded East Coast.

Mocha Latte said, "He's driving me."

"Never knew you had a driver."

Mocha Latte said, "If I dress like this and sit in a bar at an airport hotel, next thing you know, two men will be trying to kill each other to get me to kiss the winner on the cheek. My friend keeps the wolves away."

The client smiled. "Sorry I took so long. Airport security is racist. My running terrified them."

Mocha Latte said, "His name is Brick."

We shook hands. I saw a hint of concern on her face.

I said, "I'm not a police officer. I don't do any work with law enforcement."

She relaxed, exhaled like she felt safe. This wasn't entrapment.

Mocha Latte said, "He's copper-bottomed. Our conversations will stay private."

I thought they would leave right away, go do whatever they had planned to do for the next hour, but the graduate from Yale pulled up the barstool next to Mocha Latte. "How have you been?"

"I could say I've been unhappy, still struggling intellectually, spiritually, and financially, but there is always someone out there who has it worse. So, I'll just say, I'm still here. Still fighting a good fight."

"Oh, I so feel you on that. My husband . . . let's just say when you marry someone, you take on all of their issues, and all of their family's issues . . . It has been one thing after the other for five years."

"Communication is the key in every relationship."

"What's the point of communicating if it's all lies? Expecting honesty is expecting too much?"

Without a segue, Mocha Latte asked her client, "How are we for time?"

"If I get back to LAX in two hours, it'll give security enough time to harass me, so I should be fine."

"Let's get you a drink."

"Please do."

"On your American Express? If that's cool."

"Of course. I will take care of the bill. Same as before."

"A Yale graduate working at the nation's top hospital can afford a couple of drinks."

"Doctors have student loans like you would not believe. Girl, I stay broke."

Mocha Latte laughed. "Your broke ain't like my broke. Your broke incudes a mansion."

The client touched Mocha Latte's thigh. "That's a dress made for undressing."

Mocha Latte bounced her leg. "You have your room key?"

"I have it."

"Should we go upstairs?"

"Someone is anxious."

"Was just trying to be considerate."

The client whispered, "When I am with you, I am nervous. This is different, you know? I text you provocative messages, say bold things; then when I get here, I get so very nervous. This conflict is not an easy one to resolve. I always want you so badly. Crave to feel your hands embracing me, and your hugs feel so good. All day I have imagined the taste of your tongue and wanted to suck your lips. Turns me on to be naked in front of you. Miss the way you snuggle with me. Enjoy feeling your skin, your legs intertwined with mine. Your touch, the slightest touch from you makes me wet. I try to control myself when I'm with you. Sometimes, like now, I feel like I want to scream. I could make love to you all night and then all day."

She said those things the way I was accustomed to a woman talking to a man, or a man to a woman.

Mocha Latte leaned into her. "Touch me."

"First, do that thing you do with your tongue. Make it touch your philtrum, then, you know."

Mocha Latte took a breath and made her tongue snake from her mouth. It touched the indent just above her upper lip; then it wiggled to the tip of her nose. The client hummed, remembering a good time. After that, Mocha Latte made that flesh go beyond the bottom of her chin. She made it do the wave, rolled it like a taco, then made it move like a snake. They grinned at each other, both biting the corners of their lips. Mocha Latte uncrossed her legs, put the client's hand in her lap, then discreetly under her dress. Mocha Latte's eyes tightened; she hummed like a soft fire on a winter day. Her client hummed and licked her lips, famished.

Mocha Latte whispered, "That feels good."

"You are an oyster with a hardening pearl."

"You're the same."

"I feel like an animal with you. Animals don't know sin. Animals are free."

In a sultry voice Mocha Latte said, "Hour starts when we get in the room."

The client licked her fingers, then put her fingers in Mocha Latte's mouth for a quick second, then took her hand back and grinned.

Mocha Latte asked, "Mind paying for my driver's drink too?"

The client flagged down the bartender and went to take care of the tab.

Mocha Latte leaned to me, whispered, "The dignified woman across the bar is still checking you out."

"The MILF? She probably has a thing for sexy chocolate like you."

Mocha Latte winked at me. "I'll be upstairs. Go investigate."

"My job is to wait in Barstow while you go to Vegas. I'll be right here until you're done."

The client wrapped up the bill, then eased off her barstool. Mocha Latte did the same, adjusted her black dress, then finger waved good-bye to me. Her client looked back, and her hijab framed the kind of smile that told me she hoped I was as discreet as the beautiful black woman she was renting by the hour.

As soon as they disappeared, I googled BDE, saw what it meant, then smiled at the compliment.

I took in the people at the bar dealing with their two wolves, strangers in need of aged alcohol and a new friend for a few hours, felt the heat between them all, felt capitalism and biology at play. Biology kept the escorts of the night in business. Biology kept wedding chapels booked and divorce courts filled with people ready to try again. Biology made burn victims run back into another blazing fire. Biology had sent me to Penny when Penny had called me to soothe her pain. Biology had sent Mocha Latte to two men and made it impossible to decide on one. Biology had sent Christiana to an unfaithful husband, a man she didn't know as well as she had assumed. That same biology had sent Christiana's sister to that same stranger. Biology had sent Dwayne to Frenchie, or Frenchie to Dwayne, depending on whose version of their complicated love affair you believed.

Biology whispered in my ear, voice like honey, then gently kissed my face.

To shake it off, I responded to a message from someone in Santa Monica interested in buying two bottles of high-end wine. I scheduled a meeting with them at the Farmers Market in the Grove tomorrow.

Anything to distract me from biology.

One of the televisions in the bar was on CNN. Twenty million people without food. I was reading the closed captions when my phone rang. It was Mocha Latte. I didn't recognize her voice at first. It was deep. Husky. Fifteen minutes had passed. She said the code phrase so I'd know everything was okay, but something must have gone wrong for her to call so soon.

Mocha Latte took a breath, let out a little moan. "My date wants you to help us do something."

"What does that mean?"

"Room 1237. Come up in ten."

"My job is to wait in Barstow. I'm waiting in Barstow. Enjoy Vegas."

"Come to Vegas in ten. You'll be done in two, and you can go back to Barstow."

Mocha Latte hung up. I sat back, sipped my Corona, and within seconds, my phone rang again. It was Coretta. My heart stopped, and I was going to let it roll to voice mail, but I answered.

She hesitated, then said my name like it weighed a thousand pounds. "Brick."

Her name weighed twice that. "Coretta."

"That was a surprise. Stepping out of Roscoe's and *bam*. There you were."

I said, "Only took six months for us to cross paths again."

"I guess LA is shrinking."

"Coretta, are you drunk? You fell off the wagon and bumped your pretty little head?"

She made a nasty sound. "You never asked me to come back. Not once."

"You landed on a softer pillow. Two softer pillows based on her cleavage."

"Do you even care that I left you? Did you ever care?"

"You're drunk."

"Do you think you were fair?"

"Flip this shit; give me your résumé, say I was spending and not paying one bill, not paying rent, say you had no idea how much money I made, if I had any savings, what my portfolio looked like, and your girls would've told you that was too many red flags. They would have told you not to marry me, to break up, and walk away running."

"We were living like we were married. I was cooking for you, making you breakfast seven days a week, washing your laundry every Friday, sucking your dick on demand. Your dick was the first dick I ever sucked. I don't like dicks like that, but I did that for you. I even tried to swallow. For you. On your birthday. I spent months putting up with your OCD, then all of a sudden you needed to look over my check stubs, credit cards, and see my fucking tax forms like you worked for the muh-fuckin', goddamn IRS? You actually wanted me to have your accountant, someone I didn't know, look over my personal life, so you could decide if I was good enough to marry you? Who does that?"

"Smart people who don't want to be outsmarted by love."

"Brick."

"If you were going to be part of my life forever, was that too much to ask?"

"I made you breakfast every goddamn morning. And you *never* had to ask."

"All I asked you to do was put it all on the table. Same as I had done. I didn't hide anything from you. I operated under full disclosure, but you hid your shit like you'd colluded with Russia."

She slurred, "Maserati Mama ain't complaining. She'll do anything for me. She'd save two million dollars to get Beyoncé to perform at our wedding, if I wanted her to. That's how much she loves me."

"Give it time. What you have is still new and she's blinded by the feel-good nights."

"You're jealous. You live off Crenshaw. Nigga, I'm living in Fox Hills now. Being chauffeured in a luxury car. Eating crab legs whenever I feel like it. Ain't nobody got time for a dumb-ass credit report. That whole credit system is used to keep black people down, and you wanted to come at me with that stupid shit as a deal breaker?"

"Are we done here?"

"Are you capable of loving anybody unconditionally?"

"I let you move in. You paid no rent. I took care of you. That meant I loved you."

"Not un-fucking-conditionally. If people love each other and want to be together, then they will be together, no matter what. It doesn't matter if it's man and woman or woman and woman. Love doesn't care about a damn credit score or student loans or a nasty toilet. Why were you such an asshole? I would have walked across Northeast Greenland National Park in flip-flops and a thong to be with you."

"You are really drunk."

Coretta sipped her poison. "I need to arrange to get the things I left at your funky little apartment."

"To the right, to the right, everything you own is in a box to the right."

"I should have never dated you, never should have made you breakfast."

"Don't forget to flush twice. And add some roughage to your diet. And bleach will get rid of that brown ring."

I hung up. She was plastered, crying out in pain, and I hung up on her.

I headed toward the elevator, my mind stuck on Coretta. Those mornings she woke up in need, she'd reach back, stroke me until I was awake, then mount me, that intense look on her face as she went up and down, riding strong, sweat dripping down her back, scarf coming loose on her head, heat from each ragged exhale warming my face, taking dick like she owned dick. By the third minute she was coming, and by the fourth minute, I was coming hard while she came her second time. The earthquake inside her created a tsunami inside of me. Morning sex was quick—she had to get to work, and I had to get to my white-collar gig at the widget factory in Santa Monica. It was before the cancer, before I took off work. Then at nighttime, Coretta put on a negligee and wanted to be three levels deep as soon as the sun dozed off. Some weekends we didn't leave the crib, and it was wine, food, and nymphomania meeting satyriasis. The sex was off the chains, never a bad session, but outrageous sex almost on the daily wasn't enough to keep us together. If sex kept people together, divorce lawyers would be out of business.

Everybody needed love. We were born crying for love, crying to be nurtured. We never stopped crying. We just learned to cry in different ways. At five o'clock every bar in the city was packed with people who were crying out to the world, using martinis or Jack and Coke as their evening pacifiers while they searched for someone to take them to their bosom and love them through the night. People just needed to make it through the night.

Every night since Coretta left, I've needed to make it through the night.

My wolves were growling, growling, growling.

My duality howled to be set free.

I almost called Coretta back, wanted to go to her, take her, fuck her senseless, get this rage out of me, put my dick so deep inside her she couldn't help but to love me the rest of her life, but the door to the elevator opened and the sudden brightness cleared my motherfucking head. Six months ago, she moved to Fox Hills and moved on and fed one of the wolves growling inside her. Sex had been good, but business was bad.

I still missed her.

CHAPTER 22

BRICK

ROOM 1237.

Mocha Latte opened the door and hurried me inside the suite. She was nude except for high heels and an impish mask like the ones they wore at Mardi Gras. She saw surprise in my eyes and shrugged. She had been oiled and her dark skin shined like a diamond, oiled so well there was no ash in the crack of her perky little ass.

Mocha Latte handed me a cell phone. "Record."

"What?"

"Mostly her face. Her expression. Keep it erotic, not nasty. Well, not too nasty."

"What about you?"

"I'm cool. This hair. This mask. No one can recognize me."

"Okay."

"Bring that BDE this way."

Mocha Latte fluffed her purple Afro. I followed the out-of-work engineer. Lights were off, but scented candles had been lit. Her client was on the bed, hands up over her head, a cat on a hot tin roof. She squeezed her thighs together, moaned like she had been close to orgasm when Mocha Latte left to answer the door.

The client moaned, "Who dareth to knock at my door while I am in such a distressed state?"

"It was the knight thou requesteth."

"Return to me at once and hark to the sonnet I sing when you take me beyond the heavens."

Mocha Latte pushed the client's legs apart, crawled on top of her. They caressed, took deep breaths. Soft kisses. Heavy breathing. I aimed the phone at them. The client pulled Mocha Latte's face to hers, kissed, kissed, kissed. I chronicled their meeting at the first order of the sewing circle.

Mocha Latte was wicked with her tongue. It surprised me, seeing her do that, work it like that. No one knew a woman like a woman. She was methodical, slow, comprehensive. The client's arousal was outstanding. Her moans were a love song. Mocha Latte took it slow, like it was a Sunday morning ride down Pacific Coast Highway. I studied her technique, learned. She focused on a circular motion that made the client say things in her original tongue mixed with things in her second language, a mellow ride to a searing orgasm.

Mocha Latte looked my way, voice soft, "Art thou recording our queen in her splendor and beauty?"

"Right, right."

I had gotten caught up watching, felt heat and arousal, then swallowed, tried to shake it off. Biology ran its fingers up and down my spine, sucked on my ear, dared me to ignore its touch.

The client grabbed the sheets and moaned. She also wore a mask. It was secure, not slipping from her face.

Mocha Latte paused and told me, "Come hither, Lancelot. Sucketh her toes. She'll reward you handsomely."

Phone in hand, still recording, I asked, "Sucketh her toes?"

"Art mine own words unclear?"

I went to the prestigious doctor who matriculated to and graduated from Yale, and while Mocha Latte pleased her, I took the client's small foot in my nervous hand. My touch made her jerk like she felt a new level of stimulation. Her nerves were alive. Her senses were heightened. Her toes were manicured. Feet soft.

Mocha Latte whispered, "It's okay. She wants this. She said she's attracted to you."

I rubbed the client's foot against my nose. Clean. That woke up my fetish. A foot fetish. Since I was fourteen, when my teacher had turned me out, I'd had a foot fetish. I kissed Yale up and down her calves, kissed to her heels, licked across her feet, and finally took her small toes in my mouth, sucked till her back arched.

Mocha Latte teased her lips. Rubbed her hands down her thighs, played with her inside and outside with her tongue. Tongue, thumb, middle finger, all worked in concert, and that concert made the client sing like a symphony.

Mocha Latte paused. "Put the phone down for a second. Let it keep recording though."

"Put it where?"

"Give it to our queen."

The client held the camera, stared into it, amazed and aroused by her own erotic expressions.

I rubbed the client's legs, felt her softness, her response to my touch sensual and encouraging. It made my nature rise. I got into it. The energy moved from her body into mine, and I made love to her foot.

Mocha Latte whispered, "Isn't Queen Guinevere beautiful?"

I exhaled. "She is. She glows like she is hotter than the sun at summer solstice."

"Thou art Shakespearienced."

"I am, my melanin-blessed lady."

"I'm supris'd. Thee hoyday me at ev'ry freakin' turneth. I did study the bard in univ'rsity as an elective."

"Mine own fusty'r broth'r is in the theat'r, a thespian, and that high-sighted lover of Shakespeare forced us to holp learneth his lines, and ov'r the years that gent did teach us much about the most famous of all bards as well."

"Would thou make love to her?"

I took a breath. "The king wouldst behead me."

"How dareth thee mention King Arthur?"

"Please forgive me for casting his shadow against the mure."

"My mistress needeth to asketh nay one. If't be true the lady hests, 'twill beest done."

"Then with her permission."

"Doest thou want to prithee the queen, Lancelot?"

"It's up to the queen."

"She wants thou. Pull Excalibur from its sheath."

"The queen has to say she wants me to doeth that, not thou, lest I be beheaded at once."

The client nodded and moaned. "Taketh it out."

Mocha Latte said, "Remove Excalibur from its sheath."

The client moaned again, demanded. "Taketh it out at once."

"The queen wants to seeth thine sword; test thine weapon while I please our queen."

"I shall reward you handsomely. I only want to see thine sword, nothing more."

I was scared, but I was excited. Afraid and aroused. I was caught up in this. It was like I had committed to something by entering Vegas and the only way out was to see it through to its conclusion.

I unzipped my pants. Did that like I was in a trance.

Mocha Latte saw my cock and whispered, "Wow."

The client said, "Excalibur is beautiful."

She reached for me, touched me, held me, stroked me. I felt a hallelujah rising in my soul.

She shivered, gyrated, moaned in Arabic, then sang, "Ooooo-oooo."

Mocha Latte teased her. "What is your desire? What else?"

"To feel Excalibur awaken the neglected love in my heart."

I moaned, felt both dizzy and over-aroused. I wasn't supposed to be in Vegas. My job was to wait in Barstow, maybe Victorville. But I was in Sin City. I needed to dial this back, but it had too much momentum.

Mocha Latte stared, surprised, momentarily mesmerized. She moved me away from the client, out of her reach, left her writhing and demanding to feel me in her hand again.

Mocha Latte whispered, "Do thou want to feel Excalibur again?"

The client whispered, "I am your queen and I shall have that which I deserve."

Mocha Latte said, "To experience Excalibur, Queen Guinevere, that wilt cost extra."

"My demimonde, and what doth I receiveth f'r mine own wage?"

"Thee shall receiveth Excalibur."

"Bid me thy most wondrous off'r."

Mocha Latte massaged the client, kept her aroused, did the upsale and cross-sale, told her the fee to have Excalibur, as if I had no say, as if I was on the auction block. Or just on the block. Whoever Mocha Latte was now, she wasn't the woman who'd made blueberry pancakes the other morning. Not the woman who was walking in her sleep, not the woman who hated being an escort. Her fire made the sun seem like ice.

The client demanded, "Bringeth me Excalibur."

She took me in her mouth and made me coo. Mocha Latte recorded the client's distorted face. Then Mocha Latte put the phone down. The client had me weak. I tried not to moan, but I moaned. The client set me free.

"Removeth thine armor. I want to seeth thy body in its truth."

I hesitated.

It was like it had been with Dwayne at breakfast, when he had ordered food and a hoodie, had made a promise he couldn't fulfill, and I paid to keep him from being embarrassed. Mocha Latte had promised something, and I felt like if I backed away, she'd be shamefaced. All I had to do was turn around, walk my erection back to Barstow.

I came out of my clothing, then fell between our queen's generous thighs. She put my cock inside her, no pretense, no hesitation. I was inside a woman I'd met less than an hour ago, a woman who had never told me her name. We were strangers. Not knowing me, controlling me, this shit excited her. She moved like she was possessed, danced with the heat of the devil as she glowed like an angel. The client positioned herself, moved so she could have us both at once. She wanted the GFE-BFE she'd paid for. Mocha Latte stared at me while the client pleased her. I pleased the client. Mocha Latte looked into my eyes, and we exhaled, had a moment, and despite the third set of moans, it felt like it was just us in the room. Mocha Latte moved, had a small orgasm, not sure if it was real or pretense, and the client rolled away, aroused. On fire, I grabbed Mocha Latte, pulled her to me, turned her over, was about to take her from the back, rubbed my erection against her slit, against dampness, heard the sweet, sticky sound. She jerked like feeling my hardness shocked her back to reality, and she moved away from me, shaking her head. I had imagined something downstairs, some connection, some desire that didn't exist.

"We hast nay contract, Lancelot. If thee putteth Excalibur inside me, we shall hast a problem."

"Touching thee in such a manner, it wast mine own misprision. Mine own mistaketh to desire to please you as I do the queen, my lady. I didst not meaneth to enter thee; if't be true yond wast not to beest. Mine own cock wast anxious, out of controleth, but now things art cleareth."

The client laughed at us and mounted me. Her full figure amazing, her softness supreme. That feeling was gold. I sank inside heaven, and she moved like she needed to come or die trying. Mocha Latte kissed her queen's legs, sucked her breasts, then came to me, looked me in my face while the queen sang in ten octaves, touched my lips, smiled, winked. Mocha Latte had me stop for a moment. She got on her back, had the client get on top of her, so they could be breast to breast, kissing, inhaling and exhaling, while I took the client from the back.

The client kissed and bit on Mocha Latte as if Mocha Latte was rocking her to heaven. The client was pulled into Orgasmland. Soon, she was three levels deep. Lost in her climaxes, trembling, moaning, moving, grabbing, scratching, biting, coming, coming, coming, then shuddering like she was experiencing the phenomenon called Catatumbo lightning, riding more lightning than struck Lake Maracaibo in Venezuela. Mind, body, soul, she was mine.

CHAPTER 23

BRICK

THE GLOWING WOMEN were on the bed together, in the center, panting. The scent from three had blended into one decadent aroma. The client had her phone out again, and they took a few selfies; then they took their masks off. They giggled the way young girls did after sex. I rested at the foot of the bed, like a wench, a bed warmer, a phallic, an accessory to their impishness. Objectification done, I had been moved aside, put on a low shelf.

I didn't know if I should stay in Vegas or stagger back to Barstow, but since no one said for me to leave, I stayed.

In a dreamy voice that carried a fresh huskiness, the client said, "That was unexpected and amazing."

Mocha Latte wiggled like she was tingling. "Any other fantasy I can help you with?"

The client wiggled in her own way, hummed. "I really want to have sex with two handsome men."

"A Devil's Triangle."

"Is that what it's called?"

"I can set it up for you. Can be there too, to keep you comfortable, if you want. Fly me to wherever you are, and I'll be yours. Would be great to do that out of the country. Maybe in Paris, next time you go."

"Let me think on that before I commit. Maybe it could be one man and you can wear the strap-on like you did the last few times. That could be interesting. Or maybe this undertaking might be where I draw the line."

"Just let me know, and I can make it happen."

The client looked at me. "Kiss me."

I did, slow and easy. She bit my lips, sucked my tongue, moaned into my mouth.

The alarm on Mocha Latte's phone sounded. Mine went off at the same time.

Almost at the same moment, we moved and turned our phones off.

"Time is up," Mocha Latte said kindly, yet professionally. "Unless you want to pay for more."

"Don't tempt me. I'm calculating how much time I have in my head. It would be cutting it close."

"Never know when we will hook up again. Especially like this."

The client squeezed her thighs, hummed, looked at the clock. "Another half hour."

"I only charge by the hour."

"You're going to have me so broke."

"Once again, your broke and my broke are not the same broke. The one percenters' broke means they have to put their Lamborghini in the shop and drive the Porsche to the pier to board their mega-yacht."

They kissed some more. Soft, sweet kisses. Mocha Latte was working her. She looked at me while I watched them, and she winked at me. This wasn't real. Not for Mocha Latte. It was real for the client.

Mocha Latte said, "Another two hundred for my friend, if you want him to stay with us."

"That was spontaneous. Inviting him. Hadn't planned on that."

"Yeah."

"I enjoyed him. It felt genuine, like he was really into me. I liked that."

"And if he can rise to the occasion, you can enjoy him some more before your flight."

"You enjoy him?"

"Our relationship is professional."

"You're sexy. He's handsome. You looked like the perfect couple at the bar."

"You watched us?"

"For a couple of minutes. Saw you two laughing and talking. It looked very intimate. I wasn't sure if he was a customer, or if you had met someone while waiting. Was nervous about coming to you."

Mocha Latte hummed, wiggled again. "You ready for more?"

"I have a better idea." The client grinned. "I want to watch him make you climb the damn walls."

Mocha Latte stopped wiggling. "He's here for you, not for me."

"You've been with me in ways no other lover has ever been with me. You watched me with him. No one has ever watched me before. Now I want to watch you with a man; see what you're like with a man."

"He's here for you."

"Everything has a price."

"He's your treat, not mine."

"How much would that cost?"

"I'm serious."

"So am I. To watch him please you, how much?"

Mocha Latte inhaled sharply. "That will cost a lot."

"Is there a problem?"

"Twice my normal rate."

"I'll pay fifty percent more."

"Double."

"Fifty percent. Your emolument will be your standard plus an additional fifty percent."

"Seventy-five percent more is my bottom line."

"Fifty is mine."

"I'm worth it."

"Be reasonable."

"Double. You can afford it."

"Fifty. Unless you'd rather I take my coins back home, or maybe elsewhere."

"Okay. But you have to do a *sixty* percent increase over my normal as a compromise."

"Includes kissing?"

"No, kissing him costs more."

"Why?"

"It's as dangerous as unsafe sex. Over eighty million bacteria are transmitted during one kiss. I could catch meningococcal meningitis. I'd die in twenty-four hours. You're a doctor. You know I'm not spitting bullshit. Eighty million bacteria passed in one kiss. Kissing is dangerous. Kissing strangers is a risk."

"You didn't get the MCV4 vaccine?"

"Eighty million bacteria."

"Never mind. Okay. Sure. How much for kissing?"

Mocha Latte told the doctor the extraordinary price for the prescription.

"Why so much to kiss?"

"I just told you."

"You kiss me."

"The fee is built into the price you pay."

"Kissing should be free."

"So should health care and college tuition, yet I have to pay for both."

"Fine. I'll pay."

Mocha Latte stalled the negotiation. "You have that much? Or should I get my credit card reader?"

"I have cash. Be worth it."

Mocha Latte said, "My condoms are in my bag."

The client said, "No. Bareback. I hate watching sex when they wear condoms."

Mocha Latte paused, shook her head side to side, like that was a deal breaker, but she bit her lip, and I saw her wrestling with her financial goals and inner demons before she answered, "That doubles the price."

The client hesitated, sighed like the price was too high, but dropped more money on the nightstand.

Mocha Latte went to count the money, still naked and in high heels, her taut ass unintentionally moving in a seductive manner. I felt a chill. Talking money in the middle of sex changed the energy in the room.

Mocha Latte hesitated. "What do you want to see? MFF? Mediterranean? HTUMA?"

"Kiss. I want to see you kiss. Be boyfriend and girlfriend. Act like you're lovers."

"HME."

"Yes, honeymoon experience."

The client sashayed back to me, her eyes on fire with power and desire, took me in her mouth like she owned me. She had oral skills, was performing for Mocha Latte, and that competition had me higher than Mount Denali. Power corrupts. Absolute power corrupts, absolutely.

The client said, "I want a show. I want to see what you're like with him, with a man, my love."

"I should have brought the strap-on."

"It's not the same. Not even with butt plugs."

Mocha Latte rested on her back, waited for me. The client kissed me over and over, each kiss a sweet, gentle breeze, and each thirsty kiss took my breath away. I went to Mocha Latte, crawled to her and looked into her eyes as I traced my fingers along her marathon-running legs. This was different, being sent to make love to a woman, being commanded to make love to a woman like I had no say in the matter. We had become temporary slaves.

The client told me, "Downtown. Go downtown. I want to see that. Want to watch her face."

I looked at Mocha Latte's beautiful sex. It was smooth, a slit across faultless skin. It looked like it had never been intruded. I gave her my tongue, tasted her. The darker the berry, the sweeter the juice. I gave Mocha Latte my mouth, swipes of tongue, fingers, and lips. One at a time, her arms fell to her sides, as if an act of submission. Her breathing thickened, each exhale a sweet hallelujah. Soon she jerked, moaned my name. Flesh against flesh felt good. Her hands moved down to the top of my head. She relaxed into the heat of the fire. The client told me to stop, to get inside her, and I moved back between Mocha Latte's thighs, worked my erection inside her. It was like a firm handshake. She was tight. She made sounds like it hurt so good, like it hurt too good. I liked that.

The client whispered, "Kiss him like you're in love. Kiss her like you need kissing badly."

Kissing her felt odd, unmotivated by my own lust, but directed by the lust of another. But as we kissed, lust woke up and put its claws in her. Same happened to me. It went on and on, was powerful, almost impossible to stop. I kissed her, sucked her neck, stroked her.

Mocha Latte held my face, trembled. "Jesus, Brick. Okay. Okay. You got me. You got me."

"I got you?"

"You got me. You're about to make me come. You're gonna make my pussy come."

The client whispered, "Now pull out, stop stroking her, and go down on her again."

"I'm about to come, and it's a big come."

"Pull out before she comes."

We kissed and moved like we didn't want to stop, but the command broke that spell. It was hard to back away, but I did. Mocha Latte rocked like it had hurt for me to stop when I did. My breathing turned shallow as I parted Mocha Latte's legs again. Her back arched when she felt my soft tongue against her raging fire. She held my head, held it like she was trying to keep it in place, like she needed my tongue to go eleven inches deeper. She wiggled against me, rolled her hips, strained, desperate to come. Her whimpers and groans sounded bleak, distant, like she was falling, like she was out of control. She squeezed her breasts, shook and clawed at the bed, nails dragging the material. She covered her face, muffled her sounds, before she held the back of my neck. She put the palm of her hand to my forehead, pushed me away as she shivered, stopped me from savoring her into the heart of an orgasm.

The client went to her, touched her, kissed her. "Oh, that was nice. Now I need him inside you."

"I can't right now."

"You can." She picked up Mocha Latte's mask, put it back on her. "I paid you, and you will."

The client picked up the other mask, put it back on, then changed her mind, put it on me, made it fit the best she could. She picked up her phone and aimed it at Mocha Latte, recording. We performed facing each other. Stared into each other's eyes, inhaling, exhaling. Being inside her felt like nothing I'd ever felt before. Her nostrils flared. Her left leg quaked. She closed her eyes, panting like she was drowning. I was on top, on my knees, had her ankles on my shoulders. The client put the camera away and kissed Mocha Latte while I obeyed her commands.

The client whispered, "That's me inside of you."

"Yeah?"

"Yeah. Like the way I feel? That's me hitting it from behind, kitten. Raise your ass up for me. I wish I had my toys. Would love to see you being filled by your friend and me with my strap-on at the same time."

Mocha Latte cursed and hissed like it ached, frowned like she felt little spasms.

Mocha Latte moaned, "Stop."

The client whispered with power, "Don't stop."

"Stop trying to make my pussy come. I'm going to come too hard. Don't make my pussy come like that."

"Make her come; make her come hard."

Mocha Latte started to come, and when the orgasm was at its height, another orgasm pulled her under, held the first orgasm where it was while the second one expanded, drove her wild, had her seeing Jesus and calling God, and then while that two-level orgasm had her in a heaven she never knew existed, a third orgasm started, pulled her deeper, held the other two in place. Maybe five minutes later, she came out of the third-level orgasm, moaned and her legs shook, shook her into the second-level orgasm. She held on to me, couldn't top singing my name, had to get through that orgasm, had to ride out the first-level orgasm to return to normal. She had been to a new place.

Mocha Latte was shaken. "What . . . what . . . what just happened?"

It took me a second, but I caught my breath. "You okay?"

"Am I sleepwalking?"

"No, this is real."

"What. Happened? How did you . . . how did you . . . ? What was that? It felt like I was out of my body, like I was out in space, floating among the stars, part of the universe, a part of the Holy Spirit."

The client's voice trembled with envy and concern. "Let her breathe."

Mocha Latte panted, sweated, licked her lips, blinked a dozen times.

The client traced her fingers along Mocha Latte's smooth skin. "Let her catch her breath."

Mocha Latte's alarm went off. The thirty minutes was over.

The client looked at her watch, thinking, then said, "I paid for a full hour, right?"

Mocha Latte licked her lips. "You. Could be late. For. Your flight."

"That'll be my issue. Thirty minutes. Ride him again. Give me what I paid for, my love."

The client put me back inside of Mocha Latte.

Mocha Latte moaned, "Jesus, Jesus, Jesus. My pussy fixing to come hard again. My pussy gonna come so damn hard."

Mocha Latte's expression, the gaze in her eyes, told me what I knew, that I didn't have a small cock. Hadn't ever had a small cock, not that I could remember. In school, when I was in PE, when other boys saw me naked in the communal shower, or getting dressed in the locker room, many wanted to see it; not in a sexual way, but in a way that said they hoped to have a dick like mine one day. Girls heard about it and giggled in the hallway. Some girls wanted to see it, touch it, or, on a dare, taste it. More than a few wanted it inside them. Teenage girls could be fast whether they were white, Mexican, or black. So could women. When I was fourteen, my middle school teacher had heard gossip about my cock, had heard fast little girls talk about it getting hard as a brick and being a fat one, and she wanted to see it. She told me I had a cock like most men would never have. I was fourteen, and I had become overexcited, had lost control when I came, had tried to bang the fire out of me, and I had made her bleed. I learned to be better, and she taught me not to jackhammer like I was all about the nut. I learned to watch the woman, feel the woman, listen to her moans, read her body, and take her to orgasm. I watched Mocha Latte, felt her, listened to her moans, read her body, and took her back to orgasm. The first time I had made a girl come, it scared me. The way she howled and trembled. Mocha Latte did that now. Was again in an orgasm wrapped in an orgasm wrapped in an orgasm. I'd been with women who had no problem with my size, like Christiana. Like Penny. But the ones who did, I had to be careful never to use it to make them feel more pain than pleasure. One level deep. Two levels. Then three.

The client cried out, moaned that she wanted to feel what Mocha Latte was feeling. She pushed Mocha Latte away from me. The client mounted me. I took her from hurricane level one to three, soon to five. Then, as she became the second warrior splayed out on the battlefield, she saw I was in distress, that there was only one true resolution to my agony, and she gave me permission to set free the bloat of orgasms that had become a monster of storms inside of my body, but she told me to do that with Mocha Latte, directed me to come inside her. She paid the additional fee for that too. Finally, I allowed my strength to become my weakness, and I started to come. My moans, my growls, were like a starved bear coming out of hibernation. I needed to bust a nut before I lost my mind. She coached me as I took Mocha Latte back to level two, made her lips quiver, made her body quake. The client kissed my neck as Mocha Latte came, held on to me until the end, as I did what was commanded, as I let out hums that made me sound like a man in pain, as she moaned my name while I busted the nut of all nuts and rocked the room. The alarm sounded.

CHAPTER 24

BRICK

Mocha Latte, the client, and I rushed to clean ourselves, hurried to get dressed, and left Room 1237 like we'd heard the starter gun for the LA Marathon. The women waited out front while I retrieved Miss Mini; then I sped the client to LAX. She was in the back seat with Mocha Latte, getting soft kisses, the kind that shared bacteria, and they made promises to meet again soon. The client hopped out at Delta like a paratrooper being dropped behind enemy lines, running like her marriage, job, and life depended on it. Mocha Latte moved up front, and I drove away, not saying a word. Right away, Mocha Latte counted the money she'd made, then stuffed it into her bag.

When I hit the madness on Century Boulevard, Mocha Latte said, "Brick. Can you drive around for a few?"

"Sure. Where?"

"Anywhere safe. I need to clear my head. I need to deal with my thoughts. My demons. My doublethink. I need to deal with my contradictions, my hypocrisy, the lies I tell myself."

I doubled back, took us down Sepulveda, and headed north toward UCLA.

Mocha Latte was in the same foul mood I had seen two nights ago, when I met her. Her demons had arrived, screaming her name. She pulled the purple wig off, then threw it out of the window. She did that as if she were throwing away that personality, as if she were jettisoning the woman who had been buck wild in the hotel room.

Her hair was short, curly. Now she looked like a professional money-hungry woman out on the town.

She took a breath, and in a delicate tone said, "I told you to stop."

"You told me to obey the queen. The queen told me to keep on keeping on."

"I didn't plan on doing the Roc and Shay with you."

"Well, I was in Barstow minding my own business."

"She did that to control me." She took a deeper breath. "Never seen that insecure bitch act that way before. It is always just me and her. Women are hypocrites. Women are abusers. Women are liars. Just like men."

"That's what money does. Money is power. And man or woman, the powerful act the same."

"I don't give a fuck how many letters you've earned behind your name, I'm not a slave."

"You were good with her. It seemed natural. She is crazy about loving you."

"I don't even like women like that. Had to learn. It felt like a better choice, to be honest."

"A better choice in what way?"

"Safer with women than with men, on many levels. But women . . . we are so emotional."

"I never noticed."

"Shut up."

———

A HALF HOUR later, I pulled up to valet parking in front of Sweet Chick, another hot chicken and waffle spot, this one gourmet and cofounded by hip-hop legend Nas. Mocha Latte didn't ask any questions. She just eased out of the car when the valet opened her door and followed me inside like she was my woman. The moment we stepped into the restaurant, it felt like we were in the hippest part of New York City. The place was small, but swanky and sexy with the sweetest music playing. Joyce Wrice finished singing "Good Morning" and Mahalia started singing "Sober."

After we were seated, Mocha Latte ordered the Quinoa Bowl: poached persimmon, macadamia nut, Greek yogurt, kale, roasted tomatoes, and curried vinaigrette. I ordered the grilled chicken sandwich with heirloom tomatoes, pickled shallots, iceberg lettuce, and Kewpie mayo with a side of fries. She ordered a glass of pinot noir and was done with the wine before the food came. When our feast arrived and we started to throw down like we were beyond famished, she looked at me. We stared at each other, knowing what we'd just done.

She commanded, "Don't tell Christiana any details about what happened between us tonight."

"How does this work with y'all?"

"Tonight? I set it up. I worked with her last night and didn't feel like dealing with her tonight. She works my nerves sometimes. Tonight, this is my money. All of it. Her hands aren't in my pocket on this one. If she sets up something, I pay her a percentage. If we work together, we split it down the middle. She's fair."

"Okay. You don't scream, I won't holla. We cool?"

"Okay, yeah. We're cool."

"Regrets?"

"Always. I have the best intentions, but I never make the right choices. They seem right at the time, but I always open the wrong door. So yeah, I have regrets." She nodded, then said, "But the client we had . . . I had tonight, she pays well. She's a good tipper too. So I made more money to put in my house fund."

"You have a house fund?"

"I need to claim my life; the life I deserve."

"What kind of house you have your eye on?"

"The crib I want costs four hundred thousand. Culver City. I don't want to live in a black area. White areas have better grocery stores, better restaurants, better parks, and the type of black people I like."

"That's up to you."

"But in some parts of Mississippi, I could buy three homes for that amount and it would be on the coast with what feels like an ocean view, well, the Gulf of Mexico. I can get a nice house for one hundred."

"Yeah, but that's Mississippi. Confederate flags and old racism that's being rebranded."

"I can handle it. I'm from Texas and can stand my ground same as they can."

"How and where you invest your money is your business."

"But I like it out here, if for no other reason than the weather. Hardly rains and can wear summer clothes in the winter. If I can save enough for a down, then get another steady job, if I get another chance to be an engineer, or go figure out how to get to law school, then I can quit this life, be back on my feet, and move my life in the direction it should be going. Even without a king, I'm still supposed to be a queen."

"House. Engineering. Law school. You don't know what you want to do, do you?"

"I feel stuck. I'm in a nightmare trying to get back to a sweet dream."

After a moment of silence, she reached into her purse and finally handed me what I had earned.

She said, "Not bad for an hour, huh?"

"Did you set me up for this? Did you and Christiana play me?"

"The client went on and on about how she wished you had come up with us. I asked her what it would be worth to her if I called you. She wanted to be recorded, so yeah, I used that as a reason to get you to Vegas. I didn't want to leave this much cabbage on the table. Tonight, my client was pleased. Never saw her so happy."

"Your client is in love with you."

"They are all in love with the false version of me that is presented, the version they pay for and control. That version of me shows up, acting like I always want to have sex, like I enjoy pleasing strangers."

"You sound like you did things you didn't want to do."

"I entertained a woman. I'm straight, but I give women the GFE."

"Need to talk?"

She whispered, "I'm disgusting."

"What?"

"I'm a sex worker, not a goddamn sex slave. No matter how much you pay to lease this black pussy, I still choose what I want to consent to. I don't care if you live in a five-million-dollar house on a lake."

"Ever turn down anything and walk away from the table?"

"All the fucking time. There have been plenty of times I've said no to some disgusting request."

"Like?"

She made a nauseous face. "Let's not talk about that while we're eating."

We finished our meals and our plates were taken away, but she took her time finishing another wine. I took in the room, a congregation of alligators, a sleuth of bears, and a glare of cats mixed with a coalition of cheetahs.

I told her, "White boy at the bar is breaking his neck checking you out."

"I know. He's real cute. Tall, dark, handsome. My type of guy too, aesthetically."

"Want to slide him your digits?"

Mocha Latte looked at him as he smiled at her; then she turned back to me. "Nah."

"Sure? He's looking at you like he loves Frrrozen Haute Chocolate."

"My head is filled with velleity after velleity now."

"And that means?"

"When you make a wish that you know can't come true."

"We can talk about it."

She shook her head. "You have me a little mixed-up now."

"How so?"

"Really? I mean, really? My legs are still weak from you being in Le Chocolat Box."

"You can tell the white boy I'm your cousin."

"Then I'd start the relationship with a lie. It looks like we're on a date too. I don't want a man who thinks it's okay to see me with another man on a date, then get my number. If I made a move, he'd think I'm just another thot."

"He won't. You look professional. Like a powerful lady, because you are a powerful lady."

"I'm with you. He'll ask me if I ever slept with you and that would be complicated. What would I say then? That I did, but it was professional, not personal? Say some bitch just paid me a king's ransom to have sex with you? Say you made me have an orgasm that I can't quite shake? But it meant nothing because we're strangers too?"

Her phone rang again. It irritated her, but she put on a business smile and answered.

Her nostrils flared. "No, no, no. For the last time, I don't accept Bitcoins for any services."

She ended the call.

I asked, "You okay?"

"Entitled rich boys are a trip. Those fatherfuckers overpay white girls and underpay us. They want you to go around the world bareback, let them come wherever, and pay half of what they give white girls."

"Fatherfucker?"

"Because my dear, sweet, bourgeois-ass momma ain't got nothing to do with this."

Her phone rang again.

She put on her fake smile and answered, "Hello, love. You make your flight? You missed it and now you have to spend the night in Los Angeles? Aww. I can't come back. As soon as I left you, I booked an all-nighter. Well, I can't bail on them. I am with them now. Until noon tomorrow. So sorry, baby. So sorry. My driver? He dropped me off and went home. I think he turned his phone off. Sorry, my love. Yes, next time."

She hung up, then massaged her temples.

"Mocha Latte?"

"She went too far. Tonight, she went a bridge too far."

She ordered another glass of wine. Drank it slowly.

I asked, "Want to go to a comedy club?"

"Are you asking me out on a date?"

"I think we need to laugh."

"I read that children laugh three hundred times per day. I'll bet I used to laugh two thousand times a day. I used to be a very happy person. My incidents of laughter have decreased to an abysmal level."

"Yes or no? I can get us in for free. One of my brothers is a comic."

"There are more of you?"

"Two more."

"Right, right. I saw the picture at your apartment."

"I share a dad with one brother and a mother with another."

She hesitated. "No. Not in the mood for comedy."

"Want to go back to Savoy? Or we could roll up to Hollywood and listen to some music."

"Take me home. Well, to the place I'm crashing."

I paid the bill and we stood to leave. The white guy at the bar was still checking her out as we exited. He liked what he saw. She smiled at him. Ball was in his court now. He didn't come to her. She didn't go to him.

Stalemate.

We didn't go straight to valet. Cool Cali night. We walked Fairfax, passed all the shops.

She shook her head. "Mind if I address the elephant in the room, then never speak on it again?"

"Sure."

"Three levels. Jesus. Two times like that with Penny."

"You're mad at me."

"Dogs get mad."

"You're angry."

"It was like I was gone from my body, existing inside a duet from the opera *Figaro*, and I resided inside every note. I felt you, the way you made my nerves come alive, how you made me feel spiritual; you were the instrument that inspired my aria. Three levels deep. Was like Wolfgang Amadeus Mozart was orchestrating my orgasms while Luciano Pavarotti held me tightly and sang lovingly in my ear, a song only for my soul to feel. That was how that felt. I felt something I never knew existed."

"Orchestrated."

"And you were a damn good conductor. Not only in the way of being the leader of a musical ensemble, but also a conductor by its other definition. It was like you were magical, some unknown and undiscovered object that permitted an orgasmic series of electric currents to flow through my soul."

"Wow."

"It was a Five Point Palm Exploding Heart Technique for sex."

"Double wow."

"You made me orgasm like a pig."

"Triple wow. And you know a sounder of swine can orgasm for like thirty minutes, right?"

"And my legs are still shaking. I see why Penny is batshit crazy when she gets around you."

"She was that way when I met her."

"And to be honest, I know why you get a little crazy around her."

"You know her."

"She gets going and makes Bruna Surfistinha look like she's the rookie of the year."

We made eye contact, then smiled a knowing smile.

We made it to the corner at the same moment a Tesla stopped at the red light, its music up high, jamming "Best Part" by H.E.R. like they had been sent to be our personal DJ. Baby-making music washed over us and I took Mocha Latte's hand, touched her waist, eased her to me, slow danced on the sidewalk.

She said, "Really? You really going to do this?"

"I'm doing this."

"You just tried to send me to a white boy, and now you all up on me like I owe you money?"

I held her close, and she rested her head against my chest. The red light changed, and our DJ drove away, but we didn't stop swaying. Traffic zoomed by, people yelled at each other, and we danced. Eyes dreamy, she took terse breaths. Permission was in her eyes. I kissed her again. It was short, sweet, greedy, and stirring. She was easygoing in my hands, soft here, firm there. I held her just above the curve of her ass and inhaled her as she did the same. Lips against hers, I looked at her, saw only the engineer, the woman with roots in Bakersfield and Texas.

We kissed again. Kissed and danced and let thirst lead the thirsty.

She whispered, "Brick."

"Yeah?"

"Words do things to a woman, more than sex."

"I say something wrong?"

"'Beauty is an aphrodisiac of which you are not in short supply. I see an abundance.'"

"Should I apologize for being honest?"

"No apology is required. Now I know what I need the right man to whisper in my ear. I know how the next man I fall in love with should make me feel in bed. He has to take me three levels deep."

"I feel like I did something wrong. On every level."

"You won MVP tonight. We were definitely like Roc and Shay for a minute."

"You're mad."

"No. Just have a heart that's filled with so many little wishes right now."

"Yeah?"

"Yeah."

I said, "The most expensive bottle of wine in the world is a bottle of Romanée-Conti Grand Cru, and one bottle of said wine costs about eighteen thousand dollars. It is considered the perfect burgundy and tastes of rich fruit and exotic spices with black cherry aromas. That's what you taste like. A bottle of Romanée-Conti Grand Cru."

She held me tighter. "Words, Brick. Words."

"Why does it bother you when I compliment your superlative natural beauty?"

"Because I am a black woman and grew up down south receiving more pejoratives than compliments."

I tasted her again, kissed her until she shuddered and pulled away from me.

She was chocolate. I loved to eat chocolate. I whispered, "One more."

"Damn you."

I kissed her again. Passersby blew their horns and cheered for late-night romance.

We both needed something, something that was beyond sex, something more profound and intangible.

After the dance, after a dozen kisses, my car was waiting at valet. She moved with charm school sophistication, and the valet opened the car door, let her ease in like a lady, bottom first, knees together, and that southern girl swung around properly. As we drove away, her left hand covered my right; we interlocked fingers while I drove, no words spoken between us while we were stuck in the Ethiopian area's one lane of traffic. Over and over, her middle finger tickled my palm.

CHAPTER 25

BRICK

Twenty minutes later, I parked Miss Mini on Stocker. Not until then did Mocha Latte let my hand go.

Like a gentleman, I opened her car door, let Mocha Latte out. She stood tall, adjusted her clothing, sighed at the world that had been mine for a few years, some judgment about me or her life passed but kept to herself. Mocha Latte stood motionless and beheld the Afrocentric neighborhood where she was squatting. So many thoughts were on her mind. She snapped out of her trance, adjusted her secondhand dress, then took slow steps, moved like a sophisticated lady, like she was Jackie O., as we walked up the worn stairs to my sixty-year-old apartment building.

I asked, "Want to come over and kick it on my oversize classic sofa a bit?"

"Uh, no. No need to ask me to Netflix and chill."

"I didn't mean it like that."

"What happened in Vegas, well, that was Vegas."

"You can have the bed. I'll crash on the oversize classic sofa."

"Keep it professional. I'll go and let Christiana watch over me."

"I can watch over you. I know you sleepwalk. I'll keep you safe."

"I'd misprize to waketh up from mine own deep catch but a wink with thy cock in mine own that from which we speak, down mine own throat. Or I wouldst waketh up with thee consuming mine own pussy."

"I wouldn't do that. Hashtag I support Time's Up. Hashtag I support Me Too, too."

"You know my secret. You know how I sleep. It could happen, and it would be my fault."

I shook my head. "It wouldn't be."

"Besides, I need to sleep so I can pick up my Rubicon in the morning. I left it parked before the job with Christiana and Penny."

"I'll drive you. No charge."

"Nah. Uber. I don't need you. Might kick it in the Valley. Or drive to Santa Barbara to get away. Guy on a dating website wants to meet. He responded to that corny stuff about going to movies."

"You met somebody."

"Told him I might do a daytime-brunch thing, just to connect, see what he's about."

"Who is he? Okay to ask that?"

"He's an engineer too. I get to be a nerd again, for a while."

"Smart, like you."

"He's a mechanical engineer at Aim Systems Network."

"You didn't say that earlier."

"I know. Was on a date with you and didn't want to spoil it."

"Was it a date?"

"For about five minutes it felt that way. You took me to Sweet Chick. Paid for it. Kissed me. Danced with me in the streets like we were Ginger and Fred. If that's not a dream date, I don't know what is."

I paused. "Hope the rendezvous works out for you."

"A favor, please?"

"Yeah?"

"Wine?"

She followed me to my crib but stayed in the front door. I gave her the Château Margaux Red '98. It cost seven hundred a bottle retail. It was my favorite wine. I'd hoped to one day open it and share it with a woman who loved me as much as I loved her. Men fantasized too. We were just as foolish as women.

She dug into her purse. "Twenty-five dollars cover it?"

"Sure."

"May I smoke here? I need to get my head right before I go across the way to Penny's place."

"Sure."

"Won't take but two seconds. I only puff a couple of times and I'm good."

Mocha Latte sat on my classic sofa, opened her purse, took out an ink pen, then took out a strip of aluminum foil. She put the pen on the foil, used the pen to roll the foil into a tube, then bent the tube in half. She reached into her purse and took out a small plastic container. Popped it open. She had balls of Orange Kush. Mocha Latte rolled up a joint and fired up the weed. She took three hits, inhaled hard each time, exhaled slowly, and when she was done self-medicating, she put the fire out, put everything away, stood, and headed for the door.

In a humble tone, Mocha Latte asked, "Do you think I'm lovable?"

"Of course you are."

"I miss kissing. You made me realize how much I miss . . . I miss swapping and swallowing bacteria."

"Me too. I miss risking getting good old meningococcal meningitis."

"I could kiss for the sake of kissing and kiss all night."

"Me too."

Mocha Latte hesitated, the broken staring at the damaged, almost too nervous to ask. "Could you love me?"

"I could."

"We blew it."

"Did we?"

"Love has to be built from the ground up, from the first smile, from the first laugh, from the first dance, from the first kiss. Not by fucking first, not by being paid to have sex with each other, then trying to reverse engineer it from there. You don't start a relationship with sex, then try to reverse engineer and see what's there to hold both of you up. If it starts with sex, then sex is your foundation, and sex is never a good foundation."

She rubbed her nose, tsked, hummed, sighed, took a breath, made eye contact with me.

I nodded. "What do you want?"

"To be in love, to be loved, and have raw sex with the same person forever. I want the love of my life."

"Me too. Maybe the love of my life got stuck in a condom. Or was a slow swimmer."

"Mine probably got swallowed."

"Or ended up on some woman's tits."

"Or up her ass."

Again I nodded.

She whispered, "You made me miss being loved."

The eye contact remained as she rocked from one foot to the other, licking the edges of her lips.

She whispered, "Part of me wants to stay. You want me to stay, so I'll stay under one condition."

"What's the condition?"

"If you can answer one question correctly."

"Okay."

"What's the flattest state in America?"

"Texas."

"You blew it."

"Wyoming?"

Wine on her breath, smelling like Kush, bottle in hand, she headed toward Penny's apartment.

I stood in the cool air, watched her go inside Penny's spot. Once the door closed, I took a deep breath, sauntered away. I sent a text to André, told him I might come back to his comedy show, the third show. Then I texted Dwayne, checked in, tried to find out if he wanted to meet me in Long Beach. Before I made it to my apartment, Penny's front door opened and closed again. Christiana hurried out and called my name like it was urgent as fuck.

CHAPTER 26

BRICK

CHRISTIANA WORE GRAY slim jogger sweatpants. Black CUBA T. Unadorned, she looked ten years younger, like a breathless, sweaty teenager.

I asked, "What's going on?"

She raised her phone. Showed me a photo of a woman of a certain age.

I stared at Christiana. "I saw her tonight. She was staring at me all evening."

"She saw you at the bar. She went there to see you in person. To assess your energy."

"You're as persistent as I am irritating."

"I know other men I can message, and they will go in a heartbeat. But she wants you."

I asked, "Who is she?"

"In due time. Names will not be important. Only the date. I sent her your photograph. That was how she knew who to look for at the hotel. I knew you'd wait at the bar when Mocha Latte went on her date."

"So Mocha Latte knew you were going to put me on the auction block."

"Don't be upset with her."

"How did you get my picture?"

"From your Facebook page. Very nice photo of you in a suit."

"Why me? Hotel was filled with good-looking escorts. They probably have an app for that too. There has to be a GrubCoochie or InstaDick or WineDineSixtyNine app out there by now."

"It will be her first time too. She loves your name. Brick. It conjures images of something sturdy, arouses her curiosity, and rhymes with what she longs for. She will want more than your company if you consent."

"She had on a wedding ring."

"Her husband betrayed her, and she will take a lover. It's what she deserves. She wanted to see you first before booking. She is old-fashioned. You will be her treat. This is her revenge, and she has rules. Strict rules."

I paused, spoke as if talking to the winds. "Why would a man become an escort?"

"Some for fun. Some for debt. The money is tax-free; you get to keep it all and not share with the IRS. Some to help others like family. Some to be like clients and feel revenge from being rejected by someone they trusted or loved. Maybe I should ask you. You have been betrayed. You have been hurt. You are the man and only a man knows what causes a man to do the things a man does even when he has a wife who would have loved him forever."

Her past rose in her eyes, and a tribe of tears fell.

I thought about love. That was no longer existent in my life.

I thought about my debts. Those had to be handled to achieve any of my dreams, and I wasn't ready to slap on a white collar and go back to the widget factory. I was still out on disability. I could ride that train a little longer.

I asked, "When?"

"Soon. I have to see when she will be back from Washington and available."

"Okay."

"Just in case, I will get you prepared this week. Physiologically as well as physically."

"*Psychologically.*"

"Psychologically. It is a hard word to remember and say. For me it is."

"But you can say 'entrepreneur' with no problem."

"It is that way, learning a language. One day I forgot the word to say 'chair.' I learn words that are of a higher level in order to gain more respect. I learn to talk like a true entrepreneur, not a street person."

I nodded. "What do I need to do?"

"I will wax your body. There should be no hair from your face to your feet."

"Anything else?"

"No sex until then."

"Why no sex?"

"The client wants you capable of having a substantial orgasm."

"What's that about?"

"Her request."

"Anything else?"

"I will arrange a haircut."

"I have a barber."

"I have a stylist. The person I use charges three hundred dollars to groom men."

"They charge three C-notes to cut hair? Get the fuck outta here."

"She cuts your hair, waxes hair from your nostrils, gives you a facial, neatens your eyebrows, pops pimples, and exfoliates. Your skin will glow, and you will see the difference immediately."

"Three hundred dollars?"

"I will pay for it this one time."

"Pimp."

"I am an entrepreneur, and I am altruistic. Another word I love to say. *Altruistic.* I help everyone, and I want to help you. There is no obligation. It's up to you if you want the experience. And the money."

"Never forget the money."

"I know other men I can call. Many men do this, and I could send one of them to meet her. You're curious about what goes on in Vegas. Think of it as an experience for yourself, and you will get paid for carnal knowledge."

AS I DROVE away, my cellular rang. It was Penny. I didn't want to be bothered. I was in that mood where I wanted the world to go away and leave me alone for a while. I answered with a negative attitude.

Penny asked, "What the hell happened tonight?"

"What do you mean?"

"Was there an issue with Mocha Latte and her client?"

"I sat at the bar. Her client came. They went upstairs. Her client came. Two hours later, she left the hotel."

"She's getting on my nerves. All attitude. This bitch doesn't know me like that."

"If she's too moody, send her to my place. Tell her I'm not home, so she can have some space."

"Mind if I go over there?"

"Sure."

"Where are you going right now?"

"I need some air."

"Want some company? I can ride with you. I need to get away from everybody. Maybe we could ride down by Dockweiler."

"No. I'm good."

"Rejection. Payback."

"I'm not being petty. Just don't feel like I'd be good company right now."

She took a breath. "You're really going to let Christiana book you for a trip to Vegas?"

"She told you."

"Is this my fault? What if I don't want you to, would that matter?"

"I'm a grown man. I make my own decisions. And like you, I have financial obligations."

She took a deep breath, was about to say something, but decided to hang up on me.

RIDING WITH AN anger that refused to sleep, I drove to Fox Hills, where a half million duckets bought a one-bedroom, one-bath condo. I parked, remembered that Saturday I'd been insulted at a barbershop in front of a league of black men, took a knife out, and went to the Maserati. It was the least I could do. I stabbed the rear passenger-side tire once. Coretta's luxury car was there too. I stabbed her back tire; killed it. Then I got in Miss Mini and drove away.

CHAPTER 27

BRICK

A NO-NONSENSE VOICE called from the other side of the door, "Who is it?"

"Frenchie?"

"Wrong answer. I'm Frenchie. And just to be clear, Frenchie is strapped and in a bad mood."

"It's Brick."

Frenchie opened her front door, lantern in one hand, small gun in the other. Every nation had a bomb, and in America, urban or suburban, there were enough guns for everybody to be strapped.

She said, "You here to help or chastise and criticize?"

"Let me in."

There was enough light from when her neighbor's motion sensors kicked on for me to see her unfriendly expression. She had a face that reminded me of the girl next door, if you lived in Malibu. Her golden hair had been dyed a rich shade of violet with violent maroon streaks. Even the colors in her hair looked like they were in a civil war. When her hair was all blond, she looked like she should be on Hermosa Beach playing professional volleyball.

Her look and attitude had changed. Life had put her through some changes.

Frenchie had been an actress. She was a singer before that. She'd had a hit song once, "Everybody Knows." It was an R and B number that peaked at number eleven on the soul singles chart, number four on Billboard. There was a nomination for a Grammy. She lost, and no one hung on or followed a loser. Music industry dropped her. The pop star went to stage to try to reinvent herself as a legitimate actress. Dwayne had met her when they were touring. Frenchie had been married. Not many knew it, unless they looked on Wikipedia. She'd been on the road for six months, then went home to a new marriage in Vermont and found out she was three months' pregnant by Dwayne.

I said, "Heard you had some damage over here."

"What, are you the inspector? Or you calling the cops on me too?"

"You gonna shoot me or let me in to get a better look to see if I can help?"

"Dwayne with you?"

"No."

"Don't play with me."

"It's just me."

"I will shoot you."

"You know I'm not worth the bullet. Now, take that misplaced anger and get out of the way."

She stepped aside. I stepped inside.

Carpet was fucked. It had been flooded, then dried out, that sour stench soft but present.

She said, "Pipe had burst in the ceiling over the kitchen. See that big hole?"

"Yeah."

"The furniture had water damage."

We moved toward the epicenter of the damage.

I said, "Ceiling will take some work but can be patched up. After that, you could redo the walls with Behr paint. They have a paint and primer in one. No odor. Hallway looks like it needs paint too. Paint one part of the house the rest will look bad, so I'd redo everything. Start fresh. Mexican and Central American day laborers that hang out at Home Depot can do it better than me and will be a lot cheaper than a contractor. One thing at a time. Don't need electricity to do that. I'd just rip the carpet up for now. You need to make sure you're not sitting on a nest of mold."

"I can't afford it, so it will have to stay like this until whenever I can come up with some extra money."

"Your mortgage?"

"Don't worry about it. I talked to Chase and I'll get that worked out some way."

"You have equity?"

"At least three hundred thousand. At least. But I don't want to borrow."

"Why not?"

"That equity is college money for Fela, worst-case scenario. We have to rough it out."

I headed back outside, stepping over overgrown grass, into the fresh air. Frenchie followed, that torchlight swinging like a night watchman. She was embarrassed, frazzled, and stressed, and it showed on her face.

She put the gun in her waistband and marched me back toward the street, got me off her property, a sign she didn't want me going back inside of her home. It didn't occur to me until that moment that dropping by this late, uncle to her son or not, might have been taken the wrong way. Or maybe she moved me from the house because her power was off and the street lighting was better. I saw she had on blue Juilliard leggings and a light gray Juilliard cap.

She said, "I'm working, hustling, doing this and that."

"What kind of hustling?"

"I work at a place called Plots to Die For."

"Clever name. You're writing movie plots? Screenplays?"

She cringed. "I sell burial plots."

"Not so clever. Actually, that's kind of morbid."

"I buy and sell real estate for people as dead as my acting career. Oh, how far I have fallen."

"It's honest work."

She said, "And I just applied for a job teaching theater at Cerritos Community College in Norwalk."

"Community theater?"

"They have a great program. Underrated."

"So what happened here? Dwayne not paying his child support?"

"My accountant. She stole everything."

"Fuckin' serious?"

"She had access to all of my accounts to pay my bills, then took all of my money."

"Just you?"

"Did the same favor for her other clients. Now she's living on an island and we can't touch her. I found out she hadn't paid my property taxes or my mortgage, had just stolen all of my money and left for the West Indies."

"The money, all the child support Dwayne has sent you—"

"Stolen. And I can't afford to hire anyone to do anything."

"White-collar crime. Low priority. Get in line behind Madoff's victims."

She laughed. "Karma made its rounds and finally got to me. I had a series of unfortunate events."

"What else happened?"

"After the pipe burst? Refrigerator went out. Then I started a load of clothes when we were leaving one morning, and the washing machine didn't shut off, ran water for six hours, flooded our service porch, kitchen, living and dining room areas, flooded the whole damn house when I was gone. Then the dishwasher went out."

"Fuck, Frenchie."

She sighed. "And the air conditioner died during the hottest summer on record. One thing after the other. Because I depended on my accountant, and she hadn't paid my home insurance, I'm fucked."

"Sorry to hear that, Frenchie."

"Then we were dead broke. Lights got cut off."

"Why didn't you call somebody?"

"Don't tell Dwayne any more than he already knows. Don't give him any ammunition."

"He needs to know how Nephew is living; nothing personal against you. Nephew is stressed."

"I'll never forgive you. If he writes this in court documents, if the judge asks me how this happened and makes me sound like I'm irresponsible, or stupid, or incompetent . . . I won't forgive you."

"He loves his son, Frenchie. He's his parent too. He wants Fela to be comfortable."

"But not me."

"That's his son."

"I love my son more than I ever loved Dwayne. Dwayne loves my son more than he ever loved me."

"Circle of life. Dwayne wants to be a dad to his son, so let him do it, in his own way."

"Fela is my responsibility. Full custody."

"He has a dad."

"A Disneyland dad. Me and my son, we're a team. We have been a team since the day he was born. The ups and the downs. I'm letting him down. This problem. My bad luck. I'll find a way to fix it."

"You've been living this way for months. Why didn't you reach out? I'm just a few neighborhoods away."

"Independent woman. Too embarrassed. Too angry. This shit is numbing."

"Why didn't you tell Dwayne how bad it was? He found out from Fela. The boy is hungry, Frenchie."

"I don't want to hear his fucking mouth. All he does is figure out how to tour more and more and still pay less and less. I don't want him to be able to use any of this against me. If he knows, I know he will."

"He's got it rough too."

"He's all over the country, taking pictures with fans and posting them on Instagram, at bars with the cast tweeting how good life is, probably fucking as many fans as he can fuck, or fucking someone in the company, and I'm here, trapped, having a hard time with a kid I'm responsible for. I do all I can and all I get is backtalk from that boy, but Dwayne sends a fucking text message and gets treated like he's a king. Dwayne isn't going to doctors' appointments and dealing with teachers like I am. Some boy called my son the n-word, and I had to deal with that bullshit. Not Dwayne. He's the famous dad and his son loves having a famous dad. If you look at the pictures Dwayne posts, you'd think they lived in the same house. He's a social media dad, sends a text to check in. I'm the one here every day making breakfast, doing laundry. Even when I'm dead broke, stressed, crying through the night. What Dwayne doesn't understand is that nobody cooks for me. Nobody cleans for me. Nobody makes me meals or does my laundry. Nobody makes sure I'm okay. Nobody caters to me, period. A woman is always looked at as someone who needs to take care of everyone but her-damn-self. I take care of Fela, Brick. This is my struggle. I'm dealing with this the best I can. I just have to figure out how to get more money somehow."

"Can Nephew get a part-time job at the mall or something, to help with expenses?"

"I need him to *stay* in his books. This year is the most crucial year."

"Just asking. Don't bite my head off."

She measured me, then asked, "You have kids yet?"

"Not yet. Had a scare or two, though the scare didn't scare me like it did her. One day."

"Don't. They're dream killers."

"Well, for some that's part of the dream. The thing that bonds or breaks couples."

"Do you have any idea how many women have given up their dreams so a man can pursue his?"

"A lot, I'm sure. But men also enslave themselves to work so they can take care of everybody."

"All of my friends from my acting days are starring in shows on Broadway, or getting parts in major films, and here I am, following them on Twitter and Instagram, like a groupie. I was supposed to be the next Bernadette Peters on Broadway and be more influential than Regina Baptiste in Hollywood. At least I was in my head. When my old friends pass through here, the ones who remember me comp me tickets. I go to their shows, sit in the audience. *In the audience.* I'm not used to that point of view. I used to go see them as much as I could, to be supportive, but last time I was introduced as the girl who used to be an actress. *Used to be.* I was no longer part of the group. My membership had expired. No Golden Globes. No Grammy. No Emmy. No Tony. Just me and my Fela. He's my award now. I love my son, but kids are dream killers. At least they are for women like me more than they are for men like Dwayne. If I'd abandoned my son and had gone off to pursue my passion, if I had taken that call to go tour, or had snagged a part in a Broadway show, as a woman with a kid, as a mother, as the mother of a black son, I'd be called all sorts of names, least of all being a suck-ass parent. Brick, your brother is a suck-ass parent. No shade. I will tell him that to his face."

When she was done venting, I said, simply, "I'm not going to try to argue with that or defend him."

"He drops a check once a month, late most of the time, and walks away like he's done enough."

"You know your truth and how you feel. I'd never mansplain or challenge that."

"Dwayne tell you what happened? He just got kicked off a show two weeks ago."

"He said the show was folding, and that he asked to be let go so he could get unemployment again."

"Bullshit. He went off on the lead and ridiculed the musical director."

"He was probably stressed."

"Stressed or not, he wasn't professional, not when it counted."

"He has depression."

"And I don't?"

"They let him go."

"Yeah. He was sent home. I know someone on the tour and they reached out to me on Facebook and asked if he was all right. Don't worry, I didn't reply. People can be so damn malicious. It's real suspicious he was let go right before we're going to court, so now he can claim he's back on unemployment, between shows, and has no income. I bet we fight in court, he gets his reduction, and then magically he'll be booked in a show the next week."

I backed away from that topic. "Where's Nephew?"

"He's sleeping. He ate so much he passed out from the shock."

"How much of the food did he eat?"

"Damn near all of it."

I laughed. "Why are you keeping Nephew locked up like a rebellious slave?"

"You can't do slave jokes with me. Do those with your brothers or my son, but not with me."

"I'm sorry. Why is Nephew on lockdown with no phone?"

"You're barely a part-time uncle, if that, so it really isn't any of your business."

"Is he on punishment?"

"All these hot-to-trot girls are DMing him booty pictures and naked pictures and talking about blow jobs. One girl sent a video of her masturbating. *At sixteen*. And then there are the horny bitches at our church."

"At church?"

"And when did getting *choked* become part of sex? Bitch texted my son and said she wanted to drive over when I was sleeping so he could let her sneak in his bedroom window late at night, so he could stroke-and-choke her. I had words with her momma. Shit. I'm keeping my son from making the mistake I made."

"Well, I'm going to come pick Nephew up to hang out more often. Maybe this weekend."

"Ask me how I feel about that offer after we go to family court and hear the judge's ruling."

"Don't keep Nephew from his family."

"Family? When was the last time any of you Duquesnes came around here, Brick? Who has called me and offered to pick Fela up from school when I'm sick or keep him a weekend or take him for the summer?"

I almost told her I'd been sick awhile, that André had been on the road, but I kept the excuses to myself. I understood because I'd felt the same way, like I was out there alone, like the world had gone on and left me to suffer.

"Okay. After you and Dwayne go to court, I'll swing back by."

She said, "Your big brother called the police on me."

"I heard."

"You know how embarrassing that was? My neighbors saw, and the police saw what I didn't want anybody to see, looked at me like I was a bad mother, shaking their heads. I should have called Dwayne and cursed his ass out while they were here. It hurt and mortified and scared and disgusted me. I thought they were going to take my son from me. I fucking cried. Dwayne called the fucking cops on me. How low is that?"

"He was scared. He fucked up. He knows he fucked up. Don't blast him on social media."

"Why would I do that? First, I'm emotionally mature. Second, this is between Dwayne and me, and I have always kept it that way. I don't even involve my son. I don't mention how he was supposed to take Fela to do this or that but booked a show and reneged. Third, he's my son's father. Like it or not, we're part of the same family tree for eternity. If I blast him on social and the world hates him, that fucks with his money, and that would fuck with my money, and I'm not doing shit to mess up my son's inheritance. But don't tell Dwayne that. Let him think I'm that kind of weak, immature, bitter girl. Let his ass be scared of my Twitter finger. Understand this, Brick: Dwayne and I were friends before all this. I ruined a perfectly good marriage to be with him, and because of the way I left my marriage, I wasn't entitled to any alimony. I felt like a fool warmed over twice, and I said and did some things that can't be taken back, wrote things to the court I wish I hadn't, and now those things are forever part of the public record. I've never wanted him to fail. If I am stuck here in mommy mode, I need him to act, sing, dance, and be very fucking successful so he can pay his goddamn child support on time, and not ten and fifteen days late like he's been doing."

It was a lot to unpack. She'd overwhelmed me, left me speechless.

"So, Brick, I heard you broke up with my play-cousin."

"You keeping up with Coretta?"

"I ran into Coretta at the movies, up at ArcLight. We had coffee after."

"Who was she with?"

"Maserati Mama. She got away from her long enough to gossip."

I nodded. "What did she say?"

Frenchie laughed. "Did you really ask Coretta to show you her tax papers and her credit report?"

"Is that a bad thing to ask when you're talking marriage?"

"What was that lack of trust all about?"

"Showing that was the ultimate trust."

She laughed. "That's more personal than sex."

"Asking for a credit score is more personal?"

"You ever hear about someone showing a FICO score on a first date? Fucking on a first date? Yes. Every night. FICO? No. Too personal. Too revealing. And asking that comes off as a bit odd."

"When money starts to mix, you eventually need to know things."

"Things like?"

"If your credit is bad, then we need to make all the major purchases on my credit before we get married and yours is taken into consideration. If you're neck-deep in credit card debt, then I need to get the house before we're dealing with a combined debit-income ratio and have to pay off all of your cards to get a loan. I need to know how much money it will take me to reach my dreams with you at my side. I have dreams too. Shit like that."

"You and your practical thinking will have you living alone until the end of days."

"Someone has to be practical. Two fools can't steer a ship in the right direction."

"That part."

"From where she stood, everything looked okay, but I was paying the tab on all the bills."

"As men should."

"If you're paying for someone to be in your life, that's not a girlfriend."

"What is it?"

"An employee."

"That one of André's tired jokes?"

"Shut up. Your no-lights-no-water-having ass. At least I can flush a toilet. You and Nephew are probably doing like the ancient Romans and sharing a poop sponge like they did in public bathrooms."

She gave me the middle finger. "My life isn't perfect, but I'm thankful for everything I have. You may see me struggle, but you will never see me fall down and not get back up."

"You're a strong woman."

"My son needs to experience this. He'll know how life can be and know not to count on other people."

"I get it, but there is a line. Don't let your self-flagellation be his torture for too long."

She hummed, thinking, and changed the subject. "How much did you and Coretta have sex?"

I laughed. "A lot, at first, but it came to a screeching halt when finances came up."

"She didn't look like the type who had sex without looking in a mirror at the same time. She looks like the type of Barbie doll who would get her hair done, have makeup on, record herself having sex, and be looking at her own face in the camera the whole time, like she was making love to herself, and then drink wine and look at the recording all day, smiling, happy with herself and how beautiful she looked while glowing and having an orgasm."

"She was in my top three; maybe top two."

"Honestly, I thought she left because you weren't having much sex, or it was god-awful."

"We had sex a lot."

"Did you trust her?"

"Trust, but verify."

"But why?"

"Her shopping sprees and spending habits had me concerned. She was buying red-bottom shoes, new wardrobes. She bought a new Benz, then traded it back in for a BMW, did that in three months."

"Why?"

"Because the new BMW was *cuter*. Cost thirty grand more and was a nicer color, one that went with her complexion. She bought a new car and, on the way home, bought a wardrobe to match the color of her car."

"Not good."

"She lost at least ten grand on that trade-in deal. She didn't take me and got ripped off."

"Ten grand. Jesus. I didn't know all that. I could redo my house with ten grand."

"I never had no idea how much money she made, never pried, just observed and knew that Monday through Friday she looked like a CEO, but she had over twenty charge cards and used them all."

"Okay. Red flags."

"I needed to know if she was living off credit."

"Everyone lives off credit, Brick."

"I wanted to know how much she was saving, what was in her 401(k), and who was handling her investments before we got married."

"That's a lot to ask."

"That's family stuff, Frenchie. It would all have to be addressed at some point. I wanted to sit down and put all the debt on the table, so we could see where we were before we amalgamated our brands."

"Your brands? Really? You have a brand now? What's next? A mixtape?"

"You know what I mean. I needed to see if the relationship had legs."

She chuckled. "A wedding is a smart idea. Marriage rarely ever is, not in the long term."

"You should know. I defer to you as the expert in that field; heard your wedding was massive."

"If I could've had the wedding without the marriage, life would've been better. The honeymoon too. Oh yeah, the honeymoon. After the honeymoon, couples should go back to being single, or at least have that as an option."

"You went on tour right after?"

"Which was like going back to being single with a paycheck and my own room."

I said, "You're funny when you want to be."

"I'm hilarious and have the reviews to prove it."

"You're not onstage. Don't push it."

"You're special. Coretta said you don't own more than three hundred things, you buy wine for resale but never really resell any, and you refuse to get a bigger car."

"She had so much stuff I barely had room for one hundred paper clips."

"You miss her?"

"She's taken her sexual fluidity to Maserati Mama now."

She wagged a finger. "You knew how she was from the get-go."

"I knew."

She chuckled. "It probably excited you."

"Probably did."

"You hoped she brought home a girl for both to have some next-level sex."

"Undoubtedly."

"Did she?"

"Nah. But we talked about getting a random from a strip club."

"You didn't care about a credit report then."

"Checkmate."

"Answer me. Do you miss her?"

A hundred images of Coretta flashed in my mind. "I do."

She twisted her lips. Her voice cracked. "It hurts to miss someone."

"Without a doubt."

"Sometimes it never goes away, Brick. That's the worst kind. It's torture."

"Been there, done that, bought a ticket, and a T-shirt, then rode the merry-go-round."

"With Coretta?"

"Long before Coretta, and now again with Coretta. So, this pain ain't new. I know how to deal with it this time, and I'm sure I'll handle it better next time, and the time after that, and the time after that."

Frenchie said, "Coretta's new boo, it won't last. Two women that pretty will never make it."

"They looked happy."

"Coretta misses you."

"She's happy."

"She was happy with you."

"Now she's happier."

She sighed. "I've missed talking to you, Brick."

"Same here, Frenchie. Same here."

"You met anybody since Coretta?"

"Saw a girl. She played chess. Pretty, smart, and snarky."

"You say anything?"

"Wish I had. Will probably never run into her again."

She whispered, "Thanks for the food. That made me cry, knowing you care."

I said, "Let Dwayne see Fela before you go back to family court."

"Why should I?"

"They need each other. If it were a mother and daughter, would that make more sense to you?"

She paused. "You love your brother."

"I do. I won't defend what he does wrong, but I have to support him no matter what."

"You love my son."

"I do. And I love you too, Frenchie."

"First he buys me chicken, then he says he loves me." She nodded. "Okay. I'll send Dwayne a text."

"You're the best, Frenchie."

"Don't make me regret this, Brick."

"You won't."

I reached into my pocket, took out some cash, part of the money Mocha Latte had just given me.

I pushed it into Frenchie's hand.

She pushed it back and said, "No."

I said, "Yes."

"Brick. Fela is not your responsibility. This is not your mess to fix."

"Shut up."

She thanked me with a smile, then said, "I'm thinking."

"About what?"

"The cost of love. About what you paid to be in a relationship, and my cost of being in a foolish love. You're looking at your credit cards. We all pay. It's not money, but we all pay. We get mad when we can't recoup what we've lost financially, but also what we've lost emotionally and spiritually. A bad relationship can lead to sleepless nights or sleepless years or permanent insomnia. Love spares no one. We all pay. If men want to get their money back, women want to get back time lost, to unbreak a broken heart, to find a cure for the bitter taste left in their mouths."

"So, it's a wash. Everybody pays."

"Everybody pays, but not everybody pays the same amount or in the same way. For some, the loss isn't felt, while for others it's emotional bankruptcy. But everybody pays. Love changes us all."

I asked, "What if love is theater created by the gods, for their amusement, to watch the foolish struggle while the gods drink and make bets on how long before humans realize it's all a farce?"

"Then the gods are thoroughly entertained. And will be amused perpetually."

CHAPTER 28

BRICK

MOMENTS LATER I was standing outside Room 1237.

I knocked twice and the doctor answered, glass of red wine in hand. She looked surprised, then let me into her suite. Now she had on Yale Bulldogs pajamas, her hair damp, fresh out of the shower. Mocha Latte's voice was behind her, mewling and moaning. The doctor's Samsung was on the dresser, the video of her and Mocha Latte playing, the volume up loud. Mocha Latte was having a level-two orgasm on the screen. The client took my hand, and I followed her. The video played on, sensual, erotic sounds audible. We sat on the rumpled bed, watched Mocha Latte ascend as she earned her duckets. The client winked at me, grinned, then looked back at the video and frowned.

She said, "I went through so much trouble to see her. I lied to my job. To my husband. I sat on the runway for hours. When she was here, I paid her well. I needed her. She knew I needed her. She could have canceled her next fucking appointment and made me feel special. I would've compensated her. She's cheating on me right now."

"I'm not her, can't offer what a woman has to give, but what can I do to make it better?"

She went to her purse, put money on the dresser.

I was about to tell her that I wasn't here for her money, only her company, but she spoke first.

She said, "BBFS. Greek. K9. Around the world. DATY. I'll DT and give you a BBBJNQNS."

"Outside of Greek, I don't know what any of that terminology means."

"They call you Brick."

"Most people."

"With that name, the way you fucked us both, were you really her chauffeur?"

"I know nothing about what happens in these rooms. Not before tonight."

"My name is Maureen. Maureen Asuryasparsh."

"Nice to meet you, Dr. Asuryasparsh."

"Maureen."

"Maureen."

"Mind a little role-play?"

"What did you have in mind?"

"Let me pretend I'm the escort. I'll show you everything from AR to 69."

I nodded. "I need to shower."

"I want you just like this. I want to smell and taste her on your body."

"What do you want me to do? Without all the acronyms, acrostics, and abbreviations."

"Take me back to Camelot."

"Camelot it is."

She smiled. "How longeth can thee stayeth with me?"

"Until sunrise, if't be true thee shall has't me."

We took to the bed, and she took control. My cellular rang. As the client moaned, she handed me my phone. I think the client had hoped it was Mocha Latte calling me, and she wanted her jealousy and disappointment known. It was Coretta. She jumped right in, cursing, going off. Said someone had vandalized her and her lover's cars.

"Look, Coretta, whatever that's about, I'm on a date right now."

She paused. "Are you smashing?"

I held the phone as the client entered level three the second time, her hallelujahs strong.

Coretta sounded all shook up. "You're smashing some bitch right now? *Brick, seriously?*"

"Why do you keep calling me? You're a millennial. You're supposed to send text messages."

"We're done, Brick. We're so fucking done."

"We were done six months ago."

I hit the red button, ended the communication.

When I was about to blow my load, the client suckled me until I was too sensitive and had to push her away. That time it had lasted seventeen minutes and thirty-seven seconds. She pushed me down south, and I pleased her for six minutes and some change. She panted, held my head, and cursed. I'd had enough of her. I prayed we were done. I imagined this was how Penny, Mocha Latte, and Christiana felt. I was her whore. This was what she had paid for.

This was Vegas.

I could do this. Keep it professional. Stay out of my feelings. Walk away unscathed. And caked up. I could get the kind of cake needed to buy paint at Home Depot. I was learning to see life the way Christiana did.

CHAPTER 29

BRICK

THE MAIN ROOM at the comedy club in Long Beach fell apart in laughter. It was the next night, after midnight, and André was onstage. I was in the back, sipping on a beer. André finished his set to explosive laughter and a standing ovation; then he made his way to where I was seated, shaking hands and giving high fives along the way, the emperor of comedy.

I congratulated him. "Contemptuous. That last bit about lazy white people was scathing."

"You know I was a big fan of George Carlin. Still study Pryor's concerts."

His phone buzzed.

He said, "Have to go see this girl. Joëlle. She lives in Culver City."

"Same girl you were riding around on your bike last time I saw you?"

"New girl. Her daddy has a blues bar out in Riverside. She's an engineer at Dan L. Steele. She's a rebel, wild as fuck. Loves to cosplay and loves to role-play. Should see her dressed like Storm."

"Engineers and librarians, Comic Con nerds . . . aren't the square ones all wild as fuck?"

WHEN I PARKED Miss Mini in front of my apartment, Penny was outside, and she wasn't alone. She was holding flowers, arguing with a guy who was tall enough to play for the Lakers. It was her ex. He was back, the one who had ruined her financially. It was his fault that she spent time on her back to get back on her feet.

She snapped, "What do you want, Javon? Why are you bringing me flowers?"

"I miss you, Penny. I want to see if we can work something out."

"Go miss your wife, Javon. Only reason you should be here is to pay me what you owe me."

I walked up the steps. "Penny."

"Brick."

"It's almost two in the morning. Everything okay?"

Javon said, "What, you're friends with Coretta's nigga now?"

I warned, "Javon, I suggest you shut the fuck up; otherwise your wife will collect you from the emergency room, and what will be left of you will fit in a shoebox."

"What the fuck you gonna do?"

"Try me, motherfucker. Say one more word. One word."

Penny stood between us. "Brick, I got this."

Javon asked, "You fucking this nigga, Penny? You messing with Coretta's nigga?"

Penny snapped, "Javon, we're neighbors."

I took my daddy's gun from the small of my back, and that move startled him. I kept it aimed at the ground. I took my temper inside my place, left the lights off, stared out at Penny and Javon as they argued like lovers. She walked him back to his car. Kissed him good-bye. Ran back to her place, tears in her eyes, flowers in her hands. This time next week, I wouldn't be surprised if he had moved back in.

Not long after, Penny knocked on my door. I didn't answer. She used her key and came in. I was at my dining room table, in the dark, glass of eight-dollar wine in front of me.

She said, "You're mad."

"You still love him."

"Like you still love Coretta."

"I'll get over it."

"I will too."

I shrugged. "I was out of line. Nothing to be mad about."

"I do love you."

"I know."

"As a friend."

"I know."

"We never should have had sex."

"But we did."

"Too bad I didn't meet you before I met Javon."

"Yeah. Too bad."

She poured herself a glass of wine, sat with me, and drank.

I asked, "How much longer will you work with Christiana?"

"Not long."

"You feel safe?"

"As long as you're around, yeah. Doing this scares me, but you make me feel safe."

"I only did this, the only reason I got involved driving you, was to make sure you were safe."

"I know." She sipped. "Should I spend the night?"

"Really?"

"Just to cuddle. I'm sure Mocha Latte and Christiana will be over here in your bed before long."

"What does that mean?"

"You make us all feel safe."

CHAPTER 30

BRICK

FRENCHIE PUT OFF letting Dwayne see Fela. Said she needed another week or so. She wanted to tête-à-tête with her expensive lawyer first. Dwayne was left in an indefinite holding pattern. For the next few days, I stayed busy as a beaver with the pace of asses. Christiana kept the client list growing. She was the most ambitious woman alive.

The next weekend we mixed with celebrities and had breakfast at Beverliz Café in Beverly Hills. We ate poached eggs, pancakes, egg white omelets, and the best lox ever. Living in luxury, we talked up a storm.

Mocha Latte swallowed the last of her orange juice. "If Christiana had it her way, we'd have more regulars than the number of tourists that go to see whatever it is they see at the Grand Canyon."

Christiana picked some omelet from my plate. "We are a better sight to see. And we'd be richer than rich."

Mocha Latte laughed. "We'd be more tired than tired."

Penny added, "With worn-out coochies that look like mud flaps."

Christiana picked at her spinach. "We'd be able to afford vaginal rejuvenation."

I said, "That's a thing? Can you autotune a coochie and get rid of years of bad remixes?"

Christiana said, "We could make it brand-new and so tight we'd be virgins all over."

I asked, "Would that be tax deductible?"

"Of course. Like if you use Viagra, you can deduct that as a business expense."

"I was joking."

"I do not joke about money."

At the same time Penny and Mocha Latte said, "We know."

LATER THAT EVENING, watching the pace of asses get dressed in all white was an intimate affair. An erotic privilege. They adjusted one another's saintly dresses, made them sit right on one another's butts, adjusted tits, touched one another's hair. I watched them gild the lily and put on makeup. I took in the show as they helped one another with lipstick, mascara, perfume, blush. Women owned a level of closeness never shared by men.

Penny seemed different now. She had two new best friends. Girls who understood her plight.

The pace of asses wore incredible plunging dresses, kinds that if they coughed once would fall off and leave them as buck naked as Eve before she bit the apple. The pace looked like they were heading to the red carpet at the VMAs. Those dresses gave their toned figures bear hugs that would make men groan as they passed.

I said, "Y'all are putting in the work, staying in shape."

Christiana said, "Physiques are our calling cards, the determiner of our worth in a capitalistic society."

Penny whistled at me. "You're looking very handsome, Brick."

I rocked a two-piece single-button white linen suit accented by beige, paired with brown shoes.

We hopped in Miss Mini. Christiana was up front with me, in control of the music and chatting me up while Penny and Mocha Latte had their own conversation. I chauffeured the pace of asses about nine miles, from inland to the edges of the Pacific Ocean. Christiana had arranged clients for them all at the Viceroy Hotel. The hotel was so sophisticated, I was apprehensive. As we walked in the joint, soulful music throbbed like it was our theme song, Ari Lennox singing "Whipped Cream," the bass line seductive and erotic.

Mocha Latte sang along, "Yo deceiving, receiving, non-giving-head ass."

I strolled behind the pace and entered a world decadent enough for the king of Rome. We mixed with six hundred upwardly mobile, melanin-blessed professionals wearing all white.

I said, "Ladies, you already know my rules; I'm not going to repeat them."

"Whatever."

"Sí, papi."

"Go to hell, Brick."

Very serious, I said, "My phone will be on. I will be down here waiting in Barstow, just in case."

Christiana said, "We will be fine, Ladrillo. Enjoy yourself until we return."

Christiana headed toward the elevators, and the attorney from Cuba vanished with a middle-aged black married couple. He was a watcher. Penny left with three black men, an embarrassment of pandas smiling, talking, and flirting with the college student. One was getting married tomorrow. Mocha Latte was greeted by a distinguished gentleman, and the out-of-work engineer left, hanging on to his arm like a happy daughter. The pace of asses headed to the swank luxury hotel's seven-hundred-dollars-a-night suites that had pillow-top beds and ocean views. I knew them all, knew them all in intimate ways. Jealousy stirred in my heart, for all three. Each was a unicorn in her own way.

I heard an arrogant voice I recognized booming behind me. People hurried toward where a stage had been set up. The way everyone in white hurried, it was like a flock of angels scurrying to Jesus.

"Santa Monica. My people are looking good tonight. Give yourselves a round of applause."

I stood and watched my little brother draw the crowd in. Baby Bro was onstage. Dressed in the royal color of the kings of France, his shirt trimmed in kente patterns. I cursed André for not telling me he'd be here, then cursed myself for muting his overtweeting ass on social media. I moved back into the crowd and away from the side with the stage. I didn't want to be seen tonight, not when I was working with Penny, Mocha Latte, and Christiana.

The crowd opened long enough to let the help push a cart loaded with more exotic foods toward the extravagant set. During that two-second interruption, I saw an old girlfriend of André's. I'd met her a couple of times. Never asked her name. Another woman was up front, laughing like she was André's biggest fan. She was in super-sky-high heels and white shorts that showed off her amazing thighs and legs, all accented by reds and pinks that flowed with her red-and-yellow hair. Just like Nameless, her eyes and smile were focused on André, a curvaceous woman in awe.

Soon as I checked my phone to make sure all the girls had messaged me saying they were okay, someone tapped me on the shoulder. Startled, I jumped. When I turned, *fuck*, I was facing Dwayne. He was in all white for the affair too. We were surprised to see each other and made it known. We hugged, then turned to watch André.

I said, "Didn't know you were coming here."

"I didn't either. Agent got me a ticket at the last minute. Cost a grip to get up in here."

"The three-hundred-a-pop cost at the door weeds out the chavs and the riffraff."

At that same moment, across the open space, I saw Coretta and Maserati Mama. They were just arriving. Short skirts. Plenty of cleavage. Dressed like twins. Holding hands. They didn't see me. Even if I wanted to, I was here working, so I couldn't leave to get away from a memory that kept showing the fuck up everywhere I went.

When we could hear each over the hilarity, Dwayne commanded, "Buy me a drink."

"What do you want?"

"A greyhound. Vodka. Meet you at the food. Going to get a bowl of fruit cocktail and glass of chili."

As Dwayne headed away from me into the crowd, my phone vibrated, and it was a 911. One of the girls had a problem. I had to get there now, but six hundred drunk and party-minded people were in my goddamn way. I fought to get to the elevators. People were coming in, standing room only, and I was a salmon going upstream.

I spotted Frenchie in a white skirt and shimmering top, talking to a black guy who smiled at her like she was the one. Couldn't believe she was here too. She saw me, looked surprised, and we waved as I squeezed through the crowd. I wanted to tell her that Dwayne was here, wanted to ask about Nephew, but now wasn't the time.

I bumped into two guys from my neighborhood, Ken Swift and Jake Ellis. They were in a hurry going left and I was in a hurry to go right; had to fight my way through the sea of black dressed in white. Then a few steps later I was face-to-face with Eigengrau, Dwayne's ex from back in the day. She was at least six months pregnant and was holding hands with a handsome guy ten years her junior, one who looked like an underwear model. This was the biggest party of the year. Right now, I wouldn't be surprised to run into Dwayne Sr. up in here with a sister one-fourth his age on his arm. Then I was finally out of the thick of the crowd, could maneuver without knocking a drink out of someone's hand. I raced for the elevator. My phone rang as I moved.

I heard the issue and said, "I'm on my way up. No, don't call the fucking police."

CHAPTER 31

BRICK

ONE OF THE pandas with the bachelor party opened the door. He looked like he'd been through hell, and I knew that was because he had laid hands on Penny and she had fought back. If I had my gun, I would've double-popped, but instead I'd have to go Krav Maga to neutralize the threat that might come from three pandas.

Right eye swollen, the panda frowned at me. "You with that crazy African?"

I had no idea what he meant, and I didn't care. I hit him in the face right away. My blow made him stagger backward and plop on his fat ass. He raised his hands to hide his wounded face from any more blows.

"C'mon, man. I'm getting married tomorrow morning. You can't jack up my face up like this."

My heart thumped hard. "The girl."

"Bathroom."

The suite was tossed: TV smashed, art ripped off the wall. The other two pandas were on the floor, one by the bed, the other across the suite, both half-dressed with bloodied faces. The biggest one was balled up in the fetal position, moaning and groaning with his agony, his virtuous snowy outfit spotted in bloodred. His front tooth had been knocked out. Lamps were broken. The desk was flipped. Unopened condoms were scattered all over the floor.

Penny's clothes were neatly folded, resting on a table.

I went to the bathroom door, called out, "Penny."

Penny opened the bathroom door fast and hard. She was dressed in pink lingerie. Her makeup was smeared, her hair as wild as her wide eyes. She held her high heels in her hands like weapons. She ran into my arms and held on to me, clung to me crying and shivering, terrified like I'd never seen a woman terrified before.

"You okay?"

"Two black guys. They came in kicking ass. It was horrible. Something about a debt owed to someone in San Bernardino. It happened fast. I ran into the bathroom, locked the door, and called you, Brick. Brick, I called you over and over and it took you forever to answer your damn phone. Took you forever to get up here."

I had to pry her off me. Had her wait in the bathroom. I went and got Penny's clothes, handed them to her, told her to get dressed, to fix her face. I went into the jacked-up suite. Six terrified eyes looked at me, three of those eyes uninjured, three swollen as big as a fist. The groom was going to have an interesting wedding.

"My girl has been both traumatized and inconvenienced. She has to be compensated."

Pandas dropped money like leaves falling from a tree during the change of seasons.

I said, "And her tip."

Again, the pandas opened their wallets, shook the money tree, and made it rain.

I told them, "Whoever did this to you, for whatever reason—"

Panda one groaned. "Goddamn African."

Panda two moaned. "And his crazy-ass friend."

I said, "We had nothing to do with that."

Panda one. "What am I going to tell Brianna?"

Penny rushed out, dressed, shaken, and stirred, hair redone the best she could. I took her hand like she was my woman, and we split the scene, left the embarrassment to deal with their own problems.

As soon as we hit the hallway and headed toward the elevators, there was another surprise. We ran into Penny's ex. Javon was heading into a room with his wife. Penny saw him looking happy as he took his wife to a seven-hundred-dollar bed. She held my hand tighter, said nothing to him, but the wife's eyes were on Penny.

The married woman snarled like a dog, then mumbled, "Bitch."

That set Penny off, and she went after the woman. I had to catch her and pull her back.

Penny shouted, told her to tell her husband to stop calling and texting and coming to her apartment and bringing her flowers and begging to come back because he despised the bitch he married.

I had to drag her to the elevator, and her ex had to hold his wife back too.

THREE HOURS LATER, we were back at my apartment, karaoke machine on, sipping expensive wine, pulling names of old-school songs from a hat, and singing out loud. Penny pretended she was okay, tried to be strong, but I saw the levels of trauma in her eyes. I didn't know if seeing Javon or what had happened with her clients had upset her more. When the singing was done, she showered, put on *Doctor Who* pajamas, and stayed in my bed, slept wrapped around me all night. We woke up the next morning to the scent of blueberry pancakes being made.

CHAPTER 32

BRICK

THE NEXT MORNING, I drove Mocha Latte to the Coral Tree Café in Brentwood.

She wore her hair natural and dressed like everyone else on that side of the 10 freeway did, like she was going to a gym that served infused water. I found free parking by the Brentwood Veterans Memorial Building. The streets were filled with homeless veterans, an encampment large enough to make the problem on my side of town seem insignificant.

I parallel parked right in front of a homeless man, a man of European descent, and his just-as-homeless girlfriend. She was on her side, using her hands as a pillow, as her worry-faced man covered her with a soiled blanket. Both were under thirty, with dirty faces, faces so dirty it made me wonder if they were trying to do blackface. Worn and dirty military backpacks and duffels were at their side. It was eighty degrees, hot as fuck, and he was covering her with a thick blanket. She was in bad shape. I locked my ride, then headed down San Vicente to the café.

Mocha Latte frowned back at the row of snowy homeless veterans, saw it went on forever, then shook her head and asked, sarcastically, emotionally, and rhetorically, "How's that American dream working out?"

Everybody inside the café looked clean and moneyed. The only things black in the eatery were me, Mocha Latte, and the Latino servers' uniforms. I checked out the spot. There was a nice-looking woman in her twenties at a bistro table by herself, MacBook open, law school books stacked next to her. She was dressed in a pretty, sleeveless, flowered minidress and sandals, her long hair pulled back. The woman's dress was the tell, the sign of whom to look for. Mocha Latte went to the woman, smiling like an old friend. They sat and talked over iced coffees and muffins, ate and warmed up to each other for twenty minutes. They were all laughs and smiles. A moment later Mocha Latte left with the woman. She sent me a text as they headed out the door: the one-hour appointment was now a two-hour deal.

Today the café was my Barstow, one with a sweet view of both the rich and the disenfranchised. While I relaxed under cool air and ate the best omelet I'd had in recent memory, I waited.

Twenty minutes after Mocha Latte left, Frenchie messaged me, told me that she was ready for Dwayne to meet with Fela, and it had to be now, for breakfast, while she was feeling good on a sunny day and in this mood. I sent the message to Dwayne. Marked it as *urgent*. This would be his only window. He'd messaged me earlier, angry that I had vanished from the Viceroy party, said his broke ass was looking for me all night, thirsty for that greyhound I had promised. He had seen Frenchie with her date, and he had also seen his ex, the woman he'd cheated on with Frenchie. Chickens had come home to roost. Seeing Frenchie had had the biggest impact. I knew that had thrown his anger and jealousy meter into the red zone, same as Penny seeing her ex had done to her, and my seeing Coretta had left my heart rattled and unsettled. He didn't start a scene, though. He was too close to seeing Fela.

My eyes were on the juxtaposed lifestyles. I watched the wealthy kissed up against abject poverty. I thought about the sick girl out there on the pavement, and all I'd been through, alone and in silence.

I grabbed a menu, hurried back to the homeless couple, offered to order them whatever they wanted to eat and drink, then bring it back to them. My treat. Brentwood Medical was half a block west, maybe eight hundred feet away from where they had been forced to make nasty concrete their pillow-top hospital bed. I told them that if the woman needed medical attention, I'd get them to Brentwood Medical. Two soldiers who had done multiple tours of duty, a man and a woman, both of whom had faced imminent dangers and confronted armed enemies abroad, both of them broke down crying. I was on my haunches talking to them, seeing them, as people walked by rocking two-hundred-dollar workout shoes and Lululemon gear. I felt their suffering. Those who had suffered understood. They were in an overpopulated world and still felt alone. I was glad she had somebody. When I had suffered, Coretta was gone. André was on the road and never noticed. Dwayne was doing his Broadway thing. We FaceTimed, talked, but they didn't know. The thing about cancer was you could be sick and still look well. Chemo three out of four weeks each month, and no one noticed I was sick; only had days when I was tired. I was glad she didn't have to be sick by herself.

I said something out loud to them, to strangers, that I'd never said before: "I'm a cancer survivor."

Their empathetic tears for me were profound, made me wish Christiana was with me so she could hug and console the ailing woman as I hugged the man and shook his hand like he was a brand-new brother. I acted as her proxy, became the representative of an ambitious and altruistic entrepreneur.

The man who ran Tres Dwaynes would've spat on them before he helped them.

After I had gone back, ordered food for the homeless soldiers, and taken it back to them, I made it back to the eatery, eyes on phone, checking time, looking at the GPS location Mocha Latte had sent when she made it to the client's mansion, more concerned with her than anything. I copped a squat at a table that was being cleared, then sat sipping on a fresh latte, but the energy in the room felt off. I glanced around and damn near spilled my drink from the surprise. Coretta was seated four tables away, close enough to spit and have some of it rain on me. Maserati Mama was holding her hand across the table. They glared at me in a threatening way. I glowered at them and went back to my latte. They had stopped eating whatever the fuck they had ordered, now too busy grumbling about me. I'd fucked up their romantic morning by being in their space. That ache in my chest was once again strong. She was too close to me. I inhaled, smelled Coretta, and I was once again disturbed.

Mocha Latte came back through the door, just as my alarm sounded. Two hours had passed to the second. I went to her. She was freshly showered. I kissed her cheek, then with an accent said, "Mine own pussy-eating ex-girlfriend is h're with h'r new lov'r, across the cubiculo, but behold not. Those braches art watching me."

"If the witch is h're, kisseth me f'r real. Kisseth me. Alloweth h'r t' seeth thee kisseth me."

I kissed Mocha Latte, gave her my tongue, then took her hand like she was my new and improved woman and led her back to the exit. I opened the door for her like a gentleman, put my arm around her, and we strolled away in Cali sunshine, laughing. I heard Maserati Mama's curses, felt Coretta's eyes stabbing the back of my head.

When we made it back to Miss Mini, she had two flat tires, both on the passenger side.

My lips curved up into a smile.

Checkmate, bitches.

Checkmate.

CHAPTER 33

DWAYNE

DOWNTOWN MANHATTAN BEACH.

I was cut off by an arrogant fuck rocking a black convertible Porsche, waxed and glistening in the sun. In the bumper-to-bumper crawl down Highland Avenue, a Gomer cruising in a showroom-new, pearl-white, drop-top Rolls-Royce let me in traffic. I found a metered space on the roof of a garage behind the restaurant called the Kettle. Every eatery was packed and had a line running thirty feet out front. For every Lupita and John Boyega, there were three hundred Emma Stones and Jonah Hills. Droves of locals and tourists marched uphill from the beach carrying surfboards or hurried downhill for a volleyball tournament. Women in colorful bikinis and men in Speedos mixed with men in Dockers shorts and svelte women in pretty dresses that showed off their suntanned figures.

I saw my son in front of the Kettle waiting for me. I hurried to my boy and he hurried to me.

"I've missed you."

"Missed you too, Dad. Missed you too. But don't break my back, okay?"

We laughed. I was carrying a hoodie. I handed it to him, his gift.

He said, "A Leimert Park hoodie? Cool. This is dope af, Dad."

I smiled. "Love it when you call me Dad. You know that? I smile every time. Trying to earn that title."

"Bruh, you already have that title. From day one. You gave me life and are helping me through life. You're here. You left your show for me and came back just when I needed you the most, and I love you for that."

I almost told him I was let go. I never wanted to lie to him. He had texted me that he was hungry, told me that they had no lights and the water had been turned off, and I freaked out, snapped on the next motherfucker in the show who said something sideways to me while I was trying to call the police to go check on my son's well-being. It was my burden. Wasn't his fault I'd lost the plot. I would never want him to think anything was his fault.

As he wrapped the hoodie around his waist, I asked, "Hungry?"

"You have to ask?"

"How much time we have?"

"Mom said one hour."

"Let's break bread."

"She's going to meet me right there where she dropped me off."

"Why couldn't we have met down at Venice Beach instead of here?"

"You love Venice Beach."

"I can find free parking there. Took me an hour to get a space here."

"She said it's cleaner, safer. She's always wanted to live on a nice beach."

"With white people."

"Is there any other kind of nice beach in Southern California?"

FELA ORDERED THE French Quarter burger and a large soda. I got a stack of pancakes and chicken sausage.

As we enjoyed breakfast, I told him, "Don't turn on me."

Fela bit into his hamburger, chewed, swallowed. "What you mean, Dad?"

"I know me and your mom have problems, but that's me and her. If you have problems with me as a dad, as a man, as a human being, tell me. Keep the door open; never burn the bridge between us. I love you and you're all in this world I love. Kids grow up and somehow things change and dad and son become bitter enemies."

"Like you and Grandad."

"I don't ever want for us to be estranged and not in touch or not talking."

Fela hesitated, his eyes watering. "Are you dying or something?"

"Of course not."

"Then why you being dramatic af?"

"Boy, I'm trying to be a better dad. Therefore, I need you to let me know what you need from me, what to do to make sure you're okay and we're okay and . . . I know I'm not the best dad, Fela. I know that. But I'm trying."

"There are worse."

"Shut up."

"You better not be dying."

"Now who's being dramatic? And whassup with you saying *af* all the time now?"

"Got that from Mom. She's the queen of saying *af* all the af-ing time."

"Stop it."

"What's going on? That look on your face is the one you get when you're stressed."

I got to the point. "I have to go to court again. I don't want to, but my accountant tells me I have no choice. Not making enough money, so I have to ask for a reduction. You want me to go to court and fight for full custody?"

"You mean, to make it legal for me to come to stay with you? You moving back?"

"In Florida. I've been renting out my house, but I can get my spot back with a sixty-day notice."

"All my friends are here. I'd be the new kid. No one wants to be the new kid."

I asked, "Sure you don't want to move to Florida with me?"

"My friends are here."

"After you graduate. When you're a legal adult."

"Dad. Florida. Stand-your-ground state."

"Yeah."

"Where they make up reasons to shoot black people."

"Son."

"A crazy man can follow me, harass me, shoot me, kill me, and blame me, even though he was stalking me. No, thanks, Dad. No, thanks. People with guns will shoot you because you're black and a male. Police, neighborhood watch, random person who is mad that your music is too loud. It's scary. Especially in Florida. I'd rather avoid the Crips and Bloods and the LAPD in California. I don't need to go where every fool is strapped and shooting blacks."

That ended that.

I said, "Okay. I'm trying to do what I think is best for you. My conditions are better; that's all I'm saying."

"Mom would be upset with me. It wouldn't be fair to her."

"Okay, Son. I wasn't trying to stress you."

"No matter what, I can't leave Mom. Besides, you know she won't sign off on that idea."

"I want you to know I'll fight for you. I'll spend my last dime to make sure you're okay."

"What good would spending your last dime do if that left everybody broke? We'd be worse off."

"I'd do what I had to do. I'd take out loans. Sell my house to pay to make sure you're okay."

"Dad, eat your pancakes and let me enjoy my juicy burger and fries, please?"

"I'm trying to be your dad."

"You showed up. You always show up. Job done. Now, eat."

Another moment passed. "I'm your dad and I'm supposed to give you sage advice."

"Shoot your best shot."

"Be humble. Be hardworking. Be kind. Be generous. Be curious. Be trustworthy. Be forgiving. Your time is limited, so don't waste it living someone else's life. Work hard. Have to say that twice. Enjoy being young. Time will go by fast. Feels like I was your age yesterday. Above all, be yourself. Be yourself and know you have a dad who loves you unconditionally and beyond the grave."

He asked, "What else you got? Keep going, Pa."

"It's unavoidable, but you're going to get your heart broken one day. Happens to us all, whether you deserve it or not. One day a friend will not be your friend anymore. You will lose a job and it won't be your fault. You will fail at something, some test life throws at you. There will be moments where people will make you feel less, and guess what. I'll always be here for you. No matter the ups or downs, I'll be here for you, Fela. I will always do my best."

"Not too bad, Dad. Not too bad."

I paused. "That's all I got for now."

"Hashtag listening to my dad's advice. Hashtag getting emotional."

I smiled. "What are you studying? Which class is the hardest?"

"Theories of Deviance. Have to do a paper tonight. I'm working on a short story too."

"Short story? Didn't know you were writing."

"Runs in the family."

"Can I read it?"

"Yeah, but you'll be too harsh."

"Mom see it?"

"She's not as critical as you. I get it, Dad. I'm a black kid. You're harsh with me because you see that as toughening me up, getting me ready for this cruel white world. I get it. Especially when I'm with you."

"People treat you differently when you're with Mom?"

"Well, people used to think she was the babysitter or had kid-napped an African American baby."

"Anyone ever call the cops? They call the cops on black people in a heartbeat."

"She's white. She could kidnap Africa, and no one would. Wait, the white half of my bloodline did that. My bad."

"You got jokes."

"Self-deprecating humor helps me get through the day."

I asked, "What do you want to do in life?"

"I don't want to do what you do. You're gone months at a time, and Mom hates it."

"You hate it?"

"Used to. I'm used to it now. We text and stuff, but I'm not used to being face-to-face." He laughed. "You're like a plane that's flying around the world, going city to city, and I'm just an airport layover."

That joke stung. "You're used to me not being here."

"You're used to not being here. You get home and you get antsy like you need to leave again."

"Being on the road gets in your blood."

"It's like you live in a different city every week. I have to track your show online to know where you are."

"You're not used to being around me; is that what you're saying?"

Fela shrugged. "Like this. It's odd."

"Frenchie got a boyfriend?"

"Why?"

"I'm not here, so was wondering if you . . . had another male role model. It's important. A black child needs a black man to help navigate him though this white world. Would be great if she . . . had a friend like that."

"She goes on dates, I think."

"You think?"

"She doesn't tell me anything except to stay home and study until she gets back."

"She stays out all night?"

"No later than midnight. She likes to go to bed early."

"Often?"

Fela shrugged. "Maybe once a month."

"Okay."

"Dad. You have a girlfriend?"

"Nobody special. Never in one spot long enough to make anything work."

"All those women in those pictures you take online?"

"Just random people. Nobody special. They all go away in the end."

We finished eating and went outside to walk around and browse the shops.

Fela said, "Dad? Why didn't you marry Mom?"

That jarred me and I was silent for a few seconds. "I don't know. Just didn't work out that way."

"She said that being married to a white woman would've been bad for your career, would've destroyed your black fan base, made black women hate you, and left you talented but broke, and ostracized."

"I never said that."

"She said you were ashamed to be seen with her outside of the tour."

"There is a lot she didn't tell you. I'm not the only ingredient in this gumbo."

"Dad."

"You know she was married when I met her, right?"

"She said you had a girlfriend."

"*Your mother was married.*"

"You cheated on your girlfriend."

"*She cheated on her husband.*"

"Chill, Dad. You look like you're ready to flip a table. I read that the average person falls in love seven times before getting married. Maybe you hadn't fallen in love with enough people before you met her."

I took a breath, reeled it in. "The child becomes the teacher."

"I'm not a child."

"My bad."

"No offense, but I'm watching you and Mom to learn what not to do."

"Are we that bad?"

"I'm sure there are worse."

"Burn."

"Some of my friends would be glad to get *one* text from their dad, let alone *see* him. For a lot of them the word *dad* isn't in their vocabulary. I get to use the word *dad* every day. For them Father's Day is some kind of anti-holiday, a day of hate or ridicule or remorse or bitterness. You try, Dad. You're in my life. I always know where you are. You answer when I call. Plus, you send me bomb presents and the swag is poppin'. Means a lot to me."

"I'll do better."

"Have I really cost you a million dollars so far?"

I sighed. "That wasn't why I showed you that. You thought I had never paid your mom any money for some reason. She misled you. I just wanted you to know I was being responsible. I'm not a deadbeat dad."

Fela took a second. "I'm the reason everybody is broke."

"Stop it."

"To be clear, you know I'm not paying you back, right?"

Laughter pulled us together, father and son, and my heart felt lighter and hopeful. My laughter was strong, but short-lived. It ended when I saw Frenchie heading our way, resting bitch face in full effect.

CHAPTER 34

DWAYNE

FROM THE MULTITUDE of tourists and locals Frenchie sashayed our way. My child's mother wore a sheer, crotch-high tunic over a two-piece bathing suit. Heart-shaped lips, the kind many women paid to get installed. Solid legs. Just enough hook to her bottom. Memories stood up, danced, made some decisions seem like regrets.

Frenchie asked Fela, "You eat?"

I said, "You're not talking to me?"

Sarcasm on one hundred, she replied, "Scared if I speak, your punk ass might call the cops."

"I did what I had to do."

"That was fucked-up."

"Mom. Language."

I said, "So is having a starving child. If I didn't care, I would have done nothing."

Fela said, "I'm not starving, Dad."

"Should I show your mother the text messages you sent?"

Frenchie said, "*You called the cops.* Be glad I feel like being nice today."

Fela snapped, "Everybody chill."

I told Frenchie, "I want to show my son Bruce's Beach."

Frenchie added more resistance and attitude. "I'm sorry. Did I hear the word *please* in that sentence? You make requests, cleared by me, and don't you dare show up making demands. I'm the full-time parent."

"Sure. *Please*, may I show *my son* the historic Bruce's Beach?"

"What's that, where is that, and why does he need to see it with you?"

"Used to be a black beach until . . . until the KKK . . . until it wasn't. Do I have your permission?"

"Can't you just spend time with your son instead of making it a field trip about racism? A day like today, a day this beautiful, and that's what you want to do with your son? A son you haven't seen since—"

"*Ma.*"

"Racism will be here tomorrow, Dwayne. Enjoy your son and the weather today. Because we both know another storm is coming soon. If you've forgotten, have your attorney ask my attorney for details."

"Ma. Dad. How about I cut myself in half and you both get a piece?"

That shut it down for now. Family court would resurrect ghosts and open old wounds.

Frenchie asked, "Where is that beach located?"

"Walking distance. Highland and Twenty-Seventh. Want to show him the overlooked marker that looks like a dead culture's tombstone and teach him about the racial history of black people down here in Manhattan Beach."

Frenchie said, "You can go with your dad if you want to go, Fela. That's all I was saying. If *you* want to. Don't be afraid to tell me or Dwayne that you want to do something, or don't want to do something."

Frenchie smiled at Fela, and he nodded a nod that said that he wanted to come with me because that was what I wanted to do with him. His expression begged his mom not to continue an argument in public. Cops a few feet away slowed and watched us, evaluated the bad-tempered situation. Black man. White woman. Arguing over a teenager, his hue somewhere in between, his hair radical. Hashtag moment. Frenchie waved. The cops nodded, then moved on. Her tribe. Her privilege was being used to protect and serve the black life in her life that mattered.

She told Fela, "Two hours. Meet me over there. You have your phone?"

"In my pocket."

"Two hours, Dwayne. Respect my wishes. Two hours or it's my turn to call the cops."

CHAPTER 35

DWAYNE

AFTER GOING BY Bruce's Beach, we ran back toward the pier, passed the skaters, bicyclists, joggers, and walkers on the paved trail, hiked the sand, laughed and jested, until we found Frenchie. One hour and fifty-nine minutes had passed. My son's mother saw us coming. I nodded at Frenchie. She went back to focusing on her workout. She was on a low concrete wall. Frenchie stood like a gymnast and did a backflip, hit the desert's warm sand, and did thirteen more backflips, half of them handless. Performed like it was no big deal. She wore her bikini top and thong bottom, everything Speedo tight, like every female volleyball player. Her body was show-business ready.

She used to do those across the stage during rehearsal, effortlessly, for kicks, for attention. That was how she had caught my eye. She had done a set and grinned at me. She was married back then, showing off, flirting. Her enormous talent had me as in awe of her as she was of me.

We'd given each other that attention and praise that all entertainers needed. We had fed each other praises until our bellies were filled and we both needed to be burped.

Frenchie did handstands, cartwheels. When some music came on, when "Level Up" jammed from a nearby speaker, she danced like Ciara. Fela ran over and joined in. They tried to outdance each other. Fela didn't stand a chance. Frenchie had been performing since she could walk, and it showed. I watched the former pop star and thespian show off, watched her be a peahen and garner applause. Mother and son were like brother and sister.

Their bond was strong, unbreakable. I felt my absence in Fela's life, and it hurt like hell. I'd worked hard, provided, worked in shows I hated to keep the cash coming in, and I had still managed to fall short.

I wanted a do-over, but there were only do-overs in theater, where each night you got to repeat the same show, you got to fix any mistakes, to rewrite dialogue, to change entrances and exits.

Life wasn't that way.

Frenchie looked better now than fifteen years ago.

It disturbed me, the sensuous way her legs moved, their rhythm.

My million-dollar kid came to me, hugged me, said he had to go. I wanted to hold him there. I grasped for a conversation that would make me worthy of being his dad, something that acknowledged he was no longer a child.

"Do I need to talk to you about being mixed race?"

"I *abhor* being called mixed. Makes me feel like a science experiment."

"Any problems?"

"Same thing as most kids who are like me. We get picked on more. Mostly by blacks. Whites are afraid to call me names to my face because they'll be called racists. But black people. Mutt. Half-breed. Corny stuff."

"It's fucked that we even need to have that conversation. This isn't anything new."

"Girl I like, she was telling me about all the racism her parents went through."

"Who is this girl?"

"She's biracial. Her last name is Greene but we call her Chavers. She has red hair. Her mom is a famous artist, and her dad is a big-time engineer or something, like Uncle Brick. She's older, but I really like her."

"What you like about her?"

"She is woke af. She vibes to Badu and twerks to Boosie."

"How much older is this intellectual-yet-twerking woke girl?"

"One year. She goes to the Ramón C. Cortines School of Visual and Performing Arts."

"You having sex with this freckle-faced redheaded biracial girl who looks like Ella Mai?"

"Dad, I'm still a virgin."

"Really?"

"I'm not smashing. Don't do the stereotypical thing and think that since I'm a black kid over five years old I'm having sex. Virgin. For real. Girls know I'm pure and are coming at me. They made a bet who can hit this first. They be coming by the house trying to get in my window all through the night, especially on Saturdays."

"Be coming?"

"I'm half-black. Let me be all black af and wreck verbs for fun when I'm in that state of mind."

"What I just tell you about saying *af*?"

"Let me be black af like Chavers. I'll speak the queen's English and use *af* on the way home."

We laughed. I remembered him the day he was born. I remembered him in diapers. He was a young man now and needed me as much now as he ever would. I gave him a hundred dollars.

He asked, "You sure?"

"Take it before I change my mind."

He hugged me like he loved me just as much as he loved his mother.

I didn't want to let him go, but Frenchie came to rain on the end of the celebration. She took his hand and stole him away from me.

I walked behind them, in the horde of faceless people, like I was a goddamn stranger. As we stood at the light to cross the street, Frenchie gazed over at me. Sighed. Considered me. It was her first time looking me in my eyes since New Jersey. She regarded me, and the hard edges softened up, but her lips turned downward.

Fela broke in. "Mom, stop scowling. You're being twitchy af and weird af all of a sudden."

She rehabilitated her expression like she recalled New Jersey again. I cleared my throat, adjusted my mind, did the same.

CHAPTER 36

BRICK

THE NEXT DAY as I slept, someone used a key; then my front door opened and closed hard.

A pained voice called out, *"Briiiiick?"*

I ended my nap and opened my eyes.

That pained voice called out again, *"Briiiiick?"*

"Coming."

She groaned. "Don't yell."

"I'm not yelling."

I was home, in my bed, early afternoon. I followed the distressed voice to my kitchen.

Mocha Latte had on dark running shorts, dark bra, and a dark wifebeater. She was sitting in a kitchen chair, bent over, elbows on the old wooden table, holding her head, leg bouncing like a jackhammer.

She raised her head when I came near her and made a face like some-one had dropped an anvil on her foot.

I grabbed a bottle of water from the fridge. "What's wrong?"

She took a breath. "Migraine. I told you I get stupid-bad migraines."

"How stupid-bad is this one?"

"Don't drink the water so loud."

"Loudly."

"Go to hell."

"Sorry."

"I was trying to masturbate to self-medicate and make my head stop aching. Can't focus."

"You just masturbated?"

"Tried."

"Oh. Did you need my bed?"

"Was about to ask you for a favor."

"This is a joke, right?"

Her face showed me the intensity of her pain. "Orgasm turns off the migraine pain. I need the endorphin rush or I'll go crazy. I would pay you. It would be a professional service. Don't get it twisted."

"Are you serious?"

"I decided that wasn't the right move."

"Great. Now I have a migraine in my balls."

"Was up all night. I messed around and didn't take medicine in time. I should take medicine every day, but it messes with my digestive system. So, I try to fight my way through. But this time, it's really bad."

I asked, "Where are Penny and Christiana?"

It was hard for her to speak. "They're at Venice Beach. Roller-blading."

I asked, "Should I call them to come back and help?"

She shook her head. "They can't do anything for me."

"You sure?"

"Look in my purse. Tell me which medicines I have inside the green bag in there."

"Where is it?"

She struggled, pointed to the kitchen counter, then went back to bouncing her leg with the pain.

I said, "Found it. "Co-codamol?"

She made affirmative sounds. "And get the Tylenol."

"How many?"

"I don't know. Just . . . just . . . just give me two of each."

"That will be about two thousand milligrams of mixed medicine."

"When it's this bad, it only works for me if I make a cocktail."

Mocha Latte took her cocktail, then grabbed a pillow and crashed on the oversize classic sofa.

I got back into bed, stared at the ceiling until sleep found me.

Mocha Latte made a pained sound from the living room and woke me up.

I called out, "How's the migraine?"

"Fuckity fuck. Fuck. Okay. This is too much. Meet me in the bathroom."

MOCHA LATTE SLAPPED two hundred dollars in tens, twenties, and fifties down on the bathroom counter.

She picked up her phone and said, "Siri, set timer for thirty minutes."

"What am I doing?"

"Hands and mouth, that's all. Fingerfuck, French kiss me there, fix this migraine."

Mocha Latte sat on the edge of the counter. I left her long enough to grab a pillow from the bed. I came back, dropped it on the floor, got down on my knees. I pushed her legs apart, patted her sex, looked up at her face, saw pain and the need for me to hurry up. I touched her vagina, fingered the outside, felt she was dry, then moisturized her with my tongue, took in that salty sweet taste of a woman. I got her wet and worked her with two fingers. She sat up to make sure I got in good, got the angle right. I pressed my left hand against her belly and worked her, massaged her insides with the fingers on my right.

I'd fingered Coretta right here, just like this, more times than I could remember.

"Ah ah ah ah ah ah ah ah ah ah ah ah ah."

I was so into doing this, so in my zone. I had done this to Coretta, had done it often, but it had never felt as good as this. Pleasing Mocha Latte satisfied me as much as it was a curative for her. She tasted so good it almost made me come. If I had to eat one thing for the rest of my life, Mocha Latte would be my soup du jour. I looked at her face, at her beautiful dark skin, at her underlying glow, her desperate expression, and I felt the army of twitches, the orgasmic sensations gathering up and beginning to explode, rolling throughout her trembling body. I gazed at her as she held on to the edges of the counter. She shuddered and held on like she was on the edge of the sea cliffs along the western coast of the Canary Islands, with no option but to surrender to orgasm's gravity, to let a thousand little deaths loosen her hands and make her let go and force her to fall sixteen hundred feet and sink into the warm sea.

She moaned, "You got me you got me you got me you got me you got me damn you got me."

She sat up straight, then slid down off the counter to the cool tile on the bathroom floor. I massaged her slowly, rhythmically, backward and forward without pause, took her higher as she moved to get on her haunches, fingered her as she held the sink and bounced, as she moved up and down on my hand.

"Oh my God, oh my God, oh my God, yes yes yes yes."

That beautiful woman made ugly expressions that let me know her dark and lovely face was on fire. She fell away from my face, stood up, told me to come with her. She dragged me into the bedroom. We hurried to get in bed. She pulled me on top of her, her toned legs wide open. Her ankles hooked around me as she reached for my cock.

I stopped her. "You paid for fingers and tongue. That thick Brick dick costs extra."

"Really? Fucking really? I mean really, you're going to do an upsale, fatherfucker?"

"This is a professional service."

"One hundred."

"Two hundred."

"One fifty."

"Two."

"One sixty-five."

"Two."

"Okay okay okay, two fucking hundred."

"Cash. Plus tip."

"Fifteen percent."

"Twenty percent. Plus blueberry pancakes in the morning."

"Get a condom. And I want repeats."

"No repeats."

"No repeats, no pancakes. And I want that level-three shit you can do, or no goddamn pancakes."

"Okay, one repeat at level three."

She said, "Damn you. Siri, set timer for one hour."

I countered, "Oh, hell no. Siri, set timer for thirty minutes."

"Charging me another two hundred and pancakes? Fatherfucker, you better smash this migraine to smithereens."

CHAPTER 37

BRICK

TWO HOURS LATER Mocha Latte shook me out of another dream.

"Brick. Wake up. I need you to drive me to meet my date."

She'd showered, was rocking a wig that made her hair jet-black and bone straight and was dressed like an astute businesswoman. Penny and Christiana were in the living room. The television was on. *Family Feud.* I smelled dinner cooking, and it smelled so good my stomach growled. I went into the kitchen. Christiana had made a five-course Cuban meal of black bean soup, *croquetas*, shrimp with cilantro cream, garlicky chicken, and salad.

She said, "I try to cook something that everyone will like. *Buen provecho.*"

I said, "You're spoiling me."

"Let me know if I am overstaying my welcome."

"If you leave, wherever you go, I'm going too."

She said, "I love it here. But we could all put our money together and lease a nice condo in Playa Vista, or maybe a high-rise in Marina del Rey. I did some investigating, and I hope you don't mind."

She took out brochures, put on her excited smile, passed them out to all of us. The booklets showed three- and four-bedroom condos, each bedroom with its own bath. Each unit had a private elevator. Kitchens by Poggenpohl. Granite countertops. Miele double oven paired with induction cooktop and hood. Dishwasher and Sub-Zero refrigerator. Eleven-foot ceiling with floor-to-ceiling glass windows. Wraparound glass balconies.

Each property was breathtaking. Made my place feel like the junk-yard on *Sanford and Son*.

Christiana said, "No one would have to work more than once or twice a month to pay their part of the rent. If you worked twice that, each month or so you could vacation in Barbados or Belize. We could schedule in-calls then. No more driving three hours in traffic to work an hour. Time is money. Think about it; no need to discuss or commit now. I know Mocha Latte has to go to work soon, and it's a long drive to get from here to Newport Beach in this horrible traffic."

Penny hummed. "Marina del Rey is a very expensive zip code."

"It's all about location. We can earn more for doing the same thing, and it will be done in the safety of our own condo, not in random houses or in hotels. And when we are not working, we have that ocean view. We can relax, and Penny can study, and we can do it all with fresh ocean air blowing in our windows every day, and after we watch the beautiful sunset, we can sleep in its coolness at night. Plus, we'd save many dollars on gas money. Gas prices are ridiculous."

Christiana had been transformed, like the lead character in the classic movie *Caged*. Sweet innocent girl went to jail, locked up for a crime her husband committed, and came out hardened. All that mattered was what was in it for her. Life in Cuba with an unfaithful husband had been Christiana's cage. If her marriage hadn't gone south, I wondered what the attorney would be doing now. She would have a kid, or kids, be a mother, be living a different life, one that she didn't almost drown trying to escape. Love no longer mattered to her. Winning was all that mattered.

I GASSED UP Miss Mini; then Mocha Latte and I hit the freeway. Had to go forty miles south in grim traffic to Newport Beach. In constipated traffic. Mocha Latte had an overnight date with a man who lived on a yacht.

Mocha Latte was still looking at the brochures that Christiana had given us, captivated by the lifestyle she'd been offered. As we moved through LA toward the tiki torch part of Southern Cali, we chatted.

I asked, "How's the migraine?"

She laughed.

I smiled. "What was that strange little laugh all about?"

"Learn to negotiate. I would've paid you at least five hundred. You had me. When you have a client stressed like that, you can get them to buy you a house just to be licked one more time, especially the way you eat pussy."

"Didn't mean to be a cheap date."

"Migraine gone, as if it never were. That three-levels-deep shit you can do is both scary and—"

Her phone rang, and she took the call.

She said, "Sorry, but I'm a soft dom. Because I really don't like violence. Sorry. Because I'm not into that. It's not about raising the price to feed your fetish. What? Well, fuck you too. Your momma."

"And scene."

She ended the business call and sighed. "These fatherfucking fatherfuckers. I try to be professional. Some people don't hear a soft, polite no. Then you give them a hard no, and they call you asshole, bitch, and cunt."

A look of disgust came and went.

I asked, "Everything okay?"

"You make the girlfriend experience feel real for me. You make GFE feel real."

Mocha Latte frowned, hummed, and rested her soft hand on mine; our fingers interlocked.

She asked, "What do you think about Christiana's proposition?"

"She's focused. She's about the money. An altruistic entrepreneur."

"Made us that big-ass Cuban dinner and softened us up before she put that proposal out there."

"I noticed. She made me imagine getting homemade meals like that on the regular."

"Everything with her is calculated."

"What are your thoughts?"

"It scared me, being in that deep, but it sounded like the life I deserve. Those properties . . . I want that life."

"We all want that life."

"Would be nice to wake up with a view of the ocean. Barnes & Noble is a block away. I could chill there and read. There are two dozen restaurants in walking distance. And at least two movie theaters. And a swank grocery store. All the mainstream coffee shops. DSW to feed my shoe fetish. I could get so many more runs in because the beach would be a mile away. And Christiana's right, in that zip code, I could triple my fees for companionship."

She let my hand go, the affection she had for me gone, replaced by a new ambition.

She asked me, "What are you up to tonight? Are you going on a date?"

"Nope. Dropping you off, then heading back to Leimert Park. Why?"

"Because you packed up a picnic basket of food like you're going on a hot date."

"Just taking some relatives some food."

She stared out the window like a woman looking for her true love in the darkness.

I asked, "We good?"

She whispered, "'Beauty is an aphrodisiac of which you are not in short supply. I see an abundance.'"

"I meant that."

"Liar."

"I'm not lying."

"You had me twice and haven't asked me my real name once."

"Paid services each time, so technically, I've never been with you romantically."

"You didn't ask when you danced and kissed me in public like I was Cinderella."

"You never asked mine."

"*Yours was on your mail.* At least I know who I've been with. You have no idea. Never asked."

Annoyed, I asked, "What's your real name, Mocha Latte? Cappuccino? Hot Chocolate? Tell me."

"Doesn't matter. That was the last time, Brick. Never again, not even for a stroke-level migraine."

"I know your goddamn name."

"What is it? What is my name, Brick? Who am I?"

"First name Simply. Last name Beautiful."

"Know when to stop joking."

"Am I laughing?"

"Never again."

"Cool by me."

"Fuck. Jesus. No. I've become a goddamn Penny. A fucking Penny after two times."

"Are you serious? You're a goddamn riddle wrapped in a mystery inside an enigma."

"You don't know my name. You never asked. So I don't matter to you, nigga."

We went back and forth like an old married couple, but soon we held hands again until her phone rang. It was the mechanical engineer she'd met online, the decent-looking nerd with the PhD. She sent the call to voice mail. She took my hand again, restless. I saw that conflicted look on her face. She was struggling with her duality.

She asked, "Penny okay? That night at the Viceroy scared her to death. She was talking about quitting."

"It was a watershed moment. For both of us. Never saw her so terrified."

"I was talking about quitting too, while I'm ahead. Before this becomes a career."

"Then what?"

"Malakoff. There is a tractor there with my name on it."

"Too bad this had no foundation. I'd drive you to the real Vegas and make you my wife."

"Too bad it can't be reverse engineered."

"Marry me anyway."

"Sure, Brick, if you can tell me this. Which is the first element on the periodic table?"

"Carbon."

"You blew it. Last try. Which Spanish town is completely surrounded by France?"

"Damn you."

She laughed and held my hand tighter.

"Brick. Tell me about this experience you had with cancer."

"Why?"

She held my hand a little tighter. "Because I care."

We had bad traffic and a good hour to go to get to Newport Beach. I took a breath, told her all about it.

Chemo, three days in a row, then three weeks off, five cycles.

The pretending to not be weak.

The opioids for pain. The medicine for nausea.

The fear when I dropped twenty pounds in a week.

The mornings I cried alone, then faced the world and pretended to be perfect.

The days I didn't have enough energy to get out of my fucking bed.

André was on the road telling jokes and Dwayne had been touring with his stage play.

Dwayne Sr. wouldn't have cared, would've thought I needed his financial help.

I didn't worry my momma or my stepdad. We talked on the phone, but I hid my issues.

Frenchie had been going through what she was going through, and I was going through my own shit.

God had everybody too occupied, had us thinking everybody else was doing just fine.

We'd all been suffering in our own way, doing it in silence.

I hadn't told anyone that much detail.

She held my hand and cried.

CHAPTER 38

BRICK

LATE EVENING, I met Dwayne back at Hot and Cool Cafe. He was dressed in distressed denim, a pure-white T-shirt, and a big brown fedora. He was drinking a chai and ranting while he flipped through the pages of *Backstage*.

"How in the fuck have I paid a million dollars and my son is still starving? Hasn't Frenchie saved one dime over all these years she's been sweating me and bleeding me for every penny she can get?"

I almost told him what Frenchie told me not to tell, but instead I said, "Checkmate. New subject."

"What does she plan to do when Fela turns eighteen and I make the last payment?"

"Get your laptop, open up a new file in Word, and write out your anger. Say all the negative shit you want to say there. Call her names. Tell her how you really feel about her, about the situation. Then e-mail that six-page diatribe to yourself. Read it ten times, then delete it. Because once it's said, it can't be unsaid."

Then my brother shifted gears, started a new conversation, asked, "The girl you broke up with . . ."

"Coretta."

"Bad breakup?"

"Bad enough."

Dwayne said, "Not all breakups are bad. Sometimes when you break up with somebody, it hurts but it forces you into a better place. Know that. Sometimes it's better to push the reset button and start over with somebody new, as opposed to dealing with something that is never going to get any better. Pussy good, relationship bad, then relationship bad, even when the pussy is good. Learn to let go of the pussy, no matter how good."

"Funny how you get your heart broken, but you'll take them back instantly just to ease the pain."

"New poison is the cure. A new poison will make you forget the old poison."

"Sometimes poison is just poison."

"A brokenhearted man is a broken man, so he does things to make himself feel like a man worthy of being called a man again. Be careful what you do to make yourself feel like a man again."

I realized that Dwayne was always listening to me. Even if he didn't respond, he heard me.

I nodded. "I'm proud of you. You've fought this battle over Fela for over fifteen years and you've never given up. Even though I'm tired of hearing you talk about that shit, I'm not tired of hearing how you feel. I care how you feel. I'm learning how to be strong too, how to not give up. You taught me to not give up, to be persistent, and most of all, to love. Sometimes men go away, run away, so they won't have to be a father. Your son loves and respects you because you love and respect him. Unlike my dad, our dad, who was horrible at taking care of that which he created."

Dwayne said, simply, "I'm glad you're my brother."

"We almost didn't meet. Never would have if it had been up to Dwayne Sr."

"Nigga Daddy."

"He didn't want it this way."

He said, "I hated being an only child. I was so happy when I accidentally found out I had siblings."

"Accidentally."

He nodded. "My mother had written your name down, as my brother, on a document for social security. She knew and wasn't going to tell me. Yeah, I remember when I first found out that I had a brother that my dad had never told me existed."

"You were eleven and I was six years old. I remember it like it was yesterday."

"I found your address and I rode my bike to your parents' front door, knocked and asked for you. They asked me who I was, and I told them I was your brother, and I was coming to meet you. You were six and had a baby brother by your momma and her new husband. André."

"Our mothers could easily pass for sisters."

"Yeah. Seeing your mother look so much like mine surprised me. Both were educators who had fallen for a businessman on the rise. My mother is smart and beautiful and vulnerable at the same time, almost sad and glamorous all at once. After I found out about you, I was scared to meet you."

"You never told me that."

"Fear of rejection. You were surprised and happy to know you had an older brother."

"I showed you all of my comics."

"Yeah. We sat down in your room and you were so excited to show me all of your comic books. You had at least five hundred comic books in a box. Every Saturday I'd come by to pick you up, and André would look at us, see us about to walk to the corner store to get cookies or whatever, and start to cry because he wanted to go with us."

"You picked him up."

"He clung to me. I asked your momma and stepdad if André could go with us because you were my brother and André was your brother, so that made André my baby brother too. I went from being an only child to having two awesome brothers. I lived for Saturdays. Had to take y'all and show my younger brothers off to everybody."

"We went everywhere you went. Barbershop. Hoops. Track. Piano lessons. Singing lessons. Dance lessons. We did what you did."

"Sure did. André could barely walk, but he was right there, trying to keep up."

I said, "You showed up at my doorstep forming a link that shaped our lives and didn't even know it."

"Caused drama with all the parents. All the lies had to be confronted because of me."

I gritted my teeth. "Fuck them for lying. You were more adult than the adults."

I wanted this conversation with Dwayne Jr. regarding Dwayne Sr. to end as abruptly as it had started.

He took a breath. "Anything else going on with you? I've been gone too long and came back stressed out with my head up my ass. Was just so focused on Frenchie and Fela that I forgot the world don't revolve around me."

I regarded my older brother, felt like confession was good for the soul and was about to finally tell him I'd been sick for a few months, but was better, much better, and like him, I had my own bills to catch up on. I wanted to tell him how I needed to get back to my full-time job now that I was off the magical juice from City of Hope and Kaiser, but I wasn't one to complain. He hadn't told me that Frenchie was having a hard time until he had to, and Fela knew I was a text message away, yet he never reached out. Men were like that, none more than the Duquesne men. Black men were like that to the grave. We were treated as adults from the womb and seen as warriors with no weaknesses. We suffered in silence, handled things on our own. We didn't really sit around and powwow our problems over wine at a pity party. We just handled it. We were about solving issues, not pointless conversations that offered no solutions.

He saw things his way; Frenchie saw them hers; same as I saw things my way and Coretta saw things hers.

He said, "Fela asked me why I didn't marry his mother. That question hit me hard."

I asked, "Why didn't you marry Frenchie? I mean, you did knock her up. Legit question."

"Loved her, but I knew I'd miss being in the arms of a black woman."

"That's not why."

"But it's an ingredient in the soup somewhere. I would've missed Eigengrau too much back then."

"Is there a word for that?"

"Word for what?"

"Should be one for longing for the love of a black woman."

"Should be. Would have helped me describe my issues to my therapist."

"In German, *Fernweh* means 'feeling homesick for a place you've never been to.' Can't say I've ever suffered from that malady, but there should be a word for the psychological condition, for the strong feeling, of needing to be in the arms of a black woman again, if not for the rest of your life, then only for one night."

Seconds passed before he said, "Part of being free is the freedom to choose who you love."

"I know."

"I knocked up Frenchie and destroyed Eigengrau. I destroyed her love for me."

I said, "Eigengrau was a smart one. Not many actresses have advanced degrees."

"She was Dorothy Dandridge and Lola Falana wrapped in one."

"She was a hot one."

Dwayne exhaled. "I loved Frenchie, but I was already suffering from

Eigengrau withdrawals. Hard to explain that shit. I was with Frenchie and missing Eigengrau day and night, but I still loved Frenchie."

I understood the battle in his heart. "You see Eigengrau at the Santa Monica party?"

"I saw her. I went over to her. Told her I was happy for her, then nodded and walked away."

"Pregnant. Married. She's moved on."

Dwayne took a moment, overwhelmed. "My therapist. I need to schedule a session."

"For now, keep talking to me. Talking to me is free, though I will accept donations and tips."

"I need a professional. My stuff runs deep, way deep, too deep. Black men are abandoning their young like T. rex, and even though I'm trying to be a good dad, I'm still doing it all wrong for some reason."

"Man can't work the job you have and be home at the same time. Same for André."

"What I do is all I know how to do, and doing anything else would leave me depressed."

I wanted to ask him about being let go from his last tour, but I didn't. He'd have to bring it up. Boundaries. I just knew that I had two brothers who were entertainers, and show-business people were a special lot.

I said, "Your script."

"I'm not changing it."

"You were right. Don't gentrify your creation. You were right, and I was wrong."

"What in the Samuel L. Jackson is this?"

"It's pro-black to the bone. If they still see being black as being radical, then be radical. Don't sell out. Don't limit your imagination to match their version of us. We need that voice. We need your black perspective. First things first, though. You said you need to get your head right. How much is a therapy session or two?"

"As much as it costs to talk to a lawyer, except lawyers cost more because they charge to answer e-mails, DMs, or texts. I get charged for every freakin' second, and it's rounded up to the next half hour."

"Just to listen to you talk about the same shit you've been talking about for fifteen years?"

"You don't understand therapy. Not many black people do."

"I do understand. I need to find a Groupon and get a few sessions for myself."

He exhaled. "I'll be okay, Brick. I'll be okay."

I gave him money. A stranger had paid me for sex, and I gave that money to Dwayne like I was trying to get rid of it, like it didn't have the value of real money because of how it was earned.

I said, "You can either talk to somebody or get Nephew's water and lights turned on. It's up to you, and if you choose the latter, don't put my name in it. Say it all came from your pockets. I want you to be his hero."

He pushed the money back to me. That was a first. I told him to hang on to it and decide.

I said, "If you have it this time next week and your pockets are hot, give it all back."

We sat there a moment, him considering his options. Finally, he took the money.

Dwayne went to the piano, performed a song from *Phantom of the Opera* to calm his anger and angst. The café was packed. A few people went and sat on the big red sofa near the piano, up front for the concert.

This get-together at Hot and Cool Cafe had been my idea. I had used Big Brother as a cover because I had hoped to see someone else. Uber-for-One hadn't left my mind. No matter what I had done, no matter how I had evolved, or devolved, she was on my mind every day. I asked one of the owners if the beauty in the Uber for one had been back. They remembered her but hadn't seen her. I wished she had dropped a glass slipper.

A text came in from Mocha Latte letting me know all was well in Newport Beach.

For her it would be a night of champagne wishes and caviar dreams.

André whipped up on his yellow-and-red BMW. He parked right out front. He had an apple booty rocking pink-and-red high-heel motorcycle boots on the back. That wasn't Nameless. This body was a little bit fuller, had a touch more this, that, and the other. When she dismounted and took her helmet off, I saw the same flaming red-and-yellow hair I'd seen on a hot number wearing short white pants back at the Viceroy in Santa Monica. The thick, sweet-breasted, full-figured, bad-bodied brown girl dressed in tight jeans and a yellow hoodie with African kente prints.

Dwayne had also noticed André's arrival and returned to the table. I asked him, "Who is she?"

"Joëlle."

"What happened to Nameless?"

"They had a big blowout in Santa Monica. Joëlle showed up uninvited. Came to see André. Nameless showed up uninvited. Came to see André. He left with Joëlle. It was a butt-ugly moment."

André came in and pulled Dwayne back over to the piano. They started playing "Stairway to Heaven" and I flipped both of them off. Left alone, his girl sashayed to the counter, placed an order, then sat down at a bistro table at the other side of the café, smiling as André sang with Dwayne. She was totally enamored.

I went to them, joined in on the keys, asked, "How's it going, André? Looking tired, bro."

"Shit. Monday, Tuesday, Wednesday, Thursday, Friday, twice on Saturday, thrice on Sunday."

Dwayne chuckled. "The new temporary one won't give you a break."

I asked, "What she do?"

"She was a double-E major at Berkeley."

"Double-E majors come built like that nowadays?"

"She's smarter than she is fine. Smart, nerdy, cosplay-loving girls are the best in bed for damn sho'."

We all high-fived one another.

I said, "Dwayne, show André your script for that Stanislavski-level movie you wrote."

"There better be a leading part for me in that bad boy."

I motioned. "It's in his bag; chillax here and read it to your new girl."

André told me, "Call Mom, Brick. She hasn't heard from you in a few days and you know how she gets."

I nodded. "Will call her later."

"She wants us to fly out there for a weekend so we can go fishing again."

"With the Afro-Mexicans?"

"Our people, Brick. Whether we speak Spanish or not, they're part of the diaspora, and our people."

Dwayne dug into André's pocket, pulled out his wallet, and took three hundred bucks. He handed the money to me, then took another five hundred dollars, put the cash in his pocket, and tossed André his wallet back.

Dwayne proclaimed, "Now you owe me seven hundred, André. Brick, we're even Steven."

WHILE MY BROTHERS talked, I took André's keys, grabbed his helmet, and took off on his iron horse. It was his turn to deal with Dwayne. I zigzagged the neighborhood to avoid the construction for the Metro train and headed toward Wilshire, suit coat flapping in the desert air. Then I took it another twenty minutes to the 105 freeway before heading back toward Hot and Cool, with one thought stuck in my mind. Christiana had me booked, and the day for that date was almost here. Penny was ready to get out, same with Mocha Latte, just as I had fallen in.

I'd become an accidental escort. Four times I had been paid. That was four times more than 99.99999 percent of the men on earth. The first time had been accidental, a setup, a test, but any occurrence after the first time had to be seen as intentional. I'd become a reluctant gigolo and had no idea how this shit had happened. At first, I was driving Penny to make sure she was safe. Now I was like Penny, had become a regular in Vegas. I understood how Penny had felt the first time. I understood why Christiana saw this as the way to salvation and redemption. I understood why it disturbed Mocha Latte but she kept answering the calls when they came in. It was nothing I wanted to do all my life. But the money had come so easily. Every dollar could be tax-free. It paid more than buying and reselling wine. Even paid more than my old white-collar job, the one my master's degree garnered me.

As I white-lined my way through traffic and dodged potholes as deep as a ditch, I passed more homeless encampments than I could count. I wondered how much fucking it would take to pay all of my bills and break even.

CHAPTER 39

BRICK

THE PEEPHOLE AT the presidential suite went dark. A kaleidoscope of flaming butterflies danced inside my stomach. I should've turned and hurried for the elevator. The door opened, and I faced a familiar Amazon, the gorgeous politician I had seen at the hotel bar with Mocha Latte, a woman who was as shapely as Big Barda. She looked me up and down, no smile. Maybe she didn't recognize me, or her taste in escorts had changed. Just in case, I had a novel in my hand. That was our signal. The book was *1Q84* by Haruki Murakami.

In a tone that said she was the boss, she snapped, "Both candidates are *sycophantic.*"

She wasn't barking at me. The dignified woman wore a blinking earpiece and was sipping white wine as she yakked on the phone, free hand flying like she was either Italian or landing ten planes at once.

"Yes. I was valedictorian at my high school, graduated from Princeton and Harvard Law. Yes, I saw online where professors described me as being off-the-charts brilliant. Yes, I won the US debating nationals. I argued cases in front of the Supreme Court. Will I run for president? We will see."

As she did her interview, she inspected me, the next words for my ears only.

She said, "I need your identification. Two forms of ID, both with recent photos."

I handed her my driver's license and passport. She put her call on hold long enough to snap photos of my identification with her phone; then she handed me a sheet of paper and a black Movado pen.

She said, "An NDA *must* be signed before we proceed with this interview."

I put the book down, signed the NDA, then handed the legal document back to her. She compared the signature to the signature on the license, then handed my identification back to me. As I put away my driver's license and passport, she went back to her call.

The clock on the wall said it was 5:11 P.M. An hour from now this would be over.

She motioned for me to follow. The hotel room was an ostentatious display of power and wealth.

I wanted to back out of this deal. But the money had been paid in advance. I'd been bought and paid for.

"Yes, I know the system. I grew up in the system. My mother was incarcerated, my father MIA. When elected, I will make the proper changes and will be the champion for all of our displaced children."

I waited, hands folded in front of me like I was still an usher at church.

She said, "Use the photo that was e-mailed to you. The one where we are all in white shirts on the rocky shores of Devil's Bridge in Antigua. The Atlantic Ocean is behind us. Because I'm Antiguan, that's why."

She objectified me with her eyes and snapped a finger at me. That meant she wanted me to follow the next part of the instructions. I eased out of my suit coat and took my clothing off, leaving only my boxers.

She whispered her command: "Everything."

The client watched me strip to my b-day suit as if to prevent me from stealing anything. I was smooth like a bodybuilder, didn't have any body hair now. For seconds that felt like minutes, I stood nude with her evaluating me in my most vulnerable state. I expected her to come over and check my teeth for cavities. Maybe check my prostate too.

She snapped her fingers again, motioned for me to come over to her like I was her Solomon Northup.

While she ranted about a senate race, about the lead she had over her opponent, she took my limpness in her hand, inspected it for cracks, pimples, and faults. Her hand was cold from holding her wine. My instructions had been to enter the room and not talk. If she approved of what she saw, if she was as thrilled now as the first time she'd seen me at the bar at the hotel near LAX, she would take it from there. That done, she let my cock go and sashayed away, still ranting, hands waving, landing planes. The money had been paid in advance. I wasn't sure how it would have worked out if she had looked at me and didn't want what I had to offer. She looked back at me, nodded as if to say what she saw matched what she had ordered, then did a bevy of rapid finger snaps and motioned toward the bathroom.

"Shower."

I headed for the fancy bathroom. It was luxurious, cavernous, had a chandelier, a large bathtub, an enormous shower, his-and-hers sinks, and fixtures that cost more than a hilltop house in Chino.

"Be sensual."

I turned the shower on. Set the temperature to 105. I was naked, self-conscious, and nervous.

She hung up the phone and walked into the bathroom. She stripped, put everything on wooden hangers. Her body confirmed she was a thousand-dollar-luxury-wax type of woman. She slipped on a shower cap, then eased into the shower with me. She rubbed my chest. It was smooth. She touched my cock again. I imagined that once the pace of asses had been paid, their clients felt like they owned them, could touch them anywhere, any way they desired.

"Bathe me. Wash away my stress, my anger, my disappointments."

I lathered her, cleaned her body, washed between her legs and the crack of her firm ass. I cleaned her so good she held the wall and moaned. I touched her between her legs, rubbed her right there, and she moaned louder, softened up, transformed from being as hard as diamond to being as pliable as gold. The pit bull became a kitten; her moans were girly, young, velvet soft. She stood on her toes, gave me space to fill her with two fingers, and cooed a silky coo.

She whispered, her voice almost begging, "Use that fat cock. Make me come."

With her face against the glass, as water rained down on us, I took her from behind. She had paid for bareback, BFE.

I'd met her fifteen minutes ago, and she had invited me inside of her body.

"You feel so good inside, my love. Use that big dick. Punish me good."

I fucked until I looked beyond us and saw we were being watched. A man stood outside the bathroom door. He was tall, wore a blue suit. Heart thumping, I withdrew my cock and backed away from my client, a flock of fear in my gut.

Startled, the politician opened her eyes, saw him, stumbled, covered herself the best she could with her hands, and looked at him, her frown strong, then raised her voice, "What the fuck are you doing here?"

The tall man took three steps and stood in the bathroom's door-frame, his lips turned down.

In a dark and unhappy voice, he said, "You're being intimate, showering with him?"

"This is not what we agreed upon."

He scowled. "I should stay."

"Was I there with you when you had your affairs?"

"That was years ago."

"Was I, Wakefield? *Was I?*"

His jaw tightened. "Be quick with it."

"Were you quick with it?"

"Victoria."

"Interrupting me will only make it take longer."

"He's younger than our son."

She snapped, "And your mistresses were younger than our daughter."

He swallowed. "How many times will you do this to punish me?"

"Leave."

"Use a prophylactic."

"You didn't. Hence your secret baby. Hence the secret checks that went on for the last ten years."

"Use a prophylactic."

"Leave."

"*Use a goddamn prophylactic.*"

"*Leave.*"

He frowned at me. "Be gentle with my wife. Don't hurt her."

The door slammed behind him. She left the shower, jogged to the other room, and slapped the deadbolt on the presidential suite's door.

When she marched back, her nipples weren't hard, and I had all but gone soft.

She got back in the shower, eased down on her haunches, and became a goddamn Hoover. Then she turned around, put her damp face against the wall, bent over, and spread her cheeks.

She moaned, "Give me my therapy."

CHAPTER 40

BRICK

ON THE BED, the politician made grotesque faces that spoke of unimaginable gratification. She unquestionably owned me, rode me like I was a horse not to be let to get water and rest for at least thirty hard miles.

"Look at me, lover. Look into my eyes. See me. Not some other woman. See me."

With her left hand on my right clavicle and her right hand on my left thigh, she rose and came down hard. She was feral. She was as flexible as a contortionist and could move like a ballerina. Orgasm weakened her and the Amazon collapsed on her back, struggling to inhale and exhale. I looked toward the time. I had entertained her for twenty-six minutes and eleven seconds. She crawled back to me. Soon I was back inside her love, made me get on top and held my ass, had me banging like a carpenter. She put my fingers around her throat and held my hand tight. I choked her. She trembled. Her legs shook as a level-three orgasm overwhelmed her. She put her nails into my skin, held my ass, held my back, bucked against me, swam in a liquid orgasm, treaded those heated waters until she was pulled under again. She was stranded at level three, inside an orgasm that was inside an orgasm that was inside an orgasm.

I remained a man at work until I felt it was me dancing by myself.

Her hands fell away, first the left, then the right, left her posed like a woman crucified. I looked at her. I shook her, gave her a gentle slap. Nothing. I put two fingers on her damp neck, searched for a pulse. Couldn't find one.

My words came out in a panic. "Fuck, fuck, fuck, fuck, fuck."

Looked like she'd had a heart attack. Her face wasn't slacked, so it wasn't a stroke. Had to be her heart.

I ran to the bathroom to get a wet towel to clean her with, then wondered why I was doing that. The moment I turned on the water, there was a sound like an old woman who had stubbed her toe. I hurried back to the bedroom. Her left hand was twitching. I stepped closer. Her chest began to rise and fall. I moved closer. She licked her lips. She raised her right hand, put it on her left breast like she could feel her heartbeat.

"Jesus. What in the hell was that?"

She coughed like she was choking on a fish bone. At the same moment the door to the presidential suite opened again, but was caught by the security bar. Her husband was out there, desperate for this to be over.

He called out, "Victoria? Victoria? Victoria?"

"What? What, what, what?"

"Are you ready?"

"Almost."

He slammed the door and left again.

She whispered, "I'll be done when I am done, and I am not ready to be done."

She pulled me back on top of her, put me back inside her, again behaving like she owned me.

Hips rising, short nails in my back, heated breath on my neck, she commanded, "Do that shit again."

THE POLITICIAN STAGGERED back into the shower, then called for me to come help her wash her body again. Ten minutes after that, I sat on the edge of the bed, naked, a damp towel across my lap. She wrapped a towel around her body. I watched her redo her hair. It was like watching Picasso create art. She was meticulous.

She picked up her phone, made a call. "Beverly? Have you and your husband arrived?"

The politician went back to the bathroom, back to being girly, fussy, and doing her makeup.

She told Beverly, "A bet is a bet and a promise is a promise. I'm serious as a heart attack."

Then she ended the call.

Soon she was fully clothed, in a dazzling outfit. She stood in the mirror evaluating her figure, the shape of her round ass. The Amazon picked up her designer purse, took out four one-hundred-dollar bills, eased them onto the dresser. She went to the door, then hesitated, and came back to where I was seated on the edge of the bed.

The client put her finger on my chin and raised my face until my eyes met hers.

She gave me a slow kiss, again wiggling, breathing like she was aroused.

Her phone rang and all that was sensual, all that was erotic, was shut off. She checked the message, then went from zero to pissed in two breaths. She made a call, frenzied, back in damage-control mode.

She barked, "Scrub the damn files. Everything. *Everything*. I want no blowback or else I will take everyone on this ship down with me. I'm at a fucking event all evening."

She opened the door to leave, and jumped, caught off guard. Her husband was there, waiting.

Her voice trembled, was urgent and shaky. "We have a problem."

"I know."

"What should I do? Should I tweet something now?"

"I've prepared a few powerful and profound tweets for you to look over."

Their conversation faded as they went toward the elevator. I took deep breaths, picked up my tip from the dresser, pocketed it, then retrieved my phone from the drawer, powered it back up. Right away, it buzzed with alerts.

My phone rang at the scheduled time. Voluntary enslavement hour was officially over.

I said, "Hey, Christiana."

"Code phrase."

"Your cockeyed momma eats Mexican food and farts the third verse of the national anthem. I'm used to this shit being done in the other direction. I'm used to being the bodyguard."

She exhaled. "I'm glad to hear that. How is it going, Brick?"

"I'm done."

"Congratulations, Brick. You are official. Your first time. Your official first time."

"She's gone. I'm to wait thirty minutes after she is gone, then leave, right?"

"Those were her initial instructions."

I said, "I'll shower, get dressed, and be downstairs at the bar soon."

"You're not done yet."

"She's coming back?"

"No. Another opportunity has been offered."

My altruistic friend told me to stay where I was until I heard from her again. She had to talk to the politician regarding my services. I went back to the shower. I turned the water on, lathered my body, scrubbed my skin. Felt like I couldn't get clean enough. I banged on the wall a few times, hit the tile hard enough to hurt my hand. When I looked to my left, I saw I wasn't alone. The politician's husband had come back. The angry man stood tall, like a stilt walker, a moko jumbie, hands in fists.

CHAPTER 41

BRICK

I STEPPED OUT of the shower, water and soap raining from my flesh. It was just me and him. I was naked, big fat black dick swinging like an elephant's trunk stunt-doubling for a pendulum on Big Ben.

Like he was the boss's boss, he pulled out a chair, sat down, crossed his long legs, put his hands on his knees, gritted his capped teeth.

He barked, "Did you enjoy yourself?"

"I was paid so she would enjoy herself."

"You're a tough guy. A real tough guy."

"Tougher than some."

"If I were your age—"

"You'd end up beaten half to death. I don't fight AARP members. Looks bad on the résumé."

"I could make one call and LAPD would flood this room and take you away."

"Call the cops. Tell them your wife hired me to fuck her for an hour. Let them know you approved it. Let's see how that plays on CNN."

He snapped at me, "Get out. Get the fuck out of this room. You low-life piece of shit."

I went for my clothing. He had political power. I was Stormy Daniels. I knew that I'd end up incarcerated while he went home.

The tall man said, "Don't."

"What's that?"

"Don't go."

"What's your problem?"

"She'll know and then she will be angry. She'll take it out on me if you do."

He stood, wiped his eyes.

He asked, "This is how you make a living?"

"You offering me a better job? Or looking to change professions?"

"Do you know who I am?"

"You're the man who should know that I'm the man who doesn't give a fuck who you are."

"*That's my wife.*" He came toward me. "*She's my wife.* I love her more than anything."

I stepped toward him, trunk swinging. He saw my hands become fists and backed the fuck up.

He cleared his throat, said an almost incomprehensible, "I'm sorry."

"Speak up."

"I set the wrong tone for this conversation."

The Dwayne Sr. in my blood came to life and I barked, "*Talk like a man talking to a man.*"

"*I apologize.* I love my wife. My emotions and my jealousy got the best of me."

He stood before me as if it were my turn to speak, grief and suffering written all over his face.

He dabbed his red eyes and stammered. "I can give her everything."

"Again, speak up and talk like a man talking to a man. Look me in the eye when you talk to me."

"I can give her money and help her obtain political power, can give her everything except . . . except . . . except for one thing. I can break into ten hells and rob a hundred gods blind, and that would still not be enough to satiate her. I am unable to be a man with her. Do you have any idea how incompetent that makes me feel?"

"Your wife is your issue. Decide if you want to become mine."

"An affair came back to haunt me. And the irony is, I can no longer be unfaithful. My prostate."

I understood. He had lost the ability to be a man to a woman during the midnight hour.

"I have repented. I have fallen to my knees and asked for her forgiveness every day. She tells me that forgiveness is the fragrance the violet sheds on the heel that has crushed it. She tells me that through my indiscretions, I have crushed her. Every day, none more than today, none more than tonight, she lets me know that while she is beautiful and delicate in her own way, she is not a flower. No one steps on her."

Nothing filled the air as my balls tightened and my dick swung side to side.

"Don't tell her I came back up here. The issue between my wife and me is not your issue."

He extended his hand to shake. I looked at him like he had lost his mind.

I said, "What, you walk in uninvited, insult me, make threats, and we're gonna be BFFs now?"

He withdrew his hand. "Let's keep this unfortunate moment between the men."

"You're on my dime. I'm at work. You've taken up my time. Pain and suffering are due."

We stared at each other. He opened his wallet, dropped three hundred-dollar bills on the table.

I didn't reply.

He dropped two hundred more. Dropped it like it was nothing but taxpayers' money.

I nodded.

"Now get out before you get the same thing I gave your wife."

I didn't mean it, just wanted to sound Eastside. That prison tone shocked him.

Impotence stared and a potent man, a younger man, a stronger man, stared back. The tall man adjusted his expensive suit and trudged out the door. I took a deep breath. Glad that it didn't get any uglier than it did. A moment passed before I picked up the money, counted it, added it to his wife's tip, stuffed it in my suit coat.

My phone rang.

It was Christiana.

She said, "Next client will be there in twenty minutes."

"Are you serious?"

"You're a birthday gift from the politician."

"You are serious."

I told her about the politician's husband.

She said, "That will be taken care of."

"I need to change rooms."

"No, stay where you are. I will make sure the old card key no longer works."

"Don't make me catch a case."

"Things have changed. You used to look out for me, and now I am making sure you're safe."

"You've handled me. From the moment I met you, you've handled me."

"Stop saying that."

I popped five twenty-milligram sildenafils, then called housekeeping and asked them to change the linen pronto. I showered again. When I came back to the bedroom, housekeeping had been there and gone. The room was immaculate. I had just picked up *1Q84* and read a page when the door opened again.

CHAPTER 42

BRICK

IT WAS A woman of a certain age, a silver fox. Five foot four. Nice physique. Her body said she could afford to eat at Whole Foods and Trader Joe's. She wore a beautiful dress and sexy high heels. The toned arms and defined legs said she was a gym rat, that or paranoid of being the size of the average woman. California paranoia.

She said, "Brick?"

I nodded. "Brick."

She whispered, "Oh my. Victoria isn't punking me."

I sang, "Happy birthday to you; happy birthday to you."

"So, this is true? Victoria actually . . . you're my gift?"

"Tell me what you want, and I'll make it happen."

She came to me, looked me over. "My, my, my. I have to be back downstairs soon."

I put my hands on her hips, did that gently, looked for permission in her eyes and body language.

She whispered, "This is for real."

This time I was in control. I kissed her, kissed her neck, spine, thighs, sucked her bottom lip. I took her clothing away. I picked her up like she weighed nothing, carried her to the bed, and eased her down. I gave her a ten-minute massage. Put lotion on my hands and rubbed her down from her neck, across her ass, to her feet.

She asked, "May I touch you? Or in this situation, do you do all of the touching?"

"It's your birthday. You can touch me any way, anywhere you want to touch me."

She bit her lip, then touched me where I grew when aroused, held me in her small hand.

She sang, "Oh my. My, oh my. You're blessed."

She made it grow as I put kisses on her stomach, kissed her inner thighs.

I asked, "Anything special you want?"

She said, "Just don't mess up my hair. Whatever you do, don't mess up my hair."

"Then you'd better get on top."

"I'm not that good on top."

"I'll bet you are. I'll bet you have no idea how good you are on top. I'll hold your hips and guide you."

WINDED, THE SILVER fox touched my chest and my stomach, dragged her fingernails over my skin like I was a dream come true. She kissed my chest over and over, sucked my nipples, touched my softening penis.

Suddenly she sat up and said, "The event. My husband. I have to return to my friends and constituents."

She hurried to the bathroom, washed herself, redid her face, put on perfume. She pulled her gown back on, kindly asked me to help get her back in order. I did, then stepped away, gave her room. She shifted from side to side to look at herself from all angles. I stood behind her with my hands on her hips, kissed her neck, then nibbled her ear.

Breathless, she said, "Thank you."

"Happy birthday."

"Our song was lovely. You made me chant unique verses. It was very moving. Magnificent."

"If you want to see me again in the future, it can be arranged."

"This would be better, more comfortable for me, in the privacy of my home."

"Aren't you married?"

"Technically. Public appearances, but separate homes, and mostly separate lives."

"Sounds complicated."

"Life gets complicated." She pulled her lip in. "I just want to have a good time. We could do this, not rush; then we could lie in bed, talk. I would like to know who you are, know all about you."

"Sex isn't required. It's about you. About what will make you happy. You can define that."

"No one ever asks me what will make me happy. No one has ever asked."

"I want you to enjoy yourself, to have fun."

"Was this fun for you?"

"Did I do or say something wrong?"

"Sex makes me like people more than I should. I could get attached to a very young man based on sex."

"I've done the same before, only with a slightly younger woman."

"Then you understand."

I offered, "Let's play it by ear."

"Young man. Do you know who I am?"

"No, ma'am."

"Let me tell you."

"Okay."

"More or less, I have been with the same man for over thirty years. Since I was seventeen. He isn't the only man I've been with. When I was at the University of Texas at Austin School of Law, I had a few spring break moments, moments he knows nothing about. Alcohol, music, weed, sand, beaches, and taking a week away from studies to live life to the fullest was a must. I was young and energetic, idealistic, nice, and diplomatic when required. At times I wish I had had more affairs, or only had had more boyfriends, and never taken a husband. But you can't live your life like it's spring break. I was twenty-two when I married. I made life serious so soon. My husband was with me, was in my bed most nights, when he didn't travel, when I didn't travel, but I think he had mentally left me within five years. When I was twenty-eight, I used to blame the petite Pakistani girl with an accent. Then when I was thirty, I blamed the girl from Spanish Harlem. When I was thirty-two, I blamed myself for working, for having a mind of my own, for not capitulating to almost every argument the way my mother did with my father. I said it was my fault. Blaming myself was easier. We all want someone to blame. We need to have the blame focused. It is never one thing. Fires can be traced to a source, and then you can point your finger at the cause of the destruction. The disintegration of love can't be traced so easily. It's muddled in time, spread out over many events. Our best times were at the start. We were like Marvin Gaye singing a love song, and it was all about the need for sexual healing and wanting to get it on to get rid of our inner-city blues. I used to live for him being inside of me, lived to bond with him, but that all went away. After the children. After a million pointless arguments. You wake up one day and it all feels like a chore. I became just another chore to him, and he became just another chore to me. We married out of love, but now we stay married for legal reasons. I suppose we love each other, but we are chained together more by law than by our hearts. Now I am almost fifty. Sometimes I laugh and hear the laugh of a twenty-one-year-old woman. My reflection tells me the truth, shows me I still look young but am aging gracefully. I see my mother's face. When she was my age, I thought she was old, but now I realize how young she was. It feels like life is just beginning for me, but I am on the other side of the halfway mark in my journey. I have fewer days left than days I have already spent alive. I feel as if I have to grab what's left of the young inside me before the old takes root and spreads like kudzu. I ask myself if I would do my life over, and the answer is no. Not the marriage. Not the kids. I love them but could do without them and their father. The best part was when they were young. We want babies, not children, not teenagers. They need you for a while; then they become insolent and no longer need you in their lives, only your money. I love my spoiled brats, but I experienced it once and that would be enough. I might even have skipped all of those rigorous years in university and had more fun in life. I've always been chained to something or someone that wasn't equally committed or chained to me. Now I am longing for something else. I am finally yearning for something for me, but the sad thing is, I have no idea what that thing is."

I listened. Some clients paid to be heard. I listened to learn. There was wisdom in her words.

She said, "I was ambitious. Had to have a certain type of man. Had to have the biggest house. I might have been just as happy being a barista with Friday night dates that led to Saturday morning breakfasts on the beach."

Birthdays made people reevaluate their lives. I witnessed her reevaluate hers.

She said, "That is the *Reader's Digest* version of who I am. My life crammed down into a monologue I wish I could undo. I've never been so honest. That is who you just undressed and kissed and . . . and took on spring break."

"I'm glad I met you."

"I know nothing about you, nothing of your values."

"Ask me what you what to know."

Her smile was nervous. "Yeah. This was fun. I've seen more sunrises in the past than I will see sunsets in the future. Every day is precious to me. Maybe not in this way, but I must be daring. I want to have more fun the rest of my life."

"Maybe fun is all you need. Make every day your birthday. Or have a birthday party once a month."

"I deserve love. Love is what I need. If not love, then maybe an insane amount of sex."

"Well, I can help on the latter."

"Is this the way men do this sort of thing? I just walked into a room and engaged myself with you like I was still a young, intoxicated girl, a freshman in Austin, living out loud during spring break. I tried to recapture who I was then. She's gone. That randy, naïve girl is gone. I am no longer her anymore. This is who I am now."

"Then why did you come to see me, if not for what we did?"

"I made love to you on a dare."

"On a challenge?"

"I talked the talk. My bluff was called. I wasn't prepared for this. Maybe that was better. I didn't have time to think about this. Victoria handed me a room key, told me where to go; then I just walked into a room and did it with a stranger much younger than I am. I have been *cougared*. I have been naughty on so many levels. Two hours ago, doing this would never have occurred to me. Peer pressure. Let's just call it middle-aged peer pressure."

"Peer pressure. Because your friend gifted me to you, and you felt obligated."

"She called my bluff from a personal conversation we had weeks ago. We were by the pool, and I think I had had too much to drink. We talked about men. Old lovers. Spring breaks. I had jokingly said that I would love to be gifted a young, strong, handsome man half my age for my birthday. She said she would find me one. She said he would be young, handsome, and sexy. I told her if she did, I would have sex with him in a heartbeat, without even knowing."

There was a knock at the door. Birthday Girl stopped talking and moved toward the bathroom. She was afraid. She didn't know who it was, and neither did I. My bet was the moko jumbie was back. There was an electronic beep when a key card was placed in the sensor. I guess Christiana hadn't changed the key cards yet. The door opened. It was the politician again. The Amazon was alone. She sashayed in like she owned the place and called out to the birthday girl, didn't acknowledge me. I was just the present. A man objectified.

"Victoria." Birthday Girl came out of the bathroom. "You startled the Jesus out of me."

"How did it go?"

"You made me behave like a bad girl."

"Good girls might make breakfast, but they don't make history."

"Drought over. I have to reset the celibate clock."

"I'll take 'Things Husbands Never Say' for ten thousand, Alex."

"Let's not go there."

"I want the details later."

Birthday Girl nodded. "What have I missed?"

"A soporific conversation. Same old bullshit arguments. NRA. Cops killing blacks. Immigration."

"Aren't they all bullshit and soporific? After a while, aren't they all?"

The politician inspected herself in a mirror. "Do you need to tell your birthday present good-bye?"

"Give me a moment. We were just winding down."

"No need to tip. I paid for it all."

The politician's phone rang, and she answered the phone cursing, going off on someone, chastising them for their incompetence. Birthday Girl grinned at me, and the silver fox kissed my cheek.

She whispered, "Spring break."

I nodded, whispered, "You were good on top."

She smiled.

The politician ended her call. "Let's go. Beverly, they are looking for both of us by now."

The Amazon and the silver fox left talking like professional women, as energized as a leap of leopards rushing back to their pitiful husbands. I turned my phone back on, called my favorite altruistic entrepreneur, and checked in. As soon as Christiana answered, she told me to shower again and prepare to entertain another client.

I said, "You're joking. How the fuck do y'all do this back-to-back-customer shit?"

She told me I would have to change rooms this time.

I said, "Women can lube up and fake this shit, but I'm almost out of juice."

"One more, but it is up to you."

"Who is she?"

"First-time caller. You would be her first. She's younger, in her twenties. A Mensa."

"Pressure, pressure."

Her voice smiled. "Shall I confirm the appointment, or pass it on to someone else?"

"One more. Will do my best."

"Get dressed and be ready. I will call you in ten minutes and let you know the new room number."

CHAPTER 43

BRICK

WITHIN THIRTY MINUTES, I was in a different posh suite. Already it felt like I had better control of the situation. First, I heard a dog bark; then there was a soft, tentative tap on the hotel door. I adjusted my suit coat, did the same with my necktie. When I spied out the peephole, only the top of someone's head was visible. I cleared my throat and opened the door, hoped this wasn't a sting by the police.

Her Afro was parted in the middle, untamed. Her nose was small, lips full, eyes light brown.

A black purse was on her arm and a chessboard was in her lap. Her little dog was at her side.

She said, "Hi. I'm Dr. Allison Émilie Chappelle."

I lost the ability to speak, found it, shook her hand, then managed to say, "I'm Brick."

Her dog barked twice like it remembered me. I barked back. Her dog growled. I growled.

The client said, "Strawberry, hush."

She wore a black dress that was tight and showed off her curves. But her shoes. She rocked traffic-stopping, metallic-gold, thigh-high Balenciaga boots that had a razor-sharp pointed toe. Those boots were a fashion statement's fashion statement. She wore no makeup. When a woman wore no makeup, she wanted to be accepted as she was.

She said, "You look surprised."

"I think I'm in love."

"We haven't met."

"I meant with the dog. Reminds me of a girl I dated in high school. Only the dog is cuter."

She laughed. "Bet she was a bitch. A cute, expensive, fun bitch to be around. Right, Strawberry?"

The dog barked like it was laughing.

I said, "Now, so far as you. This is like Adam being sent a gift from God."

"Stop it."

"I'd give up a rib. A real rib. Not a McRib."

"Stop it."

"I'd give up a slab of ribs, the coleslaw, sweet tea, and the corn bread."

"You'd give up the corn bread?"

"I'd give up the corn bread."

She smiled, let loose a small exhale. She looked into my eyes and saw something I couldn't hide.

She asked, "Have we met?"

"You haven't met me."

"The way you look at me. It's like you know me."

Dr. Allison Émilie Chappelle wheeled herself over to the desk area, and we set up the chessboard.

She said, "They told me you played chess."

"I try. Been playing on a few apps."

"I tried those. Chess Live, iChess, the King of Chess. I prefer playing a human being."

We got right into it. She started the game by moving her pawns to the center. Like the day I'd seen her at Hot or Cool Café, she had an aggressive strategy.

She asked, "What was the last book you read?"

"*Binti*. Love that series. Rereading *Brixton Rock*. *How Not to Get Shot* by D. L. Hughley. You?"

"*Redemption in Indigo* and *Les Contes d'Amadou Koumba*. Reading both at the same time."

"I usually read one book at a time. Takes me forever. Not wired for literary multitasking."

"Last movie you watched or saw at the theater?"

"Haven't been to see a movie in a while. Maybe *If Beale Street Could Talk*. You?"

Dr. Allison Émilie Chappelle said, "*Bienvenue à Marly-Gomont*."

"A French film?"

"On Netflix. I speak French, but it has pretty accurate subtitles. It's called *The African Doctor* on there."

"Okay. Will check it out."

"Chess players? Who do you like?"

"Magnus Carlsen. You?"

"Mikhail Tal was a genius."

"Probably the most creative attacker of all time."

"Oh God. He was brutal. He exposed his opponent's king, demolished the entire kingside."

We fought a good war. It went on and on, move after move, going for the king when it was exposed, refusing each other a decent counterplay. When she became über aggressive, I made a move that made her raise a brow.

She said, "You're good."

"You're better."

"The way you play, I'll bet your opponents don't even realize they are losing."

I couldn't take my eyes off her. She had dimples, high cheekbones. Her skin was stunning.

She smiled at me. "You okay?"

I put my eyes back on the war, made a strategic move. "Check."

She made her move. "Checkmate."

"We're tied. One game each."

"Again?"

"Again."

"The way you look at me."

Her phone rang and jarred us.

She asked, "Do you mind?"

"Go ahead."

She took the call, talked science and physics, then told the caller, "In the theoretical case that the universe is stationary, homogeneous at a large scale, and occupied by an infinite number of stars, then any line of sight from Earth must end at the very bright surface of a star and therefore the night sky should be completely illuminated and very bright. Exactly. This contradicts the witnessed blackness and nonuniformity of what we call night. There are so many stars in the universe, more than there are grains of sand on all the beaches in the world, and actually there are five to ten times more stars than there are grains of sand on all the world's beaches. So, there's your quick answer, and that means that if it weren't for all the interstellar gas and dust and space pollution blocking your view, the night sky would appear almost entirely bright white. No, not exactly like a midnight sun. We can discuss Olbers' paradox in detail tomorrow. Yeah, I'm in the middle of a chess game. Of course I'm winning. What? Well, was busy being an ambassador so couldn't get back to you right away. Sure. Anytime, day or night. I'm here for you."

She ended the call and turned her phone off.

I said, "That was intense."

"My niece. She starts university next year. She's fourteen. Plans to rule the world by the time she's twenty."

We continued our battle.

She asked, "Intelligence or beauty? Which do you prefer?"

"Beauty if they are intelligent, and intelligence if they are beautiful."

"Between aesthetics and intelligence, I don't think I'd want a smart *ugly* man, or a *dumb* handsome man. I've met them both before, dated both, tried both, and it went nowhere. But then again, I am the common denominator in all my relationship problems."

"You have someone?"

"I did. I had somebody. Before . . . before. I was engaged, almost got married."

"I was almost engaged once."

"What went wrong?"

"I asked one question too many."

The dog came to me, and I rubbed its coat, made the mutt smile.

She said, "Strawberry likes you. That's a good sign. She hates everyone."

We talked for a moment, the dog at her feet, resting, watching me, wagging its tail.

I said, "You're an ambassador?"

"For an African NGO dedicated to training medical personnel involved in caring for mothers and children. I just returned from Uganda on a humanitarian mission."

"I really need to start working on becoming an overachiever."

"African parents make us all overachievers."

"You're African?"

"Mother is from Seychelles. Dad is Equatoguinean. They met in South Africa. I'm first generation born here."

"You do a lot."

"Since I can no longer run track, I try and keep myself occupied. I still train. I came in sixth at the LA Marathon. The wheelchair portion, of course. Came in tenth in Boston. That was disappointing."

She shifted in a provocative way; then she turned and put her brown eyes deep inside of mine.

She asked, "Did I tell you what I do for a living?"

"No. We skipped that part and went to war."

She was an actuary but was ready to move on and do something else more challenging.

I said, "You have a PhD."

"I do."

"What are your interests?"

"I want to be become a neurosurgeon."

"You're a badass."

"I feel like I am out of my league."

"Why is that?"

Dr. Allison Émilie Chappelle grinned. "This is not what I normally do. I've never done this before."

"I'm new to this too."

She held her grin. "Well, I won't ask how new is new."

I let that ride, then said, "PhD, it also means you are a doctor of philosophy."

"Yeah. Not many people know that. Not many people care."

"You know what? I've always found it odd, because even if you don't know all that much about philosophy, you're still called a doctor of philosophy. But I guess it's one of those things you accept, even if it rattles your brain."

She hummed. "Yeah, being named doctor of philosophy is a bit off, but it is what it is."

"A medical doctor might have earned a PhD in immunology and infectious diseases, though they don't actually need one to treat patients with infectious diseases."

"Look at you. Now who's the smart one?"

I smiled, then winked at her.

She said, "I haven't had this much intellectual stimulation in a long time."

"Neither have I."

"Talking like this makes me want to stand up and dance."

"Then let's dance."

"I was joking."

"I'm not."

Dr. Allison Émilie Chappelle laughed. "Did you not notice I am in a moving chair? Daleks don't dance."

I went to the television, turned it on a music channel with old-school slow jams; then I reached for her hand. She hesitated, then extended her fingers. I picked her up, held her in my arms, moved around the room slowly. She pulled her Afro back, rested her face next to mine, cheek to cheek. My hunger for her pulled at the chains, and I held her and kissed her cheek, then kissed her lips, gave her a slow and easy French kiss without asking.

She whispered, "I wanted to do that twenty minutes ago."

I asked, "Why didn't you?"

"I was winning."

"Those lips. I wanted to kiss you from the moment I first saw you."

"Why didn't you?"

"Barking dog."

"Strawberry has warmed up to you. She stopped barking. That means she trusts you."

"Do you?"

"Yeah. Yeah, I think I do. Yeah, I do. I thought this would be awkward, but it really isn't."

"So, I have permission?"

"Yes. You have permission, but if she barks, you'd better stop. She will bite your ankles."

I carried her to the king bed. She opened my shirt, sucked my nipples. We kissed, first lips, more lips, then tongue. Every woman was different, every kiss was different, and every session was different.

Each time I learned something else about women, but each time I learned more about myself. I was able to adapt, adjust, be generous.

She said, "The way you look at me, from the moment you opened the door."

I took over the kissing. "And?"

"I didn't tell them I was in a wheelchair. I mean, you did notice the wheelchair, right?"

"You mean, your Uber for one made by Tesla?"

She paused. "That joke. That's my joke. Do I know you?"

"You are a combination of Aphrodite, Helen of Troy, and Lupita."

"Wow. I like this. This is scaring me, but don't stop scaring me. It's a good scary."

The timer went off and the kissing went on, until my phone rang. I didn't answer the call.

Her cute little dog barked at us, tail wagging, like it was laughing.

My client moved like she was about to gather her things. I stopped her.

I told her, "Don't go. Stay another hour."

Dr. Allison Émilie Chappelle smiled.

My phone rang again, and I answered with the code phrase.

I asked Christiana, "We good?"

"You're done for the night. The room is paid for and yours until morning."

"Everybody okay?"

"Everybody is working until morning. I'm about to meet a client."

"See you downstairs at breakfast."

Then I ended the call.

Dr. Allison Émilie Chappelle pulled away her jacket, then gestured for me to come to her. I pulled her sexy little black dress up enough to expose her breasts. Her breasts were wonderful, perfect, full and firm, full C-cups; her nipples were thick as a thumb, dark like Belgian chocolate. Both grew harder under my tongue.

She moaned, whispered, "I am a thinker. I know the place this is coming from. I understand my motivation, the emotions that have led me to you, Brick. I know my reality, and I know truth."

"What does that mean?"

Dr. Allison Émilie Chappelle undid my shirt, then pulled at my belt, unzipped my pants and hurriedly pulled my pants and underwear down to my knees. She gave me head, the kind that made me groan and weak at the knees. Whenever a woman did that, it always astonished me. Her lipstick was glossy, glittery, shined on her full pillow-soft lips. Amazed me how a woman dressed up her mouth and made her lips look so seductive, so sensual. So erotic. She gave me head and for a moment her beautiful lips looked like a sideways vagina. A swollen vagina that felt better than the real thing. It was an odd thought and left me fascinated, holding her hair and watching her work me toward a poor man's heaven. Those lips. Those goddamn lips. She looked up at me, teabagged me and stroked my penis as it grew in her hands, then kissed her way north, licked my nipples like that was her fetish.

She said, "Talk to me. Tell me what you like. Tell me what to do to please you."

She took care of me, hugged my erection with her mouth, as I kicked my shoes off. She fellated me as I undressed. She paused, and I kissed her, ran my fingers up and down her legs. She responded. She felt my touch. I helped her out of her four-thousand-dollar boots, then smiled at how good she looked unclothed, and took her to the shower. I sat her on a stool and cleaned her, then dried her off and put lotion and oils on her skin before I carried her to the bed.

She said, "Dogs can smell the subtle changes in your natural aroma, and that lets them know how you are feeling. Strawberry knows I am happy now. She won't bark when she knows I'm happy."

I went down on her, stirred her, made her talk to God. She tasted virtuous, tasted wholesome and sweet.

She pulled me back to her, kissed me like she was overwhelmed with greed to savor our combined flavor, tasted herself on my tongue and moaned like that turned her on so much she couldn't wait to have me inside her.

She said, "I brought my own protection."

"How would you like me to start?"

"On my stomach. I love being on my stomach. My spot is easier to reach like that."

"Okay."

"I'm not delicate. I won't break."

"Okay."

"Do we need a safe word?"

"Just say stop and I'll stop."

"I wish I had brought along sex wedges. They are better than soft pillows."

She told me she would be able to feel me inside of her, would be able to have an orgasm.

She chuckled. "But I won't be able to twerk it."

I told her. "I got this. I'll twerk, wukkup, and whine you so good you'll think we're in the West Indies."

She put her face into a pillow, muffled her sounds. I rubbed her butt awhile, then did a slow stroke. Twerk. Wukkup. Slow whine.

"Ahhhhh ooooooo-oooooooo-oooooooo."

I didn't go fast until she was wet, until her moans begged for more, until she was one level deep. I went from being halfway inside her to all the way.

"Ooooo-ooooooooo, ooooo-oooo."

I held her waist and rocked her, twerk, wukkup, whine, kept it steady until she was down two levels.

"Ahhhhh, ooooooo-oooooo-oooooo-ooooooooo-oooooo."

Her sensuous cries and the bark from her dog mingled when she was feeling level three.

"Mmmm, ooooooo, that's what I'm talking about, right there, right there, yes, ooooooo, yes, ooooooo, right there, oh my, oh my God, mmm mmmm, oh yes, oh my God, like that like that like that like that."

For thirty-six minutes and thirty-four seconds it was more than sex, and I was living in my feelings. I felt like I loved her. I had loved her before I touched her, had wanted her before she knew my name, before she knew I existed.

CHAPTER 44

DWAYNE

THE LIBRARY IN Manhattan Beach was another world. The two-level library had no scent, and all I heard inside was the soft hum from the air conditioning, no street sounds, because the tall, floor-to-ceiling windows were double-paned. When I made it upstairs, I gazed out at the seaside city built on a sand dune for a moment; then I walked around until I found Fela. He was next to a window at a high-tech table for two, the kind with built-in outlets.

He saw me, smiled, and whispered, "Dad, thirty more minutes and I'll be done with homework."

"Cool beans."

"Here, read my short story. My own little *Hunger Games*."

He handed it to me and I smiled. "'Lottery: A True Game of Hunger.' Interesting title."

I was glad to be included in this part of his life. I read the two-thousand-word story in a matter of minutes. It was good. I'd created the teenager who had written this. I had enjoyed it. He had included parts of his life in his fiction and I saw his struggle on the page, saw what was beneath the words. I saw the fears and pain of a black teenager.

I needed him to never be hungry, or feel hunger, ever again. It made me feel like a failure.

I looked out at the pristine city. I had just driven down La Cienega, the highway between two well-to-do black sections. The median had looked like a dumping ground. Manhattan Beach was spotless. I was looking at a banner advertising a Catalina Classic Paddleboard Race when Fela came over and stood next to me, pulling on his backpack.

He pointed at the banner and whispered, "Mom wants to do that paddleboard race."

"Where's my hug?"

We embraced each other, kissed cheeks.

I asked my one and only heir, "Hungry?"

"Bruh."

"What do you want?"

"You know what I want."

"Hamburger."

"Give the man a door prize."

We headed to the elevator, rode down a level, then went out of the public library into the sunshine. I had parked in the back, probably the only place in the city that had free parking, and that was for only two hours.

"Dad, question. I don't want to ask Mom, well, because she's a girl and might be offended."

"What?"

"Is a blow job sex? I know it's called oral sex, but is it really like sex-sex?"

I took a second. "Can't make a baby that way, so I'd have to say no."

"Okay. I'm still a virgin."

"Well. Okay."

"Dad, one more question. And don't judge me. If I finger a girl, is she still a virgin?"

"Uh. Well. Yeah, I guess. Can't make a baby that way, either."

"Okay. She's still a virgin, too."

"So, you're still interested in the red-haired freckle-faced biracial girl?"

"And I found out she's very interested in me."

"Do I get to meet her?"

"Awkward."

"You made it awkward. Up to you."

"One day. I really like her. I told Chavers I had the coolest dad on the planet. I showed her videos of you singing in a bunch of shows on Broadway. I even found a video posted of you and Mom singing together."

"Where did you find that?"

"YouTube."

"Get the fuck outta here."

"Language. Swear jar. Keep swearing and make me rich."

"How did you find that?"

"I put in your name and Mom's name and it popped up. You and Mom doing a duet."

"Back to the Chavers girl. You really like her?"

His grin was wide. "A lot."

"In love?"

"Think so."

The conversation rattled me, but I didn't show it.

When we got to my rental, Fela looked inside. I had forgotten to clean it out and hide my stuff.

"Dad, why do you have so many junk-food wrappers in the car?"

"I need to take it to the car wash."

"All the dirty clothes in the back seat. Your luggage. Looks like you've been living inside this car."

"Let's get you to the spot where we're to meet your mother."

"Her text said she'll meet me by the Apple store in two hours."

"Why does Frenchie bring you to a public library this far from home?"

"It's a lot nicer down here. This library is amazing, like a museum with books."

"It's white and this zip code has a tax base that—"

"Dad."

"Never mind."

"Thank you."

"She loves to have you in white areas."

"But a lot of black people are here, more blacks than anybody, not just me and you."

"I see. Don't think I didn't notice that."

"Black people like nice stuff too."

"If they build it, we will come, invited or not."

"Mom fantasizes about living on the beach, so we come down here all the time and hang out and walk around acting like we live here and not in Inglewood. We play make-believe. And with the number of black people down here studying and reading and surfing and playing volleyball, Mom's not the only one with that kind of fantasy."

I TOOK FELA to Manhattan Village Shopping Center on Rosecrans and Sepulveda. The mall was a small, relaxed community with loads of clothing shops, restaurants, and bars. It had a Macy's anchored at both ends; the one at the west end was a men's store. We entered the mall there and browsed around on the first level.

"Those jeans are popping. Want me to buy you something, Fela?"

"These prices. I'd rather go thrifting, Dad. I can get a lot for a little. I mean, a *lot*."

"Thrifting?"

"Goodwill is the bomb. Especially the ones around here."

We hit the Apple store next. He played with all the latest iPhones while I checked out an iPad. Fela went to the back of the store, browsed headphones. He picked up a pair and smiled like it was the jackpot.

He said, "Chavers has some of these. These are awesome."

I asked, "Want me to get those for you?"

"Dad, no. Maybe a refurbished pair, if they're mad cheap, but not a new pair. Cost too much."

When we left the Apple store, Frenchie was standing at the fountain, arms folded, checking her watch, waiting for her son. She wore slim jeans that hugged her body, Chucks, and a shocking-pink FEMINIST AF T-shirt.

I said, "I'm not late, am I?"

"I'm early. Didn't want to end up stuck in traffic trying to get here."

"We're about to grab a bite to eat at Islands."

Fela said, "Eat with us, Ma. I don't think we've ever sat down and had a meal like a family."

There was a moment of hesitation; then Frenchie looked at me. I nodded that it was okay.

We headed toward Islands, Fela walking between us, no one talking.

We were put in a large booth, one big enough for six people, under pictures of surfers, ocean waves, and Hawaiian girls. I sat facing the three screens high on the walls, a different sport on each channel.

Fela sat next to his mom, was all up under her like a momma's boy.

"Ma, this is a historic moment, one I'll tell my kids about. I'll need proof. Okay, selfie. Everybody in. Smile like you did before I was born, because I know both of you've been frowning ever since."

Frenchie said, "I'm not in a picture-taking mood, Fela."

"Get in the picture with us, Mom."

"Why?"

"Because I don't have a picture of all three of us together. Because it would be cool to have one like all the other kids at school do. It would help me feel normal for once. This is not an option, parents."

We considered each other, then shook off the discomfort. I went to their side of the large booth, put Fela in the middle. Frenchie and I leaned in and took the selfie, all smiles, like we were a happy family.

I hadn't seen Frenchie smile since before New Jersey. She still lit up a room.

Fela showed us the photo.

Frenchie scrunched her face. "I look horrible."

"You look fine, Ma. Not like you have another face you can use."

"Delete it."

"Not deleting it. Like the way you look or not, that was how you looked. Don't blame my iPhone, and this one-of-a-kind photo is how we looked ten seconds ago. It's a moment that will never happen again."

"At least let me take another one I like." She opened her purse and took out her lipstick, then redid her hair. "I know it will be all over social media. I'm your mother, but I don't need to look like a mother."

Eighteen selfies later, Frenchie was satisfied. She'd always been persnickety about her photos. That done, I went back to my side of the table.

"Love Is a Battlefield" played on the restaurant's sound system. First Frenchie started singing, then I joined in, then Fela came in, using plastic utensils as drumsticks. He threw in some Drakeish, improvised rap about his girlfriend, Chavers, on the break.

The waiter came for our order, eager to give the kind of customer service that came with the zip code.

Frenchie said, "Turkey burger lite. Fries. Gluten-free bun. Strawberry daiquiri. A double."

Fela hummed. "Pipeline, the chili burger. Fries. Mojito."

At the same time Frenchie and I snapped, "Really?"

"Sweet tea."

Frenchie said, "Fela, don't make me lose my religion."

"It was a joke, Ma."

"I know you sneak and drink my wine."

"Once, and you will not let me forget it."

I said, "Maui burger, no cheese, lettuce wrap. Fries. Mai tai."

Frenchie said, "Can you make mine a lettuce wrap too?"

The waiter nodded. "You have a good-looking family. Like a Hall-mark card of happiness."

We nodded, all of us caught off guard by the comment.

Fela said, "We've been called many things, but we've never been called a family."

My son's phone buzzed.

"Ma, I'll be back. Going to the bathroom to wash my hands."

"And sneak and text that Chavers girl. I hear your phone vibrating. Don't be long."

"I'll tell her you said hello."

"I'll tell her about all the other nasty-ass fast girls chasing your ass."

"Mom. Don't be a hater."

He hurried away texting, left me and Frenchie alone.

"Nobody" by Keith Sweat came on; Keith sang how he wanted to tease and please and show his lover he needed her. I sang his part, to not feel so awkward. When the girl part came in, Frenchie sang how she wanted the night for her and her lover. She promised to give it to him just the way he liked because no one could love him like her, her voice soft, yet high enough to carry. She sang as if she wasn't even aware that she was singing, like being a vocalist was in her DNA. When the song ended, the people at the next table applauded us.

We made eye contact. She looked unapproachable.

I asked, "When you look at me like that, what are you thinking?"

"You don't want to know."

"That bad?"

"You don't want to know."

"I can take it. I probably deserve it."

"Best for both of us if I allow some thoughts to remain thoughts and not become words."

"Tell me."

Frenchie said, "You went on tour and left our relationship on the cutting-room floor."

"Did I?"

"You've never forgotten about Fela. I appreciate that. Thanks for not leaving him on the cutting-room floor."

"He's my son. He means everything to me, always has."

"It hasn't been easy."

"I know."

She twisted her lips. "I saw you, Dwayne."

"Where?"

"Venice Beach."

"I didn't see you."

"You were walking on the boardwalk. I spotted you in the crowd before you spotted me."

"You were there? You hate that beach. You've always hated that crowd."

"Dwayne, I was there, on the boardwalk, singing with the losers, weed heads, and freaks."

"Singing? What do you mean?"

"Things were tight, so I put my ego on the shelf, dusted off my guitar, and I went down there during peak hours and sang for tourists and whoever would listen to a has-been sing her old songs and cover hits by others. I had to make us some money to buy food. I saw you and freaked out. Didn't want to be seen. This is my low point, and I saw you, the former child star, the man theater loves. I was singing and begging for tips."

"Jesus. Why?"

"Needed to pay my mortgage and keep up my son's health care.

Did what I had to do. Fixed expenses eat up a lot of the money. Have to deal with food insecurity, medical bills, utilities."

"Damn, Frenchie."

"And I started selling real estate for the dead on the side too."

"Graves?"

"Yeah, my shit was so grave I started selling graves. I'm at a low point. Doing what I have to do to stay afloat. Living ain't free and dying costs a grip. Next stop will be Third Street Promenade. Then I guess I'll get a job bagging groceries at Trader Joe's with other celebrities who used to be famous in the nineties."

"It is honorable work."

"I did the research. It has what I need: living wages with the potential of a ten percent raise annually; health, dental, and vision insurance; paid time off; in-store discount. My big fear is that someone will recognize me and try to shame me on social media. Or TMZ will show up and not see the courage, humility, and dedication in what I'm doing. You are one of the lucky ones, Dwayne. Very few actors can fully support themselves from their craft. We all have to rely on unemployment and, when that ends, hope we can find honest work to offset those dry periods."

"I had no idea. Fela never told me any details. Just that he was hungry."

"He is hungry. I'm hungry. He knows not to tell anyone. It's our secret, our struggle. Mine and his."

"Well, that explains a lot."

"I'm doing my best." She rocked and her voice cracked. "I wasn't made to have a nine-to-five; always saw myself as being self-employed, singing, dancing, but I'm adjusting and doing my best."

"I know. We're entertainers. The world's playtime, their evenings, weekends, and holidays, are our stage time. We sacrifice, work hard to make strangers feel good and relax and have a good time."

Her eyes teared up. She poked her tongue in the inside of her jaw, shook her head, and chuckled like it was incredulous. "From Juilliard to Broadway to sitting on the beach with a plastic bucket in front of me begging for spare change. I was where people juggle chainsaws and walk broken glass to earn their dinner. Felt like I was part of a traveling circus that's too poor to go on the road. I broke down and joined the freak show. The Venice circus."

"I heard you, but I assumed it was someone else covering your old songs."

"A few weeks ago, I saw your father down at Venice."

"Nigga Daddy?"

"Don't. Not with me."

"Dwayne Sr. You saw him?"

She nodded. "Saw him again when he walked into a bar in Century City where I was a singing waitress."

"Wait a minute."

"Yes, I was a singing waitress, too. Your father walked in with a young African girl on his arm."

"Singing waitress? Are you serious?"

"Yeah. I did that a few weeks, to get extra money, until I was fired."

It was a lot to unpack. "I'm listening to you. I don't miss a payment, Frenchie. What's going on?"

She told me about her accountant stealing all she had and vanishing to the West Indies. I was stunned. I felt like everything was my fault. I let down my wall, spoke from my heart.

"Frenchie, I'm sorry. For everything. Sorry I didn't marry you. We should have been a family."

She raised her hand like she didn't want me to say another goddamn word. Those soft words, my excited utterance, had rocked her. Frenchie opened her mouth to say something, moved her lips, but no words emerged, as if she were searching for the right language to express the foreign sensation she felt, but there was no such language.

With tears in her eyes, she stood and stormed away from the table.

I wiped my eyes too.

Fela came back. "Where's Mom?"

"Bathroom." I was just as rattled. I told Fela, "Let me go wash my hands too."

When I made it back to the table, Fela and Frenchie were laughing, already eating. Frenchie had three mai tais. I only had one, but it felt like I'd had four. I could tell she was buzzed. Swimming in emotions and buzzed.

"Ma, can Dad give me a ride home?"

She shook her head. "That wasn't the plan. You have a hard time following rules, Fela."

"Please? My beautiful mother, mother I love dearly, please, Mommy, please?"

"Sure, hang out with Disneyland dad." She laughed. "Don't be out too long. School in the morning."

"Can we catch a movie?"

"Fela."

"My homework is done. I'll be home before my curfew."

"If you're not, I will not hesitate to call the police on your police-calling father."

"Go with us."

"No. Not this time. Lots on my mind right now. I'm going home to sip on some wine."

Frenchie didn't say anything else to me. When we were done breaking bread, she kissed Fela, rubbed his wild hair, then left, headed toward the Macy's at the north end of the mall, the one that sold women's clothing.

We headed in the opposite direction. I didn't look back for fear of turning into a pillar of salt. I assume Frenchie didn't look back either. She'd never been the type to look back, had always been good at moving on.

FELA AND I hit the Goodwill in Manhattan Beach. I took my teenager thrifting. He scored some funky clothing and found a headset he liked. Everything cost forty bucks. We hit the theater, saw an action movie, and I got my son home on time. We said good-bye; then an hour later I called his mother's number. I was parked near LAX on Lincoln, watching planes come in from the east. I'd been rattled since dinner at Islands, so rattled I couldn't let it go.

"Frenchie? Why did you leave the table like that?"

"I was trying to spare you your life."

"I apologized."

"And that left me stuck with sixteen years of anger festering inside me. What am I supposed to do with this anger now, Dwayne? It disarmed me. You can't just apologize like that. It's not fucking fair. I fucking hate you."

"Frenchie."

"You said what you said, said you wished we had married, said you wished we had been a family, and it stirred up old feelings. We were supposed to be a team greater than Sophia Loren and Marcello Mastroianni. I see old pictures of us and they remind me that we used to be so intimate, and I remember everything you did, everything, all we did together, all the stuff that you said you would do with me forever, and I recall all the late-night exchanges and phone calls, and I reminisce about all the good things and bad things, and I remember now that all the good times are just a memory and there's nothing left for us now but bad times henceforth until the end of time. I've learned not to feel sad over someone who gave up on me, even though they gave up on someone who would have never given up on them."

"Frenchie."

"What, Dwayne? What do you want this late at night? Why do you keep disturbing me?"

Her tone was as hard as a diamond, anger stronger than graphene.

Disturbed, I sat in the dirty rental car that doubled as my motel, my heart drumming inside of my chest.

"What do you want, Dwayne?"

Sixteen years of bitterness, resentment, attorneys, judges, court orders, and disappointment was the wall erected between us. I should've hung up. I should've handled it all in court as we had done from day one. I should've let my three-hundred-dollar-an-hour attorney talk to her three-hundred-dollar-an-hour lawyer. But I didn't.

CHAPTER 45

DWAYNE

MEMORIES OF NEW Jersey, of being in court, of being lied on, they all danced in my head.

I steeled my nerves, swallowed, and asked Frenchie, "What if I come back to your house?"

"Dwayne, it's late. Playtime is over. Fela had a long evening and is in bed sleeping."

"To talk to you, not to my son. I want to talk to you."

"This late?"

"You have company?"

"Would I answer if I did?"

"Are you expecting company?"

"Not your business."

"Can I come back to Inglewood?"

"Can you?"

"May I?"

"You may have your attorney talk to my attorney and we'll work it out in court as usual."

"Frenchie."

"What, Dwayne? What, what, what, what, what do you want? Why are you calling my number?"

I also had memories of the days, weeks, months, before New Jersey. "I want to see you."

"You just saw me."

"Not the way I want to see you."

It was there, in the statement. I waited for her to hang up on me.

"You want to see me?"

"Yes."

"Not Fela."

"I want to see you, Frenchie."

"Why?"

It was hard to say the three words, but I did. "I miss you."

Her voice changed, softened. "You miss me?"

"Yes. And I've missed you a long time."

Then her voice was diamond hard again. "No, you don't."

"Yeah, I do."

There was a long pause, and I expected her to either curse at me a hundred times or burst out laughing.

Her tone tendered. "You miss me."

"I miss you."

She hesitated. "You want to see me."

"I want to see you."

Again she hesitated, then sounded perplexed when she asked, "For what purpose?"

"Frenchie."

She understood; it was in her breathing. "My son can't see you come into my home and definitely not into my bedroom. So you'll have to sneak around back and come through my bedroom window."

"You're serious?"

"Are you serious about missing me or just . . . you fucking with me, Dwayne?"

"I want to see you."

"Dwayne, I've been drinking. Don't call me and mess with my head."

"Just me and you, Frenchie. Just me and you. Like we used to be."

"We're being honest here?"

"Yeah. We're being honest."

"Okay. I don't like you but still have feelings for you. My desire for you is stronger than the dislike, and I hate that. I almost told you that tonight when we were at Islands. Almost was foolish enough to say that out loud."

"Serious?"

"You looked so good that day at the beach."

"So did you."

She exhaled, stressed. "Wait, wait. We have to go to court in a few weeks."

"I know. We'll be back in the ring fighting through our high-priced lawyers."

"Not a good idea. Things are ugly enough as it is, Dwayne."

"I'm coming back. I'm coming to see you, Frenchie. I need to see you."

She hesitated. "Give me thirty minutes. I need to shower and make sure my son is sound sleep."

"He's my son too."

"And you can't be noisy. If we have ex-sex, you have to make sure you are quiet. I'm serious."

"So, are we having ex-sex?"

She groaned. "Shit. Is that what you wanted? I'm sorry. Or just to talk."

"I wanted to talk. But yeah, I want you like that. Since we're being honest."

She asked, "Or are you just saying that now since I slipped and said ex-sex?"

I took a breath. "I'll knock on your window."

"Tap, don't knock. *Tap.* My bedroom is the first one. My light will be on. Well, I'll light a candle."

"Okay."

She said, "And you can't make me be noisy either."

"We've never not been noisy."

"Park up the street. Not out front of my home. And no talking, not a word when you get into my room."

"I have to be silent?"

"We will both be on vocal rest. No speaking, singing, or whispering."

"I get it. I'll head in that direction now."

"Bring a condom."

"From where?"

"They make a million condoms a day; I'm sure you can find *one.*"

"Condom or condoms?"

"Condom. The thin kind. Non-latex. I'm allergic. Ribbed if possible."

"One and done?"

"One and done. And this better not come up when we go back to court."

"Frenchie."

"What, Dwayne? What now?"

"Sometimes I touch myself, just to feel me, and imagine me filling you to my balls."

"Sometimes I drink too much and imagine you down my throat."

"Jesus."

"I'm imagining that now." She swallowed. "Get a condom and get here."

CHAPTER 46

BRICK

Dr. Allison Émilie Chappelle put her head on my chest. I had my hand in her incredible hair, an Afro that smelled like coconut. My fingers massaged her scalp. Her dog jumped up on the bed and rested next to her.

She stared at the wheelchair and said, "You didn't ask if I've ever been able to walk."

"You said you ran track, so I assumed you were able to walk, not just run."

"I walked for twenty years. I ran track for fourteen years. I hiked in twelve countries. Played volleyball at a professional level. And was a scholar. Did it all. Owned the world. Until a car accident."

"How long ago?"

"Four years ago. Was with my fiancé. He died on that rainy day."

"Sorry to hear that."

"He died, and I woke up in the hospital thirty days later."

"You were in a coma?"

"When I woke up, he was dead and buried. They had taken me off life support. They had written me off. Then said it was a miracle I survived. A miracle. I ended up in a wheelchair, and they called that a miracle. I didn't see it that way. Sometimes I sit in my chair and watch people run and I want to cry."

I said, "Doc, you okay?"

With a hard face and a soft voice, she said, "I'm okay, boo. I'm okay."

She yanked her wheelchair to her. She plopped herself in the seat, then took herself to the bathroom. When she came back, she eased back onto the bed, inched back to me. I kissed her face a dozen times.

She asked, "How often can I see you like this? For chess and whatever happens to happen after?"

"How often do you want to see me?"

"Once a week. On Mondays. I don't work Mondays."

"I could be yours from midnight to midnight, if you wanted me. Same rate."

"I will need a lower rate. I have to budget."

"We can work something out. It will be to your advantage."

"You accept Groupons?"

"Groupons, coupons, any discount you can think of. I can make an exception for you."

"Should I be ashamed?"

"For what?"

"For paying for this."

"No more than I should be ashamed."

"How many times have you done this? Hundreds?"

"You are number three."

"I was almost your first."

"Almost. You had an opening and middle act. That makes you the headliner."

"You're my first. Like this. I can count the number of men I've been with on one hand and not have to use my thumb or my pinky or my traffic finger. Wasn't an easy decision to make, but I thought, why not?"

I held her. She mumbled, nodded off.

I stared at the ceiling, tired but not sleeping. It was funny how fate had worked out. I had been searching for her, and she had ended up needing me. Not me, but a man she now perceived me to be, for only one night.

I wanted to make her breakfast, then lunch, then dinner, then breakfast again.

I whispered, "I don't know you, but I could love you, and I really, really, really need to love somebody. Someone as amazing as you. I adore you. Your mind is amazing. Everything about you is amazing. Be mine. Just give me a chance, one chance, and if we break up, it won't be because I cheated. I'd never cheat. I'd try to work things out, and then if it doesn't work out, we tried, and we just go our separate ways, but it won't end over infidelity. So, tell me, actuary, what are the odds of a woman like you giving a guy like me a chance at happiness? Long shot. I'm not a man who needs or craves a lot of women. I just want one I can call my own. A remarkable, stunningly fine woman like you."

Listening to her smooth breathing, fantasizing, I fell asleep too.

CHAPTER 47

DWAYNE

As instructed, I parked a few houses away, then tiptoed through the overgrown grass on the side of Frenchie's crib. I tapped the bedroom window twice and it eased open. Like Romeo creeping to see Juliet, I crawled into Frenchie's boudoir, then stood before her holding a box of chocolates and three roses from 7-Eleven. She softened, surprised by the romantic gesture. She stood in candlelight and soft music, Teena Marie singing "Portuguese Love," and she put her finger to her lips and shook her head. Hair down, Frenchie wore an Italian infinity cross lariat necklace. Stainless steel earrings with Swarovski crystals. Pink lingerie. She smelled like heaven, like mangoes. The girl from Vermont looked vulnerable now. Just a girl waiting on a boy. No grudge, no chip on her shoulder. Trembling like a virgin on her wedding night.

Frenchie took the chocolates and roses, eased her gifts on her dresser, then tiptoed toward me. She put her hand on my chest, touched me, her first time touching me since before Fela was born. She kept her hand there a few seconds, on the rise and fall, felt my energy; then Frenchie backed away, went and blew out the candle.

She stood in front of me and I was nervous, both of us asking if we were really going to do this.

I wanted her.

I pulled her to me, sucked her lips. She shuddered, gave me her tongue, kissed me like she was famished. It was as good now as it had been the first time. At the midnight hour, I quivered from my head down to my liver.

The kisses were dizzying. I took my tender kisses to her ear, down her neck, to her breasts, sucked her nipple as she made "wanna cry but don't stop because it feels so good" faces. I kissed down across her belly, pushed her back on the bed, opened her legs, went down on her, gave her my tongue with an urgency. My tongue made her body dance. She made sounds like it felt too good, covered her face with a pillow, then panted into the pillow. I held her suntanned ass in my eager hands, pulled her toward me, went deeper. Frenchie muffled her moans the best she could, but my tongue made her jerk like she wanted to hit Mariah Carey high notes. I took my tongue away and left her squirming. I undressed and took out the box of condoms, ripped it open, pulled out one, dropped the box with the remaining two, rolled on a condom as fast as I could. She watched me, anticipating, waiting on me to come back. I eased down on top of her. My weight eased down on hers. She was wet. Wide open. Swollen. I moved inside her and opened up more memories. She slapped her hand over her own mouth to muffle her suddenly savage moans. Vocal rest was being tested to the max. Her throaty groans roared in my ear, and it was arousing. I swallowed; then I moaned like a man dying from lust. She clamped her hand over my mouth to hush me. I moved against her, grew harder as I slid deeper inside her, made her feel me while I filled her.

The sex was Tennessee whiskey: smooth, harsh, and needed. No sounds, but our faces told all. The headboard tapped the wall a half dozen times. Frenchie gave me a panicked expression, made me stop. It hurt for me to stop. Hurt for me to pull out of her. We grabbed pillows, yanked the comforter from the bed, rushed to the floor. She got on her back, legs open, and without guidance, I sank inside her again. She whimpered to God and Jesus. I wanted to shout. It was too much. The wonderful feeling was too much to bear. I stroked her so good. My low, guttural moan tickled her ear. Being on the floor was so much better. She could move against me. She didn't have to hold back. Floor didn't give. More intense faces were made in vocal silence. She held me and started to come. Her breathing was dense. The pillow fell away. I let out another low moan. She let out a soft whine. Together we struggled. We were almost there, close to coming together, our ragged breathing the perfect duet. The lines in Frenchie's face, the way her lips were pulled in, the way she clenched her jaw, the way she bared her teeth, showed how bad she wanted to curse. Her wicked expression was pure swearwords, the kind you made when pleasure was too much. I stroked her, and she gave it back to me as good as I was giving it. I gave her my urgency, gave her the desperate, out-of-control stroking a man gave when a man was about to come the come of all comes. I pushed so far inside of her she almost screamed. She felt me coming and that heat set her on fire, made her move like she had the Holy Spirit.

I slowed my stroke, but she didn't slow hers. I rode her the best I could, until she stopped bucking.

As we panted in each other's arms, Frenchie sat up like she'd heard something. She hurried, yanked on a robe, peeped out her door, saw no one, then listened. She tiptoed to Fela's bedroom door as if Fela was the parent and she didn't want to get caught. She came back and closed her door, still nervous. Frenchie slipped off her robe, got back down on the floor with me. I took the condom off. She wrapped it in tissues and put it to the side. No words. I sat up. One and done. I reached for my pants. She touched my shoulder as she gazed into my eyes. She reached for my penis, then motioned at the box of condoms. I nodded.

Message received. She licked her lips, still hungry, nodded. I ripped open another condom. She stopped me from putting it on. She bit her lip, touched my face, kissed me as she stroked me, then went down on me, made me grow inside the warmth of her mouth. Frenchie made me feel so good it was my turn to bite and chew into a pillow to keep from howling at the moon. The second round of ex-sex started slow, kisses sweet like strawberry wine, then evolved, hands over mouths, light moans, soft giggles hidden by the music that she'd left playing, both of us struggling not to break vocal rest as the passion elevated. We came and tried to recover from another orgasm. Frenchie was glowing and radiant. I took her right foot in my hand, massaged it gently. Frenchie cooed. I massaged her calf, then her foot again. In that post-sex haze, I wished I was a male alligator, forever erect and aroused, and I'd spend the rest of my life inside Frenchie. A man lost himself in the things he loved. He found himself there, too. She took her foot away, crawled to me, and kissed me over and over and over.

CHAPTER 48

DWAYNE

EXHAUSTED, I GAVE Frenchie a deep fairy-tale kiss, then climbed back out of the window. By the time I made it to where I had parked my rental car, my phone vibrated. It was a text message from Frenchie.

COME BACK. PARK IN FRONT. I'LL COME OUT.

I wondered what I'd done wrong. Or maybe I'd forgotten something, left some evidence behind.

I drove over and parked in front. Frenchie had come outside. She peeped in the rental car's passenger-side window, then went to the trunk of the car and leaned against it. I got out and sat on the trunk next to her.

I asked, "What I do wrong?"

"Who said you did something wrong?"

"Well, what's on your mind?"

"Was thinking about all the sex we'd had. Morning sex. Afternoon sex. Before-the-show sex. During-the-show sex. After-the-performance sex. After-dinner sex. After-lunch sex. Day-off sex. Mad-at-you sex."

"Monday sex. Tuesday sex. Wednesday sex. Thursday sex. Friday sex. Saturday sex."

"Sunday-before-the-matinée sex."

"Sunday-after-the-matinée sex."

"Sex-because-we-liked-having-sex-together sex."

"Sex-because-I-loved-you sex."

"We made a mess of things. We hurt other people. And we ended up hurting each other."

"We did."

"I was married to one man and pregnant by another. I was so scared."

"I was scared too."

Nothing was said, not for a while. Our most tranquil moment in the last sixteen years.

She asked, "Is it true?"

"Is what true?"

"Fela said you're sleeping in your car. Don't lie to me."

"Let's just say I'm camping. I'll be okay."

"Dwayne."

"We've both hit rock bottom."

"Why aren't you staying with your brothers? Both have apartments."

"They had guests. I didn't want to impose. I feel . . . To be honest . . . I'm too old to be couch surfing."

"André owns an apartment building."

"All the units are leased and he keeps a pair of hot legs in his bed damn near every night."

"A beach for men doesn't need lifeguards because if a man is drowning, he won't ask for help."

"I'll make it, one way or another."

"Gurgle, gurgle, drown."

I said, "It's just another rough period."

She paused. "We have water again. We have running water."

"Yeah."

"Did you pay to have it turned back on?"

I didn't answer, just said, "Glad it's back on."

She wiped away a tear. "Where have you been crashing at night? Everywhere is dangerous. People are getting held up at gunpoint at Coliseum and Crenshaw, not too far from where your brothers live. Nipsey got gunned down in front of his store. It's crazy out there."

"Parked here and there. Parked by Monteith Park in View Park one night; parked by Rueben Ingold Park the next. Let the seat back. Cracked the window for ventilation. Hoped I didn't get jacked."

"Why didn't you use that money to get yourself a hotel room? Plenty of cheap motels on La Brea."

"I can't be in a motel living large when my son . . . and you . . . don't have water."

"It's cold until I get the power back on. The water is cold af, but every drop is appreciated."

"Give it a day. It will warm up."

"Dwayne."

"Frenchie."

"Thanks."

The door opened and Fela came outside, using his phone as a flashlight, stretching. He came over to where we were, stood next to us, scrunched his nose, then stared at the sky, clocked an airplane heading into LAX.

Frenchie said, "Fela."

"I know, Ma. It's past my curfew."

"It's fine, Fela. Tonight, it's fine." She hummed. "Mind if your daddy sleeps on the couch?"

Fela smiled. "Cool. He can drop me at school. The million-dollar kid wants to show Dad off to the teachers. Some of the older ones are his fans. Maybe he can chat to the class about Broadway and Hollywood stuff. You come too, Ma. You have a lot of fans there too. Every time 'Everybody Knows' comes on, Jesus, the older teachers come running to me. I want everybody to see us together for once. That would be better than Christmas."

Fela told us good night, yawned again, and staggered back into the house.

Frenchie whispered, "He heard us. I knew I heard him in the hallway. He heard us."

"He heard you."

"I won't be able to look him in the eye tomorrow."

"Me either."

Frenchie sighed. "What did we just do?"

"I have no idea."

"I feel foolish."

"Yeah. Feels like . . . like it did back then."

Frenchie hummed the Teena Marie part of "Fire and Desire." I sang the Rick James part.

Frenchie said, "It's getting cold out here."

"Nothing like these desert nights. I miss this coolness when I'm in Florida."

"Bring your stuff into the house."

"You sure?"

"No. But bring it in anyway. Clean your car out. It looks disgusting. Just turn it back in. Use mine."

"One car for two people in LA? You sure that would work for you?"

"I'm not sure about anything other than going to court is going to be interesting."

"Very."

She bit the corner of her lip, nudged me. "One condom left."

I nudged her back. "Waste not, want not."

"Then we can go back to hating each other."

"I missed you."

"Missed you too."

We went to Frenchie's bedroom.

After a dozen kisses, we took turns and showered in cold water.

The chilling water wasn't enough to put out fire and desire.

We locked the bedroom door, opened the last condom.

I took Frenchie to the bedroom floor, and we put vocal rest to the test one more time.

CHAPTER 49

BRICK

By **TEN IN** the morning, each time a lift opened, it was packed with frowning politicians who dared me to squeeze into an already crowded sardine can. I let three elevators go by before I accepted the challenge. Most were heading to the express checkout, a few in a hurry to get to breakfast and pig out on the taxpayers' dime before catching flights across the divided nation. When I exited the people pulley at the lobby, I strutted like a maverick who'd broken free from a stud of pale horses. My swagger took me to the hotel's five-star restaurant. Penny, Mocha Latte, and Christiana were already there, seated in the midst of a malapertness of political peddlers. The pace of asses were dressed in dark business suits with American flags on their lapels, like they were lackeys for the politicians.

I'd left Dr. Allison Émilie Chappelle in the well-appointed hotel room. At sunrise we'd played chess and she'd beat me in three out of five games. It had been a wonderful night and an even better morning.

I grinned at the pace of asses. "Well, if it ain't the good, the bad, and the ugly."

Penny rubbed her nose with her middle finger. "Wow. You look good in that suit. Democrat or Republican?"

"Independent. Hard to choose when in the end all you're doing is picking a devil you hope to be kinder."

"That haircut is sharper than a kitchen knife."

I said, "The stylist was meticulous. She waxed inside my nostrils and checked my prostate."

Christiana said, "I waxed the rest of Brick yesterday. Now I have waxed all of you."

The pace had worked here last night. They had been put in suites by clients, then waited for their customers to come to them. They laughed about how old men paid top dollar to just sit and look at women more beautiful than their wives. They said that the men who paid the most were knocking on the doors of impotence, or already impotent, but flexed their financial power. If they could come once, it took forever to get it up, then forever to get them to come, and when they did, they were done, down for the count, and probably done for the month. They wanted a woman younger than their daughters at their side for the night. They wanted to eat out a beautiful woman and see her naked.

I said, "No issues?"

Penny laughed. "No one broke into a room and kicked everybody's ass."

We got comfortable amid the pale male power. The table to our right was filled with men older than Moses. They talked unemotionally about human trafficking and sex slaves. The table to our left was filled with millennials, Fox News–type pundits, who used Black Lives Matter as a punch line. They were huge fans of a racist president who lacked self-control and tweeted like an emotionally immature, hor-monal thirteen-year-old going through puberty.

Penny said, "So, Brick, you're actually doing this."

"Gave it a try last night."

Mocha Latte shifted, kept her opinion to herself. Judge not, that ye be not judged.

Christiana smiled like she had found a new source of gold. "He received five stars from his clients."

Penny said, "Clients?"

"He had three."

"Damn, Brick. Damn."

We ordered like king and queens, sipped mimosas, talked about irrelevant things.

We all noticed Mocha Latte. She smiled, but we saw that mood had her once again. Her demons.

She said, "I should go back home, get baptized again, rededicate my life to Christ, start over."

Penny asked, "And forget about us heathens?"

"I won't look back, but I will remember you, Brick. Jesus was friends with the common man, with thieves, with Mary Magdalene, no mat-ter how her reputation had been tarnished. He was friends with people like us."

I said, "Texas. The Deep South. Where slavery began, and its impact still resonates."

"I'm going to look at a place on the Gulf of Mexico. A brand-new house in that part of Mississippi costs less than two hundred grand. If I live there, I can drive my Rubicon back and forth to Malakoff to see my folks."

I said, "Hurricanes and floods will turn that house into a boat that don't float."

"They're building the houses higher now. Living room is on the second level."

Christiana shook her head. "The humidity will make you sweat like hell. Mosquitoes bigger than your fist."

"I'll buy a shotgun, sit on my porch like I'm skeet shooting."

Penny asked, "What's to do there in Mississippi, besides leave in a hurry and never look back?"

"Eat at Dunk's. Get doughnuts at King's. Get drunk at Rum Kitchen. Get crayfish at C&R's Bar and Grill. Go to church. Walk out on the pier holding hands with someone you like. Help people repair the damage to their homes from Katrina. Build something more than a house from the ground up. Fall in love. Real love. The kind that is really scary. Make beautiful babies. Pretend this part of my life never was. Ain't no love in this life. No love at all."

When we were about to pay, the waiter told us that the six-hundred-dollar tab had been taken care of, tip included. We didn't ask any questions and headed toward the valet.

Bellies full, we headed home in Miss Mini under the warmth of the California sun.

Mocha Latte sang a tune by Elizabeth Grace called "Perfect." She had a beautiful voice. Surprised me. When she was done, I cranked up some Bruno Mars and we turned the ride into a hard-core carpool karaoke.

Happiness only lasted so long.

When I made it back home, the enemy of all enemies was demanding an audience.

A Maserati was in front of my building like a stalker waiting on me to return to my castle.

CHAPTER 50

BRICK

MASERATI MAMA'S IMMACULATE ride was parked outside my building when we made it back to Leimert Park.

Christiana said, "The fuck. Brick, isn't that Coretta's lover's car?"

"Yeah. Miss Intergluteal Cleft seems to have gotten lost in my zip code."

Mocha Latte asked, "What are they doing here?"

"They probably came to hit me in the head with the claw part of a hammer."

Penny said, "Keep away from them, Brick."

"I'll be fine, Penny."

Mocha Latte added, "Said many a man right before a woman blew his brains out."

I parked. The pace got out and headed to Penny's crib, scowling back at Maserati Mama's ride. Maserati Mama stepped out of the car. I waited for the passenger door to open. It didn't.

Maserati Mama was alone.

She stood tall, regarded me, took a hard breath, then sashayed my way like an angry model. Her hands were open, a good sign. I walked toward the Nilotic woman dressed in her usual glamorous suit, this one a shade of purple, with reds and blacks and a slash of white. Her hair was as it had been each time I saw her, to the middle of her back, in one braid.

She said, "I came here against my better judgment."

"Your eyes are red and you smell like expensive weed and cheap wine, so I know you're not making the best decision."

"But you are the only one who can help me."

"What's going on?"

She struggled. "I don't fucking understand her. I've never met anyone like that bitch."

"Coretta?"

"Help me understand her. She's destroyed my heart. I've never had my heart broken before and I never imagined it would be broken in such a massively cold-blooded, uncaring, fucked-up way."

She tried not to weep, but it was too much, and suddenly she was crying.

"You flatten my tires and come to me for advice?"

"You flattened mine first."

"I flattened one of yours. You flattened two of mine."

"Coretta flattened the other one because you flattened hers too."

Maserati Mama shuddered and sobbed.

I took my adversary's hand, and she walked with me.

I WASN'T SURE what was appropriate, so I opened a bottle of three-hundred-dollar wine, poured her a glass, and poured myself one. We sat in my living room at opposite ends of my oversize classic sofa, facing each other, civilized, wine in hand. All that arrogance and self-confidence I'd seen in her eyes and body language was gone. I guess today Coretta was her foe, and the enemy of my enemy was my friend. Outside on Stocker, cars passed by with music bumping. Three helicopters were overhead looking for someone on the run; sirens wailed in the distance.

Maserati Mama ranted, "She's expensive. She pays for nothing and makes all the rules."

"Hard habit for her to break."

"She's a cheater-o."

"Is she?"

"I looked at her receipts for the mountain of things she bought herself. She bought a pregnancy test."

"Congratulations."

"I'm serious."

"I am too."

"My heart dropped. Dropped and shattered. A pregnancy test."

"She was never good at tests. Thank God for social passing."

She ignored my habitual facetiousness, turned very serious. "Is it yours?"

"Only if she is about eight months pregnant."

"It was negative. But still. She took a pregnancy test. I feel so foolish and threadbare now."

I dialed down the flippancy, turned up the empathy. "You gonna be okay?"

"I'm mentally drained."

"She's seeing a man. She has a side dude."

"At least one, I guess."

"And you thought she was seeing me?"

"I did. I mean, I didn't know. I don't know. She keeps changing her passwords on her social media accounts. Keeps locking me out. She defriended me on Facebook. Blocked me on Twitter. She has my passwords. I have nothing to hide, but when it comes to her phone, she always deletes everything, all her messages and texts, as soon as she reads them. Who does that but someone guilty of a crime? She texts someone through the night when she thinks I'm sleeping. One day I came home early from work, and she was in the shower and had left her phone unlocked. I found out that she has secret Twitter and Facebook accounts. Then I found she has a second phone hidden in the trunk of her car underneath her spare tire. She got busted because she left it on and forgot to turn off the ringer. Something is going on. I'm going crazy. I don't know what to think. How many ways can she lie? She lies when she cries, lies when she smiles, lies when she talks. She lies when we make love. I had a good life before her."

"And she doesn't double flush."

"She doesn't clean the bathroom, period. That's how I know she had a man in my condo."

"What do you mean?"

"The lip of the toilet had urine drops on it. I saw that filth when I cleaned the bathroom."

"Wow."

Maserati Mama raised her glass to mine and said, "A toast to the fools-o."

"Where are you from?"

"Jos, a city in the Middle Belt of Nigeria. We call it J-Town. I graduated from Unijos. Master's."

"Unijos?"

"University of Jos."

She had befriended me for the moment, gained my confidence, my truth, made it hard for me to lie, and then came the question that was burning her. "Have you been with Coretta since she's been living with me?"

"She's called because she wants a box of things she left behind, but the only time I've seen Coretta was in public and you were at her side holding her hand. I haven't seen her alone since we broke up. Not once."

"You sure?"

"I might forget my password to Facebook, but I'd remember if we hooked up."

"You pop up everywhere we go like you're jealous and following her."

"Don't flatter yourself. If I could GPS Coretta's location, we'd never cross paths."

"She's sneaky."

"Were you with her while she was with me?"

"I was. I'm sorry. But I never came here."

I nodded. "At least we know her character. No need to be angry at each other."

She rubbed her temples. "Feels like I'm loving her on borrowed time. Her love for me was never true."

"I was her fool too. Maybe the clock was ticking down from day one, but I never heard it."

"She has secrets."

"Maybe her secrets would be revealed if she had shown me her credit report or tax papers."

She laughed. "You actually asked to see her credit report and tax papers?"

"No comment."

Maserati Mama sipped. "This wine. I love it."

"Another glass?"

"Yes-o."

I poured her a fresh glass, did the same for myself.

She said, "This has been the worst six months of my life-ooooooo. But I'll be so much better for having my heart shattered by her. She has broken my heart three times a day in some way-o. I'm strong, uncontrollable, kick-ass, affectionate, kindhearted, gorgeous, and amazing in bed. I know what I deserve from a lover. I have offered her nothing but good, nothing but happiness and ecstasy-o, and all I asked for was respect, love, and to be able to depend on her. I deserve a lover who isn't self-absorbed, one who doesn't lie when I beg for the truth-o."

"When did this pregnancy-test thing happen?"

"This morning."

"What happened when you confronted her?"

"She walked out. Left me begging for answers."

"So you came here. Sat outside and waited. Probably banged on my door off and on."

"Because she vanished, turned her phone off, and I thought she was with you."

"More wine?"

"Please."

"I'll open another bottle."

This time I opened a four-hundred-dollar bottle of wine and poured her a fresh glass.

She said, "She's no cheap date-o."

"You deserve to be held by someone who wants more from you than to ride in your ride."

"Same goes for you-o. I ain't saying she's a gold digger, but . . . you know the rest."

"You love her."

"Are you still in love with her?"

I confessed, "I'm not out of love with her. Time is the novocaine for the toothache in my heart."

"One day, she'll hurt the wrong person."

"True."

"I trusted her with my heart."

"Me too."

She took two long sips. "You get the closure you need?"

"Not yet."

"I need closure too."

"I'll work it out in other ways."

"She's probably with that guy now."

"Maybe."

"Probably fucking him."

"Let me pour you another glass."

"Too bad we didn't meet first."

"Aren't you a sexual vegetarian?"

"I identify as having fluid sexuality. I'm attracted to men and women, but no one more than Coretta."

"Didn't know that."

"I just haven't been with a man in a while. Not in a long, long while."

"That would have been interesting."

"I should stop drinking before my clothes fall off. Drinking wine makes my clothes fall off."

"Okay. No more wine for you."

"Is it the wine talking, or do I sense a curiosity?"

"I never would have imagined you looking at me without eyes filled with disdain."

"I've never seen you this way, just as you are. I have felt this energy coming from you, the energy that attracts Coretta to you. I feel your testosterone. You are attractive, strong, tall. And you are kind."

"I've never seen you this way either."

She grinned, rocked, maybe surprised at where we suddenly were. "Should I go?"

I examined Coretta's lover, took in her dark mood, her vengeful eyes. "Do you want to go?"

Her voice softened. "Lover of my lover, what's on your mind?"

"You go first."

"They say if you can't be with the one you love, love the one you're with."

"They do."

"Well."

"Well."

"Your bedroom is that way, I assume. See? My. Clothes. Are. Fall-ing. Off."

CHAPTER 51

BRICK

THE NEXT MORNING at sunrise, I went to Home Depot in Ladera.

I bought five gallons of Behr paint, blue painter's tape, rollers, paintbrushes, trays, and everything I needed to patch up ceilings and walls. While I was filling my cart, I ran into my neighbors Ken Swift and Jake Ellis. They were buying chainsaws, shovels, and plastic. We chatted about quality paints. I had picked the best. On my way out, I talked to Central American day laborers who were desperate for work. Next I stopped by Leimert Park, picked up the pace of asses, and drove Miss Mini toward Inglewood. André and Joëlle trailed me on his iron horse the hue of flames. Dwayne was already at Frenchie's.

I introduced Frenchie, Fela, and Dwayne to the attorney from Cuba, the student at USC, and the out-of-work engineer. André introduced Joëlle to everyone. She and Mocha Latte became nerds and talked engineering. Two men I had talked to at Home Depot showed up. Both were from Ecuador. We assessed the damage and ripped out carpet, left it all curbside. Minutes later the lights came on and everybody applauded. Frenchie cried. Dwayne had used the money I had given him to help get Frenchie sorted. After the carpet was out, we patched the holes and painted the walls museum white. The men from Ecuador gave me a good price for labor to install new carpet.

Two middle-aged black men I had hired showed up and cut the front and back lawns.

Coretta sent me a thousand text messages. She was angry and hurt. Maserati Mama and I had taken selfies, in my crib, in my bed, and Maserati Mama had sent the evidence to Coretta. Now Coretta was blowing up my phone. Maserati Mama was petty. I, too, was petty at times, just like everybody else. Coretta had wronged us and now she felt wronged by us. She had betrayed both of us and now felt doubly betrayed. Yet I still loved her. Just not the way I used to.

I put some more money in Dwayne's hand, told him to take Frenchie to look at new carpet.

My older brother cried. He told me he'd pay me back. I told him it wasn't a loan.

I wasn't like Dwayne Sr. and didn't aspire to be. We were family. We were all we had.

My phone buzzed, and it was Maureen. Paintbrush in hand, I answered with a kind voice. She told me she had an unexpected trip back to LA and wanted to schedule a session. Just me and not Mocha Latte. I told Maureen my price to meet her for a night at the same hotel near LAX.

The second we ended the call, my phone buzzed again with a text message. Birthday Girl wanted to see me. So did the self-important politician. They wanted to try something different and see me at the same time. I sent the Birthday Girl my marked-up fee to become a three-headed beast.

She agreed on the exorbitant price. I'd learned from Mocha Latte and Christiana.

A couple of hours later Dr. Allison Émilie Chappelle texted me. I sent her a smiley face and hearts. She sent me the same. I imagined Strawberry reading the message, barking and wagging her tail.

Not long after, Christiana came to me smiling, her phone in her hand, new customers on the horizon.

While we worked, Frenchie and Dwayne were different. They were getting along.

If I didn't know any better, the way they were singing, I'd think they were flirting too.

When I stood in her bedroom door, I saw Dwayne's luggage in her room.

She saw me looking, putting it all together, then grinned and said, "Don't judge me."

WHEN I PULLED up at my apartment building, Coretta was on my porch, enraged, banging on my door. She saw me when I pulled up, realized I wasn't inside avoiding her. I got out of Miss Mini, jeans and T spotted with white paint, same for the pace of asses. They walked alongside me like they were Charlie's Angels. I told them all was cool, and they headed up the concrete stairs and went toward Penny's apartment but didn't go inside.

Coretta had her hair whipped like she was heading to the Oscars and wore a tight skirt and high heels.

Coretta gave me the ugliest face she could make and with a ton of disdain said, "I want my things."

"Good evening. You lose your home training?"

"I want my things."

"Sure. Wait right there."

"I can't come inside?"

"No."

"Why not?"

"Love don't live here anymore."

I went inside and grabbed the box of insignificant things Coretta had left behind. I went back and placed her belongings down at her feet. Mocha Latte, Christiana, and Penny milled around the courtyard checking out the scene, kissing teeth and throwing side-eyes like darts.

Arms folded and eyes watery, Coretta asked, "Did some of my mail come here too?"

"Your mail never came here."

"My tax guy said he sent my mail here by accident."

"Didn't come to my address."

I took in her long legs, her subtle curves. Her hair blew like she'd rented Beyoncé's wind machine, the same breeze bringing me her sensuous scent. She stood there looking like all the woman any man would ever need.

She struggled to not lose the plot as she asked, "Why? Why get with her?"

I calmly asked, "Did marriage scare you? Did I get too serious too fast? What did I do wrong?"

"Why did you get with her? *I asked you a question.*"

"I asked you three."

Her nostrils flared. "Why did you let her use you to hurt me? Why did you hurt me?"

I let a few seconds pass, then told my ex-heartbreak, "Take care of yourself."

She stood in front of me shaking, anger and pain in her swollen eyes. Empathy and old love rose. I should have told her the truth to ease her angst, but I didn't.

She'd earned it.

I asked, "Did you cheat on me too? Did you bring men with weak bladders into my home?"

"Don't believe shit she said. Don't you see how she used you to get to me?"

"Not a good feeling, huh?"

I owned the truth but fed her lies, same as she had done to me.

I could've told her that I hadn't slept with Maserati Mama. We'd ended up undressing, sipping wine, and taking selfies. After we took selfies, we talked, cuddled, then drifted off to sleep. When I woke up a few hours later, Maserati Mama was gone, a thank-you note left behind. She sent Coretta two dozen heart-shattering selfies.

Even if I told Coretta the truth, she wouldn't believe me. The way we looked in those photos, the smiles, the laughter, I wouldn't believe me.

I went inside my place and slammed the door. Coretta stormed away, crying, heels clicking, keys jingling. I frowned out of the window and saw she had left the box where I had placed it on the ground. Penny followed Coretta to her car, made sure she didn't damage Miss Mini. Coretta pulled away in her luxury Benz. Penny jogged back inside her apartment. Five minutes didn't pass before Coretta sent me a message, said she loved me. Said Maserati Mama was a mistake. She told me she'd tell me why she left, why what I had asked had scared her. She would tell me why she had run away. She begged to come back. I told her the rent wasn't free on this side of town, not anymore. I wasn't the same man I was when I was dealing with her. I'd never be that softhearted sucker again.

Mocha Latte knocked at my door. She'd showered, put on jeans.

The out-of-work engineer said, "You're in a bad mood now."

"Yeah. I am."

"If her dress had been any shorter, it would've been a belt. Those fuck-me pumps were higher than the nosebleed section at the Staples Center. She came here to work some black bitch magic on you, Brick. She wanted that cyclopean cock to take her three levels deep and to wake up living here rent-free again."

"She just wanted her stuff."

"Bullshit. She left that box of nothing here to have a reason to come back. She popped up like a badass, shit-kicking woman but left like a petulant brat, unable to get what she wanted."

Mocha Latte kissed me on my cheek, laughed, then headed into my kitchen, started making blueberry pancakes.

That woman from Texas knew how to make my hard frown change into a soft smile.

I said, "She has secrets."

Mocha Latte nodded. "Everyone has secrets. It's their right to have secrets. When those secrets impact you, that's when it becomes an issue. Some will lie, lie, lie and guard those secrets to their graves."

"You had secrets."

"Yup. Two engagement rings. But since you know, like you said, it's no longer a secret."

"People find deception exciting. Some people don't know how to not be cheaters and liars."

Mocha Latte nodded. "You just described most if not all of our customers."

I replayed my affair with Coretta in my mind. "She said she loved me."

"I bet dollars to doughnuts she told Maserati Mama the same bullshit."

"Every day."

"She's had months to show up on your porch because she missed you while the sun was sleeping."

"She did."

"She was here to piss off her girl, not because she loved you. Liars hate getting busted and fall apart like R. Kelly during a Gayle King interview. Your ex wanted to come in and drink wine and undress and get in your bed and take a selfie to send her girl."

I went outside, picked up Coretta's box, carried it around back to the alley, and dropped it in the dumpster. I looked at my phone. All the romantic photos I'd taken with Coretta stared at me. Each image was lie after lie. I deleted all of my photos at once because if I deleted them one by one I'd have to look at each lie one more time.

When I was on my way back, André passed by on his motorcycle.

Joëlle was riding with him, his Apollonia. He had to get to a show at the Bronson Bar on Sunset. When Joëlle was with him, she had eyes for no other man.

When I was at Frenchie's ripping out damaged carpet and repairing walls, I had spotted Dwayne's luggage in her bedroom. That spoke for itself. When everyone was busy, I'd caught Frenchie looking at Dwayne the same way Joëlle looked at André. Despite the ugly seasons, Dwayne and Frenchie had never gotten over each other.

Everybody had someone who loved them.

Even my no-good Nigga Daddy had an ingenue who loved his money enough to tolerate him.

As I headed down the walkway toward my door, Christiana came out of Penny's apartment dressed in her workout clothes. She read my feelings, knew what I needed, and gave me a hug, rocked side to side with me.

While she hugged me, Penny came outside in her USC swag, brought her emotions over, and joined in.

CHAPTER 52

BRICK

TWO DAYS LATER, Penny and I worked at a seventy-million-dollar mansion in Holmby Hills. We were in a bedroom twice the size of my apartment, a space that felt like a home nestled inside a home. We performed on a circular king-size bed. We had been hired by an octogenarian couple on their sixtieth wedding anniversary. They wore formal attire, a tuxedo and a sexy gown. The couple sat like a king and queen, champagne in hands. We did as we had been instructed, pretended we were them. We became actors, called each other by their names. The couple watched, held hands, and smiled as I took Penny three levels deep. The clock struck twelve thirty A.M. and we were at the peak stage of sex. Penny cried and moaned for Jesus. The old woman's phone rang, and she lifted it and took the call. Penny was doggy, and she shook as skin slapped skin, whimpered when I hit her spot, looked back at me with surprise and desperation. The old man enjoyed the sound of skin slapping against skin, enjoyed the magnificence of Penny's young, fit body. He inhaled like he was ingesting her moans. The old woman's attention was on me, her wishful eyes and wistful smile on my toned body. She touched me, put her hand on the rise and fall of my ass. She had the eyes of a teenager and held the phone in her hand, screen glowing, letting whoever was on the other end listen to their diamond anniversary. She wore a huge new rock on her ring finger. When it was done, they stood and applauded, as if they were at the opera. When the curtain was down and Penny stopped singing, when she had recovered from being three levels deep, the old woman turned off her phone. It was a thirty-minute job, but we were paid for two hours. Sixty years married, still in love, still freaky, fucking by proxy.

THE NEXT DAY Mocha Latte left for Bakersfield. It was a two-hour drive north through the Grapevine.

She was going to spend time with her family, touch base with people she'd grown up with. I could tell she needed to get away from us. She came back south within a week. Her attitude was different when she returned. She said she was ready to quit California and move back to Texas. Down south her money could buy a lot more. She needed to get out of this life, said she wanted to date, find a man, get married, maybe have babies.

Mocha Latte packed up the little she owned, told us all an emotional good-bye. She didn't want a going-away party. She hopped in her Jeep at three in the morning and started that fifteen-hundred-mile journey straight out on I-10.

A month later, she sent me pictures of her with cows, pigs, and chickens. She took a selfie as she drove a tractor, smiling up a storm. She was in Malakoff, back in church, and looking for a job. Her text said she was going to Waveland for a weekend. She was going to do as she had promised. Eat at Dunk's. Get doughnuts at King's. Get drunk at Rum Kitchen. Get crayfish. Maybe she'd walk out on the pier holding hands with someone she liked, then wake up and help some of the local Mississippians repair the hurricane damage to their homes. It was time for her to fall in love. Real love. The kind that was really scary. Make beautiful babies. Pretend this part of her life never was.

CHAPTER 53

BRICK

LIFE BECAME DAYS and nights of feasts at extravagant restaurants, followed by drinks in VIP lounges, then back to a hotel room. Most of the women were between thirty-five and fifty-five. They were wealthy. Some celebrated financial and political successes, some celebrated divorces, all with me as their treat. Some were dealing with disappointments and needed me to take them away. Some suffered from midlife crises.

I was chauffeured to events and showed off to other women who had their own baby-faced rentals on their arms. Many of these women had husbands and, after leasing a boyfriend for the night, slipped back into being wives, mommies, or grannies. Sometimes, we headed straight to the room: knocked boots and bounced in under thirty minutes. A few times I left so fast it felt like it had never happened.

Sometimes they told me to give them that black dick, to fuck their pussies with my big black dick, and all they saw was my black dick, as if my cock were my soul. It disturbed me being treated like Mocha Latte said she was treated on more than one of her dates. The nights I gave the BFE, I got the most respect. It wasn't like real-world dating where you discriminated by race, age, or body size. Regardless of age or size, I pretended every woman was my ideal. They, too, pretended I was their ideal man.

I took away dull days and lonely nights for my clients, but no one took away mine.

An Australian woman paid to watch me swim naked in her pool, watched me as she sipped a martini. She fed me chef-prepared food, paid three grand for me to spend the night. We never had sex. Funny how that felt like rejection. She paid me to swim, walk around naked, and be her eye candy, then cuddle with her all night.

Dr. Maureen Asuryasparsh, the freckle-faced Muslim physician from Yale, booked me on Fridays.

The Birthday Girl became a regular as well. She preferred Saturday mornings.

Every Monday, I saw Dr. Allison Émilie Chappelle. I was at her home from midnight to when Siri sounded again at 11:59 P.M. Christiana knew not to book me on Mondays but didn't know why. Gigolos get lonely too. On those days, not one red cent changed hands. She'd put money on the end table, but I never picked it up. I was in love with her, and it wasn't the kind of love I'd had with Coretta, which was a foolish love, a pointless love.

Each woman knowingly or unknowingly taught me something.

ONE RAINY FRIDAY afternoon, as sweat dried, Maureen faced me, her fingers in my hair, smiling.

I asked her why she cheated on her husband, why she was unhappy and needed me once a week.

She said, "In my home, over time I hated a room. My basement. I went into that room for years, and over time it was no longer aesthetically pleasing me. Not all at once. One day I didn't like this about the room. The next week I didn't like that about the room. *Nothing* was wrong with it. I'd seen those same walls, walls that I'd chosen to paint teal, had seen that same Italian furniture, expensive furniture I'd selected and insisted on having, had seen it so many times over the years that my once special room lost its appeal. It wasn't ugly. I needed something different. Familiarity breeds contempt. I had to create drama, create an illusion of it being somehow new. My husband was that basement. Nothing is wrong with him. I needed something different. I needed to redecorate my life. That is my issue."

"Why do we become so goddamn restless?"

"We become emotionally overwhelmed, or emotionally underwhelmed, and need a catharsis."

"I'm your catharsis. This is how you deal with the stress that comes from the choices you've made."

"You're my therapy. This keeps me sane." She nodded. "I'm restless. Many people are restless."

I kissed her lips, mounted her, took her three levels deep, came hard, then rested at her side.

She asked, "Why do you do this?"

"Because it's safe here. You know the cost. It can't trick you, not like a normal relationship."

"You left love."

"Love abandoned me. I waited for it to return like a fool waiting on Godot. I moved on. I left love."

"If you leave love, don't stay gone so long you can never find your way back."

THEN I WAS with Dr. Allison Émilie Chappelle. My standing Monday appointment. The day I looked forward to. We'd laughed and played chess for hours, then took to her bed for two hours, lights dimmed, music playing low.

She sounded bothered. "You brought me flowers. You brought me two dozen red roses two weeks in a row."

"Was that too much?"

"Brick."

"Yeah."

She sighed. "Brick, I heard what you said our first time together. I wasn't sleeping. I heard when you said you wanted to be with me, when you said you loved me, and I didn't know what to think."

"Did you?"

"You said you could love me, and you needed to love somebody. Someone as amazing as me. You said you adored me. You said that if I gave you one chance, you'd never cheat, and if we broke up it wouldn't be over infidelity. I heard you, and every word you said resonated and has stayed with me since that first day I was with you."

"Sounds about right."

"My mind is like that. I remember every word. It shocked me. It shook me."

"Then you know a woman like you is my dream woman."

"A woman like me?"

"You're amazing."

She clacked her teeth together. "I'm in a wheelchair. I am part of the halt, the poor, and the maimed. Brick, I am disabled. I am handi-capped probably for the rest of my life. I am one of those spoken of in Luke 14:21."

"I'm emotionally handicapped."

"You look fine to me."

"So do you."

"Your damage is underneath. My damage is on the surface."

"Is that a deal breaker?"

She nodded. "What good do we do each other?"

"We lean against each other, prop each other up."

"I can't stand up."

"Then I'll sit down."

She became analytical, serious. "How can you promise any woman fidelity?"

"What do you mean?"

"You're a prostitute."

"I'm a man, not an occupation."

"Have you had other women, other clients, since you met me?"

"I have."

"And they pay you for your services."

"You feel as if I cheat on you?"

She took a breath. "Brick, you're a male prostitute."

"I have a master's degree."

"You sell yourself to countless women."

"Is that all you see when you look at me?"

"You're a male whore, which is redundant. I am scarred from my ex. He was a cheater. I'm sorry."

"I can stop being an escort. I can stop today. I can stop right now."

"I'd never trust you."

"I'd earn your trust."

"This . . . once a week . . . Mondays are all we can ever be."

I held her. "If I had met you before I started doing this?"

"But you didn't. That's like asking what if we'd met before my accident. Would I be interested in you in this way if I could still run like the wind? When a woman can walk, when she can run, her options are different, her reality is different. The options for a woman who is blind aren't the same as the options for a woman who can see. I am reminded of that every day."

"The world gives perfection a pass on many levels."

She took a breath. "You sling dick, Brick. You're a professional dick slinger."

"I don't charge you."

"I am willing to resume paying at any moment."

"We do dinners. Movies. Go to Santa Monica Pier and play arcade games. That is who I am to you too."

"You do what I hired you to do."

"Okay. You came to me as a client, and you only see yourself as a client."

"First impressions are important. I live it every day. My intellect, being a polyglot, my degrees, my trophies, none of that matters once they see my wheelchair."

"I don't see you as a customer. I see a remarkable woman. Compared to you the world is handicapped."

"But you'll never be able to see me as who I used to be. You'll never know her."

"The first time I saw you, I should have come over to you and asked you to play chess."

"What first time?"

"Ask Strawberry."

"Tell me. Did we meet before?"

"I saw you, the whole you, but I was invisible to you; you didn't meet me."

"What does that mean?"

I didn't tell her. I didn't tell her because it didn't matter. She'd been firm, put me in my place.

I was unworthy because she had paid me to be her lover.

I said, "I shouldn't have brought you flowers."

"I just need things to be clear. We're just smashing for dollars."

Her phone rang. She talked to someone in French for a moment, then, as her dog barked, she turned to me.

She smiled and asked, "Chess?"

I smiled. "Sure."

She in her kimono, me in my boxers, Mozart played as we fought as if it were the final chess war, the war to end all wars, as methodical and intense as Magnus Carlsen battling Mikhail Tal. When the mental war ended, a new battle began. I gave that Mensa sex the same way, methodical and intense, like a man in battle, like a man who had to win, only it was like sensual poetry. I made her sing sonnets and haikus as she went three levels deep over and over. On the way out, I picked up the money she'd put on the dresser, enough cash to cover every session, then whispered a soft good-bye as she slept.

Change opinion when there is new information—

CHAPTER 54

BRICK

I STOOD AT the stunning ceiling-to-floor sliding glass doors of Christiana's new penthouse, gazing down at the beaches. She had a prize view of the Pacific Ocean and could watch a sunset from either her living room, or her patio, or one of the two French balconies. The former attorney from Cuba had a stunning bird's-eye view of the world. Her penthouse was split over two floors and had an elegant living room with a luxurious private pool deck. White walls. Contemporary furniture. Beautiful art. Not a speck of dust to be found. Two more girls and a guy were working with her now and living here. Like she had planned, this new zip code encouraged clients to pay triple the price.

Christiana said, "Leave Leimert Park. Move here with me, Brick. Enjoy this view every morning and night."

I took in all she presented, then shook my head. "I'm done, Christiana."

"Work with me a while longer. Do in-calls from here. Once, maybe twice a week."

"No. I'm done. Before the cops come knocking, before addiction takes root, I'm hanging up this trade."

"Why?"

"Vegas has a lot of tourists, but not everybody wants to live there. They visit and go back home. It's time for me to go back home."

"One more client. She lives in New York on Billionaires' Row, has a ninety-million-dollar penthouse, lives in an ultraluxury residential skyscraper that faces Central Park, and she would love to have you come there for two days, to go to the theater every night, to eat at the finest restaurants, to be her lover when it pleases her."

"No."

"Imagine waking up in a One57 penthouse."

"Have you?"

"I have."

"Finally making seven thousand a night?"

"Yes. I was taken to Costa Rica for nine days, enjoyed seeing volcanoes, rain forests, and beaches, and was paid seven thousand a night to be a companion. I can negotiate and get you at least five thousand."

It made me pause, but I declined that offer, and she didn't press it anymore. She knew I was done. This was but a pit stop.

The front door opened. A curvy ginger came inside, a very sexy size twelve. It took me a few blinks to realize who she was. The only time I'd seen her was from a distance, and that was the night when I met Mocha Latte and Christiana in Hancock Park. Back then she was wearing UCLA sweats. Now she was dressed like a model ready for the cover of *Cosmopolitan*. She was from Chapel Hill and used the name Sunday Domingo. She was with a middle-aged white man in a swank Italian suit. They waved, then disappeared toward the bedrooms.

Christiana asked, "What will you do now?"

"I'll put on my white collar, go back to my old job at the widget factory."

"You make more money here. You can make as much in a day here as you will in a week there."

I stroked her hair. "You should stop too. Become a lawyer again. Become an advocate."

"I don't know how to get back to who I once was. Each day I have looked for the innocent girl who once lived in Cuba, the girl who loved so profoundly she was taken advantage of, but I can't find her."

"She's inside you, Christiana. Look deeper. Where is she?"

"She drowned in the ocean. When I jumped from that boat, she drowned, and I survived."

We stood in the window, up high like gods, spying down on the world.

I smiled. "I love your place, Christiana. This is an enviable lifestyle."

"There will always be a room here waiting on you, Brick. You can have your own space. There is a full gym downstairs. A meeting room. A room with pool tables. A swimming pool. You can walk to many restaurants. We have security. It's very safe here. People are discreet. And we are two minutes to the beach."

After she finished her sales pitch, I smiled in a way that let her know she still hadn't sold me on this upgrade.

It would be so easy to stay here. It would be easy to feel like a god.

I said, "I want you to take care of yourself, Christiana."

"I will miss you. I will miss cooking for you."

"I'll never forget you. You were my first."

"You will meet a woman. You will meet the woman who is perfect for you and marry."

"I've slept with enough married women to know I don't want one. Not living in my house."

"You'll meet someone special."

"I did meet someone."

"Who?"

"Her name is Dr. Allison Émilie Chappelle."

"How did you meet?"

"I was at Hot and Cool Cafe. When I saw her, it felt like love at first sight. I was invisible to her. She was waiting on someone else, so we didn't talk. She left the café and I thought I'd never see her again."

"How did you find her again?"

"One day there was a knock on a hotel room door and she came into the room."

"A client?"

"A client."

"Wow. As if it were meant to be."

"It felt that way."

"So, you will leave here and be with her?"

"No. She knows what I do. Used to do now. She only sees me as that kind of man."

"That is a pity. She cannot see your heart as I see your heart."

"She is who I used to see on Mondays."

"How long will that last, seeing her on Mondays?"

"It ended." I gave her the details, told her that flowers had been a bridge too far. "So now, that is over."

"To make it last, Brick, as it is with all things, you must maintain the illusion."

"And if I don't maintain the illusion? If I tear down that wall and try to be who I really am?"

"All clients go away. There is nothing wrong with you, nothing at all, but they all either stop or hire a new lover to fulfill their needs. They come to us because they are bored and stay until we become bores to them."

I whispered, "They redecorate their basements."

"What does that mean?"

I didn't answer, just moved on. "I will go back to love. Before it's too late to turn back. Before I'm too cynical."

"I passed that point a long time ago, and I never realized I had. Love feels like a farce."

"It's never too late. Not for a woman as kind and as beautiful as you."

"I could not keep my husband happy."

"Happiness is an internal thing. His unhappiness was not your fault."

"I tried and failed. I was a loyal, God-fearing woman, and I failed."

"No, you tried, and he failed. He failed you. You didn't fail him."

"I must leave that in Cuba and keep moving forward."

"I know it still hurts."

"Yes. *Todavía me duele mi corazón.* It still hurts, and it will always hurt."

Keys jingled and turned in the front door. Another roommate entered, followed by a tall, well-dressed African American driver who was almost treading on her five-inch heels. The driver brought in five suitcases while she had her own cute little luggage on wheels in tow. She tipped him, and he left. She had just come back from a two-week trip to Dubai, had returned on a private plane with a chauffeur waiting to bring her back to her new address facing the Pacific Ocean. A wealthy client had taken her to the city of the future, treated her like she was Princess Grace. She looked stunning, dressed in new jeans and expensive heels, her hair whipped like a model's.

I said, "Hey, Penny."

She ran to me, arms open for a hug. "Are you moving in with us? Say yes; say yes."

I kissed her cheek, told her the same as I had told Christiana, that I'd only come to say good-bye. Penny told us about her adventure, about her trip to Dubai. She'd had a taste of Arabia in a downtown palace, ridden on yachts, looked at the old town from Dubai Creek, tanned at Jumeirah Beach, played at Aquaventure Waterpark, ridden roller coasters, skydived, had spa days, done helicopter and balloon tours, gone on desert safaris, taken in Burj Khalifa, and shopped until she dropped at Dubai Mall. She'd had a taste of what she called the Beyoncé lifestyle, a lifestyle she felt she deserved. For her, Stockholm,

Copenhagen, Hong Kong, and Singapore were the next clients Christiana had lined up. The three of us stood side by side, sipping bubbly, taking in the view.

I asked Penny, "What about USC?"

She shrugged.

I didn't know what to say, so I didn't say anything.

She was a grown woman. This was her choice.

Just like leaving was mine.

I remembered Mocha Latte's speech that time at breakfast. There was no love here. Never would be.

But even the heartbroken needed a place to rest, a place to hide.

CHAPTER 55

BRICK

I SAT IN the back of the packed comedy club in Long Beach with Dwayne, watched André do his thing.

As the crowd laughed so hard the city rumbled, I sipped my beer. "So, you and Frenchie."

Dwayne sipped his greyhound, nodded. "I'm moving in with her for a while. Just while I'm back."

"How's that work? You pay child support and rent and don't get a rebate?"

"I'll tell you about that when André stops sounding like a bigot."

"He's no bigot. White people started it with the Department of Racism."

He sipped. "I'm trying to help her get sorted. Need my snarky-ass son to be okay."

"You doing it for Fela or for Frenchie?"

"For myself. I need to be around my son. Maybe I need to be around Frenchie too."

When the third show was done, we sat in the green room.

Dwayne told us that Frenchie might leave for six months. She had an audition back in New York in two weeks, and he was sure she was going to score a part on the tour of *Phantom of the Opera*. He said it wasn't Broadway, but it had a strong cast, and it paid well. It would be a great reintroduction to show business.

André asked, "So what's the plan?"

"She goes on tour while I stay here and take care of the house and Fela."

"You get to spend time with Fela."

Dwayne nodded. "And Frenchie gets to chase her dreams. She feels guilty for doing it, but I'm pushing her."

"What about you?"

"I audition, hopefully get local parts, or become a regular on a TV show. Maybe get a spot on *Insecure*, since they're filming right here. I might sell the income property in Florida, if it gets too tough. That's my backup plan."

"The script?"

"I have an offer. Not much of an offer, but an offer."

André asked, "How much?"

"If the film gets made, they'll pay fifty thousand for the screenplay. Then I'd get an additional fifteen-thousand-dollar producer's salary, which is paid at fifteen hundred per week for up to ten weeks, so could be slightly less."

"That would be sixty-five grand on the front end."

"Shane Black sold *The Long Kiss Goodnight* for four million; Joe Eszterhas sold *Basic Instinct* for three million; Tom Schulman and Sally Robinson sold *Medicine Man* for three million. I could go on and on and on."

André said, "Movies with white casts."

"*Black Panther* was supposed to change everything, but it's back to business as usual. Follow the money. Black cast, but who got stupid rich? Wasn't the black people involved. Movie made a billion and I read on Twitter that the main black actors didn't pull a million each. They should've gotten between ten and twenty million each, at least."

"Checkmate."

"Nigga."

They laughed.

Andre asked Big Brother, "What do you have to do now?"

"In between making sure Fela is okay and well-fed, I have to spend some time breaking down the script, and I need to get some more skrilla, buy movie-magic scheduling software so I can figure out the logistics and true cost of shoot days. I need a location, crew, background actors, talent days, and meals. I have to figure out wardrobe for the characters in the background. Everything costs more money."

Andre nodded. "I'll help with all the tedious stuff."

"Big Legs gonna give you time?"

"Family first. She'll be there. If not, then she's not meant to be here."

Dwayne looked confident, happy, that hangdog look he'd worn when he'd come back to Los Angeles all but gone.

I drank my beer, listened to my brothers talk. A smile ruled my face because I remembered when we were young, running in parks and reading my worn-out comic books, remembered when we were boys and didn't carry the worries of grown men. When we were done chopping it up, we all hugged and went our separate ways.

We'd gone from being boys to being men.

André headed to be with Joëlle.

Dwayne headed to be in the arms of Frenchie.

I headed toward an empty apartment, one that had no women, no laughter. Penny no longer lived across the walkway. Christiana and Mocha Latte no longer slept in my bed.

I missed them all.

Yesterday Mocha Latte had sent me another photo. She was down at the Gulf of Mexico looking at homes. She was wearing my red T-shirt, the one that proclaimed MAJORED IN COMPUTER ENGINEERING. TO SAVE TIME, LET'S JUST ASSUME I'M ALWAYS RIGHT. I missed them all, but I missed her the most. Part of me wished I had left with her.

WHEN I GOT home, I saw mail had come to my apartment for Coretta. It was stuffed in the crack of my door. A note said it had been left in my upstairs neighbor's mailbox by accident, and they had been on vacation in Trinidad for the past few months.

It was her income tax papers, the precious documents she had asked me about the last time I saw her.

I unsealed her mail like it was my own and saw what Coretta had been hiding from me since the first kiss.

I saw the shame she had kept concealed from Maserati Mama and any other lover she'd had recently.

Clouds moved away, and I saw the truth in black and white and signed by her as being her absolute truth. Being lied to was as soul crushing as it was enraging. Enlightened, I opened a three-hundred-dollar bottle of wine, sipped, and reread her duality top to bottom and front to back, took a marker and highlighted her dark side, circled her secrets.

CHAPTER 56

BRICK

WITH A CLEAN bill of health from my team of doctors, I stopped delaying the inevitable and went back to my high-tech widget factory job. Went back to being a project manager and handling a team of fifteen. On my door was my given name, DWAYNE DUQUESNE JR. Same as my older brother's name. Here I wasn't Brick. Exercising my duality, I stood in the window to my office and looked out on the madness on the 405, looked east and took in the smog covering downtown LA.

The timer on my phone sounded, let me know it was time to head to another meeting.

The life I'd had for a short while seemed like a dream. I got to see behind their erotic and exotic curtains, heard the private thoughts they'd never tell their husbands, boyfriends, priests, or lovers. Felt them tremble, felt their hearts race, some wide-eyed like they saw the light of God. It was good for the ego to be good enough to make a woman think she loved a man she didn't know. Women wanted to feel like a woman, that definition different for each. For some it was dominance. For others, submission. For a few, it was equality. For some it was escape from the world. For others, a strong round of sex was what they needed from the world. Sex was always about some other need, or some rejection, or revenge, or acceptance. Sex was rarely about sex. So, I had had to learn to adapt and play all roles, be it spoken in Shakespearean or street slang or broken English or with extreme vulgarity or with beautiful euphemisms or done in total silence—except for the cete of animalistic grunts and intrigue of passionate groans and non-stop guttural breathing that ended at a tribe of orgasms—and then watch them come down from level three to level two to level one. Once on the ground floor, the stunned expressions were always followed by a smile, then a laugh, and the desire to pay to get back on the same ride. For them, money was an e-ticket.

It was an experience like no other.

I saw them all in my dreams, saw them separately, and at times all at once.

In my dreams I was the performer, maybe a conductor, the leader of a band of lady lovers.

I orchestrated opulent orgasms one by one but imagined the collection of clients as a choir of angels, an orchestra of beautiful women with orgasm-inspired voices. I saw them side by side, backs arched, eyes closed, staccato breathing, all being pulled under until they were three levels deep. Every client I'd been paid to touch, I imagined them working in collaboration. In my mind, it sounded like the largest choir in the world. It was so tremendous that angels wore earplugs. I had put a few to sleep at night, touched them again in the morning, showered, pampered them until the buzzer sounded, then regretfully kissed away the tracks of their tears as we said reluctant good-byes.

It was time to move on and let that go.

That was no longer my life.

Now it was mornings in rush-hour traffic, days of meetings, and evenings in rush-hour traffic.

Maybe this repetition was part of the reason Christiana's world had seemed so fascinating. Maybe that was why so many ran to her, to break the monotony of their own dull, repetitive, predictable lives.

Even with work as a project manager, I found other things to keep me occupied on the weekends.

Dwayne, Frenchie, André, Joëlle, Fela, and his girlfriend, Chavers, we all went to Disneyland.

It was interesting watching Fela and his first love. I hoped his heart didn't get broken too fast.

For everyone else life was good, and love was strong.

The money I had made with Christiana was stashed. I didn't put it in the bank because that infusion of money would cause the IRS to ask questions. They'd want their cut or incarcerate me for leaving them out of the loop. Those bloodsuckers. I had it, had every dime I'd earned, hidden in my apartment, waiting on a rainy day.

I wasn't a fool with money, not the way Coretta had been.

I still owned three hundred things. I still sold wine off and on. And I still rocked Miss Mini. Miss Mini had never let me down, had never abandoned me. I was as loyal to her as she was to me. Would be a little longer. I was considering giving it to Fela on his birthday, then getting something new for myself. It was time for me to upgrade rides.

A FEW WEEKS later, on a Saturday morning, I woke up to the smell of blueberry pancakes. It was still dark, about an hour before sunrise, and I thought I was dreaming. Then I saw a light was on in the front part of the house. I heard soft music and singing.

When I headed to my kitchen, Mocha Latte was there cooking as if she'd never left. Tight jeans, a purple THIS GIRL LOVES MALAKOFF,

TEXAS T-shirt, no shoes, hair short and curly, as decadent as the most expensive chocolate in the world. She stopped, flipped a pancake, and looked at me, then tendered a nervous smile.

"Hope you don't mind. Knocked before I came in. I kept the key."

"When did you get back?"

"Two hours ago. You were in your twelfth dream when I came in."

"Drove?"

"All the way from Texas. Did a two-day cross-country drive. Thirteen hundred miles."

"What brings you back?"

"I missed your oversize classic sofa."

"Really?"

She laughed, then tapped some papers on the counter. I went to see what it was.

I asked, "What are these?"

"My credit report and last three filings with the IRS."

I looked at her. "Really?"

"Really. Let's get that out of the way. Show me yours when you're ready."

I took a moment, absorbed what she was telling me. "You got off your tractor and came back."

"I was gone ninety-four days. I was with family and people who love me, but yeah. I drove back. Followed my heart and it led me back to your doorstep. For ninety-four days, day and night, I thought about you."

"What are you saying?"

"For you, Brick. You. I'm back for you. For the oversize classic sofa too, but mainly for you."

"For me?"

"To be your girlfriend, Brick. To give it a try. To share bacteria. I missed kissing you. Is that okay?"

"Depends. Tell me who has scored the most points in NBA history."

She winked at me. "Kareem. If you're going to challenge me, bring it."

"Name the movie. 'I don't have to show you no stinking badges!'"

The Treasure of the Sierra Madre."

"Where did Woodstock take place?"

"Oh, a slick question. Woodstock took place in Bethel, New York. Fifty miles outside of Woodstock."

"How many US states begin with the letter *A*?"

"Four."

"What city banned burials in the 1900s?"

"San Francisco."

"The least densely populated country in the world?"

"Greenland."

"First country to print paper money?"

"China."

"You're good. Damn, you're good."

"Oh, boo, I'm good at everything I do. And you know that."

"You play chess?"

"I can learn."

While we held eye contact, I said, "You know my secrets."

"You know mine. You know everything I'm ashamed of, and you still look at me . . . like that."

I nodded. "Yeah."

"Scary. But we already know the ugly stuff. No surprises there."

"Do you know what you want?"

"I'm *looking for love*. Ridiculous, can't-live-without-each-other love. I want to meet someone decent. You're decent, Brick. I want a *partner*. Someone who ain't dating everybody else. Or fucking everybody else. Would be nice to hold hands. To share bacteria. To fall in love. But I can't fall in love with you, Brick. The physics of it is impossible. You can't fall to land on a place where you already are. I already love you. I want someone to go to the movies with. I want that somebody to be you. We can take it slow, check out a matinée, and take it from there. First date will be on me. I'll buy you a large popcorn, Raisinets, and a large bottle of water. Second date we can get dinner at Katana in Hollywood, eat sushi, maybe go dance at Savoy. Third date, you know. Look in my face, forget about Coretta, and see I love you and see your future. Then we can get to know each other and eventually make babies."

"We don't have a foundation."

"We tear down what we have and build a new one—and never talk about the old one."

I went to her, hugged her. "It will take a while, but I'll save and buy the home."

"We can start with a condo."

"Or a town house. I have to have a garage."

She winked. "Maybe we can save and buy a house together. Just a dream. Am I going too fast?"

"It's okay. We can dream together."

As she held me tight, we rocked side to side a moment before she said, "I might have a job offer."

"Yeah?"

"Interview on Monday. Like God knew what I needed and finally came through."

"Yeah? With which company?"

"Dan L. Steele. Joëlle introduced me to her mentor, older guy named Tyrel Williams."

"That guy's big in the industry. Gives a lot of seminars around the world. He's major. Excited?"

"Nervous. I get to go back to the real world, and it's terrifying me."

"You got this. You're as brilliant as you are beautiful. You got this."

"I missed you. Missed talking to you. Dancing with you. Missed standing in the streets kissing like fools."

I asked, "How's the sleepwalking?"

"I haven't . . . not since I stopped. Doing that, that lifestyle, it had me stressed. I don't talk in my sleep like I used to, don't sit up and do the same motions over and over, don't scream or fall or run into things or go urinate in the closet. I'm a lot better now. Just lock the doors, don't move the furniture around or leave out things I could trip on, just in case I backslide and have a moment. I stopped taking Ambien. I think the Ambien made it worse."

"Good."

Looked like she was scared to ask, but she did. "How's . . . how's the cancer?"

"Still gone. Last scan came back clean. Next scan in a year. Doing blood work in between."

"I'll be here for you. No matter what, I'm going to be here. You'll never be alone again."

"And I'll watch over you."

"Brick, most people just want someone to care for them and watch over them."

"So simple."

"Yet so complicated at the same time."

We kissed, shared more than eighty million bacteria like each was made of pure sugar and honey.

She said, "I was surprised. My credit score is pretty good. Bet it's better than yours."

"Stop talking."

"We gonna do it right now?"

"Been too long. We're about to Roc and Shay right here, right the fuck now."

"Let me turn off the pancakes before we burn down the building climbing the stairway to heaven."

With permission I tugged her tight jeans down over her bubble, pulled those dungarees to her ankles. I eased inside Mocha Latte, broke the skin, opened her inch by inch, bit by bit, teased her, didn't rush, and along every part of that journey, as I sucked her neck, as I sucked her ear, as I felt her waking up a sleeping beast inside me, our moans danced, those wicked moans our first sounds as boyfriend and girl-friend; our desperation to feel good and please amalgamated, and those vibrations made one beautiful sound. My kitchen became the penthouse in our own private heaven. While I was inside her I stripped her naked and tore away my clothing, then took her to the classic sofa. That long, low sound of pleasure, that enthusiastic reverberation of much-needed suffering that preceded the promise of a very voluptuous orgasm, the unique uncontrollable groans as our heated bodies pulled away and rushed to collide into each other over and over, the soft wails as the flesh of a king slapped against the flesh of his queen, the curt whimpers that could not be controlled, the echoes like sobbing, the sensuous whines, the lamentation that erupted into a preorgasmic clamor, a noise that rose like a doleful cry begging for this road to ecstasy to never end, it was all followed by a command for me to not be gentle, a demand for me to not stop, and again came a chain of elongated moans that made me want to fill her up and crawl inside her to become one; as the sun began to rise and give us a new day and second chances, we lived in our sounds, swam in all of our sounds, lived in her emotional soprano moans that darkened in timber as I stroked her with a delectable rhythm. With each measured stroke that made my classic sofa give and creak like a musical instrument that needs a touch of WD-40, we united in body and spirit. She took me three levels deep. My baritone and hedonistic cries expanded as that southern girl raised her Texan hips to give me all of her as she accepted all of me. I told her I loved her as she set free epicurean moans and confessed that she loved me, let tears flow, took down her wall and confessed that she'd loved me from the first moment we'd shared blueberry pancakes. Right now with me, on this journey, in this union, as we engaged in this healing, the wildfire took control and we became the most feral of feral lovers, and together we made that rugged, off-key, heavy and harsh breathing and purring at the start of a new day sound like operatic music written in the key of lust and debauchery. We fell to the carpet and laughed and kissed and fucked like overeducated, unsophisticated demons, sweaty-bodied demons who needed love, Nubian demons who needed more than love, fiends who needed each other because we were tired of making this loveless journey alone.

We fucked hard, then slept harder.

SEVEN HOURS LATER we held hands and strolled down Degnan toward the epicenter of Leimert Park. As we passed black academics arguing if the area should be renamed Nubian Village to remove Leimert's racist name, I showed Mocha Latte Coretta's tax papers. My ex owed the IRS more than a hundred and sixty thousand dollars, was in collections, but that wasn't the biggest surprise.

Mocha Latte said, "Her status is 'Married Filing Separately'? Married? *Married?* Coretta is married?"

"Yeah. She has a husband *and* a kid out there somewhere."

"She has a secret family? I thought only men did that."

"I guess not."

"Secret child and a secret marriage, and she was shacking up with you?"

"I had no idea. Neither did Maserati Mama. But I know that if you're separated from your spouse by a separate maintenance decree, you can file as single. That means she's not even legally separated."

"Had to be something she did while she was young."

"That's why she freaked out. I got too close to her truth and she left. We were talking marriage and she was already married."

"Have you talked to Coretta since finding out she has her own duality?"

"I sent her a text, straight up asked her if she was married with a kid. Asked her if she had me looking for engagement rings when she already had a husband."

"And?"

"She ghosted me. Blocked my number and blocked me on social media."

"I won't ghost you; I'll talk so much you'll beg me to act like Casper and ghost you."

"So."

Mocha Latte laughed, amused.

"So what?"

"You gonna tell me your name?"

She grinned. "Zélie Nimota Torres-Ferreira."

"Beautiful name. Matches everything about you."

"Words, Brick."

"Get used to it, Zélie. Get used to me complimenting you day and night and day and night."

"If I have to call you by your nickname, you have to use mine."

"Whatever you say, my queen from the Nile of the Americas."

"So, you and your older brother have the exact same name? How the hell does that happen?"

"I'll tell you all about it when we get back home."

Her smile broadened. "Home. You have no idea how bad I need a place to just call home."

My enthusiastic expression matched hers. "Yeah. Home. You have a home. With me."

"I have a boyfriend." She sang like a smitten teenage girl. "I. Have. A. Sexy. Ass. Intelligent. Boyfriend."

"I haven't had a girlfriend in a long time."

"I plan on being your last girlfriend and you will be my last boyfriend. Just letting you know my intentions."

"Now you're talking."

"Keep looking at me like that and we might have to hop in Miss Mini and go to Vegas for real."

I said, "As long as we can stop in the middle of nowhere at the McDonald's in Barstow."

"Oh yeah. Their McDonald's looks like a train station and they have a cool gift shop."

André and Joëlle pulled up on his blazing iron horse just as we passed Eso Won. They parked in front of Hot and Cool Cafe. Mocha Latte handed me back Coretta's tax papers, and I dropped them in the garbage can that was overflowing with rubbish right outside the café. Then, as we went to greet André and Joëlle, Dwayne, Frenchie, and Fela came out of Eso Won bookstore cracking up. This was what we did Saturday mornings, and would do this for as long as we could. No matter what, we were a family. Today was the day I was going to reveal I had been ill, now that I was better and there was no need to worry.

For a second, I looked east, toward where a man had a shop called Tres Dwaynes. He was still my dad. I was still his son. So was Dwayne. I'd try again next year. But for now, with my brothers and their cheerful lovers, with my nephew and my tractor-riding girlfriend from Malakoff, Texas, together, we headed inside Hot and Cool Cafe, all hugs and smiles, then raced for the piano and put on a show.

Mo.
IL
Indi.
Mi
PA
Nev
Missi
Ala
Wisc
Neb
Ok
Ohio
W. Virgina
Delaware
Kentucky

Alaska
Arkansa
Arizona
California
Nevada
Washington
Oregon
N. Dakota
south Dakota
Montana
Kansas
utah
Texas
N. mexico
Florida
Iowa
Louisiana

Georgia
S. Carolina
N. Carolina
Virgina
Maryland
Massachusetts
Connecticut
Rhode Island
wyoming
Vermont
Maine
New Hamp.
New York
New Jersey
Hawaii
Colorada
Minesota
Tennesee

ACKNOWLEDGMENTS

Dear Perfect Reader,

As "Lights, Camera, Action" plays in the background . . . and I wish I could gwara gwara . . . ☺

Years ago, I had started working on a novel set in Leimert Park featuring three brothers (using the names Blue, Raheem, and André, I think), and put it aside, maybe due to good old writer's block. Eventually I saved the file, let it be a moon floating around in the Dickeyverse, and went on to create the McBrooms instead. (Love the McBrooms!)

Now I decided to give it another shot and write about three different brothers. I started off with Brick and only Brick. Initially I had no idea that I was going to add two more bros. It started with me improvising, had a guy in a car waiting on someone and I had no idea why. It became a story with Brick waiting on Penny, then being introduced to Mocha Latte and Christiana, and via good-old improvisation the novel sort of led me to this other fascinating world and took on its own life after that; eventually I added Dwayne, gave him his own conflict and POV, then added André. His story was *much* larger, and he had a killer POV, but it was all cut. The way I write, the book would've been the size of *War and Peace*. Let's just say, Joëlle took him on a wild, erotic ride between chapters. ☺

It felt like the perfect combination: three guys, three personalities, in three different types of relationships, all coming from three different places. Well, I hope it all came out fine. I hope that you, perfect reader, will enjoy this read as much as I enjoyed finally writing this one.

And to give you and the rest of the crew visiting the Dickeyverse insight into the amazing women in Brick's life, let's just say we're influenced by things we don't consciously think about—sometimes by things we read in passing that stick with us. When I was in Argentina working on *Resurrecting Midnight*, I picked up a novel from a street vendor in Recoleta. *Diario de una Prepago Adolescente* by Ale. G. It was a random purchase. I couldn't speak or read Spanish at the time. It was the first novel in Spanish I had bought, and I promised myself that I would learn the language in order to read it for pleasure. I had no idea what the novel was about; was just supporting a street vendor and a writer who was unknown to me. After I became more fluent in Spanish, I realized this was the amazing story of a girl who was down and out and reluctantly became an escort. Something about her journey and that lifestyle intrigued me, and it motivated me to try and see it from a different angle. I think that was the seed that led me to create Penny, Christiana, and Mocha Latte, and to define them not just by their occupation but as human beings facing life's challenges.

Drumroll, please!

Hear ye! I want to give a shout-out to everybody who helped, and here is the Dickey Short List.

Stephanie Kelly, my amazing editor at Dutton, thanks for once again stepping in and doing what you do. You remain invaluable. Much love and respect from me to you. Emily Canders, the publicist of all publicists at Dutton, thanks for all the hard work! Sara Camilli, my agent extraordinaire, and everyone at the Sara Camilli Agency (Hey, Ray!), we're getting closer and closer to book number one hundred! Hmmm... might be Gideon time. Hey, Gideon. Meet the other Reaper.

Kayode Disu, my London-based Nigerian brother by another mother, thanks for reading bits and giving me your feedback. Always appreciated, bro! Jason Frost, thanks for the photography tips! Sabra, my neighbor from way back when we lived in Carson, I listened, and I remembered.

Do the Mo'; do the Mo'; do the Mo'!

Special thanks to my friend and fan in Texas, Brianna Nicole Henry, and her amazing fan page @ClubEJD. You rock! Join the club e'r'body! Free admission, two book minimum, and free cyber-parking. LOL ☺ We be having fun chopping it up out there on Twitter.

In case I forgot anyone, which wasn't intentional, here's your chance to shine.

I wanna thank _____ for _____ because without their help, I'd be _____ at a _____ with _____ and wishing I was _____ in _____. You're the best of the best!

ericjeromedickey.com

@ericjdickey

IG: ericjeromedickey

Holla!

EJD

Here since '96.

19SEPT18

5:16 P.M.

Latitude: *33.9989018*

Longitude: *—118.3425759*

TURN THE PAGE FOR AN EXCERPT

From Memphis to L.A. and back again, Eric Jerome Dickey takes readers on a powerful and intense journey as Professor Pi Suleman deals with sexual assault and racism, fights being changed by his father's truths, and also discovers untruths Gemma Buckingham—a sophisticated entrepreneur who has just moved to Memphis from London to escape a deep heartbreak—has hidden for her own reasons . . .

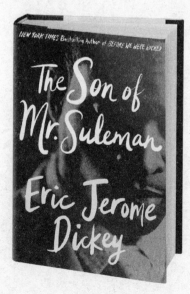

CHAPTER 1

WHEN GODS BECAME bored in heaven they walked among mortals.

The stranger to my green eyes was dressed in a skirt with stunning embellishments and intricate tailoring that rode her curves like a Chevy cruising Riverside Drive at sunrise on a Sunday morning. Her sleeveless blouse was on the same level. Voluptuous woman, thick hips, rounded backside, small waist—an impeccable figure to die for, an hourglass. About five nine without the five-inch heels, she was akin to a movie star in a room of extras. Under her gravitational pull, a victim to the weight of her presence, I watched her as I engaged in conversation with my colleagues.

She stared at this BMFM, this Black man from Memphis, with the same curiosity.

I was thirty-one, five eleven, 180 on the scales fully clothed. Hair short on the sides, six inches of trendy pillow-soft kink from forehead to neck, a radical Black man's Mohawk. Skin a light ebony brown, the complexion that said sometime after the mass kidnapping in Africa, my ancestry, the bloodline of the first mathematicians, philosophers, kings, and Moors, had been integrated either voluntarily or by force.

We were at an annual repeat of a Cybill Shepherd movie called *Being Rose* that popped off on Main Street at the state-of-the-art Halloran Centre, an astonishing thirty-nine-thousand-square-foot space big enough for almost four hundred people and open to the public. It had an amazing theater and the night was sponsored by the University Along the Nile. UAN was my alma mater, and where I worked as an adjunct. By someone determined to take control of both my career and my life, I'd been mandated to socialize.

When the open event moved to the ultraprivate reception at the Pink Palace Museum and Planetarium, we peeped at each other across the room. The UAN after-party was a high-priced classy affair with plenty of alcohol and finger food, where they played Marc Cohn's hit song "Walking in Memphis" on repeat. I took in her amber skin and cute smile. She had dimples, those beautiful indentations, plus freckles and a pronounced chin cleft that gave her face symmetry. Wide eyes paired perfectly with pillow-soft lips, soup coolers painted dark with mystery. Simply. Gorgeous. Beautiful enough to make it impossible to ignore. Her eyebrows were on point, but her lashes were an omen, two black butterflies confronting me each time I spied her way.

I went to her, but not too fast, not with thirst, introduced myself. "Professor Pi Suleman, UAN."

"I'm Gemma Buckingham, from Brixton."

She walked slowly, an invitation, and I moved with her at a snail's pace.

Without preface she said, "Meghan really is beautiful, innit?"

"Thee Stallion?"

"Meghan Markle."

"Everyone is beautiful to someone."

"Even a stallion."

British humor touched American hip-hop humor and we laughed.

I asked, "Big fan of the duchess?"

She beamed. "I'm in America. Her America. I get to see how she lived. I get to see her world."

There were murals and displays on Native American pottery, which spoke to us as we strolled with the crowd. She nodded in approval at pre-Columbian relics, the same with Clyde Parke's Miniature Circus, then became interested in the fossils and dinosaurs, mounted animals. She took in our past in silence. For thirty minutes she became a student. She wasn't interested in the displays on World War I and II, had no idea who the significant Black Memphians were, but she read the identifiers for the history exhibitions that focused on the roles of song and cotton in my city on the Nile, tuned in on the exhibit regarding the changing roles of women.

We paused in a living room with adornments from the 1920s.

I continued talking as if we'd never paused the conversation, said, "Brixton?"

"London, where American Meghan Markle moved, only to be ridiculed and treated harshly."

"Ridiculed?"

"For being mixed race. As if that means *subhuman*. They've attacked her mother as well."

I nodded. "For being gifted with melanin."

"*Incessantly.* By the tabloids. Battered on Twitter by racists. Waves of abuse and harassment."

"Racism that bad over there?"

"Not as blatant as here, but yeah. The West End is hostile. My sisters get charged twice as much to enter a bloody club. Some have had to change names to get jobs. I swear to you, it's unending. A cesspool of racism. Worse for Meghan than anyone. Being American has exacerbated the issue."

"I bet she regrets that choice, same as Princess Di did."

"What should be a fairy tale has become a nightmare. I feel her pain and depression."

"Had no idea." I stroked my soft beard. "The nasty Thames is your muddy Mississippi."

The transition was awkward, but her body language told me it was appreciated.

"Pretty much. You're landlocked here. You have the river, but that's not like having a real beach. Only a fool would get in those nasty waters. So sad you have to drive six hours to Dauphin Beach."

We stopped moving and I smiled a little more, fascinated. "You grew up on a beach?"

"No, but I could get a train from London Victoria to Brighton Beach in an hour."

"Still, we both grew up in port cities."

"Mine has over thirty bridges connecting East and West End; yours has only has two."

"Yeah. The Memphis-Arkansas Bridge and the New Bridge, the Hernando de Soto Bridge."

"So, tell me about the University Along the Nile."

Wearing my best smile, I told her what made the UAN Pharaohs stand out was the main building, which cost three hundred million dollars and was a duplicate of the defunct glass pyramid that sat on the Mississippi. We had fifteen- to thirty-foot-high statues of Egypt's pharaohs across the yard.

"How large is UAN? Sounds massive."

"UAN has about twenty-two thousand people, seventy countries represented, three hundred areas of study, one hundred seventy buildings. There are sixty statues of pharaohs, mini-pyramids, and Egyptian hieroglyphics placed over a thousand acres, which makes the campus a museum from end to end. It takes twenty minutes to walk the yard."

She said, "Wasn't there a terrifying incident at UAN a few days ago?"

"Almost. We had word some racist was on the way. He'd posted his intentions on social media. He made it on campus. The active-shooter alarm sounded, and UAN was put on lockdown for a few hours. Our security had the racist cornered by the Little Pyramid until he surrendered."

"So you're famous."

"We were mentioned on CNN."

Gemma Buckingham said, "Everyone I passed seemed to be in little groups, whispering like it's a bloody secret. They talk so loudly, then whisper concerning certain topics, but they are bloody whispering louder than their regular speaking voices. Almost everyone in here uses their outside voices."

"UAN is a proud uni, so of course we talk about the attack by a lone-wolf, southern-fried terrorist in whispers, the way southerners do all of their families' dirty laundry."

She said, "Also overheard campus police here are like the military in Israel."

"With all the campus shootings in the USA, and with a couple threats directed at UAN for some unknown reason, the university thought it was a good idea to let the security company they had contracted go and hire the Aggressive Six to protect the students. They're a team made up of steroid-chomping men built like Arnold Schwarzenegger, John Cena, the Rock, Rambo, Lou Ferrigno as Hercules, and Popeye the Sailor. They are some mean motherfuckers, no doubt paid to be that way."

She laughed at my descriptions, then mocked me, "*Motherfuckers.*"

"Pardon my French."

"In French *motherfucker* would be *enculés* or *enculées*, perhaps *connard, couillon,* or *conasse.*"

"Lots of ways to call someone a motherfucker in France."

"Because there are a lot of motherfuckers in Paris."

We laughed together.

Her scent was erotic, the kind that made a mortal fall in love with a deity.

She grinned. "By the way, love your Memphis accent."

"I thought you had the Brixton accent. My bad."

"Southern, wise, deep, intellectual. You're an African American Matthew McConaughey."

"He wishes he had my swag."

"If only you were the rule and not the exception."

"Something happen?"

She chuckled. "I took an Uber to Graceland, had the ultimate VIP tour to see your royalty. Not exactly Kensington Palace or Windsor Castle. Interesting décor, to say the least. I paid two hundred US and saw Elvis's collection of over-the-top jumpsuits, his famous pink Cadillac, the gold records, jets."

"That whole strip, Elvis Presley Boulevard, is dedicated to the King from end to end."

"Noticed that. I realized I was in what is called Whitehaven, saw a mall nearby, thought it would be akin to Knightsbridge."

"Oh boy."

"I thought the circus was in town. One fellow talked so loudly, bragged about how much he spent for his *forty-six-inch rims*. Must one have rims so ginormous it makes your car look like a bloody clown car?"

We laughed at her snark.

She asked, "What's your name again?"

"Professor Pi Suleman."

"Professor."

"Pi. Call me Pi."

"Pie? My weakness, especially a meat pie, a good posh pie. What's yours?"

"Not the food, the number 3.14."

"The mathematical constant."

"Been called worse by my own skinfolk."

"Curious. Why did your mother name you Pi, Pi?"

I paused. "Because I was born on March fourteenth."

"You were born on Pi Day. This is truly odd. Talk about odd birthdays."

"Yours?"

"April twentieth."

I laughed. "For real? You're a four-twenty baby?"

"It seems to be a big deal here in this part of America, not so much where I'm from."

"You were born on Colorado's get-high day. A day to celebrate marijuana."

"If I'd been an American, I would've been called Marijuana and teased all my bloody life."

I said, "You're a Taurus."

"And you?"

"Pisces."

"I used to be all into Zodiac signs when I was a teenager."

I asked, "What you remember?"

"Taurus needs a physical connection; Pisces are emotional. But are supposed to have *amaze-balls* sex."

"Gemma."

"Gemma Buckingham, if that is not too much to ask. Hate to bother, but I'm particular."

As we stood to the side, Blacks chatting among whites who occasionally spied our way with suspicious eyes, as if we needed to integrate for their comfort, I asked, "What's your IG?"

"Instagram? Oh, my love, I don't do social media."

"So, Black woman from London, you're not keeping up with Black Twitter?"

She turned her body away, suddenly annoyed, then tendered a UK smile that made clear being pushed irritated her. She had left the conversation, her way of telling me the gotdamn answer she gave was her final answer and to not ask her the same fucking question over and over in different ways.

The room of socialites rumbled and began to applaud.

Judge Zachary Beauregard Calhoun and Dr. Helen Stone-Calhoun came in like potentates. A squad of twelve followed like disciples.

Gemma Buckingham whispered, "I take it these are important people here."

"In the tristate area."

"Tristate?"

"Tennessee, Arkansas, and Mississippi."

"One would think King George and Queen Elizabeth had arrived on a magic carpet."

"Yeah. One would think."

To live in the past is to die in the present
Bill Bilichick

New York Times Bestselling Author

ERIC JEROME DICKEY

"Dickey's fans flock to
his readings. . . . He's perfected an
addictive fictional formula."

—*The New York Times*

For a complete list of titles,
please visit prh.com/ericjeromedickey